LION OF WAR

A MEDIEVAL ROMANCE
SONS OF CHRISTOPHER DE LOHR
PART OF THE DE LOHR DYNASTY

BY KATHRYN LE VEQUE

KATHRYN LE VEQUE
NOVELS

ARE YOU SIGNED UP FOR KATHRYN'S BLOG?

You'll get the latest news and information on exclusive giveaways, exclusive excerpts, coming releases, sales, free books, cover reveals and more.

Kathryn's blog followers get it all first. No spam, no junk.

Get the latest info from the reigning Queen of English Medieval Romance!

Sign Up Here

kathrynleveque.com

The heir to Lioncross Abbey Castle makes his presence known.

Like all sons of de Lohr, Curtis de Lohr was born for war.

As the firstborn son of the Earl of Hereford and Worcester, England's greatest knight during the reign of Richard I, Curtis grew up knowing what was expected of him, and he thrived through the pressure. But the pressure was kept buried and, with all pressure, at some point it's got to give.

With a reputation for being humorless, brutally honest, powerful, and fearless in battle, Curtis is the shining heir for the House of de Lohr. As the premier knight for Henry III, he performs flawlessly in every battle, every situation. When he is put to the test in Wales by laying siege to a castle that Henry wants very badly, the victory of that castle brings about a treaty of epic proportions—having a wife forced upon him in exchange for peace.

That changes everything.

Enid Avrielle "Elle" ferch Gwenwynwyn is a warrior woman in her own right. The daughter of the last ruler of Powys, she is a valuable commodity to the Welsh as well as to the English. She also happens to be a widow, and since the death of her husband, she has fought in every battle for the freedom of her people. That means she fights against Curtis in his quest to take her castle. A woman of mystery, Elle carries many secrets that she keeps buried. She has plans for her new husband.

One thing she didn't plan on was falling in love with him.

And the feeling is very, very mutual.

Join Curtis and Elle in a dangerous game of politics and passion during a time when the slightest swing of the pendulum could mean life or death. It's an all-out battle within the House of de Lohr to keep Curtis focused on his new command… and to keep Elle by his side when her natural instincts dictate otherwise. Can their love survive the ghosts of her past? Or will those ghosts consume them both?

Sometimes, the true enemy is within…

HOUSE OF DE LOHR MOTTO

Deus et Honora
God and Honor

Author's Note

I can't tell you how excited I am to finally be writing about Christopher and Dustin's sons. If you've read *Rise of the Defender* (and I hope you have), then you're already familiar with the House of de Lohr. If you haven't read it yet, I suggest you do it right away. While you don't need to read it to make sense of this book (all of my books are standalones), it makes the story—and characters—that much more endearing. I love me some de Lohr men!

Let's start off talking about the offspring of Christopher and Dustin de Lohr. There are several, so here's the list of kids and their stories:

- Peter (The Splendid Hour) Lord Pembridge, eventually Earl of Farringdon. Garrison commander Ludlow Castle
- Christin (A Time of End) Married to Alexander de Sherrington, Garrison commander of Wigmore Castle
- Brielle (The Dark Conqueror)
- Curtis (Lion of War) Earl of Leominster (heir apparent to the larger Earldom of Hereford and Worcester), Baron Ivington
- Richard "Roi" (Lion of Twilight) Earl of Cheltenham
- Myles (Lion of Hearts)
- Rebecca
- Douglas (Lion of Shadows)
- Westley (whose middle name is Henry and he was

sometimes referred to as "Henry" when he was young)
(Lion of Thunder)

- Olivia Charlotte (the future Honey de Shera from the Lords of Thunder series)

This book is about Curtis, the firstborn son of Christopher and Dustin. I wrote this series a little out of order by writing Roi's story first, but now we have Curtis' and it is a tale worthy of Christopher's firstborn. Curtis is kind of the strong, silent type, and I knew that going into the tale, but he's most definitely not afraid to speak his mind, and if he gets angry—watch out. He's a man you do NOT want to make angry, which is a warning shot to our heroine. As great a hero as Curtis turned out to be— and he's spectacular—our heroine, to me, is one of the better ones I've written about.

Let's talk about her.

First, let's address the heroine's name—Avrielle. That's actually her middle name. Her full name, as you will see, is Enid Avrielle, but she goes by Elle or Ellie. Avrielle is an uncommon name, and it is the name of the heroine in *ShadowWolfe*, the wife of Scott de Wolfe (another firstborn son of a great house). The truth is that the storyline for ShadowWolfe was originally meant for Curtis, which is why we know his wife's name was Avrielle (as established in *Silversword*). This was established years and years ago, before I even wrote the Sons of de Wolfe series, but when I was writing the Sons of de Wolfe, I realized that Curtis' story was perfect for Scott de Wolfe—so, it became Scott's tale and I didn't see a need to change Avrielle's name. I figured I'd just change Curtis' lady's name when the time came, but, idiot that I am, I forgot about that when I wrote *Silversword* and mentioned that Curtis had a wife named Avrielle. So there you have it. But that's okay, because there are few truly hardly used and unique names in the world. I've got two heroes named

Kevin, so why not two heroines named Avrielle?

This book is set several years before *Lion of Twilight*, the first book in the series. I didn't go with the chronological age of the sons when writing the series (for example, the eldest son was not Book One). I simply went with the book I wanted to write for the hero I wanted to write about, and Curtis' book came in second. We actually met Curtis (sort of) in *Spectre of the Sword* when Dustin de Lohr gives birth to him. He was a very tough birth that nearly cost his mother her life, so Curtis sure made his mark early on. He was named Curtis because his mother simply liked the name (and because at the time I wrote *Rise of the Defender*, Curtis happened to be my favorite name, also!).

Curtis and Elle are really two dynamically different individuals, as you are going to see from the start of this book. Curtis isn't simply the Lion of War—Elle is, too, in her own way. You'll see what I mean. If you've read *Rise of the Defender*, then you know what a rough introduction Christopher and Dustin had, as the hero and heroine. Dustin was no shrinking violet, and Elle isn't either, so both Christopher and Curtis are introduced to their wives in a rather difficult way. You'll see what I mean!

There are quite a few cameos in this novel. Keep an eye out for the sons of Christopher and Dustin, plus an unexpected cameo by one of my favorite characters—Asa ben Thad. If you've read *The Splendid Hour*, Peter de Lohr's book, then you know who Asa is—a tough little boy with his own street gang. Asa is all grown up in this book, so keep an eye out for him. There are a few other cameos, because you know I like to bring characters from other stories in for brief appearances. Pay attention because you'll recognize some of the names thrown out, even if the characters don't make an appearance. Makes it fun!

Lastly, a quick note about the de Lohr family tree—specifically, the patriarchal line. Curtis' firstborn is named Christopher, after his father. Christopher is the father of Lily, from *WolfeLord* and also from *ShadowWolfe*. Lily married Will de Wolfe, the heir to the de Wolfe empire. That's where the House of de Wolfe and the House of de Lohr connect.

Now, on to the usual pronunciation guide:

U.K. pronunciation and U.S. pronunciation is often quite different, so just to be clear on a few things –

Leominster—for the benefit of the U.S. readers, the U.K. pronunciation is Lemster.

Elle—like the letter "L"

Gruffydd—for the American ear, it's basically pronounced like "Griffith"

And with that, we're off and running. Get ready for an epic ride!

Happy Reading!

PROLOGUE

Year of Our Lord 1228
Brython Castle, Welsh Marches

"WHAT, EXACTLY, DID he say?"

The question came from a man whose query was not meant to be ignored. Not even slightly avoided. Christopher de Lohr, the Earl of Hereford and Worcester, was making the demand in the middle of what had been a horrific siege. The English, led by de Lohr, had been trying to gain control of a much-coveted Welsh castle for almost a month on the command of Henry III. Henry wanted that castle to keep it away from the control of Llewelyn, who had defeated the family of a rival Welsh prince, Gruffydd ap Gwenwynwyn, to gain the castle and a foothold on the Welsh marches.

Brython Castle was that target.

That was what de Lohr was trying to negotiate. Standing in his open tent at the base of the hill that led up to Brython, he was surrounded by wounded men, raw sewage, mud, horses, and weary soldiers who had been at war for weeks on end. There had been conflicting reports before and during the siege that Llewelyn didn't hold the castle at all, that it was some other

Welsh lord who hated the English, hated Llewelyn, and was trying to make a name for himself. Whoever it was, the English had been battling for sixteen brutal days before finally damaging the sewers and water supply enough to make a difference. Now, seven days later and with no rain in sight, the castle was starting to falter. No water, no drainage, and, undoubtedly, any food supplies were dwindling.

But de Lohr kept up the barrage.

He was a man with decades of experience in battle, going all the way back to the days of Richard the Lionheart and his bloody crusades into the Levant. There wasn't much Christopher had not faced in battle, and there wasn't a battle commander anywhere who could outsmart him. Particularly not a Welsh. He kept up with the siege engines, which had been built from the fine ash forests near the castle and then rolled up to the moat, where they could hurl any number of projectiles over, and at, the walls. Sometimes they used tree stumps covered in oil and lit on fire, swinging those over the walls and hoping to catch something on fire.

They had been successful more than they had been unsuccessful.

In addition to the siege engines, Christopher had put his men to building pontoons and ladders to get across the moat and scale the walls. Led by his sons, his men hauled wood across the pontoons and built a scaffold against the side of the eastern wall because there was enough ground footing. Dozens of men could get up on that platform at once. Christopher had been wise enough to have his men soak the wood in water so nothing flaming could burn it down. The other walls were too close to the moat, and it was difficult for any of the ladders to gain a foothold, so the focus was concentrated on the eastern wall.

As the platform was built and the siege engines were swinging away, Christopher positioned two enormous trebuchets directly across the moat from the western wall and, using those terrible engines, flung boulders into the actual wall. One individual boulder wouldn't do a lot of damage, but many boulders in successive order could do quite a bit. The western wall had holes and giant cracks as Christopher continued to beat the wall down with the boulders his men were bringing in from the nearby mountains—the rough-cut chunks of ancient black rock that could be hurled into the walls, hard enough to break the sandstone they were made from.

The holes in the western wall grew, but de Lohr's patience wasn't infinite. A month into the siege, he'd received word from Henry, demanding that he make short work of the siege by any means necessary. Also contained within that message was the suggestion that the castle not be demolished, and peace was often attained without use of flaming projectiles and swords. Hints were brought about that an alliance between de Lohr and the Gwenwynwyn family still living in the castle should be explored. Then the suggestion became plain—perhaps a marriage offer was in order.

Curtis, Christopher's eldest son and heir, was not married.

Henry wasn't hinting. He was commanding.

Curtis de Lohr was slated for the sacrificial altar of peace.

Christopher had to think about that, long and hard. Curtis was his shining star, a knight with no equal. He was big, powerful, brave, tough, and everything that came with a man of his stature. War flowed through his veins. Even now, as the siege raged onward, Curtis was working on the eastern scaffolding, supervising the rebuild of the section knocked away by the Welsh the previous night. Christopher had put it on him specifically because he wanted Curtis out of the way while he tried to negotiate a peaceful end to a siege that threatened to go on for as long as the plucky Welsh could hold out.

God only knew how long that would be.

But now, with Curtis managing the scaffold, Christopher was faced with a Welsh scout who served him, a man who knew the language and customs and had shouted de Lohr's offer to the Welsh commanders on the western wall.

The answer he received was not one that Christopher was willing to accept.

"Be plain," Christopher said when the scout was too slow to answer. "What, *exactly*, did he say?"

The scout took a deep breath for courage. "I was told that the Lord of *Castell Brythonig* would rather—"

He was cut off by Christopher. "Call the castle by its rightful name in my presence."

The scout nodded quickly. "Forgive me, my lord," he said. "It is Brython Castle. But the Welsh will only call it by the Welsh name of *Brythonig*. After their ancestors."

Christopher waved him off irritably. "Never mind that," he said. "What, exactly, did the commander say?"

The scout seemed to hesitate. "Mind you, my lord, I am only the messenger," he said. "I am told that the Lord of Co… I mean, the Lord of Brython would rather marry his daughter to a pig than an English knight."

Christopher didn't rise to the insult. He'd long learned to choose his battles wisely, because when he fought, he fought to win. He wasn't going to acknowledge the insult dealt to him by men who were on the losing end of a castle siege.

"For decades, Gwenwynwyn ap Owain's descendants had possession of this castle," he said. "Since ap Owain was loyal to

John and even Henry when he was younger, we left Brython Castle in peace. There was even a contingent of English soldiers here, and they have been for years. My scouts kept abreast of the castle's activities, but it was never one of concern."

The scout shook his head. "It was not, my lord."

"As long as it did not harbor rebels, it was of no concern to me."

"Indeed, my lord."

Christopher eyed the scout, who had been with him for many years. "In fact," he said, "you have been watching it from time to time, Glynn. Much of the information I received has come from you."

Glynn ap Gower nodded shortly. "It has, my lord," he said. "I received my information from my own family as well as from people in the nearby village, or those who had passed through, or…"

Christopher held up a hand to silence him. "I am not questioning the accuracy," he said. "The entire reason we've come here is because the castle was lost to Gwenwynwyn's enemy, Llewelyn. Henry wants it back."

"I understand, my lord."

"One question that has not been answered for me is *where* Gwenwynwyn's descendants are," Christopher said. "And by that I mean those who lost the castle to Llewelyn. The man has at least two sons that we know of. Why have we not seen them?"

Glynn shook his head. "No one can seem to answer that question, my lord," he said, rather wearily. "The castle was lost to Llewelyn over a month ago, but no one seems to know what became of the man's son."

"He possibly has a second son, I'm told."

Glynn lifted his eyebrows. "The Wraith?" he said. "No one

that I know of has ever seen him. I do not know if he truly exists."

That was true. Rumors of how many children Gwenwynwyn had were circulating still, even after many years. No one really knew. But they did know he had at least one for certain. In any case, Christopher simply shook his head.

"Regardless, we do know that Llewelyn himself is not in command of the castle," he said. "Are we certain that his men are?"

Glynn shrugged. "As certain as we can be of anything right now, my lord," he said. "I made your offer to the commander of Brython, and he would only say that his daughter would marry a pig first."

"As we do not even know who the offer was made to."

"Nay, we do not, my lord," Glynn said. "But one thing is for certain."

"What is that?"

"Whoever holds the castle is well placed in Llewelyn's court," Glynn said knowingly. "For a castle of this importance, one badly coveted by the Welsh and English alike, it is someone of wealth or ranking or both. Your marriage offer has not been made to a peasant."

He was right. Christopher sighed heavily, pondering the situation as he grasped a wooden cup of watered wine and drank.

"This is a damn puzzling business," he muttered. "Clearly, someone holds that castle, someone who has been able to hold me off for almost a month. *Me.* I would hazard to say that no one holds out against me, but that would sound arrogant."

Glynn's lips twitched with a smile. "It is the truth, my lord," he said. "The man holding Brython against you must be clever, indeed."

That didn't make Christopher feel any better, and he scratched his head in a wearied gesture. His hair, blond and full in his youth, had mostly gone to gray. It was still thick, and he still kept it cut in the same fashion he'd always worn, but that silver hair was dirty from having been kept buried under a helm since the siege began. It was dirt fed by exhaustion that covered Christopher from head to toe. The siege was getting old, and he wanted to go home, but they didn't seem to be getting anywhere. He couldn't even get a straight answer on who, exactly, was in command of Brython's defenses or his offer of marriage. In truth, he'd only offered because Henry had demanded it, but Henry didn't know warfare like Christopher did. Marriage offers weren't exactly appropriate in the heat of battle, and he'd been loath to do it, but there were too many of Henry's soldiers and knights within his ranks for him not to have obeyed a command from the king.

He'd been forced into it.

Still… something had to be done to end this siege, or he'd grow old and die here. Perhaps if a marriage offer didn't work, something else would. Anything to end this mess. He was just about to comment on that when a soldier abruptly appeared in the open tent flap.

"My lord," the soldier said breathlessly. "Curtis and his men have managed to bridge the gap between the scaffold and the top of the wall. We have breached the castle!"

That had everyone in the tent, including Christopher, running out and heading toward the eastern wall.

A chaotic day was only going to grow worse.

CHAPTER ONE

THE *SAESNEG BASTARD* tried to take her head off.

They were pouring over the eastern wall because they'd managed to get the platform repaired and ladders up, even though her men had done their best to dislodge them. They couldn't burn the platform down because the English had been clever—they'd soaked the wood with water. Flame couldn't take hold. Every time they tried to dislodge the ladders, the English archers would fire at them. She'd already lost several men because of those damnable archers.

Damn, damn, damn!

Now, the wall was breached, and she was fairly certain there was no way to stem the tide of English soldiers and knights crowding onto the wall walk. They were armed and looking for blood. That being the case, she did the only thing she could do.

"*Bylchu!*" she cried.

Breach!

The alarm was sounded. The Welsh in the bailey below began to run for the wall with anything they could use for a weapon—clubs, swords, broken pieces of wood. One man even had an iron rod from the blacksmith's forge. They were rushing to protect what they believed to be rightfully theirs, a castle that had seen its share of English and Welsh ownership. But *Castell Brythonig*, or Brython Castle, was built upon a mount that, legend said, was a gate to the Otherworld where the ancestors of the Welsh had risen from. What the English didn't understand was that not only were they dealing with a prize castle that controlled a major road in and out of Wales, but they were dealing with a locale that ancient legend spoke of as a sacred site.

Brython wasn't the castle's real name. The real name had been lost to time because there had been a fortress on that exact location since the time of the Romans. Some thought the real name of the castle was Arallfyd, meaning Otherworld, but somehow over the centuries, Arallfyd and Otherworld became Brython for the sacred place the Brittonic people had come from. They were only legends, really, but legends the Welsh had always taken seriously. The location meant more to them than it did to the English.

And that was why she wasn't going to let the English gain control of the castle.

Again.

And the woman had been charged with that task. Unfortunately, her resolve wavered when she saw big, powerful knights with thousands of weapons leaping over the wall. It seemed as if they had a thousand weapons, but it was possibly more like only one or two. She, too, was armed, but in spite of her command capability and skill with a blade, even she wasn't sure she could win in hand-to-hand combat with the English knights, who were making short work of the Welsh soldiers trying to stop them.

"Lady!" someone was shouting at her. "*Elle!* Come down

from there! You will be killed!"

Enid Avrielle ferch Gwenwynwyn heard her name being called, knowing who it was before she even looked. She knew her commander's voice, the very loud and steady voice of Gethin ap Guto. The same man who had rejected the English offer of a marriage of truce. He was frantic to get her off the wall.

But Elle wouldn't listen.

No one told her what to do. She'd established that early in her life when she didn't even like the sound of her own name and insisted on being called Elle because it sounded stronger than what her mother had saddled her with. Ignoring Gethin's shouts, she unsheathed her sword, summoned her courage, and charged forward along the wooden fighting platform that now constituted most of the wall walk around Brython. The bombardment by the English had managed to damage most of the fighting platforms and put big holes in the stone wall walks, but there were still places where one could move around on the wall.

This was one of them.

But it was a perilous wooden platform at best. In fact, most of Brython was perilous from the damage the English had inflicted, but she wasn't going to let them know just how badly they were hurt. More and more English were pouring over the wall, and her men were being thrown down to the bailey below, most of them with holes in them made by English weapons. Elle simply wasn't going to stand for it. She'd been fighting this battle from the beginning and she was going to fight it until the end.

With a roar that sounded more like a scream, she charged.

A particularly big knight was coming over the wall, and she

ran at him like a bull, lowering her head and ramming him right in the midsection as he came over the top. Her momentum threw him off balance, and he instinctively grabbed hold of her. Together, they went toppling back over the wall and crashed into several men who were coming up the ladders. The English knight had her in his iron grip, and from the way he was falling, he was taking all of the concussions.

She hardly felt a thing.

But she did know they were falling.

For a woman who suffered from an inherent fear of heights, she had to admit that tackling the knight as he came over the wall hadn't been the smartest move. As they hit the platform about ten feet below the top of the wall, she ended up falling onto her right arm and shoulder. In the process, her head hit the platform, and the helm she was wearing, which was too big for her, tumbled off her head. Blonde hair, braided, spilled out, and it was obvious to anyone with half a brain that a woman, dressed in mail and leather, was in their midst. Realizing that she had somehow lost her broadsword in the tumble, Elle began to punch the knight in his lowered visor as hard as she could.

"You... *bastard!*" she yelled, raining a furious barrage of punches on his face and neck. "I will kill you, do you hear? This is *my* castle! I will kill every last one of you Saesneg dogs!"

The knight was nearly three times her size. He was also heavily armed. His sword was in its sheath at his side, and he had daggers along the belt at his waist. When Elle realized this, she made a grab for the daggers, but he grabbed her wrists with a grip of iron. He also moved out from underneath her as she tried to kick him, since he had her hands trapped. With ease, he stood up and pulled her with him as she fought back with everything she had. The knight just held on to her wrists, making no move to strike her. He did stop the next knight passing by him, however, as the man prepared to mount the ladder to the wall above.

"Take her," the knight said, shoving her at the man with his foot on the bottom rung of the ladder. "Take her to my father. Tell him she's one of the soldiers."

"I am *not* a soldier," Elle shouted, managing to kick him in the armored shin. "This is *my* castle. Send your men away before I kill them all!"

The man with his foot on the ladder snorted. "You take her," he said. "I have my fight waiting for me. I think you've found yours."

With that, he slipped up the ladder, leaving the enormous knight hanging on to a wildcat of a woman. Elle swore she heard him sigh sharply, clearly displeased, before releasing her wrists and grabbing her by the braids.

He had moved like lightning.

One moment, he had her arms, and in the next, he was holding her hair and wrapping it around his gloved hand. In fact, his grip on her hair bloody well hurt, and she winced, but she didn't stop fighting. But her resistance had no effect on him, as he somehow managed to get her up over his shoulder and take the ladder down to the next platform, where he took yet another ladder down to the ground.

Elle fought and twisted the entire way, but it was difficult when he had her head so tightly trapped. In fact, she couldn't move her head or neck in the least, and she had to admit his grip was badly paining her. With her slung over his shoulder, but quite awkwardly because of the way he was holding her, he ended up on the pontoon bridge that the English had strung across the moat. He was halfway across when Elle twisted enough to throw her thigh into his head, knocking him off balance.

Into the moat they both went.

The knight landed on his feet, but Elle landed upside down, her head and face in the brackish water. She had water up her nose and in her mouth because she'd been unprepared for the plunge into the water, and, caught off guard, she started to inhale it. The knight didn't notice she was in the water until he was nearly to the edge of the moat, when he suddenly flipped her right side up and tossed her, nearly unconscious, onto the shore.

The knight rolled her onto her right side, pounding on her back as water poured from her mouth and she began coughing up that horrible moat water. But the near-drowning experience had washed the fight out of her for the moment, and he heaved her onto his shoulder again, dazed and limp, and marched with her to the English encampment just beyond the tree line, about a quarter of a mile away.

Elle was coming around by the time they arrived, but barely. She was gradually aware that they were heading into a tent as the knight, far more gently this time, pulled her off his shoulder and put her on a cot or a bed of some kind. Elle didn't even know what it was, and she hardly cared because she was still struggling to breathe. There was still water in her lungs. Off to her left, she could hear someone speak.

"I thought you might be interested in this one," the knight said. "She threw herself at me as I came over the wall, and we fell back to the platform. She's fortunate we didn't fall all the way to the ground."

Another voice, deep and serious, answered. "What happened to her?" he said. "Why is she wet?"

"She was fighting me and we fell into the moat," the knight replied. "You might want to have the physic take a look at her. I think she swallowed a good deal of water."

"*Who* is she?"

"That is for you to find out, Papa," the knight said. "She says this is her castle."

Elle suddenly came alive, still dazed, but the fight was returning. "I'll kill you both," she said, her eyes rolling around to the back of her head as she tried to sit up. She balled her fists, putting them in front of her. "Do not think that just because I am a woman, I cannot fight. I will fight you with one hand tied behind my back. I'll fight you with my eyes closed and I'll win. I'll kick you to death!"

As if to emphasize her point, she tried to kick out, but ended up knocking herself onto the floor. That brought the knight and the man he'd been speaking to right to her side. They lifted her up and put her back on the cot, but she slapped at their hands and tried to kick one of them. She didn't care which one—whoever was closer. But the knight pushed her back on the bed.

"Lie down and behave yourself, lady," he said. "You've done enough fighting for one day."

"Never," she said. "I'll never submit to you Saesneg hounds."

"I do not think you have a choice."

That wasn't what Elle wanted to hear. She kicked and swung her fists again and ended up on the floor once more. But this time, she crawled under the cot before they could grab her, so they didn't try. They simply backed off and left her alone. Somehow, being under the cot seemed to calm her down because it was a false sense of protection. She huddled underneath the cot as the older man with thick gray hair turned to the knight.

"Continue with your duties," he said. "I will tend to the lady."

"I do not need tending!" she shouted.

"Shut up," the knight barked at her, irritated.

"I will not!"

"You will if I come over there and put a gag over your mouth."

"Try it and I'll bite your fingers off!"

The knight started to move in her direction, but the older man stopped him. "Go," he told him, softly but firmly. "I will take care of the lady."

"I do not need to be taken care of!" she declared.

The knight waved an annoyed arm at her as if to wash his hands of her for good. He was finished arguing with a fool. As he marched from the tent, the older man moved over to a table that had a pitcher and cups on it. He poured himself some wine as Elle crouched under the cot and shivered.

"Shall I tell you what is happening to your castle now?" he finally said.

He had a fatherly, deep, and gentle voice. Elle coughed again, still clearing her lungs, but she realized her teeth were chattering.

Her situation was not improving.

"Nothing is happening to it," she said with more confidence than she felt. "My men are stopping your army from coming over the walls. You will go home empty-handed, Saesneg."

The older man lifted the cup to his lips and drank. "I think not," he said after a swallow. "As we speak, my men are in your bailey. They will soon be lifting the portcullis, and after that, the castle is ours. I'm afraid your men will all be prisoners within the hour. If, in fact, the castle really is yours."

Elle didn't want to admit that his scenario was very likely going to happen. She hadn't even let herself entertain the thought until this very moment. She couldn't stomach swallowing the reality of defeat, not after all of the fighting and planning she'd done. Not after everything she'd sacrificed.

It can't happen!

"It is just as likely that my men will repel your men," she said, trying to sound brave. "We have the advantage."

"What advantage is that?"

"We want it more than you do."

The older man shrugged as if that was, indeed, a possibility. "Mayhap," he said. "But before we continue, may I introduce myself? I am the Earl of Hereford and Worcester. My name is Christopher de Lohr. May I know your name, my lady?"

That brought a reaction from Elle. She knew very well who the Earl of Hereford and Worcester was. Everyone on the marches did because he was a very important man. In fact, knowing who he was emboldened her. She wasn't going to hide behind mystery, because her name, her family, had always stood for something strong and true. She was proud of the name. She was proud of her heritage. If this really was the moment of her defeat, perhaps being forthright with the enemy would do more good than calling him names and resisting him. To be perfectly honest, she knew that de Lohr was perhaps the one man in England other than the king who could give her back the castle.

Perhaps if she was honest with him.

Perhaps if he understood her.

She came out from underneath the cot.

"I know you to be a man of honor, my lord," she said. "I

know you by reputation. So did my father."

"Who is your father?"

She hesitated. "If I tell you, will you bargain with me?"

"I will listen to you."

She wasn't sure if that meant he was willing to negotiate with her, but she was willing to take the chance. At this point, pragmatically speaking, she had nothing to lose.

According to him, she'd already lost.

"Do I have your word?" she asked.

He nodded. "You have my word that I will listen with respect to every word you say."

That was enough for her. Since she was dealing with the man at the top and not one of his subordinates, she would tell him what he wanted to know.

"Gwenwynwyn ap Owain," she said.

Elle thought that made him stand a little taller. De Lohr had been on the marches for as many years as her father, and they'd most certainly fought at one time or another. They were not strangers to each other, and, truth be told, there was respect for a good adversary. Elle could only pray that de Lohr felt that for her father as he'd felt it for Hereford.

"I know he had a son," he said after a moment's pause. "Two sons, I believe. Gruffydd and a second son that no one knows much about. The English call him the Wraith."

"Gruffydd is my brother."

"And your name?"

Her eyes glittered at him in the dim light of the tent. "I am Enid Avrielle ferch Gwenwynwyn."

He cocked his head curiously. "I have lived here for many years and I've never heard of a daughter," he said. "Who was your mother?"

"Margaret Corbet."

He pondered that news. "I knew her father," he said. "The Corbets hold Caus Castle and are, in fact, Norman. If you are being truthful with me, that makes you half English."

Her hands found their way onto her arms as she embraced herself, trying to keep warm. "I am being truthful with you," she said. "You have given me your word, and I shall give you mine."

He studied her. "Then I believe you," he said. "But there is something more I wish to know."

"What is that?"

"Where are your brothers? Are they fighting as well?"

She shook her head. "Gruffydd is not fighting."

"What about the second brother?" Christopher asked. "Does he lead this battle?"

"There is no second brother. Only me."

"And you have been fighting this battle?"

"I have."

He paused a moment, thoughtfully, before continuing. "I would assume this is not your first battle."

"Hardly."

"Do you always fight?"

"I have been fighting since I was a child."

Christopher was a sharp man. He studied her for a moment, mulling over her reply and suspecting what she was telling him. There was something in his eyes that suggested he was onto her and everything she stood for. This lass, with her dirty blonde braids, clad in clothing that only warriors would wear. She had taken on a man significantly larger than she was when she charged him on the wall. *She* had been doing the fighting.

This pale wisp of a girl.

Pale wisp…

"You are the Wraith," he said quietly.

Elle nodded in confirmation. Truthfully, there was no use in denying it because she was hoping that her honesty would get her what she wanted in the end. In fact, she'd easily confessed everything to him, things she kept hidden from most, but she'd done it for a reason. Evasiveness most certainly would not win the trust of a man like de Lohr, something she evidently had earned. She wanted to keep it. Moreover, she had been fighting a battle against the English for almost a month, and even she knew when the fighting had to stop and the negotiating could begin.

This was the moment.

"The name Enid means *spirit* to my people," she said. "The tales of Gwenwynwyn's Wraith… That is how it came about."

There was a hint of approval in his eyes. "I see," he said. "Then ap Owain has a daughter who fights, not another son."

"That is correct."

"Where *is* Gruffydd, Lady Enid?"

Elle shook her head. "I am not called Enid," she said. "I have always been known by a version of my middle name—Elle. That is what I will answer to."

Christopher dipped his head as if to apologize for addressing her incorrectly. "Thank you for telling me," he said. "And thank you for your honest answers to my questions. I will not tell anyone you are the Wraith if you do not wish for me to."

That brought a look of surprise from Elle. "You would keep such a secret?" she said. "Your men will want to know that my father did not have two sons. Two sons can mean more trouble than a man with a daughter who learned to fight from an early age."

Christopher went back to the wine and poured a second

cup. He went over to Elle, extending it to her, and after a moment's hesitation, she took it and sucked it down greedily.

"Not necessarily," he said. "The Welsh breed strong women warriors as well as men. But you did not answer my question."

"What is that?"

"Where is your brother, Gruffydd?"

That was a question she didn't want to answer. She'd avoided it, now for the third time. As much as she would have liked to have remained evasive, the truth was that the English would discover what happened to her elder brother eventually. They would comb through Brython, search every chamber, every shadow, and eventually, they would find him. Gruffydd would have no hesitation in telling them about his sister.

Better that de Lohr hear it from her.

"In the vault of Brython," she said quietly.

If that answer was surprising to Christopher, he didn't show it. Not really. A flicker in his eyes perhaps suggested it, but that was quickly gone.

"I see," he said. "May I ask why?"

Elle extended her empty cup to him, a silent plea for more. He took the cup and poured it to the rim before handing it back to her. As he waited patiently, she drained it again, and it occurred to him that starving out the castle might have done its job. She was very thirsty and probably hungry, so he went to the tent flap to summon food and more drink. But until then, he'd continue to fill her cup and hope that a tipsy daughter might spill more secrets.

He wondered if she was aware of that.

"Would you like some dry clothing?" he said. "My wife is about your size, and there are times when she has come on a battle march with me. I could see if there is something of hers, somewhere, for you to wear."

Elle shook her head. "Nay," she said. "You are polite to offer, but I will stay in my own clothing. This is who I am, wet or dry. I will not change it."

"Nor would I," Christopher said, pouring the last of the wine into the cup in her outstretched hand. "But I will admit that I am curious why your brother is in the vault. Will you tell me?"

The full cup was almost to her lips again when she paused. She wasn't looking at him, but rather had a distant gleam to her eye.

"Because he was going to betray us," she said simply.

"What do you mean?"

She took a big gulp of wine before replying. "Precisely that, my lord," she said, her tongue loosening with the amount of wine she'd ingested in a short amount of time. "Gruffydd and my father shared the same loyalty."

Christopher wasn't going to play dumb when he already knew. "To England?"

"Aye."

He was careful as he continued, because he wanted information only she could supply. "We had it on good authority that Llewelyn had taken Brython from your brother," he said. "That was not true?"

"Nay," Elle said before taking another drink. "But I did."

His brow furrowed. "You took it?" he said, trying to clarify. "But it already belonged to your family."

She tipped her head back and gulped down the rest of the wine. "Do you not understand, my lord?" she said. "My brother and father were fools. They were forsaken of everything the Welsh stood for. They pandered to the English. To warlords like you. They were subservient to the king."

"And you are not?"

She shook her head stubbornly. "I serve Wales," she said. "Not Llewelyn or my father, but Wales. An independent Wales."

"And you have been trying to achieve that in this battle?"

"I have," she said firmly. "I was doing well enough until your knights mounted the walls. I've managed to hold you off for an entire month, and I'm sure not many can make that declaration. Does that shock you?"

Frankly, it did, because he was coming to see that this slip of a woman had held off an entire English army. Worse still, she'd held off him. Him! Truthfully, he didn't know how he felt about that, but, for some reason, he smiled. Then he started to laugh as if realizing he'd been the butt of a great joke.

He could hardly believe it.

When Elle realized he was laughing, her eyes narrowed at him. "Why are you laughing?" she demanded. "Have I said something humorous?"

He waved her off. "Nay, you have not," he said. "But you remind me of someone."

"Who?"

"My wife," he said. "You think you are the strongest, toughest woman on the marches? Think again. When I first met my wife, she fought me like a banshee until I married her. She did it to gain peace. I did it to gain a castle. I also have a daughter who has fought with men. More than that, she used to be a spy. So you see, my lady, strong women do not shock me. Not in the least. I am surrounded by them."

Elle's irritation took a dousing. "Ah," she said, eyeing him with uncertainty as he continued to snort. "But what is so funny?"

He shook his head. "The fact that you, an untrained warrior woman, have held me off for an entire month," he said. Then he started clapping, his eyes glimmering with mirth. "*Da iawn*, my lady. Well done. You have my respect."

The wine and his reaction fed her courage. "Then will you call off your attack?" she said. "I want my castle back."

Much to her surprise, he looked as if he was actually considering it. "If I do, what will you do with it?"

The question puzzled her. "Live there, of course."

"In peace?"

"If the Saesneg leave us alone, then I will not bother them."

"But what if your allies call upon you?" he asked. "Will you answer the call if it was to fight against the English?"

"Of course I would."

The food arrived. Christopher tossed back the flap to admit servants bearing trays of boiled beef and a stew of vegetables. The smell of fresh bread filled the tent almost immediately. Standing over by the cot, wet and dirty, Elle felt her mouth begin to water, and her stomach, so empty these past several days, began to growl and twist. She actually put her hand to her belly as if to comfort her own stomach at the sight of so much food. The smell was making her lightheaded.

And Christopher knew it.

"Would you like to eat, my lady?" he asked.

Elle nodded, trying not to look too eager. But Christopher didn't invite her to sit down, not yet.

He had a plan.

"Lady Elle, since you seem to know a good deal about warfare, you know that there is never truly a victory in battle, nor is there ever truly a surrender," he said. "Any battle takes compromise and negotiation, so that both armies know their place. Not everyone gets everything they want, and most especially the losing army. Would you agree with that?"

Poor Elle was starting to tremble. She only had eyes for the food, but she nodded to his question. "I would," she said. "That is the nature of war."

"Exactly," Christopher said. "You have asked for your castle returned to you, and I am willing to do that. With a compromise."

She looked at him then. She'd been shockingly adept at keeping her emotions in check, but when he said that, her eyes widened.

"You would?" she gasped.

"With a compromise."

"What is it?"

He went over to the table where the food was sitting, fragrant and hot, and sat down. He still hadn't invited her to sit. Reaching out, he tore a hunk of meat off the boiled knuckle and bit into it as she watched.

"The truth of the matter is that you are my prisoner," he said, chewing. "I am the victor and you are the loser. If you do not agree to my compromise, know this—I will imprison every one of your men, strip the castle of anything that suggests the Welsh were even there, and put an army of a thousand English there. None of your allies or enemies could dislodge them, because if you try, I will summon my own allies and have fifteen thousand men at Brython to overrun the countryside. I will punish anyone who attempts to take the castle from me, and I will kill anyone who helps them. Am I clear so far?"

Elle's trembling was growing worse. "Why are you threatening me?"

He swallowed the bite in his mouth. "Because I want you to know how serious I am about this," he said. "I have the sense that you are not agreeable to the English, in any way, and I am telling you that if you do not learn to live and work alongside us, peacefully, you will have a difficult and short life. No one will remember your name after you are gone. Battle is not about killing the enemy with no end in sight. It is always about fighting for your cause but understanding that there is, indeed, an end in sight, and that end is peace. Peace is achieved by cooperation and negotiation. Do you understand me?"

Elle was watching him put more food in his mouth. "I understand," she said. "What do you want from me?"

"Are you married?"

She shook her head. "Nay."

"Then you will take an English husband," he said, chewing. "I will not imprison you or your men, but allow you to live freely at Brython—but you will marry an Englishman, and he will bring his army to the castle as my garrison. You will live in peace and learn the ways of your enemy, as he will learn your ways. It is a compromise."

Elle wasn't so hungry or tipsy that she didn't understand what he was saying. He'd been kind to her, and had lulled her into a false sense of security until this very moment, when he lowered the hammer. She'd foolishly fallen for it. Realizing the tables had been turned on her, for she had thought she was the one being so clever, she widened her eyes and staggered back.

"Nay!" she roared. "I will not!"

Christopher abruptly stood up, slamming his fist on the tabletop and sending the food jumping in all directions. "Refuse me and I will send you to London and the king," he said. Gone was the gentle father, replaced by a snarling and terrifying warlord. "Let Henry do what he wishes with you, for I do not care. But I can tell you that you will never see Wales again, lady. If this is what you wish, then by all means, refuse me. I dare you."

Elle was so shocked, so terrified, that she couldn't even speak. She took another step back and ended up falling onto the cot behind her. She was shaking so badly that she couldn't maintain her balance. She was starving, full of wine, and de Lohr had played his game to his advantage. She was no longer in a position of respect, but in one of surrender. And that was exactly what he was demanding.

Her surrender.

It had come to that.

She struggled to push herself up from the cot.

"You cannot ask this of me," she said hoarsely, her voice quivering. "I shall not—"

He cut her off. "Shall not *what?*"

She swallowed hard, frightened by the man. "You cannot—"

He cut her off again. "I can do anything I wish," he said. "I am the victor. Bear in mind that I do not need your permission for this. I can simply do it."

She ended up on her feet, but it was shaky. "How would you feel if someone was treating your wife the way you are treating me?"

"What makes you think I did not treat her like this when I first met her?"

"And she still married you?"

"She had no choice. Nor do you."

He was right. God help her, he was right. She knew it and he knew it. Distraught and unable to conceal it, Elle turned her back to him. The tears began streaming down her face, but she didn't lift her hand to wipe them because she didn't want him to know how badly he'd upset her.

Everything was at an end.

Nothing he said was untrue. Brython was falling to the English no matter how hard she tried to keep up the defenses. God, she'd tried so hard. The truth was that she only had about four hundred men to de Lohr's thousands. They were able to hold as long as the English didn't get over the wall, but they had. The portcullis was probably already lifted and the English were probably already in possession of the castle. Gruffydd had probably already been released. Everything she'd fought for...

It was gone.

"I put my brother in the vault because he said the same thing," she said, unable to hide the fact that she was weeping. "He wanted me to marry an English warlord and create an alliance. He is allied with the English king, much like my father was, and he expected me to be complicit in their betrayal of my country. But I cannot do it. I cannot do it for him or for you."

Christopher could hear the defeat in her voice. She was no longer the stubborn, hysterical woman who had first entered this tent. Too much drink and no food was breaking her down, as he'd intended, though he had to admit he felt some pity for her. He wasn't cruel to women by nature, but she was an exception. She would probably ram a dagger into his chest given the chance. He had a fighter of a woman he'd married, as he told her, so he knew how to deal with them.

At least, he hoped so.

He'd had some practice.

"Then what is your choice for the rest of your life, my lady?" he asked, not unkindly. "To be a prisoner? Because that is what you will be if you do not agree to my terms. You will be kept by the king and, more than likely, married off against your will. You'll find yourself in France or Aragon or somewhere east. You will never see Wales again, but if this is a life that suits you better than my offer, then I will ensure you receive it. The choice is yours."

Again, he was making it seem as if she had options in this. Whatever decision she made, it would be on her head even though there was no real choice in front of her. It was hell or even greater hell. Those were her selections. The tears began to come again, no matter how hard she tried to stop them.

"You are asking me to betray my country," she whispered tightly. "You are asking me to surrender everything I am."

He shook his head. "I am asking no such thing," he said. "My lady, you seem intelligent. If you have held off my army for a month, then you are not only bright, you are clever. I want you to think about this situation from a different perspective. Can you do that?"

"Why should I?"

"Because it is important. Will you try?"

"Speak, then."

Christopher wasn't sure he had her cooperation, but he was going to try. "As the wife of a prestigious warlord, you will be in a unique position," he said. "Your men, your vassals, will see that you are willing to work toward a peaceful coexistence with England, a country that is not going away. We are not going to disappear tomorrow. We, and you, and even the Scots, live on a land surrounded by oceans, and it is ours to protect. There are so many enemies who have tried to do us harm, but we are the keepers of this glorious and unique land. Wales is glorious and unique, as is England. Separately, we are weaker than we would be if we were all united. United under one king to protect everything we have. Does that make sense?"

Elle was still tearing up, quickly wiping at her eyes because she was embarrassed that she couldn't seem to control her emotions. "I suppose it does," she said. "But Wales is smaller than England. Why should the English covet it so much?"

He began to tear apart the bread, which was cooling by now. The smell of it arose fresh as he broke off the end of the loaf. "We wish to bring peace," he said simply. "Peace for all."

"We do not need the English to bring us peace."

He cocked a blond eyebrow. "Then you can bring it amongst yourselves?" he said, his tone cynical. "Because the Welsh have been fighting amongst themselves since the world began. You still fight among yourselves. There will never be one king to unify you because you cannot agree on who it should be. Look at England—we have one king. No small, bickering kingdoms. We are united under one king, and that is what makes us stronger than Wales and Scotland. We are trying to bring that peace to you, but you are warmongers. You think war is the only way, and that is a horrible existence. Do you really want to be at war for the rest of your life?"

She had stopped weeping for the most part, knowing he was, again, correct in his assessment of the Welsh. They did fight each other quite a bit. There was no unifying king, nor was there any hope for one. Even she knew that. She could smell the fresh bread, and it was weakening her resistance, killing her resolve.

The concept of surrender was becoming easier and easier.

"I do not want to be sent away," she finally said. "To never see my home again would be worse than death."

Christopher took a knife off the table and buttered his piece of bread. "Then it would be reasonable to accept the offer of a marriage to an English warlord," he said. "You could remain here, at Brython, and you could teach your children about their Welsh blood, and your husband could teach them about their English blood. They will be children of two worlds, and they will be the seeds of peace, my lady. Your children would do great things in the history of our countries. Would that not make you proud?"

Elle was watching him butter the bread with longing in her eyes. His words made sense, but they were confusing her because she'd only been raised to understand conflict. Understanding peace… That was a difficult concept.

"I… I do not know," she said honestly.

Christopher could see that she was put off balance by his question. "Having such children would be leaving your mark upon the history of Wales far more than fighting and dying for Brython," he said. Then he stood up and went to her, holding out the piece of buttered bread. "Peace is always the better way, my lady. I believe you can become a great lady if you will only understand that."

The bread was too close, and she was starving. She couldn't even remember when she last had bread. Her pride collapsed and she took the bread, shoving it into her mouth as he directed her toward the table. Like a dumb animal being led to the slaughter, she let him guide her to a chair even as he put more food in front of her, all the food she could eat. All the food she'd been denied since the siege began. Food and drink was hers for the taking as Christopher poured wine for her himself, leaning down so he was closer to her ear.

"If you are to play a man's game, then you must remember this," he said quietly. "In battle, there is always a winner and always a loser. In this case, you have lost. This loss will be what you make of it—it can change your life to one of gratitude or one of misery. Choose gratitude, my lady. You cannot always have everything you want in life. Teach your husband about the Welsh. Show him the good things, not the hatred and resistance. Give him a reason to help you fight for your people, should it come to that. Give him a reason to defend *you*."

With that, he finished pouring and headed over to the tent flap as Elle continued to shovel food in her mouth, which was so full that she could hardly chew. Christopher kept an eye on her as he muttered to a soldier outside the tent. When the soldier fled, Christopher reclaimed his seat across from Elle and watched her eat.

Like a woman starving.

Perhaps it had been a dirty trick to play on her, withholding food when she was clearly very hungry, but he thought his tactic might have worked. At least he had her thinking.

Now, he had to get the other half of this equation thinking, too.

CHAPTER TWO

"T HERE CAN'T BE more than three or four hundred men in there, Curt." A young knight with blond hair pulled into a ponytail at the back of his grimy neck was speaking. "I believe we've rounded up almost everyone. I've got more men heading into the keep and outbuildings to make sure."

Sir Curtis de Lohr listened to the report from his brother with satisfaction. "Well done, Myles," he said. They were standing in the open gatehouse, with the burned gates and lifted portcullis in front of them. Everything was twisted and burned, indicative of efforts of the English. "Nearly a month of siege, two hours of fighting once we breached the walls, and it's all over. Seems almost a disappointment."

Myles grinned. He, too, was looking at the gatehouse as de Lohr men moved in and gangs of prisoners were moved out. There was still some fighting going on in places, but for the most part, the castle had surrendered.

"I was hoping for more of a fight once we got in," he said. "We've had no fight at all for a month, and other than building platforms and launching projectiles over the wall, it has been rather dull."

Curtis was amused. "You can always punch a Welshman in the face as he walks by you on his way to being imprisoned."

Myles shook his head. "It is no fun unless he fights back."

Curtis chuckled at his younger brother. "Agreed," he said. "Mayhap there is still a Welshman or two left who would be happy to continue the fight, but I'll have to stand aside. My squire took my sword to be cleaned already, a sure sign of the end of battle. Who is in charge of sweeping the keep, by the way?"

"Roi and Sherry," Myles said. "Sherry has Adam and Andrew and Gabriel with him, so they'll make short work of the keep. I swear those boys are more frightening than their father ever was."

Curtis snorted. "Look at who their mother is," he said. "Our dearest sister Christin could take on an entire army by herself and probably win. How Alexander de Sherrington ever tamed our bold and terrifying sister is a mystery."

Myles eyed him. "You do not favor a bold woman, eh?"

Curtis shook his head firmly. "Give me a lovely, sweet, well-bred daughter of an earl who will produce strong sons and never speak her mind," he said. "*That* is the perfect woman."

"That is a boring woman."

"Why do you say that?"

"Are you truly telling me you do not fancy a woman with a little fire?"

Curtis shrugged. "A spark, mayhap," he said. "But I do not need an entire roaring blaze. In fact, did you see what happened to me earlier on the wall?"

Myles shook his head. "I did not," he said. "But Amaro told me about it. Your knight told me that, somehow, you found yourself a Welsh warrior woman?"

Curtis sneered in distaste. "She found *me*," he said. "Just as I was coming over the wall, she hit me in the chest, and we both fell about ten feet to the platform below. Foolish woman could have gotten us both killed."

"What did you do to her?" Myles asked, trying not to laugh at Curtis' utter insult at having been knocked over by a woman. "Is she alive to tell the tale?"

Curtis grunted. "I took her to Papa," he said. "Let him deal with her."

"Who is she?"

"I do not know," Curtis said. "She kept saying the castle was hers, so mayhap she can tell Papa everything he wants to know."

Myles lifted his big shoulders. "He knows something about unruly women," he said. "He has daughters like that. In fact, he married one. But if you tell Mama I said that, I will deny it to my grave."

Curtis smirked. "I will not tell her," he said. But his smile faded when he saw his brother, Richard, whom everyone called Roi, through the open portcullis. The man was out in the destroyed bailey gripping a sandy-haired man who seemed to have trouble walking. "Who is that with Roi?"

Myles spied them, too. "I do not know," he said. "But I will find out."

Curtis nodded. "Go," he said. "I am heading back to the wall. The last I saw, there were still pockets of fighting up there, and I want to quell them."

Myles was already walking into the bailey as he waved off Curtis, who turned toward the eastern wall. He hadn't taken five steps when he heard someone shouting his name.

"Curtis!" a voice boomed. "*Uncle Curt!*"

Coming to a halt, Curtis turned to see his eldest brother, Peter, heading in his direction. Following Peter were his two eldest sons, Matthew and Aaron. Tall and raven-haired Matthew was close to being knighted, while Aaron was a few years younger, nearly as tall, but had a few more years of squiring ahead of him. Aaron was the fiercer of the two and looked more like a de Lohr, with his father's blond looks, but he was quite disheartened to be a squire. Still. Walking behind them, and bringing up the rear of the group, was Peter's brother-in-law, Asa ben Thad.

Curtis held up a hand in greeting.

"Well?" he said as the group drew near. "What kind of damage are we seeing on the western wall?"

Peter, though the eldest de Lohr brother, was not the heir. He was his father's bastard who had come to live with the family before Curtis was born. Though no one had ever treated him differently, and he was very much a member of the family, the truth was that Curtis *was* the heir. Eleven years younger than Peter, he was the one who would inherit everything from his father, including the earldom, though Peter had earned quite an empire in his own right. Ludlow Castle was his property, among a few others, and he had wealth and prestige and a gorgeous wife, born a Jewess, though she had converted in order to marry Peter. Asa was Liora de Lohr's brother, and Peter and Liora had several children and a happy life together.

There was no one on the marches more respected than Peter de Lohr.

"The western wall has folded," Peter announced. His helm was off, his cropped blond hair streaked with dirt and sweat. "My men were able to get grappling hooks into the holes we opened up and have pulled themselves through. I came to see the damage from inside."

Curtis swept his arm in the direction of the gatehouse. "Go," he said. "I'm going to take a look at the wall walk. There was still some fighting when last I saw."

"'Tis a fine victory, Curt," Asa said, his blue eyes gleaming with the thrill of battle. "I shall long remember the damage of those rocks as they pounded into the western wall. Magnificent!"

He was grinning as he threw up his arms, mimicking the concussion of rocks and dust when the projectiles damaged the wall. Then he charged off toward the gatehouse with Matthew and Aaron behind him. Curtis and Peter watched him go, various stages of amusement on their faces.

"For a man who was not trained as a knight, I have never seen someone more enthusiastic about battle," Curtis muttered, grinning. "I will never go into a fight again without Asa. The man is fearless."

Peter chuckled. "He got a late start, that is for certain," he said. "He would not come to fight with us until his father passed away, God rest his soul. All Haim wanted was for his son to follow in his footsteps and become a jeweler, but all Asa wanted was to become a knight. He is a man of two different worlds more than most."

"He fights like he was born to it."

"He was *not* born to it."

Curtis knew the story. Asa had been born Jewish, like his sister, but the man had been a fighter from a young age. It became a point of contention as he grew older between him and his elderly father, who had married quite late in life, so in order to keep the old man happy, Asa turned away from any hope of becoming what he really wanted to be—a knight—to become what his father wanted him to be. Haim ben Thad had passed away five years ago, and Asa showed up at Ludlow Castle shortly thereafter, asking to be trained as a knight.

It was his dream.

As it turned out, he was a very fine warrior, and although he'd not yet been formally knighted, and would not be unless he converted to Christianity, it didn't matter to Asa. He fought with the knights, lived with them, and served with them.

And he loved every minute of it.

"He's a good man to have," Curtis said, having grown to appreciate Asa. "Every time the siege engines launched, he cheered as if he had just witnessed the greatest event of all time."

Peter grinned. "He loves it all," he said. "Speaking of greatest events, surmounting the wall was a brilliant move on your part. You have ended this awful siege, and I, for one, am grateful."

Curtis dipped his head in thanks. "When will you be heading home?"

"Soon," Peter said, scratching his head wearily. "You?"

Curtis moved his gaze to the hulking bastion of Brython, his mood sobering. "I think I *am* home," he said after a moment. "Papa has mentioned that he wants to garrison Brython, and he wants me to assume command. He's fearful of the Welsh tide that will undoubtedly return to reclaim it."

Peter waggled his eyebrows in sympathy, slapping Curtis on the shoulder. "I do not envy you, Curt," he muttered. "In fact, I think I am going to—"

They were cut off by a shout, and they both turned to see a soldier approaching, one of the men who served Christopher personally. The man was calling Curtis by name, so Peter left him to head to the interior of the castle while Curtis went out to greet the man.

"My lord, your father has summoned you," the soldier said. "If it would not be inconvenient, he asks that you come now."

Curtis glanced at the top of the wall, where he could only see his men now. The platform, full of frenzied men less than an hour ago, was now calm as soldiers moved up and down at a careful pace. He emitted a piercing whistle between his teeth, catching the attention of most of the men in view.

"Is there fighting still?" he shouted.

The men waved him off. "No more, my lord," one of them shouted. "We have them subdued."

Curtis nodded. "Where are my knights?" he asked. "Amaro and Hugo?"

Several soldiers were pointing to the north end of the wall. "Organizing the prisoners," the same man answered. "Shall I summon them?"

Curtis waved them off. The wall was being handled by two men sworn to him, Amaro de Laraga and Hugo de Bernay. They were seasoned men from good families who served him at Lioncross Abbey, giving him his own command within his father's command. He even had five hundred soldiers that were sworn only to him. They were good men, all of them, and they were the more elite soldiers out of his father's army. Even now, they were on the wall with Amaro and Hugo, and Curtis knew they would secure the wall. He wasn't needed.

He followed his father's soldier back to the man's tent.

Sunset was approaching, and the campfires, which had burned all day, were now being stoked by squires. The cooking fires, manned by sergeants, cooks, and servants, were being stoked to epic proportions at the rear of the encampment. Food was already on the spits, being turned by young servant boys who followed the army as workers. The smell of smoke was in the air, blending in with the dampness of the coming night.

To Curtis, it was the smell of victory.

But he suspected why his father had summoned him. Probably something to do with the wench he'd dumped on him earlier. Perhaps his father had discovered something. Or perhaps he wanted to verbally swat Curtis for leaving off the banshee in the first place. As Curtis approached the tent, he removed his helm, revealing close-cropped hair soaked with sweat. He was about to enter the tent when his father emerged and caught sight of him.

Christopher came out to meet him about ten feet from the tent.

"Well?" Christopher said. "What is the report?"

Curtis handed his helm off to the nearest soldier and proceeded to remove his gloves. "Brython is ours," he said, handing the gloves over to the man who held his helm. "The Welsh are subdued and currently being gathered. Congratulations on the victory, Papa."

Christopher smiled faintly. "Victory is yours, Curt," he said. "You commanded the battle. I was simply an observer."

Curtis grinned modestly. "I did nothing without your direction and approval," he said. "I would say that makes the victory yours."

Christopher put a hand on his son's shoulder. "Then well done, us," he said, jesting softly as he patted Curtis affectionately. "As usual, we performed flawlessly, but my report to the king will be that you commanded the victory. He will be pleased."

"Good," Curtis said. "Is that what you wanted to see me about?"

Christopher shook his head. "Nay," he said. "I have something else, something serious that I did not wish to discuss with you whilst we were in the midst of battle. But now that it is over, a more important situation must be addressed."

"What is that?"

Christopher cleared his throat softly, wanting to approach this conversation carefully. Curtis wasn't a fool, but he was stubborn and obstinate when the mood struck him, and that could happen quickly. Christopher needed the man's compliance.

"Primarily this," he said. "The king has told me to garrison Brython, and I shall. The castle is yours, Curt. The tributes, the lands, and the taxes all belong to you. Anything Brython possesses has now become yours. Congratulations, lad."

Curtis had known that was coming, but he was pleased to hear the confirmation. "Thank you, Papa," he said, turning to look at the hulking structure behind him. "I wish you'd told me that before this all started. Mayhap I wouldn't have been so brutal with the siege engines, because there is a good deal of repair work to do now."

Christopher chuckled. "You can make her stronger than before," he said. But he quickly sobered. "However, there is a stipulation along with assuming Brython's command."

"What stipulation?"

This was where Christopher had to break the terrible news, the news that would change Curtis' life, so he tried to be gentle about it. "We have seen Brython go back and forth between the English and the Welsh for too long," he said. "Even as I give you the command, you know what you will be facing with this place. The Welsh will want it back. We must do all we can to discourage that because I do not want to see Brython become a never-ending battle on the marches. I want it to know peace and prosperity, as I am sure you do, as well."

Curtis was listening intently. "Of course I do," he said. "But what is the stipulation?"

Christopher gestured to the gray-stoned castle. "As it turns out, Llewelyn did not have command of the castle," he said. "It was still in the hands of Gwenwynwyn's children."

"Oh?" Curtis said, very interested. "Who told you that?"

Christopher tipped his head in the direction of the tent. "The woman you brought me," he said. "She is Gwenwynwyn's daughter. Her brother, she says, is in the vault of Brython, so make sure you free the man. He is sympathetic to the English."

Curtis looked at him in surprise. "*She's* Gwenwynwyn's daughter?" he repeated. "I did not know the man had a daughter, only two sons, including one that no one has really seen."

Christopher shook his head. "There is no second son," he said. "According to the lady, she is the one that we've heard rumors of. She is the one known as the Wraith."

Curtis was genuinely astounded. "God's Bones," he muttered. "And you're sure of this?"

Christopher shrugged. "That is why I want you to find the brother she says is down in the vault," he said. "I want to hear his confirmation that she is who she says she is, because if she is truly Gwenwynwyn's daughter, then she will be the stipulation for you taking command of Brython."

Curtis wasn't following him. "Why?" he asked, frowning. "What does she have to do with it?"

Christopher fixed on him. "Because we need Brython to be stable and secure for generations to come," he said. "Henry wants a marriage, Curt."

Curtis was still frowning. "Whose marriage?"

"Yours."

Curtis stared at him for a moment, an expression on his face suggesting he hadn't heard correctly. "Mine?" he repeated. "But I am not getting married."

Christopher sighed faintly. He could see that Curtis wasn't understanding what he was saying, more than likely due to exhaustion rather than resistance, so he needed to be plain.

"I received a missive from Henry," he said evenly. "He wanted the battle at Brython to end because he wants this castle to be part of the line of English castles on the marches. You know how important Brython is. He told me that I was to offer the Welsh commander of Brython a marriage between you and the commander's daughter, whoever that may be, to secure peace. But the garrison commander seems to have been a woman, a daughter of Gwenwynwyn, and you will marry her to strengthen the alliance with Gwenwynwyn and his descendants and secure peace along the border. Is that clear enough now?"

By the time he was finished, Curtis was gaping at him. "You mean…" he said, stammering. Then he pointed in the general direction of the castle. "You mean that… that *wildcat* who crashed into me on the wall?"

"The same young woman I have been speaking to, aye."

Curtis closed his mouth as he realized his father was quite serious. "Papa," he said, eyeing the man with horror. "You *must* be jesting."

"Do I look like I am jesting?"

"Then you have gone mad!"

Christopher was weary—too weary to argue with Curtis in any fashion, and that made his patience thin. He wasn't going to manipulate and cajole Curtis as he'd done with Elle.

He was going to get straight to the point.

"Listen to me and listen well," he said, lowering his voice. "A man's life is full of sacrifices so that he and his family may have a better and more peaceful life. Do not forget that I married your mother, quite against my will, simply to gain a castle and wealth. I did what I had to do, and so will you. If you argue with me or refuse to comply, know that it will not go well for you. I am, therefore, going to tell you this one time—you will do your duty as you are instructed to, Curtis. You will marry Gwenwynwyn's daughter."

The words were harsh, and the look in Christopher's eye was nothing short of intimidating. Curtis wasn't usually the arguing type—he was blindly obedient when it came to his father—so the tension between them at the moment wasn't usual. But Curtis could see that his father was deadly serious, and, truth be told, he knew better than to question the man because he was quite certain his father took no joy in the directive. He could see that in his expression. It was true that they hadn't spoken much of marriage over the years, mostly because Curtis had always declared he would choose his own bride, so this wasn't a subject either of them had much experience with.

And Christopher wasn't going to take anything less than complete surrender.

What Henry wanted, Henry got. Even Curtis knew that.

His heart sank.

"My God," he breathed, staring at his father. "Papa, I cannot—"

Christopher cut him off. "You can and you will."

"But—"

"It was my fate to marry a woman to gain a castle," Christopher interrupted him. "It shall be yours also. There is no more honorable reason to marry, Curtis. For peace. For safety. You understand this, so you will not disobey me."

Curtis was feeling increasingly desperate. He didn't want to argue with his father, but he sincerely didn't want any part of this. He started to huff and puff. "Do I not have any recourse in this?" he asked, incredulous. "Nothing at all?"

"Nay," Christopher said. "If you refuse, then I will command Roi to do it. How do you think your brother will look upon you, knowing you shirked your duty and he was forced to assume it? Do you think any of your brothers will respect you ever again if they know you refused to do your duty? Think carefully before you answer me. They will see you as weak and cowardly. Is that the legacy you wish to have with men who would die for you?"

It was a brutal, horrific slap in the face of the facts of the situation, but Curtis knew that nothing his father said was untrue. Absolutely nothing. If he were to refuse to marry Gwenwynwyn's daughter, the ramifications were endless. He would lose the respect of his brothers, for certain. He would lose the respect of anyone else who knew the truth. No one would follow him into battle ever again. Days like this, victorious days where he had commanded a great victory, would be at an end.

He would lose everything.

With sickening realization, he knew he had no choice.

After a moment, he hung his head, a gesture of defeat. There was nothing more he could say or do about it, so like any seasoned warrior, he simply had to accept his fate. And that was what this was—his fate.

His destiny.

God help him.

"Does she know?" he finally asked, hoarsely.

Christopher could see that Curtis had accepted the situation, at least on the surface, and he was sorry. So very sorry he'd been rough with him, but in his opinion, he'd had little choice. There was no room for negotiation, and Curtis had to know that from the start.

And here they were.

Resigned.

"She does not know it is you," he said after a moment. "But I told her—at least, I strongly suggested—that she must marry for peace. It is what Henry wants. If you wish to go into the tent and speak with her, that might be a good start. She is frightened and upset and weary."

Curtis snorted. "So am I."

Christopher's lips tugged with a smile. "So am *I*," he said. With a sigh, he softened, putting his hand on Curtis' arm. "Curtis… I love you more than life. You are my heir, my shining star. If I did not think this was an important move for you, I would have fought Henry on it. But I believe it is important, lad. I have made my mark on the marches. Now, it is time for you to make yours."

Curtis was still looking at his feet, still mulling the whole thing over. But after a moment, he nodded reluctantly. He knew his father was right.

He was struggling not to be angry with him for it.

Without another word, he entered the tent.

CHAPTER THREE

THERE WAS LITERALLY no way out of the tent.

Elle thought that she might be able to escape as Hereford went outside, but as it turned out, the sides of the tent were staked into the ground all the way around. She knew because she had checked. It was staked like that to keep the wind from blowing up the flaps and quite possibly causing the tent to lift up and go airborne, but it also made it quite escape proof.

She was trapped.

God help her.

If there was a positive side to the situation, small as it was, it was that her belly was finally full. Literally, the one positive thing about the entire situation, because other than that, she was still damp and cold and smelled of mildew. Everything about her stank. There was a small brazier in the tent, situated below a hole in the tent roof, but there was very little warmth coming out of it. Because of that, she'd yanked the coverlet off the cot nearby and wrapped it around her.

Huddled on the ground, she sat.

And waited.

She could hear voices outside the tent as men moved

around. *Damnable Saesneg,* she thought to herself. Speaking in their Saesneg language. And she was expected to marry one of those bastards? She was strongly opposed to it, even after Hereford's argument. The Welsh rebel in her thought the entire proposal was out of the question, but the reasonable side of her—the side that tended to be wise and calm—knew that she had no choice in the matter. She took Hereford's threats seriously—she didn't want to end up in France or some other place far over the horizon, with no hope of returning home. At least if she married a man of Henry's choosing, she could stay in Wales. Marriage didn't mean she had to be loyal to her husband.

It simply meant she could remain.

And continue her fight.

She had to talk herself into it, however. It was natural to rail against everything the English wanted, so she had to fight back her natural urges and convince herself that this was her best and only option, such as it was. She'd been honest with Hereford and laid herself bare, so he knew everything about her. There was nothing left for her to tell him. There was also nowhere for her to hide. She seriously wondered what was going to happen when Gruffydd was released from the vault. It had been a hell of a fight to get him there, and she'd had to betray him to do it, but she had honestly felt it was best for Brython and for the cause of her people. Gruffydd was too much like her father, too pliable to the English.

She wasn't going to make the same mistake.

But, then again, here she was.

Somewhere in the midst of her tumultuous reflections, she dozed off. With the food, and particularly the wine, she'd become sleepy and hadn't even realized it. She didn't know how long she'd been out when she heard something snap, like the flap of a banner when whipped by the breeze, and she snapped her head up, eyes open.

There was a very big man standing in the tent that she didn't recognize.

For a moment, they simply stared at each other. Elle's attention was on his face, first and foremost, and she had to admit, almost immediately, that he wasn't unhandsome. He had piercing gray eyes and blond hair, cut short, and a trim beard of nearly the same color embraced his firm, square jaw. In a world where male beauty was few and far between, he most definitely had been blessed with it. Even if he was English. But those eyes...

She had to admit that they'd give her a jolt.

A most confusing jolt.

But she tore her gaze away from his, moving down his positively enormous body and noticing the size of his hands. His fists must have been nearly as large as her head. He was covered in mail and protection, smeared with grime, and, as she studied him warily, he spoke.

"I see you are calm now," he said in a deep voice that seemed to bubble up from his toes. "At least the tent is still intact."

That voice.

She knew that voice. Instantly recognizing the man she'd hit on the top of the wall, she went into battle mode again. Her heart leapt into her throat and she tossed the coverlet off so her hands and feet would be free.

"So," she hissed. "You've returned. I'm ready for you, *Saesneg.* Try your worst."

He put his big hands up. "I've not come to do battle," he

said calmly. "Have no fear, lady. You'll get no further fight from me."

Elle was on her feet now, but she was crouched as if preparing to take a tackle from the man. But his words had her confused. Unsteady, even. She wasn't convinced he was telling the truth.

"I am not stupid," she said. "I know you do not mean it. Do not lie to me."

"I do not lie."

"Where are my commanders? My men?"

"Dead or dying or captured."

Her eyes narrowed. "You would have me believe that?"

He lifted an eyebrow. "Let us establish something from the start," he said. "My name is Sir Curtis de Lohr. My father is the Earl of Hereford and Worcester, and upon his death, I will become the Earl of Hereford and Worcester. I am his heir and, as such, hold the courtesy title of Earl of Leominster and Baron Ivington. Do you understand me so far?"

Elle struggled against further bewilderment. "I understand," she said. "But it means nothing to me."

"It should," Curtis said. "It should tell you that I am a knight of the highest order, a propertied warlord, and son of a man who has one of the greatest reputations for honor in England. I, too, share that reputation, so know from the onset that I do not lie. Ever. If I mean to attack you, you will know it. And if I mean to call a truce, I will say so. In this case, I would like to call a truce. Will you accept?"

The more he spoke, the more puzzled she became. "Why?"

He snorted ironically. "Because there is no longer any reason to fight," he said. "Because I no longer wish to fight. Will you accept this?"

She had no idea what to say to him, but she came out of her protective stance. She just stood there, head lowered and brow furrowed, feeling confused and strangely lost. So very lost. After a moment, she lifted her gaze to him.

"What of my castle?" she asked. "What has happened to it?"

Seeing that she no longer looked as if she was preparing for an offensive, he went over to the table to see the remnants of the meal. There was still wine in the pitcher, and he poured himself a cup.

"It belongs to me now," he said. "Your men are prisoners. Now, we begin the damage assessment and plan the repairs."

He sounded as if it was the most normal situation in the world. Casual, even. Elle watched him drain the cup of wine, feeling more despair sweep her.

"Where… where are my men?" she asked.

Curtis poured himself another cup of the watered wine. "I told you," he said. "Dead or dying or captured. Those that are captured are being held in the encampment."

"What will you do with them?"

He looked at her. "What would you have me do with them?"

She wasn't sure if he was being sarcastic or if it was a genuine question. "I hope you will treat them fairly," she said, forcing her bravery. "They are good men, loyal to their people."

"That may be, but they have tried to kill me and mine," he said. "I will ask you again—what do you want me to do with them?"

"Are you asking that question to be cruel? Because you do not truly wish for my guidance on the matter."

"I am asking for your guidance on the matter."

Now, her puzzlement was being overtaken by surprise. She

stared at the man, studying him closely, looking for any hint that he was trying to demean her or betray her somehow. Because she couldn't answer right away, he spoke again.

"Let me ask you a question, my lady," he said. "Let us look at the situation from your perspective. If you were the victor and had three hundred English soldiers as your prisoners, what would you do with them?"

She hesitated. "Put them in the vault."

"All of them?"

"What else should I do?" she said. "Send them home so they can rise up against me again?"

He shrugged. "Mayhap you should simply kill them and be done with it."

She shook her head slowly. "Nay," she said quietly. "Because more would rise up in their place."

"And more would rise up in their place if you put them in the vault."

The argument was becoming circular, and he was making good points, which was starting to frustrate her. "Then what should I do?" she said. "You seem to have all the answers. You tell me."

Curtis had to lower his head so she wouldn't see that he was struggling not to smile at her annoyance. "Would mercy not be the right course of action?" he said. "Show mercy and send them home. They will remember that if, and when, they are in a conflict against you again. They will know you are a woman of mercy, and they will behave kindly toward you."

"Not kindly enough not to take up arms against me again."

He shrugged. "That is the nature of the situation we find ourselves in," he said, pouring himself a third cup of watered wine, now with the dregs at the bottom of his cup. "The English and the Welsh find themselves in a battle cycle. It has not always been this way, and it will not always be this way, but for now, it is the way of things. We will continue to fight until someone shows wisdom and bravery and decides to negotiate a truce against the enemy rather than a show of force. I do not think there is any man, or woman, alive that would rather fight than live in peace."

By this time, she was listening carefully because he sounded a great deal like his father in the conversation they'd had earlier. Hereford had left the tent, and she had no reason to believe he hadn't spoken with this man, his heir. Of course he had. That was why the man was here now, speaking of peace, when at the time of their first meeting, he'd been ready to throttle her. But now, he wasn't.

He was speaking of peace.

She knew why.

"Your father has told you about me, hasn't he?" she asked.

He had found a half loaf of bread on the table and was now pulling it apart. "He has," he said as if it wasn't anything to be shocked or astounded over. "You are Gwenwynwyn's daughter."

"I am."

"We did not know he had a daughter."

"So I am told," she said. "And that was deliberate."

He glanced at her. "Why?"

"Because no English warlord will take a warrior woman seriously," she said. "We thought it better to spread rumors of a second son."

"This has been going on for years."

She nodded. "It has," she said. "I saw my first battle at fourteen years of age."

"That is very young, even for a man."

"I was born to it."

"So was I," he said as he shoved bread into his mouth. He chewed a few times before continuing. "I suppose my father told you of the marriage plans."

"He did," she said, watching him eat. "He must have someone in mind."

"He does."

"Who?"

"Me."

Her eyebrows lifted. "*You?*" she repeated. "But… surely not you!"

"Why not?"

"Because… because you are old enough to be my father," she said, her tone quickly rising. "Moreover, you are his heir. He would not marry you to a woman who could not bring wealth or breeding to a marriage. I know how the English do things."

He swallowed the bite in his mouth, a lazy smile spreading across his lips. "I am old enough to be your father if I was a child when you were born," he said. "Christ, woman, how old do you think I am?"

Elle was off balance and sinking fast. This handsome knight, who had only grown more handsome during the course of the conversation—though she absolutely refused to admit that to herself—was to be her husband. The heir to Hereford and Worcester, the largest and perhaps most prestigious earldom on the marches, if not in all of England. He was an earl already, however, as the Earl of Leominster. Elle had grown up surrounded by politics and battles, so she fully understood the worth of Hereford and Worcester, and of earldoms and their properties.

The impact was not lost on her.

"I am *not* a suitable wife," she said, shaking her head emphatically and turning away. "Your father is mad if he thinks so."

Curtis had to admit that he was enjoying her resistance. He also had to admit that beneath that dirt and sweat and filth, he suspected she was a pretty little thing. She had eyes the color of cornflowers, so bright that it was as if they had their own light source. They were beautiful. But her face and hair were smeared with dirt and grime, so it was difficult to get a sense of her beauty.

And her voice... There was a sweet quality to it, but it could also be quite loud when she wanted it to be. He sensed that she had been raised around men and spent her life around men, meaning she behaved like one. There wasn't anything ladylike about her. But if she were to become his wife, he was going to have to change that. Oddly, he wasn't all that opposed to it.

He rather enjoyed a challenge.

Even one of this magnitude.

"You've not answered my question," he said. "How old do you think I am?"

She rolled her eyes. "As old as the moon, as young as the hills—what does it matter?" she said. "Do you understand when I say that I am not a suitable wife?"

"I understand."

"And?"

"And *what*?" he said. "My father has made his decision. There is nothing either of us can do about it, so I want you to think very carefully about what happens from this point forward. I intend to be polite and respectful of you and your beliefs. You will get no grief from me. But you... you will dictate my actions, lady. You must decide how you want to build this relationship we are forced to assume. Do you want it built on battle? Or do you want it built on mutual understanding?"

Elle was coming to realize that nothing she could say was going to change any of this. Oddly, he didn't seem horribly opposed to it, or, at least, he was hiding his reservation better than she was. He remained calm while she was about to blow the top of her head off. However, given her brief interaction with both Curtis and his father, she suspected that kind of resistance wouldn't do any good. She'd exhaust herself and still be forced to go through with it, either with Curtis or with another man she'd never met. She might be worse off than she was with the heir. Not only was she defeated, she was being punished by marrying her enemy.

Demoralized could hardly encompass what she was feeling at the moment.

She felt as if she was facing death—*hers*.

"You do not sound as if you oppose this," she said, turning away from him. "Can you honestly tell me that you want a wife like me? Have you taken a good look at me?"

Curtis looked her over. "I've taken a good *smell* of you," he said, referring to that horrific mildew smell that was coming off her. "Do you always smell like that?"

She flared. "Not usually, but someone tried to drown me today."

"And someone tried to throw me over the wall today."

She was glaring at him as he tried desperately not to laugh. There was something about her in a rage that seemed humorous to him, like a wet hen. She was fluffed up and riled up and ready to peck him to death.

That thought had him biting his lip.

"If I had been successful, then we would not be having this conversation," she said. "Unfortunately, I was not successful."

He did smile then. "Your misfortune is my gain," he said. "I do not really think you wanted to kill me, did you?"

Her eyes narrowed. "Give me a dagger and we shall find out."

That brought soft laughter from him. "Do you ever stop fighting, my lady?"

"I am not your lady. My name is Elle."

She certainly wasn't afraid to speak her mind. He merely lifted his eyebrows. "You are a noble-born woman, the daughter of a king," he said. "You are a lady. In fact, you are a princess, and I will address you accordingly whether or not you like it."

She scowled at him, preparing to retort but thinking better of it. For any statement she had, he seemed to have a better answer. Now, he was forcing her to rethink everything she wanted to say.

"You didn't answer me," he said after a moment. "Do you ever stop fighting?"

She averted her gaze. The cot was behind her, and she sat on it, heavily. "Against the English?" she said, incredulous. "If you must know, I've never been given a reason to."

He suspected that might be the most honest thing she'd ever said to him, and he folded his big arms across his chest. "Are you telling me that you have never known a moment's peace?"

She looked away, becoming uninterested in the conversation because she was exhausted and defeated, two unusual sensations in her world. Here he was, asking questions she didn't want to answer after she'd already bared her soul to his father. That hadn't gone particularly in her favor. She'd hoped to gain the man's sympathy, but he took advantage of it. Therefore, Curtis' questions were beginning to annoy her.

"What more do you want to know about me?" she said, irritation in her tone. "Do you want to know that I was a daughter born to a man who only wanted sons? To a mother who hated her Welsh husband and her Welsh children? She left after my brother was born, and we've not seen her since. I was raised by a grandmother who died when I was young, and after that, I simply fended for myself and learned how to fight from the Welsh warriors who took pity on me. My brother, though he was a year younger than I, was trained by the best. My father saw to that. But me... I was ignored. When my father died, Gruffydd and I took our place with my father's men who were regent for my brother. I watched Gruffydd rise to succeed my father as *Brenin Powys* while I fought in his armies to preserve Welsh rule on Welsh lands."

Curtis learned a great deal in that angry diatribe. *Brenin Powys.* That meant king in her language, and he could hear the bitterness in her voice as she spoke. She was a woman who had fought her way to the top and struggled to stay there, the older sister to her father's successor.

"But your father was a supporter of the English king," he said after a moment. "I do not recall Powys being particularly turbulent because of it."

She smiled, without humor. "Not with the English," she said. "But, as has been pointed out to me, the Welsh fight each other quite frequently. There is little peace between different Welsh princes, my father included. He supported King John, and that made him an enemy in his own country."

"And you were put in the position of defending yourself?"

She looked at him, her eyes unnaturally bright within her oval face. "Nay," she said. "I agreed with my father's enemies."

His brow furrowed. "Then you fought *against* your father?"

She averted her gaze quickly. "I did what I had to do in order to save my people," she said. "Even if that meant undermining my father and my brother."

"Then family means nothing to you."

"Two men who have never done much for me do not have my loyalty," she said. "If that is what family means, then nay, it means nothing to me."

Before Curtis could reply, the tent flap snapped back and men were entering. He turned to see Roi and Alexander with a man between them. It was the same man that Curtis had seen with Roi in the bailey, barely able to walk. Clearly, he was a prisoner. As Christopher entered the tent behind them, the prisoner caught sight of Elle. Unexpectedly, he reacted.

"You!" he said. "*Roeddwn i'n gobeithio eich bod chi wedi marw, eich bradwr!*"

Curtis knew the Welsh language. Growing up on the marches, he and his siblings had learned it because the knowledge was imperative. Therefore, he knew exactly what the man said.

I was hoping you had died, you traitor!

Elle's eyes widened, and she bolted off the cot, rushing for the man. But as she went, she managed to grab a large iron sconce that held six fat tapers. They weren't lit because it was daylight, but the sconce was heavy enough to be used as a weapon. Curtis, however, was faster than she was—he could see that she intended to use the sconce as a weapon, and he rushed to intercept her, lowering his shoulder into her midsection. Up she went, onto his big shoulder, and the sconce clattered to the floor. Like a sack of turnips over his shoulder, Curtis had her firmly and was heading for the tent flap, but Christopher stopped him.

"Wait," he commanded. "Curt, stop. Wait a moment."

Curtis paused, but he had a tempest on his hands. Elle was twisting and growling, trying to shake herself loose from his grip.

"Let me go!" she demanded. "Put me down this instant!"

Curtis didn't move. He continued to hold her with an iron grip, looking to his father for direction. But Christopher was looking at the rather short, dirty man between Roi and Alexander. He moved into the man's line of sight.

"What is your name?" he asked him.

The man was looking at Elle with the same cornflower-blue eyes that she had. "Gruffydd," he said after a moment, tearing his eyes away from Elle to look at Christopher. "I am Gwen-wynwyn's son, Gruffydd."

"We found him in the vault," Roi said quietly, looking at his father. "He said that his sister put him there."

"I did!" Elle said, kicking her legs as Curtis tried to hold on to her. "He is a traitor to our people, and he should be kept in the vault until he rots!"

Christopher glanced at the struggling woman, speaking to Gruffydd. "That is your sister?"

Gruffydd sighed heavily. "It is."

"What is her name?"

"Elle ferch Gwenwynwyn," he said. "Take her out and burn her at the stake. She only means to kill us all."

Christopher had his confirmation that Elle was, indeed, who she said she was. That was why he wanted Gruffydd removed from the vault in the first place, to confirm his sister's identity. Gruffydd was the one loyal to the English, which was common knowledge, while his firebrand of a sister was a Welsh loyalist to the bone.

Christopher could see that, quite plainly.

He had been outside the tent while Curtis and Elle spoke, and although he hadn't been able to hear much of what was said, the situation had been calm. That was all he truly cared about. No one was trying to kill anyone. But now, he had the brother, the heir to the Powys kingdom. He wanted to know what was happening from Gruffydd's standpoint and how this situation at Brython had turned into a month-long siege. But even without that enlightenment, he could see the bigger picture—that the one they called the Wraith had held the castle against the English, imprisoning her English-sympathizer brother, but Christopher wanted to know why. He wanted to know if something greater was afoot.

He turned to Curtis.

"Take her back to your camp," he said. "Do not let her out of your sight."

Curtis nodded, Elle kicked, and he slapped her right on the buttocks to quiet her. Instead, it had the opposite effect.

She howled.

"Put me down!" she demanded as he carried her toward the tent flap. "Put me down, I say!"

Curtis didn't answer her. As they passed through the open flap, she reached out and grabbed the sides of the tent, nearly pulling that side of the structure down before Curtis came to a halt. He was trying to dislodge her, but it was impossible to do that and hold on to her at the same time, so Alexander came over and peeled her fingers off the fabric. Unfortunately, he'd peel one finger off and it seemed to be replaced by two more.

But he was patient. Eventually, he managed to pry her limitless fingers off the fabric, but that frustrated Elle so much that she slapped at him. He dodged the flying hands for the most part, watching her turn those slapping hands on Curtis as the man walked away with her still slung over one shoulder.

With a shake of his head, and perhaps a chuckle, Alexander turned back for the tent. Perhaps the battle was over for the rest of them, but Curtis was still fighting it, now single-handedly.

He had to admit, he didn't envy Curtis.

CHAPTER FOUR

NIGHT WAS APPROACHING.

On the battlements of the castle, one could gain a perfect picture of the defeat of Brython. Not only was the ground outside the castle torn up by the de Lohr army, but inside, the siege engines had done far more damage than they could have imagined. Every projectile over the wall, every flaming mass, had damaged something.

There was carnage everywhere.

Brython used to have a large stable block, but that was now in ashes. The small, sturdy Welsh ponies that the Welsh tended to favor had been housed in that structure. Most were able to get out alive, but a few had perished in the flame and the smoke. Also dead were almost an entire coop of chickens, which had also been burned to the ground by the same flames that had spread through the stables. Although there were still some chickens pecking around, along with a few goats and a cow and her calf, most everything living in the animal world had been either killed or eaten during the siege.

The English knights thought it was rather strange that there were any animals at all after such a siege. They had cut off the water supply and backed up the sewer, so the logical thing would have been for the Welsh to eat anything they could. But that clearly did not happen. What was obvious, however, was the fact that the English had a massive cleanup in front of them before the castle could even be remotely functional. In addition to the damaged walls and gatehouse, Brython was a compromised structure, and would be for some time.

Now, with the night upon them, the time had come to settle the posts for the night. The quartermasters of the de Lohr army were still outside the wall in their traveling kitchen, and the smells of food and smoke were heavy in the air. The Welsh prisoners, as it turned out, numbered nearly one hundred and fifty men. Those men hadn't eaten regularly or well since the English cut off the water supply, and many of them were quite ill. Still others had run off. The English had set up a section of the encampment specifically for the prisoners, and provided the men with decent food and fire. The de Lohr army had the reputation of being one of the more merciful armies on the marches in their treatment of the Welsh, so even the defeated could count on fair dealings from the mighty Earl of Hereford and Worcester.

But with some of the men who served him, it was a different story.

A knight with dark eyes hiding an even darker soul stood upon the wall walk, gazing over the twilight below. He was weary and bloodied from Welshmen who didn't take kindly to having their castle confiscated, but to him, any blood or bruises were a badge of honor. He wore them proudly, even if the men who had resisted were now in a pile of the dead down far below at the base of the wall. The battle had been over, and the dead were Welshmen who had surrendered on the wall walk. When the knight had attempted to throw them over the wall, even after their surrender, they'd fought back. And they'd lost.

Those wounds were his badge of honor.

Dark soul, indeed.

"Well?" A knight with fair hair, balding, was approaching from the north side of the wall walk. "Does it look like a complete victory to you, Amaro?"

Amaro de Laraga glanced over at his comrade. "It does," he said. "Another victory is ours, Hugo. How does that make you feel?"

Hugo de Bernay grinned as he stood next to Amaro, surveying the vast and torn-up landscape below. "I feel as if I want to return to Lioncross and sleep for a week," he said. "I am glad this is finally over. To be truthful, I wasn't sure if we were going to gain the upper hand."

Amaro laughed softly, clapping Hugo on the shoulder. "De Lohr will always gain the upper hand," he said. "Sometimes it takes time, but Curt is a master tactician. No one can best him."

"True," Hugo said. "But the Welsh certainly tried."

Amaro couldn't disagree. "That they did," he said, turning to look at the interior of the castle and the horrific mess it was. "It cost them dearly, I'm afraid. They should have known better."

"They have not known better for two hundred years."

Amaro nodded, looking to the battered western wall, barely visible because of the enormous keep in the way. "Foolish Welshmen aside," he said casually, "I have heard a rumor."

Hugo snorted. "You are always hearing rumors."

Amaro shrugged. "If this one is true, then we are looking at our new home."

That comment wiped the smile off Hugo's face. "What do

you mean?"

Amaro gestured to the castle around them. "I mean that Curt will be garrison commander of this massive place," he said. "Rumor has it that Henry himself wants Curt here, so we are looking at our new home. I must say, I am very pleased. No longer will we be in Hereford's shadow. Curt deserves a command of his own. We deserve the chance for glory without Hereford hanging over our every move."

Hugo looked around, puffing his cheeks out wearily at the prospect that what Amaro said was true. "This is one of the most coveted castles on the marches," he said, scratching his dirty head. "But Gwenwynwyn garrisoned it for John for many years. It has always been Welsh-held, English-loyal."

"Not anymore," Amaro said. "I am certain that William Marshal had a hand in this decision, but now Henry wants it held by the English. By a de Lohr. This will be our time to shine, Hugo."

Hugo smiled wanly. He didn't have the delusions of grandeur that Amaro had. He knew the man was ruthless and ambitious. He also knew the man had killed surrendering Welsh by throwing them off the wall. It wasn't the first time the Spanish-born knight had been brutal with prisoners, but no one challenged him. No one ever said anything. Curtis knew, but he had to weigh the man's ruthless streak against the fact that he was a truly excellent knight and a strong fighter. He was also the son of the *Conde de Zidacos*, or the Earl of Zidacos, a very powerful Spanish warlord in Navarre that Christopher was allied with.

There were a lot of things overlooked when it came to Amaro.

And that made Hugo nervous.

"I have a feeling this post will not be so romantic as you say," Hugo finally said, watching Amaro chuckle. "I have a feeling we may see daily harassment from the Welsh. They are going to want this place back."

"That is possible," Amaro said. "But I prefer to look at it is a fresh challenge. My father may be Spanish, but my mother was Norman. The hatred for the Welsh is bred into me by blood."

"Your mother was from a family closer to Scotland."

"I hate the Scots, too."

That had Hugo laughing at the man. Together, they shared a chuckle, a release of sorts and a moment of levity in a situation that hadn't seen much of that kind of thing. It also kept Hugo on Amaro's good side, something he always tried to stay on because he didn't want Amaro's ruthless streak turned on him. But the humor faded as torches were lit to stave off the coming darkness, and Amaro sighed heavily.

"I suppose we must get about our rounds," he said. "Curt will want a report."

Hugo nodded, scratching his head again. "I've had the men collect the dead from around the wall," he said. "We either need to return them to the Welsh or burn them. Curt should make the decision."

"I'll make the decision," Amaro said quietly. "Burn them. Let's pile them out there, away from the encampment, and simply burn them."

Hugo glanced at him. "That might enrage the clergy in the nearby town," he said. "Any burning should be cleared with Curt. Ultimately, he will have to answer for it."

Amaro knew that. The clergy usually greatly disapproved of burning corpses of enemies, especially in a volatile area like the marches. But Amaro wasn't beyond overstepping himself when

Curtis wasn't around. He didn't like it when his commands were questioned.

"Then find him and tell him," he said with a hint of sarcasm. "In fact, tell him that I—"

He was cut off by a shout over near one of the towers where the stairs led up from the bailey. As he and Hugo turned to the source of the noise, they could see a soldier emerging from the tower, dragging someone with him. As he drew closer, they could see that it was a woman dressed in the clothes of a male servant.

The soldier had her by the hair.

"I found this one hiding in the kitchens, my lord," the soldier said, dumping the woman in front of Amaro. "She says that Gwenwynwyn is her uncle and she is hiding because she fears for her life from the English."

Amaro and Hugh looked at the woman. She was tiny, with dark hair and dark eyes, a little slip of a woman who was clearly terrified. She put her dirty hands over her face, weeping, as Hugo crouched in front of her.

"What's your name, lass?" he asked.

The woman was a mess. Shaken and thin, she wiped her eyes with the back of her dirty hand. "M-Melusine," she said, her voice trembling. "Melusine ferch Cadwallon."

"And you are from Gwenwynwyn's family?"

She nodded, her dark hair flapping in her face. "He is my uncle," she said. Then she burst into a new round of tears. "He supported the English king, my lord. He was not the enemy. I am not the enemy!"

"Yet you hid from us," Hugo said. "Why did you do that?"

There was fluid coming out of every feature of her face. "There was fire coming from the sky," she said, shakily indicating the flaming projectiles. "It burned everything. And then she went mad, so I hid!"

"Who went mad?"

"M-my cousin, my lord," she said. "She wanted to kill me and kill her brother."

"What cousin?"

Melusine shook her head. "Elle, my lord." She sniffled. "She put Gruffydd in the vault, so I hid."

Hugo looked up at Amaro. "Do you know anything about a cousin?"

Amaro shook his head. "Nay," he said. "But we should take her to de Lohr. He will want to talk to her if she is who she says she is."

He motioned to the soldier, who took the hint. Grabbing Melusine by the arm this time, he dragged the woman off the wall. Amaro and Hugo could hear her weeping all the way down the stairs. They could see her down below, in the darkened bailey, as the soldier pulled her toward the gatehouse with the English encampment beyond.

Screams always excited Amaro.

When he heard them, he knew he was accomplishing his tasks well.

CHAPTER FIVE

"ARE YOU GOING to stop fighting?"

The question came from Curtis. He was holding tight to Elle, who was still angry, still struggling after the encounter with her brother. Curtis had hauled her to his tent, but he hadn't released her. Even though he'd set her on her feet, he'd trapped her arms behind her back so she couldn't get away from him or really move at all without causing herself pain. Even so, she kicked and twisted and cursed.

Curtis simply let her get it out of her system.

"Well?" he said. "Answer me. Are you going to stop fighting?"

Although he wasn't hurting her deliberately, he was holding her firmly, and Elle had twisted around so much that she was the one hurting herself. Her arms were in great pain from the way he had her in his grip. Knowing they couldn't stay like that all night, she was forced to nod her head.

"Aye," she muttered. "I will."

"And I have your word?"

Twisted up and in pain, she rolled her eyes. "You have my word."

"And I have your word that you will not leave this tent?"

"Would you believe me if I promised?"

"I will believe you," he said. "But violate that trust and I will never believe you again, about anything, so bear that in mind. My trust is given only once."

He couldn't see the face she made, one of utter displeasure and resignation, before finally nodding her head. Instantly, he let her arms go, and she groaned softly as they fell to her side, shaking them out because her hands had fallen asleep. Rubbing her fingers and silently cursing Curtis and his iron grip, she kept her back to him as he moved to the tent opening and summoned a soldier. The man went running for Curtis' squire as Curtis moved for the open brazier in the center of his tent. As he piled on some peat from a bucket, Elle turned to look at him.

Things were calmer now than they had been only moments earlier. Seeing Gruffydd freed from the vault had startled her. Not that she hadn't known he would make an appearance at some point, but she hadn't seen him in a couple of weeks. He looked terrible from his days in the vault with little food and no light.

But she didn't regret putting him there. She'd do it again given the chance. She thought it rather ironic that she was now the one in a prison of sorts, a looming marriage and an uncertain future. That was worse than anything she could do to her brother.

She found herself looking at the man she was supposed to marry.

Curtis was packing peat into the brazier, preparing to light it, and she watched him for a moment. Those enormous hands had held her with a grip of iron. Truthfully, she'd never known a man as big or as strong as he was. Usually, she was one of the strongest people in the room. Not by size, of course, but by personality and determination. She was used to giving commands that men obeyed. But Curtis… He was bigger and stronger and more determined than she ever had been. She could see it in his face, feel it in his hands. Everything about him screamed power and command. She was coming to think that power like that was attractive. Any man who could force her into submission, by words or by strength, had her respect, because that was something she understood.

Strength.

"That's a rather harsh stance, don't you think?" she said after a moment.

He glanced at her. "About what?"

"That your trust is only given once."

He adjusted the peat before packing in some brittle kindling. "It is not harsh. It is the truth."

He sounded final. Elle watched him light the fire, studying him. "But people make mistakes," she said. "It is the nature of man to err. If a genuine mistake happens, that destroys all of your trust?"

He struck a flint and stone, blowing on the sparks as they caught the kindling. "If you ran after your brother to fight him once you promised not to would not be a mistake," he said, "that would be a deliberate action, made by choice. There is a difference between a choice and a mistake."

He had an answer for everything, right though he may be. With a heavy sigh, Elle turned away again, and, spying a stool, she planted herself on it. As she sat there and continued to rub at her hands, a tall young man appeared in the entry. He was clad in mail and the blue and yellow de Lohr tunic, and his long blond hair was pulled into a ponytail at the nape of his neck. He faced Curtis eagerly.

"Curt?" he said. "You sent for me?"

Curtis looked at the young man. "Aye," he said. "Is my equipment cleaned?"

The boy nodded. "Aye," he said. "I was finishing with your sword. There is some grime in the hilt I'm trying to get clean."

"Good," Curtis said. "You can have this mail now, too. Help me get it off."

With that, he unstrapped the empty scabbard from around his waist and tossed it aside. The filthy de Lohr tunic he was wearing came off, and he tossed that aside, too. Then he bent over and extended his arms to the lad, who took hold of the arms of his mail coat and began to pull. He alternated tugging at the neckline and the arms. By working both positions, he was able to slide the heavy mail coat off Curtis with relative ease.

After that, the lad helped him remove other pieces of protection that Curtis wore. Soon enough, Curtis was stripped down to a sweat-stained linen tunic, leather breeches, and his boots. As the squire gathered up all of the articles of protection and clothing to take with him, Curtis stopped him before he could get out of the door.

"Put those things aside for now," he said. "I want you to go to Papa's tent and find the big chest he brings with him. You know the one—with the lions carved on the side. Buried in that chest are things for Mama. He's had them for years because she used to come along on battle marches from time to time. See if there's anything serviceable for a woman, and bring it to me along with anything you can find for a bath."

The young man frowned. "A *bath*?" he repeated.

Curtis pointed over at Elle, who stiffened up when she realized they were focused on her. "The lady requires something other than the damp clothing she is wearing," he said. "She smells like a hermit who has lived in a cave for forty years, so find soap and a comb and anything else. Anything Mama or Papa might have in that chest that the lady can use, bring it. And hurry up. I cannot stand her smell much longer."

Wide-eyed, the boy fled, arms full of Curtis' things. Elle was so humiliated by the comments on her smell that she averted her gaze, looking at her hands again. It was rare that she didn't bite back, at least verbally, but she'd been sparring with Curtis since they fell off the wall, and she was weary of him always being right. She was even wearier of him acting superior. Since she had only just calmed down, she didn't want to rise to the occasion with him.

Again.

Whatever she did, it seemed to work against her.

Elle kept her head lowered, listening to Curtis move around the tent. It was post-battle, so there were things he had to do. She could hear him rummaging around off to her right, and she dared to lift her head, noticing that he was going through a trunk. He removed a box and set it on a portable table with a chipped leg. Then he pulled a chair up to it, the only chair in the tent, and opened the box.

Interested, she watched him pull forth a small phial and set it on the table. A quill came out, and a small leather pouch that looked as if it had rocks in it. Finally, he drew forth a sheet of vellum, a small sheet, and began to write on it.

Curiosity had the better of her at that point.

"What are you writing?" she asked.

He didn't look up from his task. "An account of the battle."

"Why?"

"So we will remember what happened here."

She thought about that for a moment. "Is it something special?"

He shook his head as he carefully scripted out each letter. "Not particularly."

"Then why do it?"

"It is mostly for my father's records," he said. "He likes to keep an accounting of how long the battle took, what happened, how many men were lost. Things of that nature."

"But why?"

He did look up then. "To understand what could have been done better," he said. "To give an accounting to the king. And to keep a record for future generations."

Her brow furrowed. "The nature of war cannot be tallied," she said. "Every battle is different."

He went back to his task. "Exactly."

Elle didn't understand his response. She was trying to figure out why he should want to remember a battle at all, especially if he won it. Shouldn't one remember only the victory and not the price paid?

It made little sense to her.

"Do you always do this?" she asked.

He dipped his quill in the inkpot. "Always."

"Will you write about me?"

"You in particular."

That didn't sit well with her. "Why?" she demanded. "What will you say about me?"

He was focused on his writing. "That the daughter of Gwenwynwyn ap Owain became our prisoner," he said. Then he glanced at her. "And possibly my wife."

She deflated somewhat with the reminder of where her

future was headed. "And you still think this is a good idea?"

He paused writing and shrugged. "It does not matter what I think," he said. "What matters is the good of all. If our marriage can save lives, Welsh and English, why wouldn't we?"

Elle simply didn't have a snappy comeback for that. She'd argued with him before, and, somehow, he'd always gained the upper hand. Closing her eyes for a brief moment in resignation, she hung her head again.

But Curtis was watching her. He wasn't as detached as he pretended to be, mostly because he was weary from the battle and unbalanced from his father's directive. He was trying to figure out just how he felt about the woman he was supposed to marry, even if he had no choice in the matter. As he'd told her, his behavior toward her would, in large part, be dictated by her. She could be civil or she could build their entire marriage on a raging battle between them.

He sincerely hoped she didn't choose the latter.

"You still have not warmed to the idea," he said after a moment. "Not that I blame you. I'm not sure I have, but you and I are just small pieces of a larger game. There are those who control this game, and they tell us what must be done to make it complete. If you could save the lives of your men by a marriage, wouldn't you?"

She wouldn't look at him. "As you said, it does not matter what I think," she said. "I am going to be forced into this whether or not I want it."

"Are you opposed to marriage in general?"

Was she? No, she wasn't. But what Curtis didn't know was that she'd been married once before, to an old man. He'd been a friend of her father's, and at the tender age of thirteen years, she had been wed to him. Cadwalader ap Dai had been a very nice man, and very important to her people because he was part of the royal house of the ancient kingdom of Gwent. Elle's father had hoped that his daughter would breed a new generation of royals for Gwent, which would, in turn, become an ally to Powys. Cadwalader had been kind and gentle, but mating between them had been a nightmare because his manhood would barely become stiff enough to complete the task.

That was all Elle knew of relations between a man and a woman.

She had been young and impressionable, and Cadwalader had been old and shriveled. She could still see that wrinkly body and smell the scent of an elderly man who wasn't fond of bathing. He'd touched her as if he were afraid of her, and when it came time to consummate the marriage... Elle had found it uncomfortable and embarrassing.

Fortunately, Cadwalader had no real interest in his young wife, and Elle always received the impression that he was fearful of her somehow. It only occurred to her after his death that she represented his inability to perform as a man, because he rarely touched her, and when he did, it was yet another uncomfortable and embarrassing situation. When they'd been married six months and she wasn't pregnant, Cadwalader told his men that she was barren to save himself the embarrassment of admitting he couldn't perform well enough to impregnate her. It wasn't as if Elle could dispute him. When he finally died eight months into their marriage, she did her best to forget about a man who had been completely forgettable.

But here she was, anticipating a marriage again, but not without great reluctance. Her only experience with it had been a poor one, and she'd managed to convince herself over the years that Cadwalader couldn't become properly aroused because she wasn't particularly attractive. Curtis had no idea what he was getting into. Perhaps he needed to know, for his own sake.

Trouble was, she was so embarrassed about it that she could hardly bring up the subject.

"I suppose I am opposed to marriage in general," she finally said. "I simply do not want any part of it."

"Why not?"

She swallowed hard. "Because... because men do not like me, and I do not like them," she said, which was a lie. She did like men, but to admit she did, when they didn't like her, was shameful. "I do not want to marry a man simply so he can tell me what to do. I do not need to be ordered about."

Curtis sat back in his chair, scratching his cheek. "That is a very narrow view of marriage."

"How would you know?" she said. "Have *you* ever been married?"

He shook his head. "Nay," he said. "Why? Have you?"

He'd asked the fateful question. *If you break my trust, I will never give it again.* Those words were ringing in her head. Her relationship with the man was difficult anyway. She didn't want to add mistrust to the mix, because it would make it miserable for the both of them. She simply wasn't willing to lie to him.

She hoped she wouldn't die from embarrassment.

"Aye," she said, barely audible. "I have."

That changed his whole mood. He set the quill down, staring at her as if she'd just said something surprising. "You *have*?" he asked.

She nodded, but didn't say anything more. She told him she'd been married, so she hadn't lied to him. But, God help her, she didn't want to elaborate. She'd never spoken of it, not during or after everything happened. It was a humiliation she kept buried deep inside, and she was damn well not going to confess it to a Saesneg.

To Curtis.

But he wasn't going to let her admit something like that and not tell him the entire story. Standing up, he picked up his chair and brought it over to where she was sitting. He plopped the chair down about two feet in front of her and sat on it, facing her.

"You will tell me everything," he said quietly. "When were you married, and to whom?"

He was being surprisingly gentle. She had expected him to be irate with the news, but he wasn't. He was being quite calm and… kind, even. Elle wasn't sure if that made her feel better or worse.

"It… it was a long time ago," she said, hardly above a whisper. "You must understand that I am the last of my line. Other than Gruffydd, there are no other sons or daughters of Gwenwynwyn ap Owain. Legitimate ones, that is."

He nodded patiently. "I understand," he said. "Go on."

She couldn't look at him. "He was the last of a royal house of Gwent," she said. "He was very old and I was very young. We'd not yet been married a year when he died."

Curtis studied her for a moment. "No children?"

"No children."

"Was the marriage consummated?"

Elle didn't know why, but she burst into quiet tears. She was a lass who never gave in to emotion, but here she was, weeping in front of a stranger. It was so terribly humiliating, the question he was asking. She didn't sense he was doing it to be cruel. He simply wanted to know, especially if he was being ordered to marry her. It was his right to know. Before she could answer, however, the flap of the tent snapped back and the squire appeared with bundles of fabric in his arms. Behind him, men were lugging what amounted to a big iron cauldron.

Curtis quickly stood up.

"Put the pot over here," he said, indicating a corner of the tent away from the door. "Fill it halfway with hot water, and be quick about it."

The soldiers carrying the cauldron dropped it in the corner and fled the tent as Curtis went over to the bed where Westley was laying out some clothing.

"I found this," Westley said, holding up a woman's dress. "There were a couple of others, but they are not well maintained. I do not know if Mama knows, but Papa seems to have not paid much attention to them. She'll be furious when she finds out."

Curtis grinned weakly, inspecting the dress his brother was holding up. It was made of brown broadcloth, with long sleeves, a rounded neckline, and a tailored bodice with a big skirt. It was plain, and not particularly attractive, but he knew it was a dress meant for travel or work. His mother didn't care if it got dirty. He eyed it a moment before glancing over his shoulder at Elle, who was still quietly weeping.

"Mama is not a big woman," he said. "She's short."

Westley nodded. "She is, indeed," he said. "But she has big…"

He trailed off, suddenly embarrassed that he was about to comment on his mother's bosom. Curtis snorted at his red-faced brother.

"Aye, she has," he said. "Because she nursed a gaggle of foolish and ungrateful children, myself excluded."

Westley looked at him with confusion. "What does that

mean?"

Curtis thumped him on the head. "It means we should have drowned you when you were born," he said. "I tried, but Mama said we shouldn't."

As Westley rubbed the spot Curtis had thumped, unhappy with his comment, Curtis turned to the other garments that the lad had brought. Along with the brown dress, there was a blue one of nearly the same design, and then a couple of shifts that were wrinkled. One had a big water stain on it, from water dripping through the chest and onto the garment. It wasn't that they had been treated poorly, but merely tightly folded and shoved down into the bottom of a chest. They'd been there for years. There was also a small wooden box that contained the remnants of soap that smelled of lemons, a scrub brush made from frayed reeds, a comb, and a few other things that a lady might need, including hairpins. It wasn't much, but it would have to do.

"This is adequate for now," he told Westley. "When the lady bathes, she can borrow one of these. In the meanwhile, send for some food. I haven't eaten since early this morning."

Westley trudged out of the tent as men began to bring in buckets of hot water. They had a big iron pot near the kitchen area, bubbling with hot water to be used for wounds and washing, so seven big buckets from that cauldron filled up the pot to a little over half full. One last bucket of cold water made it so it wasn't scalding.

With the soap and the scrub brush in hand, Curtis made his way over to Elle.

"Here is soap and a brush for your bath," he said, setting them down on the chair he'd been sitting on. "I have clothing for you to wear once you are clean. It belongs to my mother, who is a little fuller than you are, but the clothes should fit nicely until you can change into something you own."

Elle had stopped weeping from his question about the consummation of her marriage, but Curtis' statement had her looking at him with a mixture of disdain and puzzlement.

"Something of my own?" she repeated. "I am *wearing* what I own. I do not come from a fine family where everything is provided for me, so what you see on my body is everything I have. There is nothing else I own."

Curtis ignored her tone because he knew talk of her previous marriage had upset her. He went over to the cot and held up the brown dress and the blue dress. "You may wear either of these," he said. "Whichever one you like. These are traveling garments, so they are not as fine as a lady should have, but they are serviceable."

For some reason, his kind gesture was having the opposite effect with her. He was completely rubbing her the wrong way with his assumption that she lived the way any fine English noblewoman lived. There was entitlement in his tone. This was a man born to privilege and raised in it, and it was the first inclination that he had no concept of how she lived or what her life was like.

If the man was still determined to marry her, then perhaps he should be aware.

"Let me be clear with you on a few things, Sir Curtis," she said, standing up from the little stool she'd been perched on. "I do not, nor have I ever, lived as a fine lady. I told you that I was born to a father who did not want a daughter and a mother who hated the sight of me. I've never owned a gown in my life. I've never had anything given to me. Everything I have, I have had to earn myself. You wanted to know if my marriage was consummated? I was given over to Cadwalader ap Dai when I was barely thirteen years of age and he had seen seventy years and six. He'd been married before, several times, and he only had one daughter as a result. My father and Cadwalader were hoping I could produce a son of Gwent, to carry on the Gwent kingdom and forever ally it to Powys. But I married a shriveled old man who could not perform as a husband should and then blamed our lack of children on me. He told everyone I was barren. Was the marriage consummated? It was, in the most horrible and humiliating way imaginable. Now you know enough about me to go to your father and tell him that we should not be wed. I've been telling you that from the beginning. Mayhap now you will believe me."

With that, she turned her back on him and sat on the stool again. The only reason she turned her back was because hot, furious tears had popped from her eyes and were now coursing down her cheeks. She didn't wipe them away because she didn't want him to see her doing it, so she let them fall.

But Curtis didn't turn away from her. In fact, he didn't move. He just stood there, and Elle swore she could feel his stare against her back. Then she could hear his joints popping behind her as he moved, undoubtedly to tell his father.

But he did something else.

"I like the blue dress," he said quietly, picking it up from the cot. "It will match your eyes. I believe my father has a screen that can give you some privacy as you bathe. He uses it to block the wind from the tent opening, but I am certain he can spare it."

Elle looked at him sharply. "Do you not understand?" she said. "I do not know anything about a noble household. I do not know anything about being a lady. You are a titled lord who will inherit an empire someday. What a sorry sight I will make as your countess."

He still had the dress in his hand as he snorted wryly. "Do not make this sound as if you are being altruistic," he said. "You are trying to make it seem like the best thing for me is not to marry you. Mayhap that is true, but I will make my own decision. You will not make it for me."

"Have I not presented sufficient evidence to help you make that decision?"

He held up a hand to beg pause while he called to a soldier and muttered something to the man about the screen. As the soldier headed away, Curtis returned his attention to Elle.

"Let us speak more when you've had a chance to bathe," he said. "Then I will make my decision."

Elle wasn't sure if she felt better or worse. "Then you understand that I am unsuitable?"

He lifted an eyebrow. "I understand that you *want* me to consider you unsuitable."

"But I am!"

"The truth is that you do not want to marry an Englishman, and for no other reason than that."

That brought her pause. "That is true," she said. "I've not made any secret of it."

"You cannot always have what you want."

Elle sighed heavily. "So I have been told."

He gave her a long look and turned away, tossing the garment back onto the bed. Then he returned to his table and writing kit, sitting down to continue recording the battle. Elle sat there in silence, listening to him scratch his quill against vellum, her attention turning toward that steaming bath. She could see the soap and scrub brush on the chair, and she had to resist the urge to smell the soap. She couldn't remember the last time she had bathed, but because she lived with men and lived as one of them, things like baths—and the lack of fine garments mentioned by Curtis—meant nothing to her, not really.

But perhaps there was a part of her that wished that weren't so.

Truth be told, there had been a time when she wished for that kind of thing, back in the days when she was envious of a woman with a pretty dress or flowers in her hair. But she knew she would never be that kind of woman, nor have pretty things, so she told everyone she didn't care. She'd said it so much that she'd talked herself into it. She had talked herself into the life that she had because there was nothing better in her future. Not even Cadwalader offered her any hope for a better future where she wasn't entrenched in regaining lands from the English or plotting ambushes for enemies.

But now...

Now, she was in a completely different world as the prisoner of the English. It occurred to her that perhaps there *was* a future ahead of her that she hadn't expected. When this day began, she hadn't anticipated it to go in this direction. She hadn't anticipated being in this particular situation, but here she was.

Life was funny sometimes.

She remained quiet, huddled on the stool, while Curtis scratched away on the vellum. He must have been writing an entire epic volume, from what she could hear. She'd been sitting for several minutes when the soldier who had been sent away for the screen suddenly appeared again, bearing the mythical de Lohr screen. It was three attached panels of wood, painted in blues and yellows. Curtis took it from the soldier and propped it up in front of the pot half filled with water that was still steaming. Silently, he went to the bed, picked up one of the shifts, and slung it over the panel. Then he went to dig around in his own chest again, only to come forth with what looked like a cloak or a coverlet.

Elle wasn't sure what it was, but she'd been watching him curiously since the screen came. She watched him toss the cloak or coverlet over the screen so it, too, was hanging. When he noticed she was looking at him, he simply gestured to it.

"You can use it to dry off with," he said. "And you can sleep in the shift."

He went back over to his table and sat down again. Unable to withstand the lure of hot water and soap, Elle stood up.

"Aren't you leaving?" she asked.

He was looking at his writing. "Nay," he said. "That is why I brought the screen. So you could have some privacy."

She stiffened. "I will not—"

"And I am not leaving you alone so you can try to escape," he snapped, looking at her. It was an uncharacteristically severe expression. "Get used to it, lady. You will do as you are told. Get into that pot or I'll put you in it myself."

That sounded much more like the knight Elle had hit in the midsection and toppled off the wall. That harsh knight with the iron grip who had manhandled her and spoken harshly to her. The man who was three times her size and far more powerful than she was. It didn't occur to her that she probably should have a healthy fear of the man, but she genuinely didn't like being ordered about.

Still...

She wasn't stupid.

Without another word, she stepped behind the screen and

began pulling off her smelly, dirty clothing. It wasn't even completely dry from having been in the moat, and as she pulled it off, layer by layer, she came across leaves and debris trapped in the fabric and, eventually, against her skin. When she was finally stripped down, with only her damp, dirty hair and her grimy skin exposed, she quickly climbed into the cauldron to discover that it was, indeed, still fairly hot. As she sat in it, cross-legged, the water rose almost to the top, nearly covering her completely.

With a sigh of delight, she submerged her entire body, including her head.

Coming up for air, she wiped the water out of her eyes and went for the soap and scrub brush. The soap was strong, smelling of lemons, which was a precious commodity in England, but she used it liberally and scrubbed every inch of her body, from her head to her toes. She even scrubbed the nooks and crannies, under her arms and the soles of her feet. Her hair, neck, ears, and face got a particularly strong scrubbing because once she started, she couldn't stop. She was determined to scrub away that nasty moat water. Perhaps she was determined to scrub away the remnants of a battle that had been unsuccessful and the turmoil her life had become. Or, more correctly, what it *would* become. Whatever the reason, she scrubbed herself silly.

And it felt wonderful.

When the scrubbing was done and she'd run another layer of the slimy soap over her skin just to be certain she was completely clean, Elle dunked her head in the water once more and came up sputtering. It simply felt good to be clean and warm for the first time in a very long time. It felt so good, in fact, that she startled when the squire returned with food for Curtis, but she didn't panic. Curtis remaining in the tent was one thing, but the addition of another man was quite another. She didn't want to be put on display as a pathetic Welsh prisoner. However, there was a screen between her and the young de Lohr brother, so she simply kept still until he left.

It was something of a relief when he did.

After that, she sat in the water until she grew cold, but Curtis didn't say a word. He ate and wrote, ignoring her for the most part. He'd probably had enough of her, and, given their interaction since their fall from the wall, she could hardly blame him. Therefore, she didn't speak to him, either, as she finally climbed out of the pot and set about drying herself with the piece of material he'd left for her. At one point, she heard him putting more peat in the brazier, warming up the tent, and she put the towel aside to don the shift he'd provided for her. It was warm and well made, a little roomy in the chest area and a little too short, but she didn't care. Elle had never worn anything so fine in her entire life.

Dry and warm, but still with damp hair, she came out from behind the screen and went to the brazier to dry her hair. It was giving off a good deal of heat, so she plopped down next to it and began running her fingers through her damp hair to help dry it. As she was doing this, Curtis stood up and went over to the bed. Elle only knew that because she could hear his movements. He was still ignoring her, so she didn't speak to him. She simply kept running her fingers through her hair until a comb suddenly appeared in front of her face. Startled, she glanced up to see Curtis extending it to her. Hesitantly, she took it.

He went to sit back down again.

It was a thick, well-made comb of tortoiseshell, and she ran it through her hair repeatedly, drying the blonde strands in the heated air. She couldn't remember the last time she had washed her hair, to be truthful, and it was drying pale blonde and shiny in the warmth. She had rather thick hair, quite straight, but it was full and lovely when she didn't have it tightly braided into four or five braids all around her head. She continued to comb and comb as it dried fairly quickly. But the warmth, the bath, and the food earlier were having an effect on her.

She was exhausted.

It had been a day to remember, to be certain. She had lost a battle, but she had gained... something. She wasn't sure what yet, but she'd certainly gained something. Hadn't she? A new perspective, a new life, such as it was. The more she combed, the sleepier she became, and she yawned several times. She wasn't sure where she was going to sleep, considering Curtis wasn't going to let her out of his sight, so perhaps she should simply sleep on the floor in front of the brazier. It wasn't such a bad place, because he had several woolen hides around the brazier rather than rushes, which would burn if sparks flew. The wool wouldn't. In fact, she was sitting on a woolen hide that was warm and comfortable. Between the combing and the sleepiness and the warmth, she ended up lying down in front of the brazier. It was too much to stay upright.

Sleep claimed her almost immediately.

Curtis saw her go down. In fact, he'd been glancing at her since she came out from behind the screen. That filthy little creature who had slammed into him on the wall walk had transformed into something quite different. With her blonde hair clean and flowing, dressed in his mother's old shift, he would have sworn that an angel had just walked into the tent. Truth be told, he hardly recognized her. He'd suspected there was a beauty underneath the grime and sweat, and he'd been right. She was exquisite.

It was a shocking realization.

He was nearly to the end of his journaling for the battle at Brython, but he paused to watch her sleep in front of the brazier. The sun was down by now, with only the light from the tapers on his table giving the tent a gentle glow. Everything else was dark. He finished off the last few sentences of his journal, listening to Elle's slow and steady breathing. She was sleeping deeply. As he finished the page, sanded it, and put his quill away, he began to feel caddish for letting her sleep on the ground.

His bed was a few feet away and unused.

Quietly, he stood up and went over to her, crouching down to scoop her up from the woolen hide. She smelled fresh, like lemons, a distinct improvement from the mildew smell she'd been harboring. But the moment he picked her up, she started mumbling.

"Dirty... *bastard*," she muttered, trying to slap something, and ended up hitting herself in the neck. "I won't let you hurt me. You smell like a pig. Why is it... so... dark...?"

She faded off as she snuggled against his chest, her face buried in his shoulder. Curtis couldn't help the grin as he carried her over to the bed and laid her down, pulling the coverlet over her. She muttered something else about it being dark but settled down quickly as the deep sleep returned. When the snoring came shortly thereafter, Curtis chuckled softly. He found himself standing over her, watching her sleep, thinking many things at that moment. There was so much about her that was foreign to him, but there was also something about her that screamed of loneliness. She seemed so very alone. She'd put her own brother in the vault, so there was evidently no love lost between them, but he didn't sense she'd done it for malicious reasons. It almost seemed like... self-protection?

Why in the world did she have to protect herself from her own brother?

The lady was, indeed, a paradox.

"Curt?" Westley suddenly burst through the tent flap. "Papa says you must come."

Curtis turned to look at his gangly youngest brother. "Why?"

Westley pointed in the direction of their father's tent. "Another woman," he said. "She says she's a cousin to your lady. You'd better go."

That struck Curtis as something of a surprise. "*Another* lady?"

Westley nodded. "Papa wants you."

Curtis glanced over at Elle, sleeping peacefully, before returning his focus to his brother. "You remain here with her," he said. "She is a skilled warrior, and she wants to escape, so be on your guard. Arm yourself if you must. But do not let her out of your sight. Do you understand me?"

Westley nodded, looking at the lady with some apprehension. "She... she seems tame enough."

Curtis snorted, but it was without humor. "The moment you truly believe that is the moment she will probably slit your throat," he said. "Let your guard down with her at your own peril. She is not to be trifled with."

Westley studied the sleeping woman for a moment before nodding. "As you say," he said. "But *who* is she?"

"Don't you know?"

Westley shook his head. "Nay," he said. "Who?"

Curtis' gaze lingered on her for a moment. "A Welsh princess," he muttered. "A firebrand. She's everything Welsh that you fear and more. Be vigilant."

With that, he left Westley watching over Elle and wondering if the lady was really all that trouble. He didn't want to admit that he was worried about being left alone with her, but he reckoned that he was more than a match for her if she suddenly woke up and got out of hand. An Englishman was always worth more than a Welsh prisoner.

Wasn't he?

Westley hoped that theory wouldn't be put to the test before Curtis returned.

CHAPTER SIX

"**W**HAT YOU HEARD was wrong, my lord," Gruffydd said as he stuffed his face with bread. "Llywelyn has never been in possession of Brython."

Seated in his cushioned traveling chair next to the brazier that was giving off a good deal of heat, Christopher watched the starving man eat.

"We've spent a month here trying to gain control," he said seriously. "We were summoned by English soldiers who had been welcomed here by your father, many years ago. It was a contingent that King John had stationed here, with Gwenwynwyn, and when Henry became king, he kept them here. That was the bargain your father had agreed to—as long as your father kept English soldiers here, the English left Brython alone. It was Welsh held, but as long as you did not cause any trouble…"

Gruffydd was nodding even as Christopher was speaking. "I know, my lord," he said. "And I was happy to keep them here because it was what my father had agreed to. Let me assure you that I am not your enemy."

"Then tell me what happened."

Gruffydd swallowed the bite in his mouth. "I assume you have already spoken to my sister," he said. "Has she told you anything?"

"She told me a little," Christopher said. "But I want to hear about this situation from you. This castle belongs to you, does it not? As your father's heir?"

Gruffydd sighed faintly. "Aye," he said. "I am his heir. But my sister… She does not think like I do."

"What do you mean?"

"I mean that she is convinced I am the enemy," Gruffydd said. "She thinks that because I honor my father's word to the English king that it makes me a traitor. I believe as my father believed—that if there is any hope of retaining control of Powys against Llywelyn, that we must ally with the English. Llywelyn is very powerful, my lord. He wants Powys. I refuse to pay homage to him when it is my right to make decisions for my people as my father did."

Christopher had a cup of wine in one hand, swirling it over the heat of the brazier to warm it. "But your sister does not agree," he said. "How did you end up in the vault?"

Gruffydd tore off more bread from the meal that had been brought to him. "It is not her fault," he said sadly. "Elle has been raised by rebels. My father taught me everything he knew, but Elle was left to fend for herself. My father simply had no interest in her. She went to live with my grandmother for a time, but when the old woman died, Elle returned to us, but she spent all of her time with the men. Men who talk. Men who were willing to teach her of Wales and of the struggles against each other and against the English. She listened well."

Christopher was listening with increasing concern. "Is that the only education she has ever had?" he asked. "From the mouths of ignorant men?"

Gruffydd smiled weakly. "Our grandmother insisted she be educated by the priests at St. Nicholas, near her home," he said. "Do not misunderstand me, my lord. Elle has a brilliant mind. She can read and write and do sums in her head. She can recite enormous passages of the Bible from memory. She speaks three languages, so she is quite learned. She will always be two steps ahead of you, in anything you do. Even though she was educated by priests and raised by soldiers loyal to her father, it does not mean she is ignorant. Not in the least. It was she who led the siege against you, my lord. She held the castle until it could be held no more."

Christopher was both puzzled and intrigued by the eldest child of Gwenwynwyn. "But why does she rebel?" he said. "Why did she send the English soldiers from Brython?"

Gruffydd took a bite of the bread in his hand before answering. "Because she is convinced that Wales, or at least part of it, can be united under Llywelyn," he said. "This is not something she decided last month, or even last year. This is something our grandmother taught her, a woman who is part of Llewelyn's family. My grandfather married her at the demand of his father, who had hoped for an alliance with the princes of Gwynedd. But instead of an alliance, it only seemed to make the princes of Gwynedd more hostile. They did not want an alliance with Powys—they *wanted* Powys."

Christopher was starting to understand. "So your sister went to live with a grandmother, who filled her head with poison," he said. "And given that your father paid her little attention, she clung to the only person who showed her any affection—your grandmother."

"Exactly, my lord."

It was certainly turning into quite a tale. Christopher sipped at his warmed wine, mulling over the warrior woman who had tried to take out his eldest son. The same woman he wanted *for* said son. Now, he was finding out more about her and was not entirely happy about it.

"How did she manage to get you into the vault?" he asked.

Gruffydd's eyebrows lifted. "There is a village to the west of Brython," he said. "It is a rather large village, and my sister is well known and well liked there. I do not know what pushed her into deciding that the English troops should be removed from Brython at this time, nor do I know what caused her to act, but someone did. She purchased a sleeping potion from the apothecary in Rhayader, put it in my wine, and when I fell unconscious, she had me taken to the vault. She purged the English soldiers from the castle, declared that it was now a Welsh holding for the people of Powys—and it was until you came along and took it back."

"And that's all she did to you?"

"That was all she did."

Christopher scratched his head. "But you said something earlier when you saw her," he said. "You told me to burn her at the stake because she only wanted our death."

Gruffydd grunted. "I was angry," he said with regret. "I did not mean it."

"Then she does not want to see us all dead?"

Gruffydd shrugged. "More than likely," he said. "You must understand how convinced she is that every English warlord is the devil. The only person she ever trusted—our grandmother—told her that. She believes it."

"You are speaking more kindly of her than you did earlier."

"She has had a difficult life, my lord. I try to remember

that."

"Even when she throws you in the vault?"

"Even then, though I could have done without that experience."

"Then you do not believe her… wicked?"

Gruffydd shook his head. "Nay," he said. "Elle is headstrong and bold, and in many ways she is more fearless than any man I know, but I do not think she is wicked. It is simply that she only knows one point of view."

"And you never tried to change that?"

Gruffydd sighed with some remorse. "She views me as the brother who received all of the attention she never had," he said. "There is jealousy there. Bitterness, if you will. But in answer to your question—nay, I never tried to change her thinking. She would not listen to me anyway."

Christopher fell silent for a moment, but it was clear that something was on his mind. Gruffydd kept eating the food in front of him, more food than he'd seen in a month, as Christopher digested their conversation. Mostly, he was digesting what Gruffydd said about Elle. Some of it was encouraging. Some of it wasn't. But one thing was certain—she was a tempest. But she was a tempest with a mind.

A rebel with intelligence.

That brought him great concern.

"I have orders from Henry to secure Brython," he finally said. "But I also have orders from Henry to secure it with one of the surest ways of forming an alliance."

Gruffydd looked up from his trencher. "What is that, my lord?"

Christopher fixed him in the eye. "A marriage."

Gruffydd nearly choked on the food in his mouth. "It is true that is a sure way of forming an alliance," he said, sputtering. "But I already… There is a woman I am already fond of, and—"

Christopher waved a hand at him, cutting him off. "Not you," he said. "Your sister. I intend to marry her to an English knight."

Gruffydd wiped his mouth with the back of his hand, his eyes wide. "Elle?" he repeated, shocked. "Married to an English… *knight*?"

Christopher nodded. "It seems no one has been able to tame her," he said. "A husband will do that. He will settle her. Marriage and children have a tendency to quiet a wild heart."

Gruffydd was looking at him in genuine horror. "Her heart isn't wild," he said. "It bleeds the Brecon Mountains and pumps the blood of our ancestors. It calls to Wales, and Wales answers. We are speaking of a woman who has been taught to hate the English like the church hates Lucifer."

"I understand," Christopher said, unwilling to give in to Gruffydd's fears. "But she is young still. She had only been taught one perspective on life, as you have said. Let someone who is patient and firm teach her another perspective. If she is as intelligent as you say she is, then she will learn and she will understand… and Llewelyn will have lost a devoted follower."

Gruffydd shook his head slowly. "I am not certain it can be done," he said. "This has been her entire life, my lord."

"We are about to change her life."

"But at what cost? And what risk to this man you shall marry her to?"

Christopher shrugged. "As I see it, we have little choice," he said. "What am I to do? Simply throw her in the vault and forget about her to rid myself of her trouble? Or do I marry her to a man who can help her see more than the narrow view of the world that she has? You said yourself that she is very intelligent. If she is intelligent, then she can learn there is more to life than Llywelyn and Wales."

Gruffydd still wasn't convinced. "I suppose the decision has already been made, my lord?"

"It has."

There wasn't much more Gruffydd could add to what he'd already said. He had expressed his fears and concerns, but in his opinion, de Lohr had no idea what he was getting into.

Or what he was asking.

"Then you do not need my approval," he said after a moment. "But you should know that my father has tried to tame her before."

"How?"

"The same way you are."

Christopher understood when he meant immediately. "A marriage?"

Gruffydd nodded. "She was extremely young," he said. "Her husband was extremely old. He died before they had been married a year."

Christopher wasn't sure he liked the fact that Elle had been married before. In fact, he wasn't sure he liked the fact that she had concealed that from him. She knew of his plans of an advantageous marriage and had every opportunity to tell him that she had been married before, yet she hadn't, and he wondered why.

"How long ago was this?" he asked.

Gruffydd sighed, thinking back to that turbulent episode in his family's life. "She was betrothed when she was born," he said. "My father did not live much longer after that. When she had seen thirteen summers, she married a man who was a prince of Gwent, and the hope was that any children from the marriage would secure a permanent alliance between Gwent and Powys, but no children were born. Her husband told everyone that it was because Elle was barren, but I suspect that was not the case. The man had been married four times before he married my sister and only had one daughter out of all of those marriages. It was unfair of him to blame the problem on Elle."

More information on something Christopher found disturbing. He certainly didn't want a barren wife for his heir, but Gruffydd seemed to think there was more to it. He believed him, because it wasn't as if the man was trying to dump his sister on the House of de Lohr. Quite the opposite. Even though he didn't like that she had been married before, he'd been ordered to make a marriage. It wasn't as if he had many choices at this point.

For the sake of peace, and an alliance with Powys, he was willing to overlook it.

"She was no more than a child when she married," he said after a moment. "She is a woman now. A marriage to a man who is not old enough to be her grandfather will be different."

Gruffydd shrugged. "Mayhap," he said. "Mayhap not. But I should like to be clear in the fact that I do not think this is a good idea."

"Why not?"

"Because you are trying to tame the wind, my lord. It cannot be done."

Christopher thought that was a rather lyrical way to put it. "That is possible," he said. "But the truth is that your sister is Welsh royalty. She and you are all that is left from the ruling house of Powys. You and your sister are quite valuable, as allies, as…"

"Commodities," Gruffydd finished for him.

Christopher nodded faintly to concede the point. "Your sister cannot be allowed to continue as she has been," he said. "The decision has been made to marry her to an earl, in fact. The Earl of Leominster."

That didn't mean anything to Gruffydd. All of the English warlords and their titles seemed alike to him. "Is he at least a good man with a heavy manner?" he asked.

Christopher chuckled. "He is the best man, and his manner his far heavier than your sister's," he said. "Have no fear—she will be in capable hands."

Gruffydd shook his head. "I do not worry for her," he said. "I worry for him."

Christopher continued to snort. "I would not," he said. "As I said, he is capable."

Gruffydd thought it was all quite mad, but he didn't protest. The reality was that his sister would cease to become his problem if she married, so in a sense, he was being rid of her, and that did not trouble him. Let her become some English earl's problem.

But as for him…

"May I then return to the lady I am fond of and wed her?" he asked. "She is from Welsh nobility on her mother's side. Her father is English. I can return to my post as garrison commander and maintain Brython as your ally."

But Christopher shook his head. "Nay," he said. "Brython will be garrisoned by my heir, Curtis. He is the Earl of Leominster."

Gruffydd's eyebrows rose when he realized what de Lohr was telling him. "You mean he will…?"

"Marry your sister, aye," Christopher said. "You have other properties, do you not?"

Gruffydd was still not over the fact that his sister would be remaining at Brython with her new husband, who happened to be the earl's son. That bit of news had him reeling, something he struggled not to show.

"I do have other properties," he said after a moment's hesitation. "But you would leave Elle here, at Brython? In the shadow of her rebellion? Is that not dangerous?"

Christopher's gaze lingered on him as he pondered what was an astute question. But it could have been something else, too. "I am attempting to deduce whether or not it is your jealousy speaking and not genuine concern," he said truthfully. "Brython is a jewel in the crown of the marches. It is very important and strategic. I realize it must be a blow to be told you are no longer the garrison commander, but you had your opportunity and you failed. I would see Brython in more capable hands."

Rebuked, Gruffydd struggled with his humiliation. "It was genuine concern, my lord," he said. "Yet you seem convinced that your son can manage my sister, so I will not say another word about it. But consider yourself warned."

Christopher was pleased he'd managed to shut down Gruffydd's protests, for they were becoming tiresome, even if they were understandable. He was confident that Curtis could handle anything Elle decided to throw at him, so there was nothing left to discuss on the subject as far as he was concerned. He simply wanted to get past it and move forward.

"Where else will you go?" he asked, changing the focus slightly. "What other properties do you have that would be suitable?"

Gruffydd realized he hadn't finished his meal. He'd been so busy discussing his sister that the food was cooling before him. He reached for his wine.

"Tywyl Castle is about ten miles to the east, in the heart of my lands," he said, then took a long swallow before continuing. "I was born there. It is the traditional home of my family."

"Good," Christopher said. "That is a better place for you, as the ruler of these lands. Brython is on the marches, on the edge, so let me keep it strong for you. Henry will be pleased that I have garrisoned it, and that will keep him peaceful when it comes to you and your properties."

Gruffydd could see what he was driving at. "And a pleased Henry will not cause me any trouble."

Christopher lifted his eyebrows to concede the point. "You understand the nature of kings."

"I know that I am one, yet I do not command the thousands that Henry does," he said before tipping more wine into his mouth. "I do not command the numbers that Llywelyn does. He wants my lands, you know. He is not finished, no matter how you convince Elle that siding with Llywelyn is not a victory for the Welsh."

Christopher sipped the last of his warmed wine. "I know that any onslaught by Llywelyn will be met by your English allies," he said. "And I have more men than he does. Is that not enough?"

Gruffydd nodded, though there was defeat in his slumped shoulders. "It means a great deal, my lord," he said. "That is why I am pleased to retire to Tywyl while your son controls Brython. He will serve it well, I am certain."

The situation was working out just the way Christopher had hoped. He stood up, stiffly, with the intent of finding more wine, and the flap to his tent flew open. His senior sergeant, an older man with a bushy beard named Becker, was in the doorway.

"My lord," Becker said. "We have a prisoner you should see."

Christopher frowned. "Who is it?"

"She says that Gwenwynwyn was her uncle."

Christopher looked straight at Gruffydd, who was on his feet at the news. "It must be Melusine, my lord," he said. "She is my cousin, the only cousin I have. She has been living at Brython too, but I have not seen her since I was put in the vault."

Christopher's features took on an incredulous expression. "Another woman warrior?"

Gruffydd shook his head. "Nay," he said. "She is… Well, she is—"

Screaming interrupted them as the woman in question appeared at the entry. She was on her hands and knees, crying and carrying on, but neither Christopher nor Gruffydd could see anything around her that should terrify her so. No one was harming her. She had no marks that they could see, no blood. She was clad in the clothing of a servant, a rough and dirty woolen tunic and hose that had seen better days. On her feet were shoes that were too large for her. On her hands and knees, she wept hysterically.

Gruffydd was the first one to move toward her, reaching down to pick her up. "Get up, Melusine," he said quietly. "No one is going to harm you."

Melusine threw herself at him, clinging to him. "Gruffydd," she sobbed. "Are you well?"

He peeled her away from him. "I am well," he said. "Are

you?"

She nodded unsteadily. "I am unharmed."

Gruffydd frowned. "Then stop weeping," he said. "You are making a fool of yourself in front of Lord Hereford."

Like a magic pill, that request caused her to instantly quiet. She looked at Gruffydd with big, watery eyes, wiping at her face with the back of her dirty hand and smearing dirt down her cheek. Then she looked at Christopher as if the man were going to eat her, but he simply indicated a chair next to the remains of Gruffydd's meal.

"Sit, my lady," he said politely. "You are safe here, I promise."

Melusine didn't seem capable of releasing Gruffydd, so he had to walk her over to the chair and force her into it. Still, she clung to him, looking like a hunted animal.

"They found me," she told Gruffydd. "I tried to hide, but they found me."

Gruffydd ended up sitting next to her because she refused to release him. "Calm yourself," he told her, trying to unwind her fingers from his arm. "Get control of yourself, Melusine. There is no need to be so frightened. You have not even greeted Lord Hereford, who is our ally. Do not be rude."

Melusine's gaze moved from Gruffydd to Christopher, who was pouring himself more wine. "Hereford," she repeated, her voice trembling. "That is de Lohr."

"It is, indeed," Christopher said. "Have you eaten, my lady? There is still food on the table if you are hungry."

Melusine's hysteria was fading, but now she seemed dazed. She looked at the food as if unsure she needed or wanted it.

"It was *your* army," she said. "Your army attacked us."

Gruffydd cleared his throat. "That is none of your concern," he said. "We have peace now, and that is all that matters."

Melusine looked at him, studying her dark-eyed cousin who looked much thinner than the last time she saw him.

She knew why.

She knew what Elle had done to him. She knew it had been at her urging. Melusine was a woman of many secrets, all of which were unknown to Gruffydd but most of which were known to Elle. They were a pair, the two of them. Poor Gruffydd had taken the brunt of the ambitious women in his family.

But she could never let him know.

"Elle," she said quietly, trying to whisper in his ear. "What happened to her?"

"She survived," Gruffydd said, making sure Christopher heard him. "She is in the encampment, in fact, but I do not know where."

"She is being well tended," Christopher said, looking at the lady. "You needn't worry."

Melusine eyed him with uncertainty. "What is going to happen to her?" she asked. "What is going to happen to me?"

She was starting to get agitated again, so soon after she had recently calmed, and Christopher went to her, handing her his cup of wine.

"Drink," he said quietly. "Nothing is going to happen to anyone tonight, so drink this. Eat something. You'll feel better."

With quivering hands, Melusine reached for the cup and took a long drink, almost draining it. She was a woman who liked her drink, even though she pretended otherwise.

"May I see Elle, please?" she asked, licking her lips of the wine.

Christopher seemed to consider that. "In time," he said.

"But first, you will tell me what your participation in the battle was."

Gruffydd started to answer for her, but Christopher held up a hand, silencing him. When Melusine saw this, she drained the remainder of her wine before speaking.

"I live with Elle and Gruffydd," she said. "Brython is my home."

"Are you a warrior like your cousins?"

She shook her head with horror. "Nay, my lord," she said. "Weapons and battle frighten me. I tend to the meals. If a man is wounded, then I care for him."

"Then you are a chatelaine."

She nodded. "Mostly," she said. "May I see Elle now?"

Christopher looked to Gruffydd, who nodded faintly. "It might make things easier with my sister," he said quietly. "Melusine may calm her down."

Christopher pondered that request for a moment before going to the tent opening and sending a man for Curtis. As he lingered over by the tent flap, waiting for his son to appear, Melusine picked up a piece of stale bread and shoved it in her mouth.

"What is he going to do with us?" she hissed at Gruffydd.

He eyed her as she continued to shove crumbs in her mouth. "Nothing," he said in a normal tone so Christopher wouldn't think they were conspiring. "I am returning to Tywyl, and I am going to marry Hawise. Elle is going to marry the Earl of Leominster and they will live here, at Brython, because it will become a castle garrisoned by Hereford. And you... I do not know. Mayhap he will allow you to remain here with Elle."

Melusine was looking at him in complete shock. "Married?" she repeated. "Elle is to be *married*?"

Gruffydd nodded, fully aware that Christopher was listening. "It is time for her to grow up and find her place in the world," he said steadily. "She will have a husband and children and a title as the Countess of Leominster. Quite suitable for a daughter of Gwenwynwyn."

But Melusine wasn't having any of it. She wasn't aware Christopher was listening simply because she wasn't that smart. Or that aware. More than that, she had her back to him. She was focused on Gruffydd in utter horror.

"Are you mad?" she said. "She killed Cadwalader! Why do you think she would not kill an English husband? She will do it, and we will be in more trouble than before!"

Gruffydd hadn't expected her to spout that very revealing bit of information. "Cadwalader was an old man who died in his sleep," he said, loudly and firmly. "Elle had no hand in it. Stop perpetuating those vile rumors."

"But she did!"

If Gruffydd could have throttled her in front of Christopher and gotten away with it, he would have. But all he could do was snap at her and pray Christopher wasn't going to change his mind about everything.

"You will keep your lips *shut*," he hissed angrily. "Shut your mouth and live longer, Melusine. You are a stupid and foolish girl. That is why none of your relatives want you to live with them. That is why you have no husband!"

Melusine turned red in the face, suddenly realizing she shouldn't have said what she did in front of Hereford. But that was typical for her—speaking first, thinking later. She further realized she could make a fragile situation worse, and from the look on Gruffydd's face, he was ready to kill her. Quickly, she struggled to make amends.

"You are correct," she said. "I... I am sorry. I do not know what I am saying. Elle did not deliberately do anything to Cadwalader, I know that. But the men said that she killed him because she was so young and he was so old, and she wanted him to bed her nightly, so it killed him. That is all I meant."

Gruffydd rolled his eyes. "For the love of God," he muttered. "Just *stop talking*."

Melusine did. Feeling rebuked and ashamed for running off at the mouth, she lowered her head and pulled scraps of food off the table, eating anything she could get her hands on simply to keep from talking. Gruffydd had his hand on his head in disbelief of what Melusine had just done, of the horrible things she'd said. He dared to glance at Christopher, who was still standing at the tent opening, gazing out at the night beyond.

But Gruffydd knew he'd heard everything.

As Melusine kept her head down, Gruffydd stood up and stretched his weary body. He was hoping that Hereford would let him go into the keep and retrieve his personal possessions, if they were even still there. Elle might have given them away, for all he knew. As he made his way to the brazier to warm his hands, Curtis suddenly appeared in front of his father.

"You summoned me, Papa?" he asked.

Christopher nodded, stepping back to indicate the small, dark-haired woman seated with her back to the tent opening. "We have found another Gwenwynwyn female," he said. "This is Lady Melusine, a cousin to Gruffydd and Lady Elle. She has been most concerned for Lady Elle's health, so I thought you could tell her how the lady fares."

Curtis looked at his father in puzzlement, and then frustration, before looking to the lady, who had turned to look at him by this time. He found himself looking at a dirty, pale young woman who in no way resembled her cousin.

"You summoned me for this?" he muttered to his father. "Papa, I should be back—"

"Tell the lady her cousin is well," Christopher said, interrupting him. "In fact, you can take her with you. It might help Lady Elle to have her cousin with her. It might ease her anxiousness, if you understand my meaning."

Christopher was trying to help Curtis with Elle's rebellious demeanor. Curtis began to understand that. Surely it would calm her to have her cousin with her. But he shook his head.

"She is sleeping now," he said. "Most peacefully, I might add. Bringing this woman—her cousin—to her now would not only awaken her, but would more than likely agitate her again, because she'd have to deal with her cousin's emotions now. Truly, she has enough of her own."

Christopher didn't want to be unkind. "Curt..."

But Curtis shook his head firmly. "Nay," he said. "She is asleep and she is calm, and that is what I wish for my own evening—calm and sleep. I do not need to watch over two hysterical women tonight. Please, Papa."

Christopher gave in, though reluctantly. "Very well," he said. "I will have Myles watch over Lady Melusine tonight. But tomorrow, they are to be reunited."

Curtis waved him off. "As you wish," he said. "I must return. Westley is watching over the lady, and if she wakes up and finds me gone, and a squire as her guard, she might give Westley a struggle."

He didn't even wait for Christopher to reply. He was heading back the way he'd come, out into the night. Christopher didn't give his abrupt behavior too much thought because the man was exhausted, as they all were.

Curtis wasn't the only one who wanted calm and sleep.

After that, Christopher summoned Roi and Myles and had them both tend to Gruffydd and Melusine. Christopher would trust his sons to tend to the Welsh prisoners, and tomorrow would dawn a better, brighter day. But for tonight, Christopher simply wanted to be alone in his own tent. It was yet another victory in a long line of victories for the mighty Earl of Hereford and Worcester, and he'd done enough today. He'd earned his solitude.

When sleep finally came for him, it was filled with dreams of home.

CHAPTER SEVEN

S HE GRADUALLY BECAME aware of sounds.

That was Elle's first awareness that the world was going on around her. She could hear a man speaking and people moving about, but she could also hear birds singing. Somewhere, overhead, a hawk was screeching against the wind. He must have been looking for a meal, because it began to occur to her that it was morning.

A new day had arrived.

Elle opened one eye and looked around a little before she opened her other eye. For a moment, she had no idea where she was and how she got there. Everything was unfamiliar. But it was clear that she was in a bed—someone's bed—and somehow, she had gotten there.

But she genuinely did not know how.

Therefore, she simply lay there and didn't move, at least not until she could figure out her current situation. She remembered the battle the day before, of course, and she remembered being captured by the English. She remembered a long conversation with the Earl of Hereford, and she remembered drinking too much. Funny that she should remember that part of it, but she had been tipsy and said more than she probably should have. She'd been hoping to play on the man's sympathies, hoping that honesty would somehow put her in his favor, but that wasn't what happened.

The Earl of Hereford had plans.

Unfortunately, she was part of those plans. Now, everything began to come back to her, and she remembered being told that Henry wanted a marriage. That child king in London somehow controlled everything, including her, and she had been selected for a marriage to an English Lord. She wasn't stupid, however. She knew that peace was made in such ways, but she never thought that she would be the one to make that kind of sacrifice. She had so many things she wanted to do, things that now might never happen. She wasn't foolish enough to think that she alone could affect change for her countrymen, but she at least wanted a hand in it.

Perhaps the only way she would have a hand in it was through a marriage.

That was something she had never considered.

As she lay there and listened to the morning around her, Elle had a fleeting moment of rebellion. A fleeting moment where she thought that escaping this morning would be the best choice for her. That woman who had been captured when she tried to take down an enormous English night was making a bit of a resurgence. But just as quickly, the woman who was fairly certain she would be captured if she made any attempts got the upper hand.

The English were not going to let her go.

And that included Curtis.

That big, handsome knight that she had tried to destroy yesterday was becoming increasingly heavy on her mind. Elle had spent her life around soldiers, rebels who taught her what they knew of Wales and its struggle for survival. They had taught her to fight and to be clever against the enemy, and many other things that were considered unseemly for finely bred woman. The truth was that although she had fine bloodlines, she had lost the hope of ever behaving like a noblewoman long ago. Her life had taken a different course from those women who were strong figures at the side of their strong husbands, and that did not include husband and children in a fine and peaceful home. It only included a hard life where she had to fight for everything she had because no one truly loved her or tried to take care of her.

She had stopped hoping for that long ago, too.

But, perhaps, that was about to change.

Curtis had discussed their marriage and given her the choice of what she wanted it to be based on. They could either build it on battle or they could build it on a civil coexistence. The truth was that all Elle knew was battle. From a very young age, she had been part of the struggles of her people. Did the prospect of peace intrigue her? Of course it did. She wondered what it would be like to wake up every morning and not have to wonder at the danger she faced or where her next meal was coming from. As Curtis had pointed out, she was indeed a princess. But she'd never felt less like a princess her entire life. The idea of actually living an existence that was pleasant and productive in a meaningful way was, indeed, intriguing.

But it was something she had never believed would happen.

Now, here she was.

A new life was beginning.

Elle wasn't sure how long she had lain there and considered the events of the previous day, but the hungry hawk had flown off, and it seemed to her that the day was deepening. Slowly, she rolled onto her back, looking around the tent but seeing no sign of Curtis. She did, however, see a tray of food and drink on the table nearby. Curious, she sat up in bed and strained to get a better look at it. When she realized she was too far away to see what, exactly, was on the tray, she climbed out of the bed and went over to the table for a close-up view.

There was bread and cheese and four hard-boiled eggs. There was also butter and drink that turned out to be a mixture of water and wine and apple juice. Suddenly very hungry and thirsty, she sat down on the nearest chair and began to wolf down the eggs. In fact, she had survived off eggs for the past few weeks because she would not let her men kill the chickens. The men weren't exactly starving, but they were eating a lot of eggs.

It was a good thing she liked them.

Elle ate everything on the tray. She drained the cup, too, and even licked up part of the butter. It was creamy and salty and delicious. Once the food was gone, she thought that perhaps she should find the comb that Curtis loaned her last night and brush out her hair. She didn't know where he was, but she did not want him to return to find her looking slovenly, having just rolled out of bed. He had gone through all the trouble of making sure she had a bath and clean clothing, and although she might not want to marry the man, his attempts to be polite and provide her with everything she needed did not go unnoticed. The truth was that she could not remember anyone being as kind to her as Curtis had.

He might have been her enemy, but there was something endearing about that.

She didn't want to be rude when he had gone to such trouble.

After leaving the tray on the table barren and the butter half-eaten, Elle moved over to the pot that still held the bathwater from the night before, now cold. She could see the comb she'd used and other things that had been laid out on a chair next to the bath. More than that, the garments that had been brought by Curtis' squire were now all slung over the side of the screen that had provided her with some privacy. Looking around, she didn't see her smelly clothing anywhere, so she had little choice but to wear what was available.

The bath she'd had last night had been the first in a very long time, and the reality of the situation was that she liked to bathe. She always had, if given the opportunity. Even with cold water. Stepping behind the screen, she stripped off the shift she'd slept in, stepped into the pot, and very quickly bathed with the last of the lemon-scented soap.

The water was very cold, however, and she gasped and shivered as she washed again and then dried off. A bath was the most luxurious thing she could think of in her world. Clean, and smelling of lemons, she put the shift back on and inspected the dresses that were hanging over the screen.

I like the blue dress.

That was what Curtis had said to her. Feeling silly, she chose the blue dress, perhaps to show him that she could be cooperative. Reflecting on her conversations with him from yesterday, conversations where he always seemed to have the right answer, she realized quickly that she was going to have to choose her battles with him wisely, and a blue dress wasn't something she wanted to battle over.

The dress went on.

The effort of being compliant began.

The dress was soft and well made, but it was a little too

short and a little roomy in the bosom area. She was able to get her hands in behind her and tie the ties that closed the seam in the back as tightly as she could, but she couldn't get all of them. There were at least three or four ties she couldn't get to because they were between her shoulder blades. She would have to ask for a female servant to help her finish with them.

Her hair was next.

It had been weeks since it had been clean, so she ran the comb through it several times. It was very long, thick and straight, so she parted her hair down the middle and fastened it in two long braids. In the items left for her next to the bath, she found small leather strips to tie off the braids.

After that, she went on the hunt for her shoes.

All she had were leather shoes she'd inherited from an old man who had been small, a loyal Welsh warrior who had eventually succumbed to a chest infection. She'd scavenged the shoes from him when he passed away because she very much needed them and didn't think he'd mind. She was just finishing tying them when the tent flap pushed aside.

Curtis made an appearance.

Elle's head came up from where she'd been tying her shoes, and, for a moment, they simply stared at one another. In the light of day, and cleaned of the battle grime from the day before, Curtis looked like a younger, fresher version of the man she'd originally met. It looked as if he had bathed, too. He was wearing heavy linen breeches, boots, and a linen tunic, but nothing more than that. No mail, no weapons, no de Lohr blue and yellow tunic.

The sight of him was a distinct shock to Elle. If she thought the man handsome when they'd first met, he appeared positively godly at the moment. Quickly, she stood up to face him.

"I awoke and you were not here," she said, sounding nervous. "I hope that you are not angry that I have dressed in the clothing from last night. I have nothing else to wear, as I cannot seem to find the clothing I wore yesterday."

"That is because I had it burned," he said, his voice deep and quiet. "I cannot stand that smell."

Elle wasn't sure if she should be insulted by that, but she figured if he really meant to offend her, he would have been more obvious about it. The man didn't seem to be one who beat around the bush.

"It was probably for the best," she said. "But, as I said, I really had nothing else, so until I can earn money and pay for more clothing, I hope you do not mind that I wear what you have provided."

He frowned. "My lady, after our conversation yesterday, I thought I was clear in what our future together is," he said. "That means that you do not have to earn any money. I will supply you with whatever you need. Can you sew?"

Her cheeks turned shades of red as she averted her gaze. "Nay," she said. "I never learned."

Curtis could see that he'd embarrassed her. "It is of little concern," he said. "I am certain there are local seamstresses. We can find one and have her make you some clothing. Meanwhile, those dresses that belonged to my mother have now become yours. How does this one fit?"

She looked down at the blue garment. "Well enough... I think," she said. "But there are ties in the back that I cannot reach. Is there a woman who can help me?"

He moved toward her. "Turn around," he said, reaching out to grasp her arm and turn her when she didn't move fast enough. He could immediately see what she meant. "I'm afraid I'll have to do. We do not have any women servants with the army."

Elle was wearing the shift, so her skin wasn't exposed, but she wasn't entirely comfortable with him so close to her. "I do not wish to be any trouble," she said. "This is a menial task beneath you, my lord."

His reply was to tie each tie very tightly, one at a time. He did the first one easily, but he pulled too hard on the second one, nearly yanking her into him. She caught her balance and leaned away from him, trying to prepare herself for another yank, and Curtis fought off a grin.

Truth be told, he wasn't at all adverse to standing this close to her.

The difference in the woman from yesterday to this morning was like day to night. Yesterday, she'd been filthy and combative, but the bath last night had shown him how well she could shine up with a little soap and water. And when he'd just entered the tent now, he was momentarily speechless at what he saw before him. She was in the blue dress that brought out the color in her magnificent eyes, and her hair was in two braids, which was incredibly charming. If he'd simply seen her in the street passing by him and had no idea who she was, he would have definitely taken a second look.

Enid Avrielle ferch Gwenwynwyn was an unusual, and exquisite, beauty.

Against his better judgment and everything he stood for as a career knight with no distractions, he could feel himself becoming intrigued with her. Interested, even. But that was solely based on her beauty. Her manner would tell the true tale of whether or not he could be attracted to her on a deeper level.

There was a part of him that was hoping it was possible.

"There," he said, finishing with the last one. "I tried to pull it as tight as I could so it would fit better. My mother is a little rounder than you are."

Elle took a step away from him as she smoothed the dress, seeing that it did indeed fit better now. "It fits quite well," she said. "I think so, anyway. I've never had a garment like this before."

He looked her over. "You were made for a garment like that," he said. "A woman of your beauty should not be wearing tunics and hose. This is what you were born for."

She looked at him sharply, her cheeks turning a darker shade of red. "If I were a finer lady born to a fine and wealthy family, that would be true," she said. "But I am neither of those things. My clothing suited me."

His smile faded. "I have offended you," he said. "I did not mean to. I simply meant to praise your beauty."

She was vastly uncomfortable. "I would ask that you don't," she said. "It… it means nothing to me."

Curtis nodded but didn't reply, at least not right away. He was quickly coming to see that flattery was unwelcome, and after their conversations yesterday, he understood why. Perhaps the surprise of seeing her clean and lovely had pushed him into easy praise, but she wasn't shy in reminding him that it wasn't something she wanted to hear.

And he was sorry.

"I hope you are at least comfortable in the garment," he said. "The truth is that I did not come here to tie dresses or spew unwelcome flattery. Last night, we found a woman hiding who told us that she was your cousin. Do you have a cousin here at Brython?"

Elle's eyes widened. "Melusine?" she gasped. "I do! Is she well?"

Curtis wanted to hear confirmation by name, and now he had it. "She is," he said. "She and your brother slept in another tent last night, but I will have her sent to you if that pleases you."

Elle was nodding before he even finished. "Aye," she said. "Please."

He went back to the flap and summoned a soldier, sending the man with a message for his father. He also summoned someone else, and Westley burst through the tent flap, eager to do his brother's bidding. Curtis indicated for the lad to clean up the tent a little, and the young man went to work, picking up and tidying up as Elle stood back and watched him. As Curtis went back over to his table and began to busy himself with a few things, the squire summoned a few soldiers, and soon, the tent was swarming with them, removing the bathing pot and the remains of the meal.

Elle realized she was unnerved with so many English soldiers close to her. As the men moved about, she backed into the side of the tent, as far away from them as she could go. She was unaware that Curtis was watching her, and, realizing she was becoming frightened, he went to stand next to her.

"I've not yet introduced you to my squire," he said, snapping his fingers at Westley, who rushed to his side. "This is my youngest brother, Westley, who happens to be my squire. But do not let his youth fool you—he is a very competent warrior, even if he is at the age where he is so annoying that I want to toss him over a cliff. West, this is Lady Elle ferch Gwenwynwyn. She is a princess of Powys and will be afforded all due respect."

Westley bowed politely to her. "My lady," he said. "It is an honor."

Elle wasn't sure how to respond, for two good reasons—the first was that she wasn't used to being around men who were so mannerly. The second was that she wasn't used to being referred to as a princess of Powys, true though it might be. Being around Curtis elevated her from a woman ignored by her family to a woman whose noble blood was acknowledged and respected. She'd never been trained in the art of conversation, or in being polite when introduced, or anything of that sort. She felt uncomfortable and embarrassed, so much so that all she could do was nod unsteadily to the squire.

It was all quite strange to her.

Curtis must have sensed it. With a slight nod of his head, he sent Westley away, thinking it might relax Elle a little, but she still looked uncertain. Cagey, even. He sought to ease her.

"He will not bite you, I promise," he said quietly. "West is a good lad. You need not fear him."

She shook her head, perhaps a little too quickly. "I do not fear him," she said. "It's simply that... You said he was your youngest brother?"

"I have five."

"And... and you like them all?"

Curtis' eyes glimmered with warmth. "I love my brothers dearly," he said. "I would kill or die for any one of them, a thousand times over."

She stared at him a moment before sighing heavily. "I do not know how that feels," she admitted. "I have one brother, and we have always been at odds. And your father... It is clear that you love and respect him."

"I do."

Elle could feel her eyes sting with tears, and she had no idea why, but she turned away from Curtis, pondering a world in which a family actually loved one another.

"I do not even understand how that would be," she said before she could stop herself. Tears filled her eyes. "My father hated me, and I hated him. I hate my brother. No one loves me except Melusine, and that is because she has no one else either. Is there really a world in which a family is truly a family and everyone gets on with everyone else?"

Curtis could hear the pain in her voice, and it touched him. She was giving him some insight into a woman who was quite an enigma so far. "There is indeed a world where that is not only possible, but probable," he said. "I live in that world. You are to be part of it, too."

She looked at him sharply, quickly wiping away the tears that were starting to fall. "They will not love me," she said defensively. "I am the enemy. I am a symbol of something they've spent their lives fighting against."

Curtis was careful in his reply. "They will not hold you responsible for that," he said. "My lady, I am going to try to explain this to you, so listen carefully. It is important."

"Go on, then."

He did. "My older sisters are both married to men who had lives before they joined our family," he said. "Neither man was perfect. One man... Well, he is a trained assassin. Alexander went on crusade with King Richard and earned himself a fairly nasty reputation. In fact, my father did not want him for my sister at all, but she loved him... and once he became her husband, we all grew to know the man beyond the reputation. He is one of the finest men I know. So you... If you give my family the chance, they will look beyond the Welsh rebel and see the woman beyond the reputation. They will want to like you. You must give them that chance."

Elle's hands were on her cheeks as she thought of that very shocking prospect. "I cannot even imagine that," she said with sincerity. "And you? What relationship am I to have with you? Do you want to like me, too?"

He grinned. "I hope so," he said. "But you must give me the chance. You must look beyond the English knight and see the man beneath."

That was an astonishing bit of advice and insight. Her hands came away from her face, and she looked at him with as much honesty as he had seen from her since the beginning of their association.

"I do not know how," she said. "I am what you see. I do not know anything more than what you see. And I do not know how to see more than I already do."

"Are you willing to learn?"

She thought on that. Hard. After a moment, she nodded decisively. "Aye," she said. "I am. But you said something yesterday that holds true for me, also. I am willing to give you my trust if you ask it. But if you betray me, I will run, and I will never come back. We are being forced into a marriage, but if it does not suit me, then I will not stay. If you betray me, you will not see me again."

Curtis understood that because he'd said nearly the exact same thing to her. "Then I was not being harsh after all?"

Elle heard her words in his reply. "Nay," she said, knowing he was right. "You were not being harsh, but truthful. I made a pretty speech about people making mistakes, but in the end, I suppose you can only trust what you know, and if someone gives you a reason to mistrust them, then you must protect yourself."

"That is very true," he said. "But I will make you a promise—I will endeavor to never intentionally betray you. Will you pledge the same?"

A commotion at the tent flap interrupted the conversation. They both turned to see Melusine being brought in by a soldier. The moment Melusine saw Elle, she let out a scream and ran to her, flinging herself at the woman. Elle was nearly toppled by the force of Melusine's momentum, struggling to keep her feet.

"Melly!" she gasped. "Melly, you are alive! Praise the saints!"

Melusine was hysterical. "You are alive, too!" she sobbed. "I was so worried for you!"

"I am well," Elle assured her, pulling Melusine away so she could look her over. "Are you truly well?"

Melusine nodded, but she was still crying. "I am," she said. But once she got a good look at Elle in the blue gown, clean and fresh, her weeping stopped unnaturally fast. "And you... What *are* you wearing? Why do you look like this?"

Elle quickly grew embarrassed, eyeing Curtis before answering. "My clothing was ruined," she said honestly. "I had nothing else to wear, so Sir Curtis gave me this dress. It belongs to his mother."

Melusine drew back, appalled. "What did you have to do for the dress?" she demanded. "He would not give it to you without recompense! What did you do?"

"Nothing!"

"I do not believe you!"

Furious at the suggestion, Elle slapped Melusine across the face as hard as she could. Melusine stumbled, shrieking, before she struck back. In seconds, a slapping fight was occurring right in front of Curtis, who stepped in quickly to defuse it, but not before being slapped himself. He ended up pushing Melusine back by the forehead, so hard that she stumbled and ended up on one knee.

"Enough," he snapped, holding out a hand to Melusine to prevent her from charging. He had Elle by the arm, and he looked at them both. "If you two cannot behave like proper ladies, then I will make certain that you are separated for good. Do you comprehend me?"

Melusine was angry, but she forced herself to pause. She didn't fly off like she normally did, before thinking. She pointed a finger at Elle.

"What have you done to her?" she shouted at him.

Curtis wasn't happy with the woman's tone or her behavior. "I gave her one of my mother's dresses to wear," he said steadily. "And if you ever speak to me in that tone again, I will ensure you never see your cousin ever again. Tell me you understand, or I will assume you do not."

Melusine was quivering with anger and a retort was on her lips, but she held herself in check. She was finally where she wanted to be—with Elle—and didn't want to immediately ruin it.

But it was a struggle.

"I… I understand," she said.

Curtis' eyes narrowed. "Any further bad behavior and you will be gone," he said, lowering his voice to a steady rumble. "This is your only warning."

Melusine struggled to calm herself, lowering her head, but Elle suddenly pulled herself from Curtis' grip and charged her cousin, pushing her over onto the floor. Curtis managed to grab Elle around the waist as he bellowed for Westley, who suddenly appeared.

"Get this woman out of my sight," Curtis said, indicating Melusine. "Take her out of here now."

Startled, Westley rushed to Melusine, who was picking herself off the ground. He grabbed the woman by her arms, and she started to fight him. Westley dragged her, hissing and kicking, out of the tent as Curtis maintained his hold on Elle.

"Let me go," she said, trying to pry his arms away from her torso. "Let me go this instant."

"I will not," Curtis said in a tone that could have very well been construed as seductive. "Not until you gain control of yourself and tell me why you slapped her. This whole incident was your fault, you know."

Elle stopped struggling, but her face was molded into a deep frown. "You heard her," she said. "She thinks that you... that we... that I traded favors for clothing. She cannot get away with that."

Curtis suspected that might be the case, and he fought off a grin. "She does not know me," he said. "She does not know I do not trade favors with anyone, at least like that. If I did not give you the dress, you would be dressed in your skin and nothing more. That is hardly dignified or proper."

Elle sighed heavily. "Melly does not consider that some men have honest hearts," she said. "Especially the English. I suppose she came to the only reasonable conclusion she could."

"But?"

"But I still won't let her get away with it!"

He chuckled and released her. "I think she received your message, loudly and clearly," he said. "But in the future, a princess of Powys does not attack people when she does not like what they say."

Straightening her dress, Elle turned to look at him. "Don't

you attack people who say things you do not agree with?"

He shook his head. "It would have to be quite serious," he said. "It is called controlling one's impulses. There are things we would all like to do immediately, like slap a cousin with a wicked tongue, but often that does not solve the problem. You should have controlled that impulse."

Elle was coming to understand what he meant. "You mean I should have asked her to clarify her statement before slapping her?"

He snorted. "Something like that," he said. "Mayhap simply asking her and not slapping her."

Elle grunted. "She deserved it."

Curtis cocked an eyebrow. "I'm sure she did, but next time, mayhap just ask her instead."

Elle shrugged. "Will you bring her back now?"

Curtis shook his head. "Not now," he said. "I need your undivided attention, if I may."

"Why?"

"Because I wanted to ask you if you would show me Brython," he said. "You would know it better than anyone, and I would appreciate you as my guide."

It wasn't a surprising request, but she didn't think he would have asked her so soon. The defeat was only yesterday, after all. But it occurred to Elle that Brython now belonged to him, and he was viewing it as a prize he knew nothing about other than it was strategic. There was no heart or soul buried in it like there was with her. Resigning herself to this relationship she would soon find herself in, she wanted him to understand that Brython wasn't just a pile of rocks to lay claim to.

It was much, much more.

"As you wish," she said after a moment. "But before I show

you, I am going to tell you."

"Tell me what?"

"About Brython and why the Welsh believe it is a special place."

He nodded as if to concede her point. "Very well," he said. "Go ahead. I am listening."

Elle paused, thinking on how she would start the story but quickly realizing there was only one place to start.

At the beginning.

"Do you ever wonder why we fight so hard for Brython, my lord?" she asked.

Curtis shrugged. "It is strategic."

She shook her head. "That is not why," she said. "In truth, it has nothing to do with strategy and everything to do with our history. The fact is that Brython is sacred."

"Why?"

"Because it sits upon an ancient gate," she said quietly. "The gate to *Annwyn*. That is the Otherworld, where our heroes dwell. It is a place where our greatest prince, Powell, lives. Someday, he will rise again and free Wales from the tyranny of those who seek to rule us. Mayhap he will not rise tomorrow, or even in one hundred years. But we believe he *will* rise again, and we wait for that day. Meanwhile, we must protect the gate."

Curtis cocked his head. "My father has native Welsh scouts who know much of Brython," he said. "They have never told him this tale."

She smiled faintly. "That is because it is a Welsh prophecy," she said. "We do not share our prophecies with outworlders. That is you, in case you did not know it."

He smiled, an ironic gesture. "I have been called worse," he said. But he quickly sobered. "So you are telling me that the reason you have fought so viciously for Brython is because it's a sacred site?"

Elle nodded. "Would you not protect such a place fiercely?"

"I would," he said. "But you were content whilst there were English soldiers here. Brython was quiet. The trouble came after you purged the soldiers."

"I know," she said. "But it was time for the English to go. This is no place for them."

"But the English have it now," he reminded her. "*I* have it now. Did it occur to you that had you never sent the English away, you would not have lost the castle?"

She shook her head. "Nay," she said truthfully. "I thought we could hold it. I tried."

Curtis' grin returned. "You held out for a month against the most feared warlord on the marches," he said. "That is quite an accomplishment."

She couldn't give in to his humor about the situation. "But it was not enough in the end."

His smile faded. "Nay, it was not," he said. "But here is something else you might not have realized. The truth is that this is a very valuable castle, and even if I decide to go away and leave it to the Welsh, there will be other English warlords who will try to take it. They may not be so kind to you or your beliefs. You *do* understand that, don't you?"

Elle lowered her gaze, nodding reluctantly. "I do," she said. "I understand that it will always be coveted."

"Precisely," Curtis said. "Therefore, it is best that you and I protect it together."

She looked at him with some surprise. "You and I...?" she stammered. "You... *you* would protect Brython?"

He nodded. "It is clearly important to you," he said. "My

lady, this marriage will be for peace. For an alliance. What kind of peace would we have if I disrespected your beliefs and treated your people like slaves? We would have a fight on our hands every single day, and that is not something I wish. I grew up on the marches. I speak your language and I know the history of your country. My father insisted that all of his children did because he felt it was important for us to understand the viewpoints of others. I want to understand your viewpoint, but in return, I also want you to understand mine. Only then can we live in true peace. *Onid yw hynny'n gwneud synnwyr?*"

Does that not make sense?

He spoke Welsh flawlessly. It was the first time Elle had heard him do it. Somehow, that elevated him in her eyes. The fact that he could speak her language meant something. It was a difficult language to learn, yet he had taken the time to do it. That told her he meant to communicate with the Welsh on their level, in their language. Perhaps he'd been forced to learn it, but he could have easily forgotten it or dismissed it. He didn't even have to let her know that he could speak it. But he had.

To her, that was a show of respect.

"*Ydy, mae'n gwneud hynny,*" she said softly.

Yes, it does.

He smiled, and for the first time since their association, Elle smiled in return. He had a very handsome smile of straight teeth, with slightly prominent canines, and the gesture made her heart do strange things. It fluttered in a way she'd never felt before. She could feel her cheeks growing warm.

It was a most unusual reaction.

"Good," he said. "I will tell you my viewpoint and what I'd like to accomplish here. And our children—if we have any—will be children who understand their Welsh heritage and their

English heritage. They will be of two worlds."

Elle had heard that before. "Your father told me that," she said. "He said they would be the seeds of peace."

"They will," he insisted. "My father was right. But I want to understand where you come from and how you envision your countrymen. I want to know how you see this land ten years from now, or even twenty years from now. Will you tell me?"

Elle nodded because he seemed genuine. "I will," she said. "But you will not like some of my opinions."

"I can only know that when you tell me."

"I will tell you that I do not want the Saesneg in Wales."

"And I will tell you that it is not your decision to make, nor is it mine."

They were heading into one of those circular arguments again, and she didn't want to do that. After last night, he had left her feeling defeated that she couldn't win an argument or dominate him with her wants.

Weakly, she smiled.

"I think we have a long road ahead of us, my lord," she said. "You may as well know that I have strong views on things. I will not be afraid to tell you."

His smile returned. "I would hope that you are not afraid," he said. "I never had much use for women who are submissive. I come from a family of fiery women."

"Then it seems you are to marry one, too."

His eyes glimmered with mirth. "Are you saying that you are agreeable?"

"As you said, we have no choice."

He grunted at what could have been taken as an insult, his smile fading. "I suppose I walked into that one," he muttered, hoping for a response that might have fed his ego a little. "I was asking if there is anything about me that would make you even mildly agreeable to this marriage. My titles, mayhap? My wealth? My devilishly good looks?"

Elle fought off a grin and averted her gaze. "I think none of those would turn my head," she said. "You are a Saesneg."

"And if I were a Welshman?"

He caught her attention with that question, and she thought about it. If Curtis de Lohr had been a Welshman, she might very well find him quite attractive. She wasn't one to fawn over men in any case, but with him…

She might make an exception.

"If you were a Welshman," she said, refusing to look at him, "I might find you… adequate."

He burst into laughter, a great, booming sound that was almost instantly infectious. "Adequate, am I?" he said. "I'll have you know I am the most handsome out of all of my brothers. I am the beauty of the family."

"Then it must be an average family."

He couldn't stop laughing. He could see that she was smiling and trying very hard not to, which told him that she wasn't serious. She was poking holes in his pride. It was at that moment he realized she had his interest, because any woman who wouldn't feed him flattery was a woman of integrity, indeed.

Without question.

"I'll pit my average brothers against average Welshmen any day," he said, wiping his eyes of the hilarious tears. "But if you think me adequate, I will accept that. It is better than being inadequate, or worse."

She was still biting her lip. "If you did not want to know my opinion, then you should not have asked."

His eyes were still warm with humor. "I think that I shall always want to know your opinion because I suspect you will never lie to me," he said. "Even if I do not want to hear the truth."

Elle looked at him then. "Honesty is all I know," she said. "I am a very bad liar. But I can be... without tact sometimes."

"I hardly noticed."

He was being sarcastic, and her grin broke through. "Since you asked me if I found anything agreeable in you, I shall ask you the same. Surely there cannot be anything agreeable about me that you've found."

A smile played on his lips. "There is, as a matter of fact."

"What is it?"

He was prevented from answering when Westley appeared in the tent opening. "Curtis," the young man said, breathless from having run. "Papa wishes to see you now."

Curtis looked at him. "Why?"

"I do not know," Westley said. "He only told me to fetch you."

Curtis nodded with resignation. "Very well," he said. "Where is Lady Melusine, by the way?"

"I gave her over to Amaro."

Curtis gave him a long look. "Nay," he said quietly. "Go and find her. Give her over to Hugo or someone else, but not to Amaro."

Westley looked stricken. "It was wrong?"

"It was wrong."

Horrified that he'd done something his brother did not approve of, Westley took off running. Elle, who had heard the conversation, approached Curtis in concern.

"Who is this Amaro?" she asked.

Curtis looked at her. "He is a Spanish knight," he said. "He is a good warrior, but he is not kind. I do not want him frightening your cousin."

It was a simple explanation, but one that sent trepidation through Elle. "I see," she said. "He will not harm her, will he?"

Curtis shook his head. "And risk my father's wrath?" he said. "Nay, he will not, but he could frighten her. It is best to give her over to someone else to guard."

Elle reached out and put her hand on his arm. "I will not attack her, I promise," she said sincerely. "Will you please bring her back to me?"

Her hand, soft and warm, was on his forearm, and Curtis found himself looking at it before he answered her. "If you wish," he said, lifting his eyes to her earnest face. "But meanwhile, my father has summoned me. Come along, my lady."

"Why?"

"Because I will not leave you here."

She didn't ask him why. She knew. There was no one to guard her, and he didn't want her to try to escape. With a submissive nod, she allowed him to take her elbow and lead her out into the sunny morning.

CHAPTER EIGHT

"THE LADY LOOKS quite… different."

That was Christopher talking. It was the voice of a shocked man as he watched Elle plow into some food that had been brought in for his morning meal. But when Curtis had shown up with this beautiful blonde creature with the brilliant blue eyes, she looked at the food so longingly that Christopher immediately offered it to her.

She'd taken it quickly.

"Aye, she does," Curtis said. He was watching her eat, too. "A bath and decent clothing can do wonders."

Christopher nodded faintly. "She's magnificent, Curt," he said softly. "I truly had no idea."

"Nor did I."

"That should make the marriage more palatable."

Curtis looked at him. "Is that why you summoned me?"

Christopher tore his gaze away from Elle and looked at his son. "Aye," he said. "Partially, anyway. I wanted to tell you that I've sent Roi into the village of Presteigne to summon a priest."

"Why?"

"Because you are going to marry Lady Elle today," Christopher said quietly. "There is no reason to wait, so let us get this done so I may tell Henry we have a marriage and Brython is now garrisoned for the English by my son and his Welsh wife."

Curtis nodded in a gesture of acceptance, his gaze moving to Elle as she wolfed down some cheese. "Things are calm at the moment," he said. "She is not unreasonable, but that is because I have been the only person she has been around since yesterday. When West brought her cousin to the tent earlier, it turned into a brawl. Nearly the same thing that happened when she saw her brother yesterday. Where *is* her brother, by the way?"

"I've sent the man back to his home of Tywyl Castle," Christopher said. "He is about ten miles to the east, and he is your ally. I would suggest you pay him a visit at some point soon. You do not want that relationship to be neglected."

Curtis lifted his eyebrows. "That will be a delicate situation," he said. "The lady has no love for her brother, so to keep him as an ally will be a supreme feat of diplomacy. I do not want to anger her, but I also do not want her trying to thrash her brother every time she sees him."

Christopher looked at his son—brilliant, strong, a truly fine example of a noble knight. He was so proud of the man that he was close to bursting every time he spoke of him. He loved his other sons, of course, and was equally proud of them for many reasons, but Curtis was his shining star. In this very volatile situation, he wanted nothing more for him than to succeed.

"If anyone can walk that fine line, it is you," he said quietly. "But I will also make a suggestion that may help."

"What is that?"

"I would suggest you bring Brython to a state of normalcy very quickly," he said. "Set schedules, set posts, and get about to the repairs immediately. A sense of routine is what you need to make your vassals feel safe and as if the situation is moving forward calmly. And you must reach out to your neighbors quickly as well. Shrewsbury, Wolverhampton, Wrexham, Trelystan... All of them. They must know that Curtis de Lohr now holds Brython Castle. And it is very important that you introduce your wife as a princess of Powys. Lady Elle's bloodlines will bring you prestige."

Curtis eyed his father with some suspicion. "As if the de Lohr name wasn't prestigious enough?" he said. "I am coming to think you are placing great value on your son marrying into Welsh royalty."

Christopher shrugged. "Would you feel better if you married a miller's daughter?"

"I would feel better if you started viewing Elle as a woman and not simply a figure of royal blood."

"What do you mean by that?"

Curtis lowered his voice. "I mean that I have had a few conversations with her," he said. "She views her royal blood not as you do. She had a father who ignored her and a brother who took what affection the man had. She was left to fend for herself."

"I know that."

"But what you don't know is that she is bright and feels deeply about things," Curtis said. "She is not proud that she is a daughter of Gwenwynwyn because she views the man and her brother as a traitor. Look at the way she is eating, Papa—this is a woman who has not had an easy life. She eats like that because she probably does not know where, or when, her next meal is coming. She's never known safety or security of any kind."

Christopher watched Elle as she chugged down a cup of watered wine. "I had a long conversation with her brother," he said. "He told me basically the same thing. She was left to her grandmother to raise for a few years, a woman who was part of Llywelyn's family."

Curtis looked at him in surprise. "Are you serious?"

Christopher nodded. "The old woman evidently filled her head with poison against the English and against her own family," he said. "Gruffydd says that Elle is intelligent and quite educated, but she has a very narrow view of the Welsh and English relationship. As Gruffydd put it, she hates the English as the church hates Lucifer."

Curtis was listening with interest. "What else did he say?"

"That you should take care with her," Christopher said quietly. "Caution would be prudent, at least until you come to know her better. Do not allow her any daggers, no opportunity to arm herself. Treat her like the enemy, Curt, because she is for now. You must not let your guard down."

Curtis digested that information. He had been feeling somewhat comfortable around Elle, but his father's words had him tensing again. He finally shook his head.

"I am marrying her, Papa," he said. "By your command, might I remind you. I cannot go the rest of my life being wary of my wife. That will be exhausting and unfair."

Christopher lifted a hand to ease him. "I am not saying that you must do it forever," he said. "But the truth is that we only captured her yesterday. Everything is still new, still uncertain. Just be careful around her for the time being. She is going to have to earn your trust, just as you are going to have to earn hers. It will take time."

That was a true statement, but Curtis was back to feeling as if he wasn't sure he wanted to marry her.

"I have asked her to show me Brython," he said. "I suppose

I will have to keep her with me constantly for a while, at least until we start to trust one another."

Christopher could hear the resignation in his tone. "If it is any consolation, when your mother and I were married, she fought me at every turn," he said. "And I do mean literally. In hindsight, I wasn't very pleasant to her, but your mother was as out of control as a wet cat. She fought with me, insulted me, disobeyed me... Everything possible she could do against me, she did. It was hell for the first few weeks of our marriage."

Curtis cracked a smile. "Mama is the Queen of the Firebrands," he said. "As a lad, she used to terrify me. She was so loving and sweet, but if I did something wrong, she wasn't afraid to swat me on the behind."

"She still isn't."

Curtis chuckled. "Nay, she isn't."

Christopher grinned alongside him. "My point is that I had to suffer with a wild woman when I first married, too," he said. "All I can tell you is that you must be patient and understanding. You must be thoughtful. That will go a very long way. But do not let her get away with any disobedience. That is something you must never accept."

Curtis sighed heavily. "I have a feeling that is easier said than done."

"That is quite true."

The conversation lagged at that point, but not uncomfortably so. Christopher went to speak to Becker, just outside the tent, while Curtis stood near the opening and watched Elle devour his father's morning meal. He couldn't say that speaking with his father had given him courage for what he must do, but at least he felt better informed for what he was taking on.

He hoped so, anyway.

Christopher returned to the tent.

"My army will be mobilizing today," he told Curtis. "I am leaving you a thousand men, however, along with Myles and Asa. You already have Amaro and Hugo, so that will be three strong knights and Asa, who wants very badly to be a knight. He fights better than some men who have been doing it all their lives. And I'll see if Sherry wants to leave Andrew with you. He could use the experience."

He was referring to Andrew de Sherrington, Curtis' nephew. He was still quite young, but he was an excellent warrior already. It would be good for him to be away from his father for a time, experiencing another castle, learning from men other than his father and grandfather. Curtis wasn't opposed to having him.

"If you think it would be good for him," he said. "I think I can use all the help I can get."

Christopher clapped him on the shoulder. "I have complete faith in you, lad," he said. "Now, will you tell the lady that today is her wedding day, or shall I?"

Curtis indicated Elle sitting several feet away. "You will tell her," he said. "You are the one making the decisions, so that is your privilege."

Taking his son's invitation, Christopher went over to the table where Elle was licking the butter from a big, flat knife. When she saw him approach, she quickly set it down, looking at him with an expression between fear and curiosity. He smiled politely.

"Are you feeling better today, my lady?" he asked. "I see that my wife's garment fits you."

Elle looked down at herself, quickly brushing away a few crumbs in her lap. "It does."

"May I tell you something about it?"

She appeared puzzled. "If you would like to, you may."

Christopher's sky-blue eyes glimmered. "That garment was the second dress I ever saw my wife wear many years ago," he said. "You see, when I first met her, she was hanging from a tree, and—"

"Hanging from a tree?" Elle said, interrupting him. "A fine lady?"

He grinned. "She wasn't a fine lady back then," he said. "And aye—a tree. I was home from the great quest to the Levant, heading toward Lioncross Abbey Castle to claim my bride, when this woman fell out of a tree right in front of me. I remember this mass of blonde hair all over the ground as she lay there and groaned, so naturally, I took pity on her and brought her home."

"This is the same woman you bullied into marrying you?" Elle asked.

Christopher laughed softly. "The same," he said. "I see that you remember what I told you yesterday."

"I do, indeed," Elle said. "I never forget a conversation."

Christopher shot Curtis a long look. "You would do well to remember that about your future wife," he said, but his focus returned to Elle. "We returned to Lioncross, where I met Dustin's mother, Lady Mary. Lady Mary was a kind, gentle creature who struggled with a daughter who was neither kind nor gentle. It was Lady Mary who forced Dustin to don the very blue dress you are wearing at our first official meeting later that day. Therefore, the garment you wear has special meaning to me and to my wife. She would be very honored that you are wearing it."

Elle looked down at the dress, trying to see it with the sentimentality that Christopher was. "If it has special meaning, why does she not keep it with her?" she asked. "Why was it here, with you, at a battle?"

"Because she would come with me sometimes on a battle march," he said. "That is why you have clothing to wear—she always kept some with me should she decide to attend me."

Elle nodded, fingering the dress that had been altered slightly since Dustin had been a young lass, wild and free. She could see where seams used to be, having been let out in the slightest. She tried to picture Curtis' mother, a blonde woman who liked to hang from trees.

"Did Lady Hereford really hang from trees?" she asked, a smirk tugging at her lips.

Christopher nodded. "Indeed, she did," he said. "She was fearsome, unrestrained in a way few women are. You remind me of her, to be perfectly truthful. You led a battle yesterday, which is something she is more than capable of doing. She is fearless, and so are you, I am coming to see."

Elle almost replied with *fearless but a failure*, but held her tongue. They already knew she was beaten. She knew she was beaten. There was no use in rehashing it every time it came up, and the truth was that it could have been so much worse. Hereford and his son were treating her kindly and fairly when they could have very well made her a prisoner and treated her as one. But they weren't.

Elle was coming to be grateful for small mercies.

"I am certain I will meet her one day," she said, because she couldn't think of anything else and Christopher's kind words had her unsettled. "I will take good care of her garment."

"I am sure you will," Christopher said, seeing that she was feeling awkward. "The reason I am telling you this is not to force sentimentality into the situation, but because you and Curtis are to be married today, and the dress you are wearing is most appropriate. My wife will be quite sad that she cannot be present, but your wearing her dress will give her comfort. She is here in spirit."

Elle looked at him in astonishment. "Today?" she said. "We are being married... *today*?"

Christopher nodded. "There is no reason to delay," he said. "Henry will have his marriage, Curtis will have a new castle and a new wife, and this section of the marches shall be settled for the time being."

Elle wasn't over her astonishment, and she didn't like the way he sounded so positive about the situation. As if this was a good thing. As if her entire world hadn't just come crashing down.

In fact, it shocked her to the core.

"You speak as if this is something good," she said, sliding from astonishment to outrage. "You speak as if all that matters is that your son will have his castle and a new wife. But what about me? I have lost everything for your son to achieve his status. I have lost my independence and my freedom, not to mention a castle I held for a solid month against mayhap the greatest warlord in England. Yet... you do not acknowledge that I had to sacrifice my entire life so your heir could have a destiny, and I find that wholly insulting."

The warm expression faded from Christopher's face. He glanced at Curtis to see how the man was reacting to Elle's statement, and all he could see on his son's face was that, perhaps, she might be right. Curtis' only response was to lift his eyebrows at his father, which told Christopher he may have been thoughtless.

He was careful in his response.

"If I have been insensitive, forgive me," he said quietly. "It was not my intention. Much like you, we have done a month's worth of battle, and I suppose I am weary and eager to return home. But I realize that although you are returning home, it will be different than it was. I should have said that, and I am ashamed that I did not. But this is the nature of war, my lady. I have told you that. There are victors and there are losers. Because I did not acknowledge your sacrifice does not mean that I am unaware of it."

Elle had to take a deep breath to calm herself. "Have you ever been on the losing side of a battle, *llew*?" she asked. "Do you even know what defeat feels like?"

She had called him the Welsh word for lion. Christopher had been known throughout his adult lifetime as the Lion's Claw, the right hand of Richard the Lionheart. A lion was even on his standard, so she knew well the man's nickname in that pleading question.

He did not take offense.

"I have seen more than forty years of battle," he told her. "How many years have you seen?"

That gave her some pause. "Not as many," she said reluctantly.

Her answer caused Curtis to turn his head away lest she see him smirk as Christopher remained patient with her. "And do you think it would be fair to say that, within that time, I have lost a battle or two?" he asked.

She shrugged. "Possibly," she said. "But I would wager not many."

"You would be correct," Christopher said. "But I will tell you something that I have learned in defeat, my lady. How you accept a loss is as important as you accept victory. A man—or woman—of humility in victory is a thing to be admired. The same could be said for a man or woman of defeat. I accept this victory with humility because I am grateful for it. I am grateful I accomplished my task, and I am grateful my losses were minimal. You can show humility with your grace and understanding and cooperation. No one is trying to shame you, Lady Elle. Please remember that, even if we are tactless from time to time."

There was a rebuke in that, but it was perhaps the politest rebuke Elle had ever heard. She didn't argue with him. She simply nodded her head. He'd been trying to tell her for two days that this was no longer her game. She was only a player in a board that someone else controlled.

It was time for her to learn that for good.

But it was still difficult for her to swallow.

"Can you tell me the worst battle you have ever lost?" she asked. "I would like to know."

It wasn't a flippant question. In fact, it was a very earnest one. Christopher could see that this young woman, who had fought so bravely, was trying to relate to him the only way she knew how. That was a lesson for him, in fact, to communicate with her in a way she understood. She understood hardship and battle.

Perhaps this was his opportunity to learn something about his son's future wife.

"It was many years ago," he said. "Curtis was not yet born. There was a battle at a castle called Tickhill. My enemy was Prince John, who had taken over Tickhill, and it was my task—and the task of the army of King Richard—to get him out. It was a very big castle with enormous walls and a tall motte. It was partially surrounded by a millpond, but on the day I remember, it had been raining horribly. The mud was so thick and deep that the chargers were in danger of breaking legs in the stuff. I remember sheets of rain and dodging the bolts that the archers were shooting from the castle walls. One, unfortunately, hit me."

Elle was listening with interest. "You were wounded, then?"

He nodded. "I was," he said. "It was very bad. I found my way to the edge of the field with what I thought was a mortal wound. A fellow knight found me, and because the battle was still ongoing at that point, he could not be spared to tend me. His horse had been injured, so he took mine, but he was nearing the castle, and the horse took a bolt. It fell over on him, and he drowned in the mud as my horse smothered him. I am not entirely sure what happened to me at that point because I lost consciousness and some people took me away to save my life, but days after the battle, my men found my dead horse and what they thought was my body buried beneath it. My wife, and the whole of England, was told that I was dead. She even married another man because I was not strong enough to return to her for quite some time."

Elle was invested in the story. "That is a terrible thing," she said. "And this was the worst battle you ever lost?"

He shook his head. "It was the battle where I lost everything," he said. "I lost my identity, my wife, the life I knew... everything."

"What happened to Tickhill Castle?"

"The castle surrendered at some point," he said. "It was given back over to Richard, and John went elsewhere to wreak havoc."

"And you were fighting for Richard the entire time?"

"The entire time."

"I have heard that was a terrible time in English history."

"It was."

Their conversation was interrupted when Westley appeared in his father's tent, dragging Melusine with him. He had her tightly by the arm. The subject at hand was quickly forgotten as Curtis, Elle, and Christopher faced the pair as they entered, but it was Curtis who spoke first.

"You have been brought back to your cousin by my good graces, my lady," he said to Melusine. "You may stay if you can behave yourself. That means you are not to antagonize your cousin. Am I making myself clear?"

Melusine looked a little unnerved. In fact, she had a rather wild look in her eye, not at all like the woman Curtis and Elle had seen earlier.

"Aye," she said quickly. "I understand."

With that, she pulled from Westley's embrace and raced to Elle, throwing her arms around the woman. It was clear she was terrified. That certainly was a change in demeanor, and Curtis suspected he knew why. He turned to Westley.

"What happened?" he asked. "What did Amaro do?"

Westley shook his head. "I do not know," he said. "I found them in the bailey, below the wall walk. Amaro had her sitting against the wall, but she did not say anything, and neither did he."

Curtis' focus returned to Melusine for a moment. He'd had qualms about Amaro guarding her from the first, and her sudden change in behavior seemed to confirm his suspicions. He had enough trouble with Amaro and male prisoners, but now... now, he had female prisoners. One was to be his wife.

He didn't like the future of trouble he was sensing.

That was something he didn't need.

"Papa," he said after a moment. "When you return to Lion-cross, will you take Amaro with you?"

Christopher's brow furrowed. "Why?"

"Because I do not want him here."

"Can you tell me why?"

Curtis sighed sharply. "You *know* why," he said, lowering his voice. "I realize the Conde de Zidacos is a valuable ally, but his son has a wicked streak in him, and most especially with women. I will have enough trouble building trust between the lady and me without worrying about a knight who can be... unpredictable."

Christopher knew that. The Conde de Zidacos knew it, as well. He was hoping that spending time with the English might show his son another facet of the world and help him mature past the petty, vindictive knight he'd been. Amaro was such a paradox with his strong sword yet unpredictable ways, as Curtis had said. Christopher had hoped that he, as the father of six sons himself, would be able to mold the man.

But that hadn't happened.

Yet.

"Not now," he said. "Keep him here with you a little while longer. You may need his sword if the Welsh decide to launch a counterattack, so I do not want to remove him yet."

Curtis didn't like that answer. "Then leave Roi with me."

"I need Roi."

"You have Sherry."

Christopher shook his head. "I am comfortable with the way my command is structured now," he said. "It works well."

"But..."

Christopher held up a hand to silence him. "Just keep Amaro for a while longer, at least until we know the Welsh aren't going to attack immediately," he said. "Then we will speak again on the matter."

Curtis was vastly unhappy. "If he cannot behave himself, you should send him back to his father," he said. "He was his father's problem until the man dumped him on you. He *knew* he was an issue."

Christopher shot him a quelling look. "You are not telling me something I do not already know," he said. "And I do not wish to speak of this any longer."

The conversation was shut down, but Curtis had a lot more to say on the subject. He wouldn't disobey his father. Still, it left him frustrated. He needed some air. Therefore, he went over to Elle, who was still in a clutch with Melusine, and took her by the wrist.

"Come," he said, sounding disgruntled. "Show me Brython."

Elle was still holding on to Melusine as Curtis pulled her toward the tent opening. "If you wish," she said. "But are we not waiting for the priest?"

"My father will send us word when he arrives," Curtis answered as he walked past his father, unable to look at him. "Meanwhile, you will show me my new garrison."

Elle went with him, grasping Melusine's hand and forcing her to follow. Christopher let them go, returning to the table that held business matters for him, including Curtis' account of the battle that the man had given him that morning. He knew his son was upset with him and he knew why, but much like Curtis with his future wife and her brother, Christopher walked a fine line between Amaro and his father.

He had for years.

In truth, he'd done to Curtis what Amaro's father had done to him—dumped an unruly and unethical son onto someone else. Christopher had made it seem as if it was an honor for Amaro to serve Curtis, when the truth was that Christopher simply didn't want the man in his ranks. Now, Curtis was increasingly vocal about not wanting him in his.

Christopher was starting to wonder if the de Laraga alliance was worth it.

In the days and months to come, he would remember that thought.

CB

"YOU MENTIONED THAT Brython is part of a prophecy," Curtis said as he led Elle and Melusine out into the sunshine. "Where is this gate to Annwyn supposed to be?"

Melusine was clinging to Elle, walking alongside her. When Curtis came to a halt at the edge of the moat, gazing up at the enormous walls, Elle came to a halt as well, and Melusine leaned against her, laying her head on her cousin's shoulder.

"It is in the vaults underneath the keep," Elle said. "Much of these lands are rocky, and there are caves about. The gate to Annwyn is in a natural cave beneath the castle, but there is water. A small pond. The gate is beneath it."

"Fascinating," Curtis said, his gaze still on the walls. "Tell me what you know of the history of this place. All I've ever heard has been from my father's scouts."

Elle still wasn't entirely comfortable with telling him everything about Brython, handing over something she deeply loved on a silver platter. Or silver sword, as it were. She had to force down the argument she'd presented to Christopher, how they were making it seem so easy when this was something that had gutted her to her very soul.

Her loss was their gain.

"It has been standing here for many ages," she said. "It was built by a prince of Powys long ago who wished to build on this sacred site to protect it. It is built from the great blue stones that are found to the west, stones with magical properties, it is said."

"Is that so?" he said as he began to walk toward the gatehouse, pulling her along by her wrist. "It seems this place was meant to be magical from the beginning."

Elle felt as if she was walking into a tomb. A tomb of her dreams, of her life, that was. She must have slowed down, because Curtis turned to look at her, but she really didn't know why until they reached the drawbridge that had been partially repaired so that a man, one at a time, could walk across the moat on three long planks to get to the gatehouse. Elle wasn't looking at the drawbridge.

She was looking at the state of the gatehouse.

He was looking at her because she'd come to a stunned halt.

"This place was meant to be magical from the start," she said, her tone soft. "My lord, I do not mean to be difficult, but the last time I was in this place, I was fighting you. I was fighting for my life. You must give me a moment to mourn what I have lost before I go in there with you. I'm simply not... ready."

Curtis let go of her wrist. "You will have to go in there sooner or later."

"Everyone is allowed to mourn a death. You must allow me to mourn mine."

He looked at her a moment before turning his attention to the castle. It was in a terrible state. English were swarming over it, mostly the gatehouse and the western wall that had been so badly damaged. They had already begun repairs. However, Curtis wasn't entirely unsympathetic to Elle's feelings. This had been her home, and she had fought hard for it. She was looking upon her failure and having difficulty with it. But even as he thought on that, something else occurred to him.

"May I ask a question?" he said.

Her focus was on the twisted portcullis that several soldiers were trying to remove from the front of the gatehouse. "What would you ask?" she said.

He gestured to the castle. "From what you have told me, your life was not a good one," he said. "Is that a fair statement?"

She looked at him. "You know everything," she said. "I have told you what my life has been."

"Then it was not a good life."

"Nay."

His gaze fixed on her. "Then why would you mourn a life that was not good?" he asked. "I can understand that you would mourn your dreams and goals, but to mourn a life where you only had one set of stinking clothing and did not get enough to eat? Why would you mourn such a thing?"

He had a point. Melusine lifted her head from Elle's shoulder, looking at her cousin to see what her reaction was going to be, but Elle didn't have an answer for him. He seemed to point out things she didn't want to acknowledge, not even a life that hadn't been the most comfortable or the kindest. But it was the only life she'd ever known, so the question frustrated her. Pulling her arm from Melusine's grip, she charged toward the drawbridge.

"Then let me tell you of this terrible place that will now become your home," she said. "Let me show you the keep where you can be comfortable. I will tell you everything you need to know so you know the quality of your prize."

She was stomping across the drawbridge, and he motioned to Melusine to follow. He brought up the rear as the three of them passed through the gatehouse and into the bailey, which was quite vast. It was longer than it was wide, rectangular in shape, and on a slightly uphill angle. This was the first time Curtis had been inside, so he found himself looking at everything curiously. All around him were the ashes of things that had been burned, ponies that were corralled up as a few men dumped grain into buckets for them because they hadn't been fed. All around them were remnants of a life that had been, a Welsh life, and the English were moving in to consume it.

Already, the English were putting their mark on it.

"There is no money here, but I suppose you already know that," Elle continued, breaking into his train of thought. "We do have ponies and chickens, and you can sell them if you wish for the money, but there is nothing else of value here. Just a broken castle and broken people."

She was verging on some kind of rage or breakdown. He could see it. Melusine hadn't said a word so far, surprising for a woman who seemed to speak first, think second, but she was looking at her cousin with sympathy. Curtis could have addressed Elle's comments, but he didn't want to get into an argument with her. Not now. He was hoping they would move beyond her wild behavior, so he chose to ignore it.

For now.

"I know we cut off your water supply," he said. "And after a month of a siege, your food supply should have been equally low. Why do you still have chickens? Why did you not eat them?"

"Because they are pets," Melusine answered. When Elle

hissed at her, she looked at the woman. "The *are* pets. The ponies, too. You would not let the men eat them. You told them that you would force them to eat each other before the animals."

Curtis couldn't help the grin that flickered on his lips as he looked at Elle. "Did you truly tell them that?" he asked.

Elle didn't find the question humorous. "We have a garden," she said, gesturing toward the northern section of the bailey where the keep was. There was another wall there with an arch. "There were plenty of vegetables in the stores to eat. We did not have to eat the animals, not yet."

"We ate eggs and turnips," Melusine said with disgust. "At least, the men did. I only saw Ellie eat the eggs and nothing more."

"That is because the men needed the food," Elle snapped back. "We could have made it last for another month at least. We would have held had the Saesneg not built that terrible platform, because then... then it was over."

She was growing agitated. That wasn't what Curtis wanted. He wanted her to show him the castle, to give him a guided tour, but he was coming to see that it was too much to ask, no matter how he or his father tried to rationalize her loss. She had asked for time to mourn what had happened, and he simply hadn't given it to her.

He was treating her like a man.

The men he knew, the enemies he knew, were seasoned men. They accepted loss as part of the cycle of battle, but Elle clearly didn't have that attitude. She was viewing it as a death, as having something she cared about now torn from her. It wasn't her life she was mourning as much as it was the location—the castle. Given everything he'd been told, he understood that she was holding the castle for the Welsh. Welsh rule, a Welsh castle. No interference from the English.

But here they were.

She simply wasn't coping.

"Come," he said, turning on his heel. "We will return to my father. He has sent for the priest, so we must be ready. We can do this another time, when you are feeling more able."

"Priest?" Melusine said, looking at Elle. "Why?"

Elle shook her head at the woman, simply grasping her by the arm and pulling her along. "Let us return to the tents," she said. "I am famished. Aren't you?"

Truthfully, Melusine was. Something was amiss, something she couldn't quite put her finger on, but she let Elle drag her back through the gatehouse as she followed Curtis. Truthfully, Melusine was inclined to be cooperative because she didn't want to be separated from Elle again. She might have to return to the Spanish knight who had been rough with her. The one who had terrified her.

Nay, she didn't want to go back to him at all.

Therefore, she kept silent.

Elle seemed to have fallen silent herself as she followed Curtis back to his father's tent, where others were gathering. Big knights with big swords, dressed in mail that was rusting or bloodied or both. Men who had fought the battle of Brython Castle and had emerged the victors. That's what the tent was full of—victors.

Melusine could smell it in the air.

Once inside, Elle dragged her over to the table where an empty pitcher and a platter with crumbs sat, but Curtis saw that there was nothing for the ladies to eat, so he sent a servant for something. Soon enough, they had bread and cheese and cold meat along with cold, boiled carrots and cabbage. More watered wine came also, along with more boiled eggs, and Elle and Melusine delved into the food as if they'd never seen food in their lives. There was a great deal of slurping and drinking and swallowing going on until, closer to midday, the priest finally arrived with one of Curtis' brothers.

Then Melusine found out what the priest was for.

A marriage.

CHAPTER NINE

"AND THEN I slapped her," Amaro said, relishing the moment. "Not where anyone could see the mark, of course, but she should have a perfect handprint across her left breast. Unless she strips to show someone, no one will ever see it. But she understands that one word of it and I will kill her. I do not care where she is—I will find her and I will kill her."

Twilight had come to Brython, and a clear sky promised cold temperatures. Amaro and Hugo were in the encampment, at the tent they shared, in fact, milling around a campfire whilst preparing for night duties. But as they donned their weapons, Hugo was listening to Amaro's boasting with some concern and struggling not to show it.

"Curtis has warned you about striking women," he said. "If he finds out…"

"He will not," Amaro assured him. "The Welsh chit is terrified of me, so she will not say a word."

Hugo sighed heavily. "He just married that woman's cousin," he pointed out. "You saw it yourself. We both did. He just married Gwenwynwyn's daughter, so if I were you, I would not strike Miasma again. Or whatever her name is."

"Melusine."

"Melusine, Miasma," Hugo said impatiently. "The fact remains that she is now Lady Leominster's cousin, and if Curtis finds out what you've done, you will be in for punishment."

Amaro stiffened. "He would not dare," he said. "Unless he wants to enrage my father, he will not touch me, and nor will Hereford. Neither one of them can do a thing, so stop your worrying. You bore me."

Hugo shut his mouth. This was another one of those situations where he found himself in a bad way. He'd seen what Amaro had done to Melusine, verbally assaulting her until she snapped back, and then he struck her. In the chest, of all places, but as he'd said, no one would see it. They'd see a handprint to the face, and there would be questions.

But no one would see a bruise on the breast.

Curtis had been married to Gwenwynwyn's daughter about an hour earlier, in Christopher's tent, by a priest from the nearby town who did the entire mass in Latin and Welsh. It had been barbaric, as far as Hugo was concerned, and hastily planned, but even he saw the value in the marriage of the Earl of Leominster with a daughter of a Welsh royal house. Perhaps it would prevent more battles, especially at Brython. Amaro had simply stood there and rolled his eyes, impatient with the entire thing, and when the mass was concluded, he rushed back to his tent, where he had been in the process of counting money he'd stolen off Welsh prisoners.

As Hugo saw it, Amaro was a problem these days more than he'd ever been.

Curtis knew it. He wasn't close to Amaro and treated him like a vassal, which he was, and Amaro hated it. Amaro tried to bend the ear of Christopher, who treated him the same way.

The man was always trying to make himself indispensable to those in command, to convince them that they could rely on his advice, but Curtis and Christopher realized what type of man he was very early on. Christopher handled him by foisting him onto his son to deal with, and Curtis handled him by basically ignoring him.

That meant Amaro was able to do things to feed that ruthless spirit that would go unnoticed. Like striking a woman in the breast. But something told Hugo that things with Amaro were going to get worse.

It was just a feeling he had.

"Curt has called a meeting with those remaining at Brython," he said, changing the subject. "I've heard Myles is remaining with us."

Amaro snorted. "Another de Lohr brother who thinks he is God's answer to a fine knight," he said. "But he's tolerable."

"He *is* a good knight."

Amaro nodded as if only slightly agreeing with him. "He'll do," he said. "He's young still."

Hugo looked at him, grinning. "You're not exactly old," he said. "You're only a few years older than Myles is."

Amaro smirked. "I was born old," he said. "In my country, men are men when they are born."

"I've never been to your country," Hugo said, trying desperately to move the man onto a more pleasant subject. "You speak of warmth so much of the year. I think that would be a lovely thing to experience."

"It is," Amaro said, looking up at the clear sky. "I never knew I could be so cold until I came to England."

"When you return home, I will come with you," Hugo said. "I do not like the cold either."

Amaro chuckled. "You will have to learn the language, my friend," he said. "How else are you to know what commands are given? And how else are you to talk to our beautiful women?"

Hugo shrugged in agreement. "And I'm sure there are many beautiful women," he said. "In fact, if I were you, I would go home now. You make it sound far more wonderful than England."

Oh, but he'd said that on purpose. He was trying to plant a seed in Amaro's mind of leaving England altogether. Hugo wasn't beyond trying to subversively send Amaro home, and he would therefore be the hero to the House of de Lohr. No one wanted Amaro here, least of all Hugo, who was forced to pair up with the man because they both served Curtis. He'd like nothing better than to be rid of him. Therefore, he carefully watched Amaro's reaction to his suggestion.

"It is, in many ways, more wonderful," Amaro agreed. "But to be honest, I think I would miss the green grass and all of the trees. Where I come from, it is dry. Very little rain."

"But you would be able to see your father," Hugo pushed. "If I could go home and see my father, I surely would."

Amaro shrugged. "In time," he said, looking at the vast walls of Brython. "But now, Curtis has his own command. This is a new land to explore, Hugo. We should not leave before we've had a chance to do so. Great rewards could be awaiting us if we will only find them."

Or great trouble, Hugo thought. So much for convincing the man to leave.

He'd have to try again sometime.

Before Amaro did something they would all regret.

CHAPTER TEN

"**Y**OU *MARRIED HIM!*"

Melusine was hissing at her. Elle didn't need her cousin spinning out of control or making her feel any worse than she already did. Quite honestly, she wasn't sure why she wasn't running about and screaming her head off.

It had been a day for the ages.

Elle had been trying so very hard to accept that which she could not change. To accept the defeat against the English, to accept that Brython was no longer hers, and to accept that, little more than an hour ago, she had married the Earl of Leominster, Curtis de Lohr. She had been trying very hard to accept all of these things, but the more the day passed and the more she watched Curtis with his father and brothers, and the other knights who were congratulating him, the more she felt her composure slipping away.

Dissolving.

Crumbling.

She had lost everything.

And now, Melusine was hounding her about a marriage she had no control over. Everyone seemed to be hounding her, pressuring her, and scolding her. She wasn't used to such condemnation and harassment. At least, she viewed it as harassment when it wasn't exactly that bad. Men telling her the course her life would take wasn't harassment as much as it was simply the way of things. But the more she listened to Melusine hiss, the more her control slipped.

Until it just wasn't there any longer.

She was in Christopher's grand tent with the flap tied open. Men were coming and going and the wine was flowing freely. Soldiers were also gathering, at least those who weren't working with the wounded or the captive Welsh, and imbibing the liquid in the barrels that the quartermasters had brought with them to battle. It wasn't fine stuff, but it did the job. It could get a man drunk.

That was all Elle could see.

Careless drunks.

Unable to stomach the display of revelry any longer, she stood up. Melusine grabbed at her, wanting to know where she was going, and all Elle could do was tell the woman to leave her alone.

Just leave me alone!

With that, she fled de Lohr's tent, out into the evening, which was becoming cold. It was a clear night, with the moon bright and cold overhead, illuminating Brython. Shadowed and broken against the backdrop of the moody Welsh hills, it looked dead, as dead as Elle felt.

All of it dead.

She had an aversion to it. She couldn't look at it and see her broken dreams. Turning away from the hulk, she found herself facing England and the darkened fields in the distance. Behind her was Wales. Looking forward was England and all of the things she had to face now that she was married to an English earl. Brython was on a rise, and she ended up wandering downhill, still looking at England, feeling more desolation than she could have ever imagined. Behind her, men were celebrating. Celebrating the death of everything that was important to her.

Her death.

Oh, God... She *was* dead.

There was a big, flat rock in front of her, one of many all over these hills. When she plopped down on the rock, grief overwhelmed her and the tears came. Tears for the loss, tears for the future. In little time, she was weeping hysterically, agonizing pain consuming her. She ended up lying on the rock, her tears mingling with the old, moss-riddled surface. Her rock, her Wales. She felt as if she was grieving not only the loss of her castle, but her very country.

The crying never ceased. The more she wept, the more she felt like weeping. It was a vicious circle. There was so much pain and regret bottled up that it had to come out somehow. It was coming out now, in buckets.

And then she saw it.

Boots.

Startled, she sat up and found herself looking at Curtis as he stood several feet away. The moment he saw that she had seen him, he put up his hands in a soothing gesture.

"I am sorry," he said softly but quickly. "You ran out of the tent, and I followed you to make sure you did not come to harm. I did not mean to disturb you."

Elle was prepared to blast him. She was quite certain he hadn't followed her for her safety, but more to make sure she wouldn't run away. But the moment she opened her mouth, more tears came. Angry, frightened, sorrowful tears.

"I could not stay in there any longer," she sobbed. "They are drinking and celebrating my loss. The loss of everything I knew. They are not celebrating a marriage, but my defeat!"

He hung his head slightly, feeling some sorrow that she was so upset on a day that would have most young women ecstatic. "They are not celebrating your defeat," he said, his voice quiet and calm. "They are celebrating a marriage and an alliance and nothing more."

That wasn't the answer she wanted to hear. "They are reveling in my downfall," she wept. "Do you not understand? This is not a celebration for me. This is not a joyful moment. This is something I am forced to do because you have more weapons and more men than I do. I am your prisoner, and you have forced me to marry you."

"You are not my prisoner," he said. "You are my wife."

"*Wife?*" she nearly shouted, bolting off the rock. "I do not even know you! You are a man who tried to kill me yesterday. In the days before that, you and your army were trying to defeat me. All I know is that you are Hereford's son, and now you are my husband. A husband I never wanted!"

She was off on a crying jag, and she plopped on the rock again. Curtis blew out a long, heavy sigh before making his way, slowly, over to her rock. He sat down a few feet away from her as she sobbed. He watched her for a moment before gazing up into the sky, to the moon and the lovely night above.

He'd tried so hard with her, harder than he'd wanted to, harder than he should have. She was right—she *was* a prisoner. She had been forced into this marriage, much as he had been. He truly thought he could make this a pleasant situation for the both of them, but he could see now that he'd been wrong. She didn't want it to be pleasant. She didn't want anything to do with it.

Or him.

Perhaps he was going to have to finally accept that.

"If you think, for one minute, this marriage makes me happy, then you would be wrong," he said after a moment. "I do not want you any more than you want me. All I've seen from you is a woman who has no idea how to behave and hates me simply because I was born in one country and she was born in another. Someone has poisoned you, and they have poisoned you badly, my lady. You have hatred flowing through your veins instead of blood. And you think I wanted to marry someone like you? Think again."

Her sobbing had lessened dramatically as she looked at him in outrage. "You came to take my home away," she said. "I am allowed to defend myself!"

He looked at her. "*You* violated a treaty between your father and the King of England," he said pointedly. "*You* started this. You had no authority to break the treaty, but you did. Arrogant and imperious, you made that decision, so you brought this down on yourself."

She leapt up from the rock again, enraged. "Is that so?"

"Of course it is," he said, standing up and facing her. "This is all your fault. The death, the destruction, is all because you felt you were important enough and strong enough to break a longstanding treaty, so don't blame me for your troubles. If there is death here, as you put it, it's because you caused it. Weep all you want, but everything is your fault. And you think I want to marry someone like you? Someone without honor? A foolish woman who cannot see beyond her own arrogance? You do not deserve me, Enid Arielle ferch Gwenwynwyn. Did you ever stop to think about that?"

She was taken aback by his harsh words. Not because they were brutal, but because they were so truthful. He was spelling out the truth of her actions and the truth of the hatred running through her veins.

Someone has poisoned you.

Perhaps that was true, but that someone had ingrained it into her long ago.

Every bit of it.

"Mayhap I do not deserve you, but I do not want you, either," she said, her voice trembling. "Mayhap this is all my doing, but this marriage is your father's doing. He could have simply told Henry that there was no woman for you to marry, but he seems to think my royal bloodlines make me a suitable wife. All he talks about are my royal bloodlines, as if they are the only thing that matter. If you must be angry, be angry at him. I did not ask for this."

Curtis sighed sharply, scratching at his forehead. "Then what do you want to do?" he said. "Do you want to return to your people? Just leave? Then go. I will not hold you here any longer. We have come to an end, my lady, and I surrender. I've tried to be kind. I have tried to be understanding. But you do not want that. You simply want to hate and point the blame at others, so do it with people who will tell you that your hatred is warranted and that you've done nothing wrong in this situation. I'll not stop you."

She eyed him in the moonlight. "Go where?" she said. She gestured to Brython. "This *is* my home, but now it is yours."

He shook his head. "I do not care where you go," he said. "Go find Llywelyn and tell him of the defeat of Brython and see if he'll take you into his household. Your grandmother was from his family, wasn't she? Go back to him and hate all you want. Let it eat you alive, because I do not care. You've never given me a reason to."

She looked at him with some surprise, but that surprise quickly cooled. "You've been speaking to Gruffydd."

Curtis snorted. "As far as I am concerned, he is the only sane and reasonable one in your family," he said. "The man has good sense, and it is a pity you learned nothing from him. But I suppose he is to be hated, too, because that's the only thing you have in your nature."

Her eyes narrowed. "You do not know what is in my nature."

He frowned at her. "Are you mad?" he said. "That is all I've seen from you since the moment we met. Since you tried to topple me over that wall, and you've been showing me ever since. Petty, arrogant, foolish, and full of hate. That is all I've seen from you, and I do not want to see any more."

Elle was hurt by his words, more than she would ever admit. She'd pushed the man, and now she was paying the price. The truth was that other than their first meeting on the wall, he'd been inordinately kind to her, and all she did was throw it in his face. He'd given her soap and she'd given him vitriol. He'd smiled and she'd frowned. He'd tried to reason with her, and all she could see was her own pain and superiority.

Nay... He wasn't wrong about anything he'd said.

Now, the situation was coming clear.

"We were married a while ago," she said. "Your father isn't going to let you walk away."

He laughed bitterly. "You let me worry about my father," he said. "I will have the marriage annulled, have no doubt. Now, go back to my tent and take off that dress. I'll not have the likes of you touching something that means a good deal to my mother and father. Hopefully, if you take it off quickly, your stench will not cling to it. You can find other clothes in my chest if you wish. There are tunics there, and hose. They will not fit you, but I'm sure you do not care. Take them. I am going to Presteigne to find myself a room for the night because I need to get away from you. You can sleep in my tent. But when I return in the morning, I want you gone."

With that, he headed off, leaving Elle standing there feeling as if she'd just been thrashed. More than thrashed—beaten. Badly. But, as she'd realized from him since the beginning of their association, he was right. He could always win an argument. She had started the downfall of Brython. She was so determined that the Welsh castle should be solely for the Welsh—for Llywelyn—that she'd disregarded her father's treaty and sent the English soldiers away.

That had been the beginning of the end.

The truth was that her father had died long ago. It had been Gruffydd and her father's loyal men who held Brython and kept the treaty. She'd been at Tywyl and Brython for years before finally taking the initiative to throw Gruffydd in the vault and purge the castle of the English soldiers, all in the name of Welsh freedom. But it had cost her everything.

Now, it had cost her the only man who had ever been truly kind to her.

Not that she blamed him.

She deserved everything he said to her.

Elle looked up into that clear, cold sky. Perhaps that tongue lashing had put her at a crossroads. He told her to leave, but the truth was that she had nowhere to go. She couldn't go back to Tywyl Castle, her family's home. Gruffydd was there. She could go north to Llywelyn, but he was her grandmother's cousin and she'd never even met him. All she knew about him was from her grandmother, how he was the only man truly dedicated to Welsh freedom, and when she'd purged the English from Brython, she was going to send Llywelyn word that Brython was now held by the Welsh without any English links. It had honestly never occurred to her that the English soldiers, thrown from Brython, would rush to Lioncross Abbey to tell Hereford what had happened. Before she realized it, the de Lohr army was on her doorstep. She'd never had the opportunity to send the missive to Llywelyn.

Now, she had nothing at all.

Did she want to be known as someone with hatred for the English in her veins? Because her hatred, and Llywelyn's rebellion against the English, had not accomplished anything. In fact, she couldn't think of anyone she knew where hatred had ultimately gained them peace and happiness. Curtis had told her to be humble in defeat, and he'd shown her mercy. He told her that he knew her nature. It occurred to her that she knew his, too.

Elle was forced to make a choice that night. When she saw Curtis heading from the encampment, heading east, she knew what that choice had to be.

She only hoped it was the right one.

☞

"HE'S LEFT, PAPA," Myles said quietly. "Curtis has left."

Christopher was standing in his tent, cup of wine in hand. Everyone else had cleared out about the time Curtis went after Elle, who had run out. After that, there was no more celebration. Roi, Myles, Peter, and Alexander had cleared out the sons and nephews, soldiers and junior knights, but Myles had gone in search of his brother and his new wife just to make sure something horrible wasn't occurring between them.

Unfortunately, that seemed to be the case.

"Where is she?" Christopher asked solemnly.

Myles gestured toward the east. "Sitting on a rock," he said. "She and Curt had an argument. I couldn't hear what was being said, but they were agitated, and you know it takes quite a lot to agitate Curt."

"He was angry?"

"I think so," Myles said. "And then he collected his horse and left."

"Do you want me to go after him?" Peter said quietly. "I will bring him back."

Christopher shook his head. "Nay," he said. "Let him be. He has been forced into an impossible situation, by me, and I can imagine that he needs time to reconcile this. I only wish he'd not left her behind. She needs to reconcile it, too. They should reconcile it together."

Peter and Alexander, two of the older and married men in the group, looked at each other and lifted their eyebrows in silent sympathy and contemplation of the situation. It wasn't an easy one, that was certain. In fact, it had been damn awkward, celebrating both a marriage and a victory when the woman who had suffered the defeat and the forced marriage had been present, watching them congratulate Curtis and each other.

But it couldn't be helped.

"Roi," Peter said, turning to his younger brother. "Go make sure that the posts are set for the night. With Curtis out, we need a commander for the evening, and that will be you."

Roi nodded, heading out without argument. Normally,

Christopher gave those commands, but he didn't seem willing to do so. Or as if he even cared about it at that moment. As Roi headed out, Peter turned to Myles.

"Watch the lady from a distance, please," he said. "Make sure she comes to no harm."

Myles headed off, leaving the three married men alone in Christopher's tent. This was a situation that only men with wives might understand, although comprehending the complexities of a woman was beyond any of them to varying degrees. All three of them had married strong, determined women, with Alexander and Christopher in particular having married women perfectly capable of battle.

Now, so had Curtis.

But the situation wasn't going well at all.

"Well?" Peter said quietly. "What now?"

Christopher shrugged. "They are married," he said. "There is nothing either one of them can do about it."

"But the marriage has not yet been consummated," Alexander pointed out. "Did Curtis ride to the nearest church to see about an annulment?"

"He wouldn't dare," Christopher said. "He knows this marriage is too important. He would not try to dissolve it, and most especially without my knowledge."

Alexander wasn't so sure. Curtis was the silent, steady type, but he wasn't beyond completely going against his father if he felt strongly enough about it. There were times when Christopher's commands had been mere suggestions to Curtis.

They hoped this wasn't one of those times.

"You cannot be sure of that, Papa," Peter said, voicing what they were all thinking. "None of us can. When Curtis sets his mind to something, he never fails."

Christopher looked at him. "Are you telling me he has set his mind to ending this marriage?"

As Peter shrugged, Alexander spoke softly. "I think the fact that he left his new wife behind speaks for itself," he said. "He is making a statement."

"Aye, he is. I would like to make one as well."

It wasn't Christopher or even Peter who answered. It was Elle, standing in the open tent flap. The three knights turned to her with various levels of surprise before Christopher began to move in her direction.

"Lady Leominster," he said, addressing her by her rightful title. "Please come in. Would you like some wine?"

Elle stepped timidly into the tent, nodding briefly to Christopher as he moved quickly to procure her a drink. She was dressed in terribly oversized clothing—a heavy tunic and hose that were far too large for her. Gone was the blue dress that Christopher had lent her. She looked quite odd, to be truthful, but she also seemed so terribly nervous in their presence. Given they were talking about her, she'd probably heard most of it— and most of the discussion on a husband who evidently didn't want her.

It made for a difficult situation.

"Since you sent one of your sons to spy on me, I thought I'd better come straight to you," Elle said to Christopher as he handed her the wine. "My lord, I would be grateful if you would allow me to speak with you."

Christopher grunted with some chagrin over the spying comment. "I sent Myles to watch over you to make sure you did not come into any trouble," he said. "You are in an encampment full of English."

"I realize that."

"May I ask what became of my wife's dress?"

She looked down at herself, realizing how foolish she must have looked. "Sir Curtis told me to take it off," she said. "I did as he asked."

Christopher frowned. "Why did he tell you to take it off?"

She cleared her throat softly. "That is what I wish to speak with you about," Elle said. When Peter and Alexander moved to excuse themselves, she stopped them. "Nay, do not go. Please. I have been speaking to Lord Hereford since yesterday, and I have only had his point of view conveyed to me. I know you are Curtis' brothers. I should like to speak to you about him, too, so that I have all the facts and not simply Lord Hereford's version of them."

Peter and Alexander looked at each other, shrugged, and silently agreed. Peter even went over to collect a chair for the lady.

"Would you like to sit, my lady?" he asked.

Elle did. For once, she didn't fight the English on anything they wanted to give her, convey, or do for her. She was at her lowest point and had no more false pride to display. Peter put the chair next to the brazier, and she sat, cup in hand, facing three men who pulled up chairs to sit with her and not simply stand over her. After a moment, she looked around as if searching for something.

"It has occurred to me that Melusine is not here," she said. "Where is my cousin?"

"I sent her to bed with a guard," Christopher said. "Sherry's sons are watching over her. They will be kind to her, so you needn't worry."

"Sherry," she repeated. "Who is that?"

"Me," Alexander said. "My name is Alexander de Sherrington. I married Hereford's eldest daughter, Christin."

Elle's gaze lingered on the man with the black eyes and dark, trim beard. "You are the assassin."

"That was long ago, my lady," Alexander said quietly.

Elle shook her head. "I did not mean that the way it sounded," she said. "I simply meant that Sir Curtis told me about you and how Hereford did not want you for his daughter. He was explaining how sometimes, people marry those who others consider unsuitable, but he went on to praise you, as his brother. In fact, he has explained to me quite a bit about his family."

"As he should," Alexander said. "You are now part of the family, too."

Elle took a deep breath, averting her gaze uncomfortably. "That is where you are wrong," she said. "Mayhap I am by marriage, but that is what I wished to speak of. You see, I have ruined everything, and I do not know how to fix it. I do not know how to… I am not sure how to put it into words that you will understand. I came here to speak to you because… because I do not know what else to do."

They weren't unsympathetic. "Start from the beginning, my lady," Christopher said quietly. "What has happened that Curt should leave you on your wedding night?"

Elle was deeply embarrassed, but she had also called this meeting, so it wasn't as if she could not tell the truth. A truth that had been twisting itself up in her mind until she could hardly make sense of it. Finally, she grunted in frustration.

"My entire life has been defined by loyalty to the Welsh and self-rule," she said. "But it has also been defined by neglect and apathy. My father was old when I was born, and I was quite young when he died. I spent my early years with my grandmother, a cousin to Llywelyn, but I am certain you already know that. She was the only person who showed me concern or even affection, limited as it was. She was rigidly dedicated to her cousin and told me that I should be, too. When she died, I returned to Tywyl Castle and my father and brother, but they were strangers. The only people who showed me any measure of attention were the servants and my father's men. I realize that is not how most young women grow up, but that was my life. It was my life up until yesterday."

"Go on, my lady," Christopher said softly.

She was trying to, but her confusion was making her doubt everything she'd always believed in, and that bewilderment came across in her manner. "Lord Hereford, when you and I first spoke yesterday, you were honest," she said. "You were not particularly kind at times, but you were honest. More than that, you treated me with respect. I thought you were viewing my royal blood as a prize, something to be used and bartered with, but it occurred to me later that you were simply showing me respect because of my father. Am I wrong in this?"

Christopher shook his head. "You are not wrong," he said. "You are a Welsh princess, my lady. I am sorry if no one has ever shown you the respect you deserve."

"But that's just it," she said, becoming emotional. "You have all shown me respect, and even though I am your prisoner, I have never had anyone be as kind to me as you and Sir Curtis have been. The food, the soap, the bath, the clothing... It seems so inconsequential, but it isn't. No one in my entire life has been as kind to me as you have, and it made me suspicious. I was suspicious of your motives. But the truth is that the life I've had is not one I should be mourning if the only people who ever showed me kindness were the men who defeated me in battle. Does that make sense?"

Christopher nodded faintly. "It does," he said. "In spite of what you have been taught, the English are not all bad."

"Nay, they are not," she said quickly. "But the innate evil of the English is something that has been etched into me. Hatred is in my brain and in my heart, yet you have all been so kind to me. It is horribly confusing because I cannot reconcile this hatred I am expected to feel. Is there such a world where I should actually befriend my enemy?"

Christopher smiled. "We would like that, very much," he said. "As Curtis' wife, you have a very important role, one that will bring you love and respect if you will only not be suspicious of it. We *want* to like you, my lady."

Elle hung her head. "He said he is going to annul the marriage," she said miserably. "He does not wish to be married to me, and I do not blame him. He has tried so hard to be kind, and all I have done is mistrust his motives. He called me petty and foolish, and he is right. I am. But he has made me think very carefully on what kind of life I want—do I want to go back to living in rags and in damp castles or the forests, rebelling against the English and living a life of ineffective transiency? Or do I want to live a life where my husband and his family are kind to me, even if they are English? Can I help Wales that way? Whatever happens, I will always be Welsh, but I do not always have to hate. I understand that much."

Christopher's eyes glimmered with warmth. "I would say that is a very big step in your progress, my lady," he said. "The fact that you are even asking these questions means you are seeing a new perspective."

"Mayhap," she said. "But Sir Curtis has told me to be gone by morning. I do not know the man well, but I suspect he means it."

"He probably did at the time, but I would wager to say that

he regrets it now," Peter said. "I know my brother, my lady. He can be more forgiving than most. But you do not know this, so you should be aware of what kind of man he is. Shall I tell you?"

Elle looked at the blond man with the intense, dark eyes. "I think I know a little about him," she said. "His behavior since yesterday shows me that he has understanding and patience. But I would like to know more."

"Like what?" Peter asked.

"For example, must he always win an argument?"

Peter and Alexander burst out laughing. "That is a de Lohr trait," Peter said. "Curt does not always have to win an argument, but he usually does because he is usually right. I think if you look back on the conversations you have had with him, you will agree with me."

Elle was reluctant to admit it, but she forced herself. Her guard was down, and it didn't matter if she admitted Curtis had been correct, in every way. Even so, it was kicking and screaming, metaphorically speaking, all the way. For a woman of considerable pride, it was a difficult thing for her to acknowledge it.

"I did not say he was wrong," she said. "I just asked if he had to win every single argument. He seems to be a man with all of the answers."

"He is," Peter said. "But he is also humble, quiet at times, and more focused and driven than anyone you will ever meet. Curtis is a man of war, my lady. That is what he knows, and that is what he does well. He is meticulous, he is clever, and he is educated. He also has a great deal of patience, as you have noted."

Elle sighed heavily. "I have pushed him beyond his endurance," she said. "I do not suppose he would be forgiving."

"I think he probably already has."

"Then why does he not come back?" she asked. "Will he truly stay away all night?"

Peter shrugged. "If you had just had an argument with your husband and he exasperated you, would you stay away all night just to make him sick with worry, so sick that he would forgive any quarrel he had with you?"

Elle's eyes widened. "Is that what he is doing?" she said. "Making it so I will be remorseful?"

Christopher held up a hand before the conversation veered out of control, because he didn't want the lady to think Curtis was playing games somehow. "He went away so he would not say anything he could not take back," he said. "He is staying away to cool his temper, which can be fearsome when aroused. Did he say where he was going?"

Elle nodded her head. "He said that he was going into Presteigne."

"Then I will fetch him," Peter said, standing up. "It should not take too—"

"Nay," Elle said, standing up quickly. "You must not go. He will think I have run to his brothers and father to shame him for leaving. Please do not go."

"She is right," Christopher said, waving a hand at Peter. "Sit back down. I fear it will only make him more furious if you find him and try to bring him back. The only person who should bring him back is the lady."

Elle nodded. "It started with me," she said. "It should also end with me. Do you think he meant the nearest English town?"

Christopher nodded. "That would be my guess," he said. "Peter can escort you there. You will bring him back, my lady."

She nodded, but her courage was wavering. "What should I

say?"

Christopher shrugged. "That is up to you," he said. "But telling him what you told us is a good start. And if it matters… I think Curt has married a strong lady. If you are willing to learn and grow, you will make a fine wife and a fine countess. You can do much more for your people in such a position than you can fighting like a rebel."

Elle thought on that. "Mayhap," she said. "But I never thought I would have the opportunity to be something other than what I am."

Christopher smiled at her. "It is a grand opportunity that few have," he said, but he quickly sobered at the look on her face. "I know it is not what you expected or how you planned that your life should be, but here we are. You must make the best of it. Fetch your husband, Lady Leominster. Let your new life begin."

The words were very true. Elle was coming to think that the English warlords were far more reasonable and wise than she'd been told. Her experience with them had been different from anything her grandmother or even her father's soldiers had mentioned, and that had her questioning everything.

What if my grandmother was wrong?

Peter was waiting for her by the tent opening. He had a cloak in his hand, though she had no idea where he got it. Politely, he offered it to her, but rather than let him put it on her shoulders, as a fine lady would have, she took it from him and put it on herself. She was an independent lass with no idea how to be proper, but somehow, it was rather endearing. With a grin, Peter followed her out into the night.

Curtis was somewhere out there, waiting.

Elle was going to find him.

CHAPTER ELEVEN

H E'D LEFT WITHOUT a word to his father.
Curtis was so angry, so disillusioned, that he'd left the de Lohr encampment with only a word to Westley, who had no idea why his brother was grabbing his saddlebags, his weapon, and heading to the corral for his horse. Curtis told Westley that he'd return in the morning and to make sure Lady Leominster wasn't there when he came back. As Curtis took off on his fat golden warhorse, Westley had gone running for his father.

Curtis had intended that his father should know that he left, but also that he would return in the morning so Christopher wouldn't send out search parties. Curtis needed time alone, and Christopher would have to understand that. The town closest to Brython on the English side of the border was Presteigne, and that was exactly where he was heading. He'd find an inn, order a good meal, and sleep in a good bed and not a traveling cot, which was never very comfortable. He'd have a fire and peace and comfort for the night before heading back to the encampment and demanding his father annul the marriage.

As he saw it, that was necessary.

Did he really want the annulment? No, he didn't. He'd

rather been looking forward to a marriage with Elle. She had moments where he could see her warmth, her eagerness to please and willingness to learn, but they were so few and far between. He didn't really mean all of those things he'd said to her. He'd said them because he was angry and she'd pushed him beyond his limit. He was angry because she seemed to be giving up on them before they even got started.

Perhaps that was what angered him the most.

She couldn't see past the knight to the man beneath.

Now, all he felt was disappointment.

Presteigne was less than an hour's ride from Brython. It was still early enough in the evening that people were still out in the street, hovering around open doors from homes or inns as warm light streamed through doorways and onto the darkened street. He could hear laughing and talking as he entered the edge of town because there were three inns on this side of the village alone. One of them seemed particularly popular, but he was looking for something quieter. He wanted peace tonight. He needed it. It was supposed to be his wedding night, but he was going to spend it getting drunk.

Unfortunately, the town's six inns and three taverns were all busy this evening. It was a cold night, so people were looking for some kind of warmth and shelter for the evening. He ended up going back to the east side of the village and selecting The Earl and the Oak, a two-storied inn that had more of a tavern feel to it because there was drink and entertainment below while the sleeping rooms were upstairs. Curtis stabled his steed in the livery behind the inn before proceeding inside to secure a rented chamber for the night.

The innkeeper, a tall man whose lower half of his left leg was a wooden peg, was more than hospitable to a knight willing to pay well. He took Curtis to the best chamber he had, on the corner of the building overlooking an alley and the livery yard. It was guaranteed to be quiet, away from the street, and Curtis ordered a meal before settling in for the night.

He suspected it was going to be a long one.

The first thing he did after settling in his rented chamber was to simply sit in silence. He had been in a month-long battle where noise filled the air both day and night. Siege engines, men screaming, and the sounds of battle had been part of his life every minute of every day. As the night deepened around him, he lit a fire in the small hearth and sat by the window that overlooked the alley.

The night above was clear, with a brilliant moon hanging in the sky. He could hear nightbirds in the distance, and all around him there were sounds of civilization as people hunkered down for the night. He could smell the evening meals wafting upon the breeze, and occasionally, he could hear a husband and wife speaking. In fact, across the alley was a small cottage with a small yard and a little barn. He watched as a child, a small boy, came out of the barn with a bucket of what was evidently milk. The child shut the barn door and headed into the house, where his mother thanked him for milking the cow.

Somehow, that family had his attention. It was a simple family, and he couldn't see if they had more than just the one son, but he could hear the mother's voice as she sweetly spoke to her child and encouraged him to eat all of his bread and vegetables. Meat was very precious to poor families, so the poor would generally eat only vegetables for their meals. But it struck Curtis that the boy didn't seem to mind that they were poor. In fact, he probably didn't even know they were poor. All that mattered was that he had a loving mother and a loving father and a warm home to grow up in.

Somehow, that depressed Curtis.

He wasn't sure what he had expected of his own marriage, but he had expected at least what his father and mother had. Even though he had heard stories, from his own father, no less, as to how much his mother did not want to get married, they were still able to put aside their differences and raise ten children. Curtis only remembered the warmth of his family when he was young and how his older sisters doted on him. He only remembered his parents being loving toward each other, and, quite frankly, that was the example set for him. Of course he should want that for his own marriage.

But it didn't look like that was going to happen.

As he listened to the mother and the father talk to their young son, he began to sorely regret how he'd spoken to Elle. He wasn't usually a man to get upset like that, and most definitely not with women, but she had hurt him. The more he thought on it, the more he realized that was why he had lashed out the way he had. He had told her to be gone in the morning, but a large part of him was hoping she was stubborn enough to disobey him. He was also thinking that perhaps he should just go back to the encampment tonight and apologize to her for becoming angry. Perhaps if he did, they might smooth things over.

But he didn't have high hopes.

His meal came several minutes later. There was an enormous bowl of stewed beef chunks with currants and carrots, plus a custard that was full of onions and baked with cheese. It was delicious. There was also plenty of bread and butter, and a big bowl of stewed apples with cloves and honey. Lastly, there was an enormous pitcher of what turned out to be warmed wine that was full of spices. He sucked down the stewed beef and the onion tart and practically inhaled the bread and butter. He didn't realize he was so hungry until he took the first bite, and after that, everything on the tray ended up in his mouth in short order. Even the trencher, a flat disk of stale bread, was eaten because it was soaked in the gravy from the stewed beef. Between bites, he drank copious amounts of the spicy wine until there was nothing left.

Stuffed and fairly drunk at that point, he ended up passing out in the chair he was sitting in. The food and the warmth of the room had lulled him to sleep, and considering he had hardly slept in the past month, his body was ready for the rest. Even though he slept deeply, he still had one ear open. It was the trained warrior in him, always listening for danger.

It was the curse of a knight.

Part of his window overlooked the stable yard, and he heard when a horse entered the yard. He could hear the steady clip-clops and the crunching of the earth. It was enough of a noise to wake him, but only because he wanted to make the transition over to the bed and not sleep in the chair. He had paid good money for that bed, and he intended to use it. His resolve to return to the encampment that evening was sliding just a bit, but he was certain he could make it back before sunrise. Before the deadline he had given Elle. But that was until he looked into the stable yard as he got up from his chair.

Elle was down there.

He also recognized Peter's horse immediately. Peter rode a horse that was as red as a sunset, with a white stripe down its face and four white socks. The horse was very recognizable. Suddenly, Curtis was wide awake as he watched Peter speak to

Elle, who was standing next to the horse. Puzzled, Curtis quickly made his way down from his room and out into the livery yard just as Peter was leaving.

His brother caught sight of him.

"Then you really *are* here," Peter said. "I saw your horse just inside the livery door, but I wasn't sure this was where you had found lodgings for the night."

Curtis' focus was on Peter for a few moments before shifting to Elle. "Of course this is where I would be," he said to his brother, even though he wasn't looking at him. "Why would I leave my horse here and not stay here?"

Peter could see where the man's attention was, and he turned his horse for the alley. "Because there are two other inns across the street, and I do not think they have liveries," he said. "You could've been over there for all I knew. But now that I have found you, I shall leave your wife here and bid you both a good night."

With that, he plodded out of the yard, leaving Elle standing there, looking at Curtis with a great deal of uncertainty on her face. It was an unusual expression for her, one Curtis had never seen before. She was full of hesitation. Before he could say a word, she spoke.

"I asked Peter to help me find you," she said, wringing her hands nervously. "My lord, I am sorry. I have made a mess out of things, and I did not want you to hate me for it. I am sorry I said those things to you, because I should not have. They are my own insecurities, and I must learn to overcome them, but I should not have lashed out at you as I did, and I am very sorry for it. If you still wish to annul the marriage, then I understand, but I could not let you do it without knowing how sorry I am."

It was quite a speech, as remorseful as he'd ever heard her.

That was surprising. Curtis' eyes glimmered with mirth and perhaps even warmth.

"There is something you must do for me," he said.

Elle nodded eagerly. "I will, whatever it is."

"Never again address me as 'my lord,'" he said. "You are my wife, and that is far too formal, even for me."

She blinked in surprise. "As you wish," she said. "What… what should I call you?"

"My name is Curtis," he said softly. "I will answer to Curtis or Curt. Whatever you wish to use, I will answer."

He sounded… calm. Calm and unlike the enraged man who had left the encampment those hours ago. Elle was unsure how to proceed at that point, because he seemed kind again, but she knew she'd upset him gravely.

"I… I said what I came to say," she said, looking uncertain. "Sir Peter has probably already started back for the encampment, so I will sleep in the stable for tonight, but mayhap you will let me travel back with you tomorrow morning."

He grinned and shook his head, glancing at his feet as he pondered her statement. "Do you honestly think I would let you sleep in a stable?" he said, lifting his head to look at her. "Ever again? Your days of smelly clothes and sleeping in anything other than the finest bed I can provide are over, Elle."

He seemed almost jovial, and her bafflement grew. "I do not understand," she said. "I came to apologize to you, and I meant it, but you've not said a word about the situation other than to pretend it never happened."

"It didn't."

"But it did," she said firmly, moving toward him. "I was horrible to you, but all I can tell you is that this entire situation has been contrary to everything I have ever been taught about the English. As I told your father, I should not be mourning my life as if it meant something before yesterday. When the only people who ever showed me kindness are the men who defeated me in battle, that should tell any sane person that my life of coldness and harshness was not a life worth living. Realizing that you are going to annul the marriage has made me understand something for the very first time."

She was close to him now, and he gazed down at her. "What is that?"

She lifted her slender shoulders. "That you have given me a glimpse of another life I never knew existed," she said. "A life where people care for one another. Your family loves one another. You have friends and warmth and understanding. All I ever knew of the English were that they were wicked and cold and greedy, but that is certainly not what I have experienced. I've never seen this side of things."

He cocked his head. "If you have come to realize that, then mayhap this incident was not wasted," he said. "All I need is for you to be fair about things. Stop relying on the lies from the past. Open your eyes to the world around you, and I promise you will not regret it."

"I will, I promise," she said quickly. "I will try very hard."

He smiled at her. "I will, also," he said. "I will never again lose my temper as I did. That was wrong of me, and if I hurt you, then I am very sorry."

The sounds of his apology were like music to her ears. "You had every right to," she said. "There was nothing else you could have done. I behaved terribly."

He waggled his eyebrows. "I would say this has been a trying situation for the both of us," he said. "When we first met, you were trying to kill me. Now, we are married. I do not know of any other married couples who have had the rough beginning we have."

"Other than your father and mother," she said.

He chuckled. "Aye, other than them," he said. "But there is hope in that. They cannot live without one another, so hopefully, we will grow to be fond of one another, too."

That made her heart flutter, just a little. "You said I should look beyond the English knight and see the man beneath," she said. "I am willing to do that as long as you are willing to look beyond the Welsh rebel and see the woman beneath."

He grinned, flashing a smile that was much like his father's. "You are not a rebel," he said. "You are a princess fighting for your countrymen. That is admirable. But now you have me, and short of saying your fight is my fight, know that I will never forsake or betray you, Elle. I want the same consideration."

"You have it, Curtis."

"Good," he said, his eyes twinkling at her. But then he seemed to notice what she was wearing for the first time, and he pointed. "That is my tunic. I recognize it."

She looked down at herself. "You told me that I could wear what was in your chest."

"Where is the blue dress?"

"You told me to take it off so my stench would not be on it."

His smile faded. "I should not have said that," he said with regret. "I am sorry, Elle. I did not mean it."

She smiled timidly to let him know that she wasn't upset. "You were right," she said. "I'm not sure one bath could clean up all of the stench I had on me. I may need another soon."

He laughed softly. "I think that can be arranged," he said. Then he held out a hand to her. "Shall we go inside, Lady Leominster?"

She looked at his big hand, hesitating. "You're not going to annul the marriage?"

"Nay," he said softly. "I did not even mean it when I said it."

With a grateful smile, she put her hand in his, and he held it tightly, gently leading her toward the rear door of the inn.

"Would it be possible for me to have something to eat with my bath?" she asked.

His eyebrows rose. "You want a bath tonight?"

"I like baths."

"Then you shall have one every night if you wish."

"But I do not have any soap."

"Not to worry," he said, pushing open the door. "I will make sure you have what you need, Elle. Always."

She believed him.

ೞ

THE BATH CAME with more food than Elle had ever seen in one sitting.

Curtis seemed to have some kind of magic when it came to getting people to do what he wanted them to do, and that included the staff at the inn. Food and drink came, and as Elle stuffed herself on the onion tart, a rather large copper tub was brought in and filled about halfway with steaming water.

She could hear Curtis outside in the corridor, speaking to the innkeeper and his wife, and very shortly, Elle had soap and combs and a scrub brush. The innkeeper's wife, a stout woman with faded red hair, also brought in a shift, well worn but clean, and a surcoat that went over the shift and tied on the sides. It was green in color, and Elle heard the woman tell Curtis that it had belonged to their daughter, who had died the previous winter of a fever. She was happy to give Elle her dead daughter's things, but Curtis insisted on paying the woman handsomely for them.

Elle found herself inheriting a wardrobe that was meant for a girl about her same size. The innkeeper's wife seemed quite happy to see the clothing put to use, and considering Elle had nothing to her name, she was thrilled to have it. There were two more shifts and three more dresses that were given to her, along with two pairs of leather slippers that were worn but serviceable. The innkeeper's wife even offered to help her bathe, something she said she used to do with her daughter, and Elle didn't have the heart to refuse her. She seemed eager to do it. As Curtis went out into the common room to allow her some privacy, Elle climbed into that big tub, both hands full of food, and ate to her heart's content while the innkeeper's wife scrubbed her down.

More kindness from the hated English.

In fact, the woman, whose name was Bess, was quite lovely to her. Elle sat in the tub until the water cooled, and then Bess helped her out and dried her off in front of the fire, combing out her hair so it could dry. Since Elle had never had a mother tend her, only a bitter grandmother in that capacity, it was strange but also weirdly wonderful to have the kind attentions of an older woman gently brushing her hair. Odd how a bath, in an enemy country, brought about some awareness. She was coming to see what she might have been missing.

Open your eyes to the world around you, and I promise you will not regret it.

She was starting to realize what he had meant.

So, Elle sat while the woman combed and combed, food in both hands and gobbling it up as if she hadn't eaten in days. Never in her life had she been exposed to so much food. She had no idea that such a thing was possible. She'd spent her entire life scraping by with the bare minimum, sleeping on the ground and eating things that other men killed or procured, and she'd truly had no idea that there was a world where food was plentiful. When she finished with everything on the tray, the innkeeper's wife sent for more.

When Elle's hair was mostly dry, the innkeeper's wife neatly braided it and helped her into one of the shifts. Since Elle knew that the woman was missing a daughter, she let her fuss. Bess had been so genuinely kind that Elle didn't have the heart to tell her to go away or that she no longer needed her. She let the woman neatly hang her clothing, touch her hair again, and then warm her bed with an old copper bed warmer. When Elle was finally finished with the additional food, she burped in gluttonous misery, which only seemed to please the woman. When Elle showed an interest toward getting into bed, Bess practically threw her into bed and tightly tucked her in.

After that, Elle was in bed to stay.

She only realized she had fallen asleep when she heard something in the chamber and startled herself awake to see Curtis moving around in the darkness. When he saw that he had awakened her, he paused regretfully in removing the daggers he'd been pulling from his belt.

"It's me," he whispered. "I'm sorry to have awoken you. I was trying to be quiet."

Elle yawned and rubbed her eyes. "You did not wake me," she said. "I have always been a light sleeper."

He grunted softly as he continued to remove his things. "That is the life of a warrior," he said. "I do not think I have had a solid night's sleep since I was a lad."

Lying on her side, Elle watched him as he proceeded to

undress. "Having a bed this comfortable is rare," she said. "It is like a warm embrace."

He smiled faintly. "I know what you mean."

He continued to undress, and it occurred to Elle why. The man was her husband, and this was their wedding night. At some point, he was going to get into bed with her, nude, and he was going to expect husbandly relations. Her stomach began to twist in knots at the mere thought of it, because the last man who had touched her intimately was Cadwalader. She could still feel his wrinkled, old hands on her body, disgusting her to the point of feeling ill.

But then something odd happened.

Curtis removed his tunic, and Elle could see his magnificent torso illuminated in the firelight. He had a beautifully muscular chest and arms, a trim torso, and broad shoulders. That was no wrinkly body. She watched him untie his breeches, but when he slid them off his hips and she got a look at his tight, bare buttocks, she quickly pulled the covers over her face. She was both embarrassed and titillated, a strange combination. She wanted to peek at him, but was too shy to do it. He continued to move around the chamber, presumably nude, but she heard him come to a halt.

"Am I that appalling?" he asked.

She knew what he meant and could feel her face grow hot. "Why… why do you ask?"

"Because you have the coverlet pulled over your head."

In the new spirit of honesty between them, she forced herself to answer truthfully. "I am unused to seeing a nude man," she said. "Surely you can understand that."

She heard his joints pop as he moved to the bed. Then he was pulling on the coverlet until her eyes were exposed. They popped open, and she found herself looking into his smiling face.

"You will never become accustomed to it if you refuse to look," he said. "I am your husband. It is your right to look."

He wouldn't let her pull the coverlet up again, so she slapped a hand over her eyes, listening to him laugh low in his throat.

"Very well," he said. "If I am so horrific that you do not wish to look at me, then I will not force you."

She peeped through her fingers. "You are not horrific to look at," she said. "It is simply... I am not *used* to this!"

He chuckled again and turned away from her. "Very well, you coward," he said. "Now that you've hurt my feelings, I'm going to climb into bed next to you and weep."

Her hands came away from her face, and she sat up, watching him as he walked around the bed and got in on the other side. "Do not be offended," she said. "My only experience with this was long ago and quite unhappy."

He knew that. He pulled the coverlet over himself, settling down as he looked at her. "I can only change your mind if you let me," he said, folding a big arm behind his head. "You were barely a woman back then. Now you are fully grown and fully lovely. And you belong to me."

She looked at him seriously, thinking he looked awfully handsome lying there on the linens. It was enough to flutter her heart again, something he seemed to be able to do with little effort.

"Have you done this before?" she asked.

The warmth in his eyes flickered. "I have," he said honestly. "Does that surprise you?"

She shook her head. "Nay," she said. "Men do not go to

their marriage bed a virgin."

"There is a reason for that."

"Why?"

"Because someone has to know what to do, or the entire situation will be a disaster."

He was trying not to smile as he said it, and that made her grin. "That is very naughty, you know."

He laughed softly. "Not as naughty as I can be."

She frowned. "What do you mean?"

He could see she hadn't a clue what he meant. Reaching up a big hand, he cupped her head and pulled her down to his lips.

"Let me show you," he whispered.

Gently, he kissed her cheek, so sweetly that Elle felt light-headed. That kiss was followed by another kiss to the cheek, to the ear, to the jaw, to the neck. Each successive kiss made her feel giddier and giddier. When he finally turned her head slightly and kissed her soft mouth, Elle thought she might faint. This was no wrinkly old man with foul breath. This was a powerful, handsome, virile knight. An English knight. Could a man's touch truly be this wonderful?

She quickly decided that she would let him show her.

This was all part of opening her eyes and letting the world in. It was part of understanding that there were people out there who were kind and gentle. Once Curtis touched her with his big, warm hands, she wanted more. It was a glimpse into something she'd never had, but something she was coming to want. She wanted to experience it all. For once, she wanted to be touched and loved. She wanted Curtis' hands upon her.

It felt like the most natural thing in the world.

The fighting was over. The hatred was gone. Curtis was kissing her now, taking the dominant position and forcing her back onto the mattress as he unfastened the ties on her shift. She could feel his hands on her waist, yanking loose the ties as his kisses grew feverish. She was breathing so heavily, trying to catch her breath between heated kisses, but instinctively, she moved to help him. All she knew was that there was a fire building in her body that she had no control over. It was a shocking realization.

Every time Curtis kissed her, the fire grew.

Her shift went over her head and she was nude against his naked flesh. This wasn't anything like her time spent with Cadwalader. She'd shuddered with disgust at every touch, but Curtis ignited a roaring blaze. Once her shift came free, his mouth left hers, seeking her neck and points farther south. He was kissing the swell of her bosom with heated lips.

The wildfire raged.

This was something she could learn to crave. He left her bosom and moved to her belly, kissing and suckling the flesh, and Elle heard herself groan in delight. He dragged his tongue over her rib cage, under her breasts, before finally capturing a tender nipple in his mouth.

Lightning struck.

Elle came alive in his arms, gasping and bucking beneath him, hardly realizing he had pulled her legs apart to settle some of his weight between them. She had her hands on his blond head, experiencing his mouth on her breasts with the utmost delight. Nothing Cadwalader had done to her came close to this, and she began to see what the excitement was about. Soldiers and servants seemed to speak freely of coupling, and she'd never understood the allure. Now, she did. Legs spread wide, she gave herself over to Curtis completely.

His fingers moved to the junction between her legs. When

Cadwalader had touched her there, however briefly, she recoiled. But she wasn't recoiling from Curtis. His fingers were stroking her, touching her in a way that made her entire body quiver. Curtis suckled strongly on her right breast as he plunged a finger into her, acquainting her with his intimate touch. But Elle didn't want to simply be acquainted with it—she wanted to know all of it. If this were coupling as it was meant to be, she realized what she'd been missing out on.

Her nubile body was prepared for him, her woman's center swollen and primed for his entry. The next thing Elle realized, his weight came down on her and he was thrusting into her gently, full and hot and hard. With a gasp, she rose to meet him, winding her legs around his hips and pulling him in deeper. Curtis' mouth covered hers, suckling her, kissing her deeply, as he tightened his buttocks and thrust into her again and again, a steady rhythm building. When their loins came together, that fire burning inside of Elle sparked brilliantly every time.

"Oh… God," she breathed. "Naughty… Is this naughty?"

Curtis laughed low in his throat, nearly fracturing his concentration. But not quite. He was on fire also.

"I told you that I would show you," he said, biting gently at her lower lip.

She gasped again as he ground his pelvis against hers. "Swear to me," she whispered. "This—you—is only for me. This belongs to me."

That seemed to feed his lust. "Until I die," he murmured in her ear. "I shall belong to you and only you. And you shall belong to me."

She nodded her head, wrapping her arms around his neck as he plunged deeply into her, causing sparks to fly. After a few such deep thrusts, she felt an explosion in her loins the likes of which she had never experienced before. Nothing Cadwalader had ever done to her could come close. Tremors radiated throughout her body, and she cried out, clutching at Curtis and driving her nails into his flesh.

Dazed, she lay there gasping as Curtis continued thrusting until he took one hard, final push and she heard him grunt. She could feel his male member inside her twitching as he released his seed. Elle continued to lie there, in a stupor, her arms around his neck, holding on to him so tightly that she was afraid to let him go. Afraid this moment was only a dream and she would awaken alone in a world that was as cold and sorrowful as she was.

Was.

She wasn't any longer.

All wrapped up around Curtis' heated body, Elle began to weep. She didn't know why, but silent tears came and wouldn't stop. They flowed down her face, touching his flesh as he lay there and held her. She was weeping because never in her life had she ever known such closeness, such warmth, or such care.

Curtis had opened that world up for her.

"What is the matter?" he asked softly, shifting so he could look at her. "Why do you weep? Did I hurt you?"

She hadn't been as discreet as she thought she had. Wiping at her face, she shook her head. "Nay," she said hoarsely. "You were quite gentle."

"Then why are you weeping?"

She almost shut him down, avoiding the question, but she thought better of it. Other than Melusine, she'd never had anyone to confide in, fearful of opening herself up. But with Curtis, she'd already established a pattern of honesty.

She wanted to keep it.

"I do not know, really," she said. "I suppose because I have spent so much time trying to push you away and keep you at arm's length that I'm fearful now that I've let you in."

He shifted so his head was on the pillow beside hers. "Am I in?"

"You've come through the door I had closed."

A smile tugged at his lips. "You mean I've managed to breach the gatehouse?"

She couldn't help but laugh. "Exactly."

It was a language they could both understand as they learned to communicate with one another. Curtis was quickly coming to be aware of that. "So I am standing at your gatehouse, yet I have no weapons," he said softly. "What are you afraid of?"

Her smile faded. "I am afraid that this is all a dream and you will leave me."

He leaned in and kissed her on the forehead. "I will not leave you," he said huskily. "That is a promise. But you must stop trying to keep me out of the gatehouse. I want to come in, Elle. All the way in, if you'll allow."

She nodded. "I know," she said. "And I want you to come in, but you must understand that pushing people away has become innate with me. If there is no one for me to depend on, then I cannot get hurt."

"I understand," he said, reaching up to wipe an errant tear from her right cheek. "But your days of being alone are ended. You have me now, and about twenty close family members who simply want the opportunity to love you. Give them that chance, Elle. Please."

She forced a brave smile. "I will, if it is what you wish," she said. "But I fear I have a great deal to learn about families and this life I now find myself in."

"Like what?"

She shrugged. "I was not raised in a fine household," she said. "I do not know how to manage kitchens or feasts or food or chambers. I do not know how to talk to English lords so they will not think I am foolish. I do not even know how to dance."

He grinned. "I can see that I have a good deal of teaching in my future."

"Do you mind terribly?"

He laughed softly and pulled her close. "Of course not," he said. "I am delighted to do it. But I do not know everything, so I think you will have a few teachers to ensure you are the finest countess England has ever seen."

"Do you really think so?"

"I know so."

The conversation ended, but not uncomfortably so. In fact, he pulled her close and held her in warm silence as they became acquainted with the feel of one another. Flesh against flesh, heart against heart. Elle was soft and pliable in his arms, and Curtis enveloped her in his strength. It was a defining moment of what their future together would be.

Breached gatehouse and all.

When sleep came for them both, it was deep and undisturbed.

It was a solid night's sleep for both of them.

CHAPTER TWELVE

THOSE FOOLISH BOYS weren't going to keep her contained forever.

Melusine had managed to sneak away from the sons of Peter de Lohr as they slept around her in a circle. It was before dawn, and she had been awoken by the sounds of the army around her mobilizing. When she tiptoed around the sleeping boys and stuck her head out of the tent, she could see that the army was packing up to leave. At least, some men were. There was a good deal of commotion going around them that should have woken up those spoiled English lads, but they slept through it.

And that was Melusine's cue to depart.

She had only seen Elle twice since the English won the victory at Brython Castle. Both times, her cousin seemed to become irate with her, and both times, they had been separated. She'd hoped to stay with Elle and help her in this strange new world that she found herself part of, but that didn't seem to be possible.

And now, there was a marriage involved. That wasn't something either Melusine or Elle had ever considered. Marriage to an Englishman was like a death sentence to women like them, women who made the resistance of the Welsh their life's blood. In fact, it was a particular problem for Melusine because she was used to having Elle's ear. She, too, was related to Llywelyn because she came from the matriarchal side of the family. Elle's bitter, old grandmother had been Melusine's grandmother, as well. She and Elle had both been raised by that rebellious, vindictive woman, and they had both spent their lives advocating for an independently ruled Wales.

Ruled by Llywelyn.

Gruffydd had long wondered why his sister had been so resistant to any English alliance, and the truth was that Melusine had a big part in that opinion. She was the one who whispered in Elle's ear, telling her how horrible and greedy the English were while fostering a rabid devotion to the Welsh cause. She was also the one who convinced Elle that Gruffydd and Gwenwynwyn were weak in their alliance with the English. Because Elle had been listening to it for so long, she didn't really realize that Melusine had been stoking the fires of hatred started by their grandmother. But now, Elle had been forced to marry an English Lord, and Melusine was concerned that her days of controlling her cousin were over.

Curtis would figure her out fairly quickly if she remained.

It was therefore imperative that she escape captivity. She wasn't entirely sure where she would go, except that perhaps she would escape to Tywyl Castle, where Gruffydd was in residence. The English had shown him significant mercy in allowing him to return home, and since Melusine had nowhere to go, she thought she would go to Gruffydd first and then figure out where to go from there. She couldn't stay in the household of a man who was loyal to England.

So, she fled the tent just as the sun began to rise, leaving the lazy English boys behind. They had been charged with guarding her, and she smiled at the thought of the punishment they would receive when it was discovered they had failed at their task. Fortunately, no one was paying much attention to her as she quickly moved through the encampment, heading for the east end so she could continue her trek into the heart of Wales. The smell of smoke was heavy, held to the ground by the mist that had developed in the early-morning hours. Cooking fires had been started, and the smell of food filled the air as she approached the outskirts of the encampment.

The western wall, the one so badly damaged by the war machines, was immediately to her right as she came through the cluster of tents. The dead, mostly Welsh dead, had been moved to this area, and the smell of death mingled with the smoke gave the entire area the feeling of hell's back acre. Because the trees and the land in general were stripped, the sense of desolation was heavy here.

Melusine was eager to get through it.

It was like walking through purgatory.

Just as she started to head toward the deforested area to the west, someone grabbed her hair from behind.

"So you think to escape, do you?" A Spanish accent was heavy in her ear. "You little cow, you belong to me now."

Melusine shrieked as Amaro pulled her back into the encampment with him. He wasn't gentle on her in the least, and continued to hold on to her hair to force her into obedience.

She knew she was caught.

Amaro had been up before dawn, separating some of the men from the de Lohr army to remain at Brython, when he saw Melusine sneaking through the encampment. Curtis had been back for about an hour after a night spent away from the encampment, and he was in Christopher's tent hammering out the details of Hereford's departure back to Lioncross Abbey Castle. Amaro didn't know why Curtis and his wife had left the night before, but he'd heard through the rumor mill that all was not well with the newlyweds. Frankly, Amaro didn't know what Curtis expected, having married a Welsh chit as he had.

He might as well have married an animal.

Amaro went about his duties as the de Lohr men gathered in Christopher's tent. Hugo was off supervising the rebuild of the western wall, which had begun in earnest yesterday, along with Asa, leaving Amaro to handle the army along with several sergeants. But when he saw Melusine trying to make her escape, he left the men to the sergeants and pursued the Welsh bitch.

Spy.

She had to be a spy.

"Where were you going, woman?" he demanded.

Melusine was in a great deal of pain from the way he was holding her. "I was leaving," she said. "Let me go!"

Amaro ignored her as he continued to drag her through the encampment. "I think you were running off to tell your Welsh rebels that Hereford is leaving today," he said. "Isn't that where you were going?"

Melusine yelped as he yanked on her. "Nay!" she said. "I was going home!"

"Home to your den of Welsh animals?" Amaro said. "Filthy, barbaric, mindless fools. And what else do you do for them, Miasma? Do you warm their beds with your skinny body?"

She gasped in outrage, trying to pull away. "Who is Miasma?" she said. "Release me. You're hurting me!"

"Good," Amaro said, yanking on her so hard that she ended

up falling into him. His severe face was inches from her own. "Now you'll have to face Hereford's justice, and you know what the man will do to spies. He will torture you and then he will kill you. And I will have the pleasure of watching."

Terrified, Melusine tried to push away but ended up hitting him in the throat as she did. His response was to slap her, as hard as he could, on the side of the head.

Dazed, Melusine gave up the fight as he towed her all the way back to Christopher's tent.

CB

SHE KNEW SHE had a stupid smile on her face.

Elle knew and she didn't care. She couldn't stop smiling as she organized the chest in Curtis' tent, the one she'd taken the tunic and hose from. She'd jumbled everything the night before in her haste to find clothing, so as he went to see his father, she carefully organized the trunk.

This is what it's like to be happy.

That thought kept rolling over and over in her mind. Happiness she'd never thought she would feel. She didn't recognize it at all. Ever since last night, and on the return home this morning, she'd had this feeling of lightness in her heart, the same lightness that was reflected on Curtis' face every time he looked at her. That was when it occurred to her that what she was feeling was joy.

Evidently, they were both feeling it.

But it was a very new sensation, so new that neither one of them could put it into words. Perhaps they didn't want to because happiness, like anything else, could be fleeting in their world. They'd had such a difficult introduction and, up until last night, a marriage that was destined to end, so no one wanted to jinx this newfound sense of bliss.

All Elle wanted to do was enjoy it.

But she felt like an idiot because she couldn't get the smile off her face. Perhaps she really didn't care in the long run, because it was a smile that was only meant for Curtis, and he wasn't here. He was with his father, who would undoubtedly be ecstatic that they had been able to hash out their differences. Perhaps she'd have the same stupid smile on her face when she spoke to Christopher, because undoubtedly, he would want to talk to her, too.

Just to make sure the joy wasn't one-sided.

Before they left the village, Curtis had procured bread and cheese from the inn's kitchen as it began to prepare food for the morning meal. Elle had ridden behind him all the way back to Brython, bread in one hand and cheese in the other, wolfing it down as she told him about the nearest town to Brython on the Wales side of the border. Because that village was relatively close to her brother's castle, she had spent a lot of time there. She knew the people and they knew her. She and Curtis had a good discussion about the town and its functions and the people in general. It had been the first real conversation they had that didn't involve angst or torment or terrible reflections.

It had been… *normal.*

Once they reached the encampment, Curtis told her that he was sorry their journey had ended and thanked her for a pleasant ride. Unused to any kind of flattery, Elle turned bright red, and he had simply laughed. But he also took her hand and kissed her, leading her back to his tent, which was now technically a tent that belonged to both of them. But he had only returned for a short while before he went off in search of his father to inform the man of his return. And quite possibly to let him know that the marriage was finally agreeable.

Elle certainly thought it was.

The whole morning had been like a dream.

In fact, it was difficult to keep her mind on her task. Her head was in the clouds. She was only half finished repacking Curtis' trunk when she wandered to the tent flap, folding a pair of breeches, looking out over the encampment in the hopes of catching a glimpse of her new husband. There was no husband, but she could see Christopher's tent. It was quite close, in truth, so it was easily in her field of vision. That big blue tent with the blue and gold standards flying above it. There were several soldiers milling about in front of the tent, and knights wandered in and out.

And that was when she saw it.

A knight dragging Melusine by the hair.

Shocked, Elle dropped the breeches in her hands and rushed out of the tent just as the knight and Melusine entered Hereford's tent. But instinct ran strong with her, the instinct to protect those she loved and the instinct to protect herself against the English, so she grabbed the nearest weapon she could find, which happened to be a piece of wood meant for Hereford's fire. There was a pile of it near his tent. She rushed toward the opening, only to hear someone shouting about capturing a spy. She could hear Melusine weeping.

When she burst in through the tent flap, Elle's gaze fell on the man who had dragged Melusine by the hair as her cousin cowered on the ground at his feet. Just as the man turned to look at her, startled that someone had come up behind him, Elle swung the wood at his head and bashed him in the face. The knight, lashing out with his hands to defend himself, caught Elle in the jaw and sent her tumbling backward.

After that, it was chaos.

Elle was dazed as someone picked her up off the ground and took her out of the tent. Someone else had grabbed Melusine. As Elle shook off the stars, she could see that it had been Hereford himself who took her out of the tent, but now he was rushing back into the shelter to prevent Curtis from killing the knight who had dragged Melusine by the hair. There was shouting going on, and some pleading, and suddenly, the entire side of Hereford's tent blew open as Curtis threw the half-conscious knight out of the tent. Quite literally, the man had been flying through the air. The tent stakes were still in the ground, but the fabric had torn as the knight hit the ground heavily. As Elle watched in shock, Curtis went charging after the knight as his father jumped in to prevent any more damage from being done.

"No more," Christopher commanded, holding Curtis back with help from Peter. "No more, Curt. Take your wife and cousin and get out of here. Go back to your tent. Please."

Curtis was like a raging bull. Peter had him from behind, holding him back, but he wasn't moving. He was like a rock, hard and immovable. Roi, who had been bent over the knight on the ground, came over as well, and between Peter and Roi, they managed to push Curtis back in the direction of Elle, who was clutching Melusine. One look at her husband's face and she very nearly burst into tears.

"I'm sorry," she said. "I'm so very sorry. But he was hurting Melusine, and I had to stop him!"

When Curtis saw her face, something changed. He'd been rigid and flushed, but the moment he saw her, his expression loosened and he pulled away from his brothers. He went to her and put a gentle hand under her chin, tipping her face up to look at him.

"Did he hurt you?" he said, trying to get a look at any marks or bruises. "His strike was hard."

She shook her head, but the tears were beginning to pool. "Please do not be angry with me," she said. "I could not let him hurt Melly. He had her by the hair!"

Curtis was oddly calm for having been thoroughly enraged only moments earlier. "I know," he said patiently, putting an arm around her and pulling her against him. "You are not to blame. He deserved it. But are you sure he did not injure you?"

It took Elle a few moments to realize that he wasn't angry with her. He was angry with the knight. She was positive his fury was directed at her, and to realize it wasn't brought a significant amount of shock.

She stared up at him.

"Nay, he did not injure me," she said, rubbing the spot where he'd struck her. "You... you are not angry with me?"

He shook his head. "Of course not," he said, but then he looked over to his father as Alexander and Roi were pulling the knight to his feet. "Get him out of my sight. If I see him again, I will kill him."

Christopher put up a hand to ease his son, muttering something to Roi and Alexander. They half dragged, half walked the knight away, disappearing into the encampment. When he was gone, Christopher came over to Elle and looked her over.

"Did he hurt you, my lady?" he asked.

Elle was becoming perplexed that they were so concerned about her health. "Nay," she said. "Melly hits harder than he does. Truly, I am well, but I suspect I'll have a bruise."

Christopher did the same thing Curtis had done—grasping her chin and tilting her head to get a look at the welt on the left side of her jaw and neck. He inspected the area before grunting unhappily.

"I will take Amaro back with me to Lioncross," he said to Curtis. "I do not want him around your wife or her cousin, and, most importantly, I do not want him around you."

Curtis barely nodded because the sight of the rising welt on Elle's jaw was beginning to feed his anger again. "That is wise," he said. "The man is fortunate he could walk away from this. If I had my way about it, he would not have."

"I know," Christopher said, holding up a hand to stop Curtis from saying anything further. "He will go with me. Meanwhile, you will need to select men to remain behind with you. Amaro was doing it. Or he was supposed to be doing it."

"Let Myles do it," Curtis said. "Where is he, anyway?"

Christopher looked off toward the south. "Mustering my army," he said. "He and Andrew are seeing to it."

"You are leaving Myles with me, are you not?"

"Aye, if you want him."

"I do."

"Are you leaving today, my lord?" Elle asked.

Christopher looked at her. "I am," he said. "But I leave you, and Brython, in the capable hands of my son. But I'm sure you are already confident of that."

He was smiling faintly, and something told Elle that Curtis had told his father that they had smoothed everything over last night. Christopher could guess what that meant. Flushing a deep shade of red, she simply bobbed her head and grasped Melusine before fleeing in the direction of Curtis' tent. When Curtis looked at his father, surprised by his wife's swift departure, they both started laughing.

"She is a paradox, lad," Christopher said. "She took that

kindling after Amaro, but speak of something romantic and she runs away."

Curtis was grinning. "Hopefully, not for long," he said. "I hope that she will be comfortable with our marriage. I hope I will be, too."

"From what you told me about last night, it seems that the rough edges have been smoothed a little," Christopher said, studying Curtis' face for any hint of what he might be thinking. "What I did not tell you is that before Peter took her to find you, she came to speak with me. Peter and Sherry were here, so they heard it, too. She expressed her great regret at how she behaved with you and how she viewed things. I believe she wants to do better, Curt. I truly do."

"As do I," Curtis said. "I only told you that everything was well between us again, but I did not tell you that she apologized to me last night. She is caught between two worlds, Papa. I can see that. But I want to pull her into mine."

Christopher nodded. "A noble goal, but take care not to completely discount her world," he said. "She will be happier if she keeps her world but understands yours. Just be patient, lad. That is all I can really tell you."

Curtis smiled. "Thank you," he said sincerely. But that warmth soon faded. "And keep Amaro out of my sight. If I see him again, I *will* kill him. And I am sorry for your alliance with his father, but no man strikes my wife and lives to tell the tale."

Christopher nodded. "I understand," he said quietly. "I think, mayhap, that it is time to send Amaro back to his father. I have taught him everything I intend to, and I am certain he has learned everything he has wanted to and no more. I am not particularly anxious to have him around your mother and sisters, to be perfectly honest."

"Then send him back," Curtis urged quietly. "Send him home and let us say no more about it."

Off to the south, the wagons were beginning to roll into formation and the army was moving in their direction, except for the thousand men that had been set aside to remain with Curtis. They could both see Roi moving through the ranks, sending men toward Brython. The duty had been Amaro's, but with the man out of commission, Roi was taking the duty.

It was time for the de Lohr army to go home.

"I will consider sending him home," Christopher replied belatedly to Curtis' encouragement. He turned to his son, putting a hand on the man's shoulder. "Meanwhile, I have my own duties to attend to. We will be leaving by midday."

"I will find you before you go to bid you farewell."

Christopher put his hand on Curtis' cheek in an affectionate gesture before going about his business. The men parted ways, each going to attend to his duties, each one looking forward to what life was to bring them. For Christopher, it was returning home, but for Curtis...

He had a wife now.

And he was rather looking forward to it.

CHAPTER THIRTEEN

Two Months Later
Brython Castle

"I AM GOING to do this one more time," Myles said loudly to the group in front of him. "Listen to what I tell you and do exactly as I say. Am I clear?"

Elle and Curtis nodded. So did Melusine, Asa, Hugo, and Andrew, Alexander's son. Andrew had seen sixteen years, but he was a big lad with his father's black hair and his mother's gray eyes. The women around Brython, especially the younger women, thought Andrew de Sherrington was quite the handsome lad. Rounding out the group was Westley and the most recent addition to Brython, Douglas de Lohr.

Douglas was the brother between Myles and Westley. At seventeen years of age, he had been fostering at Blackstone Castle in Norfolk, home of the House of Summerlin. Douglas had been there for a few years, and prior to that, he'd been at Thunderbey Castle, seat of the Earl of East Anglia, a cousin to the House of de Lohr. But his father had all of his sons home, except for Douglas, and sent for the lad a short time ago. Douglas returned to Lioncross Abbey, a skilled warrior with his father's size but the curse of arrogant youth.

Christopher had sent him up to Brython to help his elder brother.

Even now, Douglas stood across from Westley, who was three years younger, and frowned because he did not have a female partner. He was beautiful and blond and far too good looking to be paired up with his gangly, smelly younger brother. He didn't want to be paired up with Andrew, either, because Andrew was direct competition for young women's affections. Curtis and Myles knew this, and even now, Douglas was eyeing Melusine because, other than Lady Leominster, she was the only female in this particular group.

It was a dance group.

Eight weeks since the fall of Brython had seen quite a bit happening when it came to the inhabitants and the drama that tended to follow them. New knights and others had joined Curtis' ranks, and everyone seemed to have settled down admirably, including Melusine. The bitter, sometimes conniving cousin of Lady Leominster had found some peace in her new role at Brython, and that included a fondness for a certain man named Asa. The sentiment was returned, something that made Melusine think that the English weren't bad after all.

Astonishing how one's opinion could change in the face of a new love.

The only thing that wasn't dramatic, however, was the relationship between Curtis and Elle, and Elle ruled Brython with an iron fist. It had taken her some time to know, exactly, where and whom to rule, but she was getting the hang of it. The army was no longer her concern, but her husband's, leaving the keep and the kitchens to Elle.

She was learning every single day.

And that included this dance lesson. But Douglas wasn't cooperating very well, virtually ignoring Myles, so she stepped up and clapped her hands together quite loudly to stop the bickering the younger men were doing.

She looked straight at Douglas.

"You," she said imperiously. "Stop complaining and do as you are told. If you do not, it will ruin this dance, and I shall be very upset with you. Is that what you wish?"

Even Douglas knew not to cross paths with his brother's wife. "Nay, Ellie."

"What did you just call me?"

"I meant nay, *Lady* Leominster."

When they were in public as they were now, she wouldn't permit the younger knights or squires to address her informally. Douglas, conceited that he was, ignored that rule often, and the last time he'd done it, she'd discreetly stepped on his toe and nearly broken it. Therefore, he was more inclined to obey the rules these days. She smiled thinly.

"Good," she said. "I should hate to be cross with you, Douglas. You might come away missing an eye, and no woman wants to marry a one-eyed man."

Douglas knew she was jesting, but not by much. As Curtis and Myles struggled not to laugh, everyone settled back into their positions, facing one another. Myles began to clap his hands in rhythm.

"And now we go forth," he said loudly. "One, two, three, four. Left hand to left hand as you pass by one another. That's good. Turn around and go back the other way. Just like that. Douglas, put your hand up against Westley's or I'll send Lady Leominster over there to make sure that you do. Ah, good lad."

They were twirling and pairing off in a dance that was a

type of folk reel. It was the fourth dance that Myles and Curtis had taught Elle, because Myles in particular liked to dance. The man was virtually humorless, harsh most of the time, and a knight to the bone, but he had a secret love of dancing and was a good teacher. As long as no one complimented him, he was willing to do it. But the second someone mentioned dance to him, he'd stiffen up and refuse to discuss it because dancing was only for women.

So Myles said.

"Why must we do this?" Douglas muttered unhappily. "You can teach the dance without all of us present. Why must we dance?"

Myles was still clapping rhythmically. "Because your brother's dear wife has never danced in a group before, and we are helping her learn," he said. "Stop complaining and just dance."

"Do it, Douglas," Westley snapped at him. "And stop stepping on my feet!"

In response, Douglas stomped on his foot, throwing Westley off balance. Howling in pain, he stumbled into Andrew, who bumped into Asa. Asa had hold of Melusine, and she went stumbling sideways. Once Asa righted her and made sure she was well, he turned to Douglas and began balling his fists.

"You did that on purpose," he growled, heading in Douglas' direction. "I'll make sure you don't do it again."

Myles and Hugo were suddenly between them, pushing them away from one another. "Asa, you must control your temper," Myles said. "Not everything is an invitation to fight."

Asa was furious. He'd never been very good at keeping his composure, even as a child. He'd gone from a red-headed hooligan to an auburn-haired warrior who loved a good fight and always wanted to be in the middle of one. But he wasn't stupid—he knew brawling with a younger de Lohr son wouldn't exactly be a good thing. He didn't want to be sent back to Ludlow and to Peter and his sister. He was rather coming to like being at Brython and the excitement of a coveted Welsh castle.

Melusine was an added attraction.

In fact, Melusine went to him and pulled him back over to where they had been dancing as Myles went over to Douglas and Westley.

"If you two shite-brains do not stop acting the fool, Curtis is going to send one of you or both of you back to Papa," Myles said sternly. "And if he does, Mama will get a hold of you and life as you know it will be at an end. Douglas, stop being so difficult. You are causing problems when there should not be any. Were you this difficult for Summerlin?"

Douglas was frustrated, but he didn't want to display it too much to Myles or the man might punish him. "Of course not," he said. "I simply do not want to dance with my brother. Why is that so difficult to believe?"

"Wait," Elle said, entering the conversation. She held up a hand to Myles to silence him before addressing Douglas directly. "Douglas, you are helping me out of the goodness of your heart. I did not foster in a fine home like you did. I do not know these dances that Myles has been so kind to teach me. Curt has arranged for a great feast in a few days, and I am trying not to look like a fool in front of de Lohr friends and allies. Can you not help me with this? Is it so hard to do your brother's wife such a great favor?"

Douglas wasn't exactly contrite. "Nay, Lady Leominster."

Elle sighed heavily at his reluctant attitude. "Curt is trying to do something good here," she said. "He is introducing me to your allies, and we are to have a great party with many lovely young women for you to dance with, but I need your help if I am not to look foolish. I have never danced in my life because I did not have the education that you did. Now, when I need your help to make your family proud, all you want to do is complain and step on Westley's feet. Is that kind of you?"

Douglas shook his head. "It is not."

"Is it noble of you?"

"Nay."

"Then if you want to be a noble knight, the beginnings of such a thing start here," she said. "Be kind to your little brother. You may need him someday."

Douglas looked at Westley, who simply shrugged, before nodding his head in resignation.

"As you wish, Lady Leominster," he said. "Do I still have to keep calling you that? Why can't I call you Ellie?"

"You will call me what I say you'll call me."

Douglas rolled his eyes, knowing it was a punishment for the fact that he was being difficult. Elle waved her hand at him.

"Now, back up," she said. "Get into position. We must do this one more time before I go into the village to collect my new garment and shoes."

Everyone moved back into position, including Douglas. Myles got out of the way and began clapping again, a steady rhythm, as he alternately sang the tune and called out the movements. Everyone moved to and fro, changing partners at one point, before going back to the original partner and forming a circle. Everyone in the circle held hands, moving one direction and then the other. As Myles shouted at Westley for accidentally tripping Andrew, Elle and Curtis finished their dance quite smoothly. When the dance ended and they bowed and curtsied to one another, Curtis took Elle in his arms and kissed her.

"Well done, my lady," he said. "You are a natural dancer."

Elle was flushed with exertion and praise. "I hope so," she said. "I should like to do it well in front of your friends and allies. I do not want anyone going away saying you married a woman with the grace of a goat."

Curtis chuckled. "They would never say that," he said. "They fear me too much."

"Even if it's true?"

"Especially if it's true."

They shared a laugh as Westley, Douglas, and Andrew approached them. "Can we go into town with you?" Westley asked eagerly. "All of us?"

Curtis looked at the young men gazing back at him in various stages of hopefulness. The past several weeks with the trio had been exhausting, but not in an entirely bad way. Curtis found himself basically raising his younger brothers and cousin, young men who very much wanted to be great knights. Their competitiveness with each other was truly something to behold, and Curtis was starting to think that his father dumped the boys on him, much as he had dumped Amaro, because he simply didn't want to deal with them. Curtis had the patience of Job, so he was the most likely candidate to deal with women-hungry Douglas and Andrew, and then simply hungry-all-the-time Westley.

The lad ate more than Elle did, and that was saying something.

As the three young men turned their begging to Elle, Curtis simply stood back and enjoyed the view. And what a view it had been for the past eight weeks. He had watched a skinny, dirty, angry young woman transform into something angelic in every way. Weeks of good food and constant eating had put meat on her bones and filled her out in ways that made Curtis lust after her every minute of every day. Although it had taken some patience on his part, gone were her days of aggression and hopelessness. These days, she was warm and loving, firm and sometimes even stern, but she was never unfair.

And he had fallen quite deeply in love with her.

Curtis still hadn't told her that, however, because speaking of emotion tended to embarrass or confuse her. He was still trying to bring her out of the world she had grown up in, where desolation and apathy was commonplace, but it had been difficult to shake. She wasn't used to a world where people were nice and spoke of their feelings, especially when it came to love, so Curtis was still trying to ease her into a world where he wanted to tell her every day how much she loved her. Even if he couldn't yet, he was fairly certain she loved him in return.

Although she wouldn't say the words, he could see it in her actions every single day. He could feel it in her touch every single night. Elle seemed to be more of an action woman than a woman of empty words, so he took heart in her actions. Her very loving and sometimes sweet actions.

But he gave it back to her in return, tenfold. These dance lessons were part of that. He had arranged for a great feast to introduce her to his allies, and she was desperate to make a good impression. That included many things, not the least of which was learning dances that were taught to every young noble person in England. Myles had been teaching dance classes nearly every day for the past couple of weeks. Elle and Melusine had been very eager to learn, but the trick had been to convince the other young men to dance along with the women so they could see how the dance worked. Frankly, Curtis had been surprised that Douglas and Westley had lasted this long dancing with each other, but the truth was that they loved Elle, too. In spite of their pettiness, they really did want to help her.

Now, those same young men were gently badgering her into letting them accompany her to the village of Rhayader. That was the village where she had visited the apothecary for the potion that had allowed her to put her brother in the vault. Curtis had been to the village three or four times, when he could get away from his duties and accompany his wife, and in the times he'd been there with her, he could see how much the villagers loved her. They all knew her, and when she'd introduced Curtis as her new husband and Lord of Brython, the acceptance went better than he'd hoped. Elle had made it easier for him, something he had appreciated. In fact, the past eight weeks had gone far smoother with her than anything he could have hoped for or imagined.

It was like something out of a dream.

"You can go," he finally said, pushing the boys away from Elle because he was weary of their begging. "Go and have the horses prepared and we'll join you in the bailey."

The three of them tore out of the hall, nearly slipping on a section of floor that was being cleaned near the entry. Hugo followed, heading out to complete his duties, but Myles and Asa remained behind.

"You're truly going to take that lot to town?" Myles asked, shaking his head. "You're a brave man."

Curtis grinned. "They behave for Ellie," he said. "She must remind them of Mama, because they respond to her much like they respond to our mother. There will be no trouble."

Myles shook his head. "As I said, you are brave." He noted Melusine over with Elle in conversation. "Are you taking

Melly?"

Curtis nodded. "Probably," he said, noting Asa standing a few feet away. He addressed the man. "Do you want to go, too?"

Asa's face lit up. "May I?"

"Go get your horse," Curtis said. "And have the carriage prepared for my wife and Melly."

Asa dashed off, leaving Curtis and Myles smirking at one another. "You know he wants to marry her," Myles muttered. "Has he said anything to you about it?"

Curtis shook his head. "He hasn't," he said. "But how is that going to work?"

"What do you mean?"

"He still practices his Jewish religion. Melly is not Jewish."

Myles shrugged. "Then she'll have to convert," he said. "Liora did when she married Peter."

"But Peter was a knight," Curtis said. "He had a good deal to lose if he converted. It made sense for Liora to convert instead."

Myles shook his head. "I know," he said. "But if Asa converts, Papa will probably knight him. That should be worth something to him."

"Or maybe he simply wants to stay true to his Jewish religion. That must be his choice."

Myles shrugged and began to pull his gloves out from where they had been tucked into his belt. "I suppose we shall see," he said, pulling on a glove. "Now, what else do you need me to do for this chaotic orgy you are about to have in a few days? I told you that I would help, and I will."

Curtis laughed softly. "I want you to make sure that all escorts and horses and men of our guests are well tended," he said. "Keep houses that are not friendly with one another at a distance from each other. Not all of our allies are allied with each other, if you know what I mean."

Myles nodded. "I do, indeed," he said. "I will handle the guests and their escorts. But you will do something for me."

"What is that?"

Myles pointed at Elle. "Where is your wife going right now?"

Curtis glanced at Elle as she and Melusine conversed. "To fetch two garments she had the seamstress in Rhayader make for her," he said. "Why?"

Myles tried not to look too embarrassed. "Have her go to a merchant who carries perfumes," he said. "Have her find a perfume for a man that women would like to smell."

Curtis frowned. "For whom?"

"For me!"

Curtis' eyebrows flew up. "Since when do you want to smell good? For a woman, no less?"

Thoroughly embarrassed, Myles stomped away from him and out of the hall, leaving Curtis chuckling at his younger brother who would rather die than give any woman a bit of his attention. Now, he evidently wanted to smell good for the unmarried females who would be attending Brython's feast.

Shaking his head, Curtis went to his wife.

"Let us depart, my love," he said, taking her by the arm. But then he paused. "As long as you are feeling up to it. I should have asked you that before."

He was referring to the fact that she'd had a tender belly the past few days, but she shook her head at him. "I feel well enough," she said. "Not to worry. I am eager to collect my new clothing, so a sour stomach will not stop me."

He didn't think so, but he'd felt that he had to ask. "If you say so," he said. "But let us move quickly. I want to return home before sunset."

As he pulled her along, Elle grabbed hold of Melusine. "Come along," she said to her cousin. "Mayhap we can visit the merchant who carries all manner of trade goods and find a lovely scarf for you to match your new gown."

Melusine turned bright red, eyeing Curtis as they exited the great hall, out into the sunshine of a new morning. "I... I do not need a scarf," she said. "The new dress was quite enough. I do not need anything more."

As Curtis began shouting to Douglas and Andrew and Westley, who were helping prepare the horses, Elle turned her attention to her red-faced cousin. She knew why the woman was so reluctant to accept a scarf. It was for the same reason that Elle had refused, for weeks, to let Curtis purchase anything for her until he finally convinced her to relent. For women who had never had proper clothing, or any money to buy it, a new husband with a good deal of wealth was something of a bewilderment. Curtis was more than happy to spend money on his wife and even his wife's cousin, although they still continued to resist. Melusine did it more than Elle did, but the truth was that they were uncomfortable having someone spend money on them.

Curtis was trying his best to change that.

Even eight weeks later, it was still baby steps for them all.

Out in the bailey of Brython, the ladies stood together while Curtis and his men formed the escort. The castle itself had gone through a transformation over the past eight weeks that included repairing walls, fixing the portcullis in the gatehouse, and transforming the keep from something no better than a stable to something that was genuinely warm and comfortable to live in.

Brython had a big, square keep that was six stories tall, including the vault underneath it. There were two storage levels, the sub-level and the ground floor, and then the entry level and the three stories above it that were the living quarters. The first level had two rather large rooms that served as reception rooms, and the next level up had three smaller chambers where Myles, Douglas, Westley, and Andrew slept. The next floor after that had three chambers also, and that was where Melusine slept. The top floor was two chambers again, and both of those were reserved for Curtis and Elle. One chamber was where they slept and the other contained their personal possessions, like clothing and Curtis' weaponry. There was even a table there with two chairs where they sometimes took in their morning meal, just the two of them.

Elle could reflect honestly on her life before Curtis, but back in the days when they first met, she had made Brython sound as if it meant something to her. Perhaps it had because it was all she had, but the following weeks with Curtis had shown her just how desolate and depressing a place it had been. Even now, as she stood in the bailey with Melusine, she could see how much life at the castle had changed. Everything was well organized, the men seemed busy and content, but most of all, there was no hatred.

That was probably the strangest thing of all. Brython was no longer a place filled with hate. Elle had spent years with men whose only focus in life seemed to be hating the English, but the English soldiers that were now in charge of the castle never made any mention of animosity toward the Welsh. It was a completely different atmosphere, and one that had confused her at first, but one she gradually came to appreciate. Certainly, there was a sense of readiness in case they were attacked, but there wasn't the tension and the angst that she was so used to.

Strange days, indeed.

Elle wasn't sure if Curtis' life had changed that much, but hers certainly had. She was no longer expected to fight, but she had clearly defined duties. She was in charge of the keep, the kitchens, and the kitchen yard, but she really didn't know much about them. Melusine knew more, but Curtis and his brothers had taken it upon themselves to teach her what they knew about managing a house and hold.

Along with the dance lessons she had so recently been given, there was a time when Curtis had given her lessons on managing the home. Lessons on keeping track of the stores and on keeping track of costs. Luckily, Elle had received an education in mathematics, so she knew how to do her sums, and it was something she enjoyed. She learned very quickly, and soon, lessons moved away from the kitchens and to the keep itself.

That was a little more complex because there were certain protocols when dealing with the keep. For example, unmarried men and unmarried women could never be housed on the same floor. Many castles had separate bachelors' quarters for unmarried male visitors or unmarried knights, but Brython had no such quarters. That meant the de Lohr brothers were housed in the keep along with Melusine, but none except for Westley were allowed above the first floor.

The only reason Westley was allowed was because he was Curtis' squire, and also because he had only seen fourteen years and wasn't considered much of a threat, to his great consternation. Douglas and Andrew and Myles were kept on the first floor, while Asa was assigned a bed with the army. There was a troop house, a small one, that slept about one hundred of the thousand men that Christopher had left behind, and Asa had taken a bed with them. He wasn't a knight, but he wasn't exactly close family, either. The rest of the army had tents pitched near the stable yard or slept in the armory or any number of other outbuildings. Curtis was thinking about building a second troop house, but there was so much repair work going on with the walls that he hadn't yet begun that project.

In all, Brython was a little crowded these days, because there were far more men within the walls than the Welsh ever had, but they worked well together and were very organized thanks to Curtis and his brothers.

These were good days, as far as Elle was concerned, with this day being a pleasant one in a long line of days that had been equally so. She was looking forward to her journey into Rhayader, a town she'd traveled to many times before, but it was different nowadays when Curtis traveled with her. Of course, she knew almost everyone in the village—the merchants, the bakers, the men who ran liveries—because at one time or another, she'd had to deal with them. Elle was very good at bartering, and she was fortunate that she'd never made enemies out of those she did business with. They'd known her to be from Brython Castle or from Tywyl Castle before that, and everyone knew that the castles, and the family of Gwenwynwyn ap Owain, had no real money to speak of. But they also believed Gwenwynwyn's armies were fighting a righteous battle against the English, so no one much minded when Elle came to barter for food or material.

But that changed when the English came.

Now, Elle went into town with her head held high because she could pay for the things she needed. She'd even paid the leatherworker extra because there had been times when he gave help to the garrison at Brython without cost, and Elle wasn't beyond paying him for his generosity now that she had the money. The truth was that she was loved in the village, and as she and Melusine climbed into the cab of the fortified de Lohr carriage, lined with iron like a cage and with wooden sides painted blue and yellow, she could only feel contentment and pride.

Funny how life was sometimes.

The enemy was now her savior.

Curtis rode his big warhorse next to the carriage as they headed out onto the road. When they traveled into town, they usually brought at least fifty men with them, men who rode in front and in back of the escort. They also traveled on the sides of the roads and through the trees to ensure there weren't any ambushes or outlaws waiting for them.

The weather was turning colder, and the leaves were starting to turn colors as the autumn season was upon them. Dressed in a new green garment she'd got from the seamstress in town several days ago, Elle wore her husband's cloak because she didn't have one of her own yet. That was one of the things they were supposed to collect today from the leatherworker, along with the slippers he had worked on for her. With her blonde hair braided and wrapped around the back of her head, she and Melusine were enjoying the weather and the trip.

Melusine, in fact, was positively giddy.

"Asa says that he wishes to buy me a gift," she said, clutching Elle's hand. "He's very rich, you know. His father was a jeweler to King John."

Elle nodded. "I know," she said. "Curtis told me. But... Melly... you are not thinking of accepting a gift from him, are you?"

Melusine was indignant. "Why not?" she said. "He wants to spend money on me, so I will let him. He is showing his affection for me."

Elle shook her head. "You fuss when Curtis suggests you buy an article of clothing you need, yet you will freely let Asa spend money on you?"

Melusine frowned. "But he wants to," she said. "Curtis is your husband, and he should only spend money on you and not me. But Asa... he *wants* to."

Elle could see she wasn't going to get anywhere with her, so she simply looked away to the passing greenery around them. "Do not be greedy," she said. "Asa is doing it because he likes you."

"He wants to marry me, I know it."

"But he is Jewish," Elle reminded her. "I've heard Curt and Peter speaking on it. It will not make for an easy marriage for you."

"Why not?"

"Because he is not Christian."

Melusine's eyebrows rose. "And you do not approve?"

Elle shook her head. "I did not mean that," she said. "I like Asa. He is humorous and kind. But he worships differently. He is from a people who are not viewed the same as the Christians are. That is all I am saying. You are not part of his world, and his people may not accept you so easily, either."

Melusine sighed, turning her attention to the window, too. "I know," she said. "I know you like him. We all like him. You have married a *Saesneg*, and I am fond of an *Iddew*. But what does it matter so long as we love them?"

Elle thought on that statement. *What does it matter so long as we love them?* She could see Curtis outside her window, riding strong and proud. Her heart fluttered every time she looked at the man, every time he kissed her, and every other time in between if he was on her mind. Which was constantly. That flutter had started from the day of their wedding and only grown worse. Now, it was full-blown giddiness when he was around her, and it was all she could do to keep from swooning sometimes.

And he belonged to her.

Did she love him? Of course she did. She couldn't remember when she hadn't. But in her world, speaking of things like love and emotion simply weren't done. No one had ever loved her, and she'd never loved anyone, not even her grandmother. It was difficult to grow attached to an old woman who was bitter and never had a kind word. Elle had spent many years trying to please someone who would never be pleased. Could she speak of love to her? Of course not.

Could she speak of love to Curtis?

What if the feeling wasn't mutual?

He was sweet to her. So very sweet. He called her "love" and "my love" from time to time, but she was sure it was simply a term of endearment and nothing more. If he truly loved her, why hadn't he simply come out and told her? Nay, she couldn't risk telling the man she loved him only to be rejected in turn. It was enough that they smiled at one another, that he would kiss her hard and often, and that they laughed together a good deal. That was the strange part. She'd spent a lifetime hardly laughing because there was nothing to laugh about, but with Curtis, smiles and laughter came so easily.

The man who had once been her enemy.

Now, he was her whole world.

The town of Rhayader came into view shortly, an idyllic little village surrounded by gently rolling hills. They passed through the outskirts, and the children, recognizing the de Lohr carriage because they'd seen it come to town the past few weeks, began to run alongside, begging for coins. The closer they drew to the town center, the more children joined in, until there was quite a pack following them. Elle looked to Curtis, smiling, and he took the hint. He always carried a sack of silver pennies with him, a smaller and less valuable denomination than the larger silver or gold coins. Digging into a purse that was fastened to his saddle on the inside of his left thigh, he came away with a small handful of the pennies and tossed them onto the side of the road.

A cheer went up from the children as they rushed to the scattering of silver coins very excitedly, and Elle and Melusine watched with smiles on their faces. The area they were in was fairly rural and poor except for a few bustling businesses in the heart of the village. It was one of the largest villages in the Welsh midlands, surrounded by farmland and mountains to the north. In the winter, it was cold and snowy here, and in the summer, it was green and mild.

The escort from Brython was heading to the heart of the village, where there was a big stone well in the center and a pool from which women would draw water. There was also a big stone cross on one end of the pool signifying St. Nicholas, the patron saint of children and merchants, among others. Curtis brought the escort into the center of the village and called a halt, putting Asa in command of the men. Douglas, Andrew, and Westley immediately begged to go to the stall of a woman who sold sweets, and also to the alley where the blacksmiths plied their trade, and Curtis sent them off with a stern warning to behave themselves. As they rushed off, he went to remove Elle and Melusine from the carriage. Once Elle stepped out of the fortified cab, she began to sniff the air.

"Smell it?" she said. "Fresh bread. And pie. I smell pies."

Curtis knew what that meant. They had to find food. He was rather surprised, because Elle hadn't been feeling well lately, not too inclined to eat like she usually did, but he would happily take her where she wanted to go. Melusine didn't particularly want to go along because Asa was staying with the men, so Curtis took his wife's hand and led her away, following the smells of the bakers. Elle held his big hand with both of hers as they crossed the square toward the bakers' alley.

"Well?" Curtis said. "What will it be today? More bread? Mayhap the meat pies?"

Elle nodded. "All of that, please."

He grinned. "What else?" he said. "What about the woman who makes those little cakes you like with the honey and cloves?"

"Those, too," she said. "Though I am going to have to stop eating so much. My clothes will not fit me if I do not stop."

He looked at her, noting her curvy figure with generous hips, slender waist, and full breasts. "Lass, you do *not* have to stop eating," he said seductively. "I like you just the way you are, and you know it."

She looked at him, knowing exactly what was on his mind. It was on it every day, and when they retired every evening, he let her know just how much he loved the body she had developed. But it went both ways—she'd learned to crave him as well, even catching him out in a lesser-known outbuilding once and initiating what had been quite a passionate rendezvous. He still talked about it. But as he waggled his eyebrows at her, she put her fingers to his lips to silence him.

"Hush," she said, looking around. "You'll not titillate me when there's nothing we can do about it."

He laughed low. "Apologies," he said. "But the truth is that I cannot help it."

"You'd better help it or you'll make us both miserable."

"Why?"

"Because we cannot do anything about it."

He shrugged. "True," he said. "But speaking of miserable, are you feeling better this morning?"

She shrugged. "A little," she said. "I do not know why I've not been feeling well the past few days, but I feel better today. I'll feel even better once I've eaten."

"You still do not think that I need to summon a physic?"

"For what?" she asked as if it was a ridiculous suggestion. "There is nothing wrong with me. It would be a waste of money."

He simply squeezed her hand, looking ahead to the bakers' alley. There were four bakers on a small courtyard and two enormous ovens between them, going at full speed this morning. Smoke from the oven fires was blasting into the sky as the bakers worked the ovens and their stalls. Elle knew which stall she wanted, and she headed off to her right, straight into a stall where a husband and wife made braided bread with milk and honey, tarts with quince or raisins, and little cakes with oats and apples and cinnamon. Those were her favorite.

And the bakers knew it. They saw her coming in and were already pulling out the honey bread and the oatcakes. They put everything into a basket for her, and she took it gleefully while Curtis paid them well. When she wouldn't share with him, the husband gave Curtis one of the oatcakes, and he took it appreciatively. He followed Elle out into the courtyard, where there were benches beneath an enormous yew tree, and as she sat down, he shoved the oatcake into his mouth for fear he would have to hand it over to her when she realized he had it.

"What more do you wish, my love?" he asked, mouth full. "I can see if the baker on the corner has any baked eggs left."

Elle was already tearing into the honey bread. "I would like that," she said, shoving the soft inside of the bread into her mouth. "Is it wicked of me not to want to share this with Melly?"

"Nay, it is not wicked."

"She can procure her own, can't she?"

"She can," he said. "Asa can buy it for her. Moreover, you do not even share with me. If you feel wicked about something, let it be about that."

She gave him a naughty little grin, one that had him smiling back. He swallowed the bite in his mouth, patting her on the head as he headed in the direction of the baker who sometimes had baked eggs with cream and cheese. He didn't do it often, so Curtis didn't have high hopes as he entered the stall. He asked the man about the eggs and was delighted to be told that there was some left. Curtis purchased all of it, wolfing down about half before his wife saw it because once she had it in her hands, the chances of him getting anything were slim.

As he'd said, she wasn't apt to share.

Therefore, he was trying not to look like he was licking his lips when he brought the eggs back to her. The branches above were blowing gently in the breeze as he handed her the eggs, set in a bowl made of dried, woven grass. Elle was thrilled for the eggs and began eating them with gusto as Curtis looked around to the other bakers to see what they had to offer. One baker seemed to have two pieces of bread, very large pieces, with some kind of meat in between them. He turned to Elle to ask if she wanted some of it, only to see that she had vomited on the tree trunk.

Quickly, he picked up the bread and the remaining eggs from her lap as she struggled not to vomit again.

"I'm sorry, love," he said, brushing tendrils of hair away from her face so she wouldn't soil them. "What happened?"

Elle had the back of her hand to her mouth, eyes closed as she struggled not to vomit again. "I do not know," she said breathlessly. "I thought if I ate, I would feel better. Everything was fine, and then... it just came back up."

Curtis was sympathetic, grasping her arm and helping her to stand so she wouldn't get any vomit on her skirt. "That settles it," he said. "I'm going to find a physic. Is there one in the village?"

She nodded weakly. "The apothecary is also the physic," she said. "Mayhap... mayhap he has a potion to help. I suppose I am not beyond seeking something to settle my stomach."

"We shall go and see him."

Elle was upset about the wasted food. "Look at this mess," she said sadly. "I must have eaten something that had gone bad and not realized it. Now, the poison will not leave me. It is the only explanation."

Curtis had his arm around her as he walked her out of the courtyard. "That is probably all it is."

Elle felt horrible. Hand resting on her tender belly, she allowed Curtis to lead her out onto the main avenue. He took her over to the well, and although it was considered unsafe by some to drink water that had not been boiled, the well of Rhayader had its own cup next to the spring that popped up straight from the ground. Elle had drunk from it a hundred times in the past. Curtis filled the small metal cup with water straight from the spout and gave it to her, and she drank gratefully.

But she still didn't feel any better.

As she sat on the stone well, waiting for her belly to settle, Melusine caught sight of her. She rushed to Elle's side, and the situation became a conversation between Melusine and Curtis, both expressing concern that Elle was feeling poorly. Meanwhile, Elle was becoming increasingly upset that they were fussing over her. Melusine, in particular, was convinced Elle had a deadly disease, to the point where Curtis sent her back to the escort and told her to wait there. He could see that Elle was about to throttle the woman. When he was convinced that Elle wasn't going to vomit again, he took her down the street, to the lair of the apothecary.

It was most definitely a lair.

A deep, dark, and mysterious place with a wooden panel over the door that had an eye on it. Just an eye. Curtis had been here before, twice, because his wife liked to talk to the apothecary and peruse the ointments he had for softening the skin of her hands, which tended to dry and crack. She'd never really been able to afford anything in his shop before, other than the sleeping potion she'd once purchased for Gruffydd, but now that she had a nearly endless supply of coin, this was her favorite place.

The apothecary's name was Pliny.

He was a rather odd fellow, tall and thin, with stringy snow-white hair, that flowed past his shoulders. He wore black robes that smelled strangely. He was bent over a table when Elle and Curtis entered the shop, and his narrow face lit up at the sight of what was now his best customer.

He went to greet them.

"Lady Leominster," he said, using her formal title. "It is pleasant to see you again. You have brought your strong husband with you, I see."

Elle nodded. "I have," she said. "He has insisted that I see you. I told him that you are a physic, and—"

Pliny cut her off. "I am, I am," he said quickly. "I trained as a physic but found my calling to be experiments and discovery."

Elle smiled weakly. "I have not been feeling well over the past several days," she said hesitantly. "My belly has been... uneasy. I'm wondering if you have a tonic for it."

Pliny swept his hand toward a door at the rear of the cottage. "Let us go somewhere that we may speak in private," he said. Then he waved at Curtis. "You will come, too, my lord."

He was walking into the adjoining chamber as Elle and Curtis followed. The ceiling of the cottage sloped, so by the time they reached the smaller chamber, Curtis was in danger of hitting his head. As he tried to duck the beams on the ceiling, Elle explained her predicament.

"Can't you simply give me something to settle my stomach?" she asked. "I fear I ate something that must have gone bad and I did not realize it."

The small chamber had a few chairs and an enormous wardrobe in it. Pliny indicated for Elle to sit on one of the chairs.

"Let us make sure that is all it is," he said. "It is wise to know what your symptoms are before giving you a potion that may not help, is it not?"

Elle looked anxiously at Curtis, who nodded his head. "It is," he said. "It started several days ago. She feels sick during the day, but mostly in the mornings. Right now, she ate some bread and it came back up again."

Pliny looked between the pair thoughtfully. "No fever?"

"No fever."

"Any swooning or spells of bad temper?"

Curtis lifted his eyebrows as he looked at Elle. "No swooning," he said. "But the bad temper... We *are* speaking of Elle, after all."

He was teasing her, and she sneered at him as Pliny fought off a grin. "You and your wife have not been married long, have you?"

Curtis shook his head. "You would know that," he said, a knowing twinkle in his eye. "Everyone in this village knows that. We've only been married two months."

"Since the siege at Brython Castle," Pliny said.

"Exactly. It is no secret."

Pliny shrugged, looking back to Elle. "My lady, I must ask you some questions, and you will answer me truthfully."

Elle was growing increasingly anxious about the situation. "Why?" she said. "Do you think something is terribly wrong with me?"

"I will not know that until I have answers to my questions," Pliny said. "My questions will be uncomfortable."

Elle's eyes widened, and she looked to Curtis, who took her hand and nodded patiently. "If it will help you, let him ask," he said softly.

Fearful, Elle looked at Pliny. "Very well," she said reluctantly. "What questions?"

"When was the first time you had marital relations with your husband?" Pliny asked.

That wasn't a question Elle had expected, and she gasped in

outrage, shooting up from the chair. "That is a terrible question to ask!" she said. "Why would you ask such things?"

"Because I am trying to figure out why your belly began to hurt a few days ago," Pliny said patiently. "You did not feel ill before then?"

"I did not," Elle said, still agitated. "I was well. I *am* well."

"Of course you are," Pliny said, though it was tinged with sarcasm. "That is why you are here. If you do not answer my questions, I cannot help you."

Elle was fully prepared to blast the man, but she caught sight of Curtis' expression. He suddenly had the strangest look in his eye. There was softness and warmth there. Perhaps even joy. She had no idea why he was looking at her like that, but she was upset about the entire situation, worse now that he didn't seem to be protecting her from Pliny's invasive questions.

"What else do you want to know?" she said angrily. "It had better not be something vulgar!"

"You have not answered my first question yet."

Elle was gearing up for a sharp retort when Curtis squeezed her hand and pulled her into a one-armed embrace, kissing her on the forehead.

"I will answer it," he said, sounding oddly hoarse. "Aye, it was the first time we had marital relations."

Pliny could see that Curtis was more open to answering personal questions, so he turned to him. He could also see that Curtis might even understand *why* he was asking such questions.

He had a reason.

"And I would assume it was not the last time?" he said.

Curtis shook his head slowly. "Nay."

Pliny nodded. "Of course not," he said. "You are both

young and strong and virile. It is natural. But you understand that your actions will have results, as God has intended."

Curtis fought off a smile. "I do," he said. "Do you think that's what it is?"

Pliny shrugged. "That would be my guess," he said. "Does she eat a great deal?"

"Like a horse."

"And she will relieve herself quite frequently?"

Curtis nodded. "During the night, aye," he said. "We do not spend our days together, at least not for hours on end, so I would not know, but I would imagine so."

"And her body," Pliny said, gesturing to his chest. "Are they sore to the touch?"

Curtis knew what he meant. "Now that you mention it, they do seem to be more sensitive," he said. "They have grown larger, in fact, but I thought it was all of the eating she has been doing."

Elle, who had been watching the exchange with great puzzlement, interrupted them. "What are you speaking of?" she asked Curtis. "What does it all mean?"

Curtis was smiling when he looked at her, and Elle swore she saw tears glistening in his eyes. "I am older than many of my siblings, as you know," he said. "I saw my mother go through this very same thing several times, most recently with my youngest sister about twelve years ago. My mother ate a great deal, was sick on occasion, was moodier than usual. I do not know why I did not suspect the same thing with you."

Elle wasn't following him. "Suspect what?"

"A baby."

She stared at him as if she had no real concept of what he'd just said. But when she processed his words, and his meaning, her eyes widened to epic proportions. "A… a *what*?" she gasped. "You cannot mean…!"

"Why not?" He grinned. "As the apothecary says, we're young and virile. It's natural. And it is not as if we show any restraint. It's very simple—you're going to have a baby, my love. *Our* baby."

Elle was so astonished that he could have knocked her over with a feather. In fact, she plopped back onto the chair, dazed, before bursting into tears. As Pliny made himself scarce, Curtis sat down next to her and put his arms around her. As he laughed softly, she wept copiously.

"A… a baby?" she sobbed.

He held her tightly. "Aye," he murmured. "A baby. Are you not pleased?"

She was gasping and sobbing dramatically, something he found hilarious. "But I cannot be! I'm barren! Cadwalader told everyone I was barren!"

Curtis chuckled. "He lied," he said flatly. "He lied to cover up the fact that he was an old man incapable of impregnating his wife. Clearly, my dearest, you are *not* barren."

She continued to weep dramatically, and he grinned through the entire thing. It was like music to his ears. But as suddenly as the hysterics happened, they stopped as she pulled back to look at him with big, watery eyes.

"Are you happy?" she said, sniffling. "Does this please you, Curt?"

He cupped her face between his two enormous hands, kissing her gently. "I have never been happier about anything in my entire life."

"Are you certain?"

"Of course I am," he said, gazing into those bright eyes.

"But I must tell you something."

"What?"

"I love you very much."

The hysterics came again as she threw her arms around his neck and wept as if he'd just broken her heart. Or made her the happiest woman alive. It was difficult to tell with Elle, because she could be dramatic at the best of times. He let her cry for a few moments before pulling back and forcing her to look at him.

"Have you nothing to say to me to that regard?" he said, his eyes glimmering with emotion. "Or am I to go through life only admired by my wife and nothing more?"

She shook her head, running her hand down his cheek as she gazed at him adoringly. "I've never had anyone tell me that they loved me," she whispered. "Not anyone. You are the first."

"It is not painful to say it," he said, kissing her fingers as they moved over his lips. "Try it."

She sniffled, a smile playing on her lips. "I… I love you."

"I love you, *Curt*."

"I know your name."

"Then use it."

She leaned into him, kissing his mouth gently. "I love you, Curt," she murmured against his lips. "In this life and beyond."

Her mouth claimed his again, strongly and passionately, as he wrapped her up in his powerful embrace. He could taste her salty tears on her lips. She ended up on his chair, on his lap, and probably would have remained there forever had Pliny not returned to the small chamber, making his way over to the big wardrobe against the wall and throwing open the doors.

"Ah!" he said. "Here it is!"

The spell was broken between Curtis and Elle as Pliny drew

forth a small sack and approached them.

"Here," he said, extending it to Elle. "This will help settle your stomach."

Elle stood up from Curtis' lap, peering into the canvas sack. "What it is?" she asked warily.

"Licorice root," Pliny said. "Chew on it when your stomach feels poorly. It should help."

"You have my thanks," Curtis said. "Is there anything else she can do to help?"

Pliny shrugged. "She must not eat big meals," he said. "I would suggest she eat a little, but eat frequently. Bread, apples, things like that. Broth is good, but nothing too heavy. The sickness should pass in a while."

Curtis couldn't stop smiling. He took Elle's hand and kissed it before turning for the door. "You have helped us solve a great mystery," he said to Pliny. "Would it be too much to ask you to find a good midwife? I should like my wife to have the best of care."

Pliny nodded. "My sister is an excellent midwife," he said. "I will send her to you in a few days to see to your wife. Congratulations, my lord. May Lady Leominster bear you many strong sons."

Curtis grinned, removing a coin from his purse and handing it off to Pliny as he and Elle headed for the exit. They still had garments to collect from the seamstress and shoes to fetch from the leatherworker, but at the moment, he couldn't think of anything but the woman at his side and the fact that she was going to bear his child.

His son.

Funny how a journey into town turned out to be one of the better days of his life.

CHAPTER FOURTEEN

Lioncross Abbey Castle

H E WAS RELEGATED to the wall.

That was all Amaro was doing these days. Stripped of any responsibility the moment he departed Brython Castle with Lord Hereford's army, he'd been ignored and demoted, and these days he was consigned to watching the wall. He wasn't even in command of the gatehouse, as that was left to a knight who was as old as Methuselah, a Teutonic knight by the name of Jeffrey Kessler. He had been at Lioncross Abbey during the days of Lady Hereford's father, and a meaner man had never existed.

Even Amaro had a healthy respect for him.

In fact, he'd been put under Kessler's command, and the old knight kept track of Amaro every hour of every day. He watched him like a hawk. It wasn't something that had gone unnoticed by the de Lohr soldiers, who tended to shy away from Amaro because of it. No one wanted to befriend a knight who was managed by Kessler, because he was the one who always handled the men who were down to their last chance with Hereford. Men who were difficult or unruly, disobedient, or plain stupid. When Jeffery Kessler stepped in, that meant there was a problem.

Amaro knew it.

He was well aware that the incident back at Brython Castle had nearly seen him sacked. Hereford had made that clear. Out of respect to Amaro's father, however, Hereford wasn't going to send him home in shame. At least, not yet. He was giving him a chance to behave himself and to realize the world didn't revolve around him and his petty wants. Women were to be treated kindly and orders were meant to be obeyed. He wasn't permitted to make his own decisions and would leave any and all decisions up to Kessler. Amaro couldn't even take a piss without permission.

And the resentment was building.

It had been since departing Brython. Resentment toward the Welsh and the two Welshwomen in particular. Miasma, or Melusine, had caused his problems. Of that, he was convinced. But it was Lady Leominster he had a particular hatred for. She had struck him, and when he struck her in return, as any man would have, he was punished for it.

She was the one.

And he would have his revenge.

Almost two months after the fall of Brython, Curtis was holding a great feast in honor of his new wife and new command. Amaro had been at the gatehouse when the missive arrived, and he had been charged with taking it to Hereford, who had been in the keep of Lioncross, in his solar. Amaro had stepped into the grand keep, grander than any he'd ever seen, knowing that this was where he belonged, but as soon as he delivered the missive, he'd been ordered out by Lady Hereford.

Another bitch trying to tell him what to do.

But she hadn't ordered him out before Hereford read the missive and announced with some glee that Curtis was having a feast to celebrate his new command. That seemed to make everyone happy, including the younger de Lohrs. Amaro was fairly certain he would not be asked to escort the family to Brython, but that didn't matter. A feast would mean lots of people, and an open castle for the most part.

It would be a simple thing for him to slip in and exact his revenge.

That was where his plan was hatched.

He'd been spending weeks trying to figure out how to punish those two Welshwomen and the entire House of de Lohr besides. All of them deserved his vengeance, and it was something that grew in his heart like mold, clinging to everything, covering everything, turning anything it touched rancid. That was what kind of a heart he had these days.

Rancid.

It was a day-and-a-half ride to Brython, less if a man traveled swiftly enough. The only time Kessler left Amaro alone was at night when he was sleeping. Kessler had his own chamber in the enormous keep of Lioncross Abbey when Amaro was demoted to the lower levels of the wall, where old vaults where located and where some soldiers had taken up habitation. He slept in the dark, where it was damp and moldering and smelled of death, but the blessing was that Kessler wouldn't come down there because his lungs were weak these days. The dampness made him cough. He was an old man who was going to die soon, Amaro hoped.

But it couldn't be soon enough for him.

The feast, however, was something to look forward to. He knew he would be left behind to maintain watch over the great border castle. The sad part of the situation was that he more than likely wouldn't even be in command. It would be some lesser knight from a lesser family, not the son of a great Aragon warlord. It had taken Amaro two months to realize that his career in England was finally finished. He needed to go home and assume his place at his father's side, and hopefully it wouldn't be too long until his father passed away, either.

Then the de Zaragosa empire would be his.

But first, there was something he had to do.

When Hereford and his family left for Brython for Curtis' great feast, that would be Amaro's last day at Lioncross Abbey. He would also go to Brython, following Hereford's tracks, and once he reached the castle, he would conceal himself and wait for the opportunity to exact his revenge upon Melusine and Lady Leominster.

Then he'd return to his father a very happy man.

The opportunity came quickly.

A week later, Amaro was part of the group of men who organized the escort for Hereford and his family to take to Brython. Everything was prepared the day before, from the fortified wagon that would take the de Lohr women to the provisions wagons that would go along for the escort of two hundred men. De Lohr never traveled light when his wife and daughters were with him, so Amaro did an excellent job with the wagons and the logistics, leaving Kessler to tell Hereford that Amaro had performed admirably. Amaro had done it on purpose so they would be off their guard when he made his escape. So they would think he was behaving himself.

But the truth was much different.

On the crisp morning the de Lohr escort left for Brython Castle, Amaro was at his post, but before the escort could

depart, he reported feeling ill to the sergeant on duty and told
the man he was going back to his quarters to rest for the day.
He did indeed return to his quarters, but only to make it look as
if he was sleeping by making his pallet lumpy. Moving swiftly,
he collected his saddlebags and left his quarters, making his way
to the stables, where his horse had grown fat and lazy from lack
of use. Not trusting the stable servants to keep his departure
quiet, he saddled his horse personally and slipped the animal
out through the rear yard.

The postern gate was unguarded.

It was a heavily fortified gate, always locked, but because it
was so fortified, it was rarely watched. Sometimes, farmers or
merchants doing business with the kitchens or with the
stablemaster used the gate, but on this day, it was simply
unguarded and locked. Amaro unlocked it, slipped his horse
through, took the animal down the slope, crossing the small
stream at the bottom of the hill, and entered the trees on the
other side. The sentries who usually patrolled the walls had
been busy watching Hereford and his family depart and didn't
notice him.

That was what Amaro had hoped for.

But that didn't mean he wasn't seen.

A lad who had been mucking stalls on the other side of the
stable had seen Amaro move in and out. Curious, he followed
Amaro to see if he needed any assistance, only to see the man
depart through the postern gate. The stable servant thought that
was rather odd but went back to his work, until the next
morning when Kessler came into the stable with another de
Lohr knight who had remained behind. They were looking at
the warhorses, and when they noticed Amaro's was missing,
they happened to ask the lad if he'd seen the horse removed.

The servant had seen Amaro himself remove the horse and depart through the postern gate the day before.

After that, the stable servant wasn't certain why both Kessler and the other knight began to run back toward the keep, but he had a feeling it wasn't a good thing. When Kessler himself departed less than an hour later—the old man didn't normally ride out like that—the stable servant began to realize that Amaro's departure hadn't been expected. If Kessler was riding to find him, it must be very bad.

Very bad, indeed.

CHAPTER FIFTEEN

Brython Castle

I T WAS A gown of blue and gold satin.

Glorious de Lohr colors that were spectacularly presented. Standing in front of a tall mirror of polished bronze, Elle could see herself quite clearly in the magnificent dress. She could also feel every pin and every stitch that Dustin, Lady Hereford, was putting in the side of the garment. Her left arm was up as her husband's mother tried to alter a dress that wasn't quite fitting in the bustline.

A woman she had only just met earlier in the day, in fact.

But a woman she was already fond of.

"Try that now," Dustin said, helping her carefully lower her left arm. She began pulling at the top of the dress, which was formfitting and lovely. "How does it feel now? Still too tight?"

Standing around Dustin were Curtis' younger sisters, Rebecca and Olivia Charlotte. Rebecca was tall and willowy, with red hair, while Olivia Charlotte was short and blonde in the image of her mother. They were helping Lady Hereford with the exquisite garment that was simply too tight. So tight that Elle felt as if her breasts were about to spill over the top. Curtis thought it was a lovely problem to have, but Elle didn't. She'd barely met Dustin and Curtis' sisters when they arrived before Curtis was asking his mother to help with the dress. Dustin didn't need any prompting—she grabbed her younger daughters and jumped right in.

And that was where they found themselves as the sun began to set.

"It feels better," Elle admitted, trying to adjust her breasts so they weren't bulging over the top of the bodice. "Does it look better?"

Dustin stood back and inspected her work. Rebecca knelt in front of Elle and tugged at the bottom of the garment to help straighten out the fabric.

"It looks a little better," Dustin said. "But I fear with this fabric that if I try to alter it too much, you will be able to see the needle marks. Do you think you can stand it like this?"

Elle was still adjusting herself, now looking in the mirror. "I think so," she said. "But I feel that when I meet our guests, all they'll see are big white breasts right in their faces."

To emphasize the point, she turned around and made gestures over the tops of her breasts as Rebecca and Olivia Charlotte giggled. Even Dustin grinned.

"I must say that the dress is magnificent," Dustin said. "But I am surprised a seamstress with such skill was unable to measure correctly. That seems like a foolish mistake."

Elle looked down at herself. "She had the measurements correct when she first measured me, but that was a few weeks ago," she said. "I seem to have... grown since then."

Dustin was still grinning as she went to her and tried to tug at the fabric a little. "I would say you have," she said. "Curtis must be feeding you well."

Elle eyed her mother-in-law. She didn't know the woman at all, but she knew her through Curtis' eyes. He adored his mother and spoke so fondly of her. Elle hoped she could adore her, too, and would be adored in return, but her history with women was sketchy. She didn't have high hopes. But the reason for her full breasts was a very big secret she and Curtis were sitting on, a secret that not only made her nauseated on a daily basis, but fairly emotional as well. She didn't like that her beautiful dress wasn't fitting well because her breasts were becoming larger. She didn't want to look like an exhibitionist with them bursting out all over the place. Worse still, she didn't want to look fat and untidy. Unsure what to say to Dustin's comment, she felt tears begin to pool in her eyes as she quickly tried to blink them away, but Olivia Charlotte saw that she was growing red in the face. A sweet girl, she went to Elle and took her hand.

"Mama," she said softly. "Elle is weeping."

Betrayed, Elle tried to turn her face away, but Dustin wouldn't let her. She took her other hand, greatly concerned.

"I promise this is nothing to weep over," she assured her gently. "I will fix it and no one will know."

Elle's lower lip trembled. "But everyone is arriving," she said, sniffling. "I should be down with Curt greeting our guests, but instead I am here because I'm too fat for my dress."

She broke down in soft tears, and Dustin put her arm around her, hugging her gently. "Not to worry, my lady," she said soothingly. "I told you I will fix it. I promise I will."

As Rebecca ran to find a kerchief for the tears, Elle struggled to wipe them away. "I was so excited for this garment," she said. "I've never had anything so beautiful."

"It is still beautiful, and so are you," Dustin said, waving quickly to Olivia Charlotte. "Watch, now—Liv is fetching my thread. See? I will fix it right now. Please do not weep."

Rebecca returned with the kerchief, and Elle took it gratefully, wiping at her eyes. Dustin had her stand up tall so she could see where she could let the seam out just a little more, and Elle lifted her arms again.

"I think I can let the fabric out just a little right here," Dustin said, looking at a spot under the arms. "But not too terribly much or it will ruin the sleeve."

Elle sniffled, wiping her nose with the kerchief before raising her arm again. "It will not show?"

"Nay," Dustin said, concentrating on removing some thread from the seam. "No one will be able to see it."

"And you'll be able to take it in again when my breasts are not so large?"

Dustin shook her head. "It will be taken in easily," she said. "But do not think you must reduce. You have a lovely figure, Elle."

There was that secret again. She and Curtis had planned to tell his parents that she was expecting, though he wanted to do it when they were all together. Elle supposed that Dustin had a right to know why she was asking about taking the dress in. Any further talk of reducing and body shape and Elle might end up lying to cover up the reason, and she didn't want to do that. Dustin was going to find out anyway.

"I did not mean when I reduce," she said quietly. "Forgive me, Lady Hereford, but my breasts are full because… Curt and I were going to tell you and Lord Hereford tonight… But the dress does not fit because I am with child."

Dustin nearly stabbed Elle in the armpit. She gasped, her eyes wide, as she looked at the woman in shock.

"You are pregnant?" she asked.

Elle nodded, a weary twinkle in her eye. "I am," she said. "Please do not tell Curt that I told you before he had a chance to. He will be very disappointed if he knows I have."

Dustin threw her arms around Elle, a woman she had only met hours earlier, but now there was something to link them. Not only had the woman married her son and, by all accounts, seemed to have made him very happy, but now she was pregnant with what could presumably be the heir to the de Lohr empire.

She was overcome with joy.

"Of course I will not tell him," she said, kissing Elle on the cheek. "I cannot tell you how happy I am, my lady. So very, very happy."

Elle smiled weakly. "Then you will understand why I weep because my garment does not fit," she said. "I seem to be weeping at every little thing."

Dustin laughed softly as she cupped Elle's face. "Well do I remember those days," she said. "I have been through it many times, so if anyone can sympathize, it is me. But I am so delighted. I know my husband will be as well."

She kissed Elle on the cheek again, happily, before returning to work, but not before she looked to her daughters, who had heard everything.

"Not a word to anyone," she said sternly. "Not to Papa, not to Curt. You do not know anything."

Rebecca nodded solemnly, but Olivia Charlotte went to Elle and took her hand again. She was a lovely girl, clearly affectionate, and she had no problem demonstrating that with a woman she had only just met.

"I hope to have many babies," she said. "What does it feel

like?"

Elle wasn't quite used to a lass who was so overly friendly. "It feels like my clothing is getting tighter every day," she said. "It feels like I am hungry all the time."

Olivia Charlotte grinned. "Is he moving in your belly yet?"

Elle shook her head. "Not yet."

"When he does, will you let me feel him?"

Dustin chuckled at her curious daughter as Elle smiled timidly. "Of course," she said. "But I will be here and you will be at Lioncross. That is a long way to come just to feel him move."

Olivia Charlotte wouldn't give up. "Can I live here when he is born?" she said. "I can help you tend to him. I can play with him and feed him."

Dustin waved off her eager twelve-year-old, on the cusp of womanhood and so very intrigued with anything that had to do with babies. "Do not pester Elle," she said. "She has a long time to go yet, and decisions like that cannot be made now."

Olivia Charlotte might have stopped asking questions, but she still held Elle's hand, smiling at her in a way that should have made Elle uncomfortable, but it didn't. She could sense that the lass was simply a sweet, rather innocent child, curious about things that most girls were curious about. Or should be curious about. But Elle had never even considered babies or children until she became pregnant.

Now, it was all she could think of.

"I would like for you to stay with us, of course," Elle said. "But as your mother says, we will speak on it when the time draws closer. He still has a long time before he's ready to be born."

"He is baking in your lady oven?"

All three women burst out laughing. "Where on earth did

you hear that?" Dustin asked, shaking her head. "Enough, Liv. Take Rebecca and find Papa. Tell him that we are almost ready and will be done soon. And if you mention lady ovens, I will blister your backside. Do you understand me?"

Olivia Charlotte's eyes widened. "Aye, Mama."

Dustin smiled brightly. "Excellent," she said. "Hurry, now. We will not be far behind."

The girls fled, leaving Elle quite appreciative of Lady Hereford's parenting skills. When their eyes met, Elle snorted.

"Is that how I should parent our son?" she asked. "Through intimidation and adoration?"

Dustin chuckled. "If it works," she said, but quickly sobered. "I would say you parent your son with a good deal of love and encouragement. That is what children want—your love. But if you have a lass like Olivia Charlotte who likes to run off at the mouth, then sometimes, you must put fear into her so she will learn restraint."

Elle turned to watch her in the mirror as she finished with the stitch. "Olivia Charlotte," she murmured. "Why does she have two names?"

Dustin finished and cut the loose ends of the thread from the dress. "Because her father and I could not agree," she said. "I wanted to name her Olivia and he wanted to name her Charlotte. Therefore, we gave her both."

Elle grinned at the stubborn nature of her husband's parents. "I suppose if you feel strongly enough, you must take a stand."

"Precisely," Dustin said. Then she stood up and pulled Elle's arm down before tugging at the bodice again. "There. How does that feel?"

Elle tugged at it, too. "Better," she said, pulling on the skirt to loosen everything. "Much better. I cannot thank you enough, my lady."

Dustin stepped in front of her, putting herself between the mirror and Elle. Elle was an inch or two taller, but she would swear that Dustin was the biggest person in that chamber. Probably in any chamber she entered. The woman had an air about her that was positively fearsome.

"Elle," Dustin said softly. "I hope that I may call you Elle."

Elle nodded. "Of course, my lady. I would be honored."

Dustin smiled faintly. "Good," she said. "I am glad that Rebecca and Liv are not here because it gives me the opportunity to speak with you alone. I want to let you know that Christopher has told me everything about the first day or so after Brython fell, after the siege. He has told me about his conversations with you and what transpired."

Elle couldn't look the woman in the eye any longer. She lowered her gaze. "It was a difficult time, my lady," she said. "I had—"

"I know," Dustin cut her off, but not unkindly. "I know that you were called the Wraith. I further know that you held the castle against my husband for an entire month, and I must say that you have my great respect for that. Greater warlords have fallen much more quickly against him than you did. You are to be commended."

Elle smiled wanly. "But the castle still fell in the end," she said. "I did not hold out forever."

"Nay, you did not," Dustin said. "But do you know what you did?"

"What?"

"You proved your worth to my husband," Dustin said, a twinkle in her eye. "You proved yourself strong and capable in

Christopher de Lohr's eyes. Why do you think he was so determined for you to marry Curtis? He knew that such a strong and capable woman would make a magnificent Countess of Leominster and a magnificent wife to our firstborn son. I know the first few days of your acquaintance must not have been a pleasant one, but I have heard that Curtis is very happy with this marriage. I've not yet spoken to him, but from the brief moment that I did when I first arrived, he looks happy and content. That is your doing, my dear. I want to thank you."

Elle could lift her eyes again, feeling touched at the woman's praise. "He has made me happy also," she said softly. "I… I do not know how much you have been told about my life, Lady Hereford, but before I met Curt, it was a dark and terrible thing. The Wraith… That woman no longer exists. Curt has shown me another life I never imagined."

Dustin touched her arm gently. "I was told about your up-bringing," she said. "I know this has been a drastic change for you, but I hope Curt has been helpful."

Elle grinned. "He is the greatest teacher I could have hoped for," she said. "And Myles is a wonderful teacher, too. Douglas and Westley… Well, they are young, but they are good in their hearts. You have raised fine sons, my lady."

Dustin shook her head in resignation. "You mean that Douglas and Westley are foolish and pesky," she said. "I know they are. They have always been like that when they are thrown together, and I did not want Douglas to come to Brython, but my husband insisted. He said that they boys are growing up and must learn to work together, as men. I suppose he is right, but that means they have been your burden, and for that, I am sorry."

Elle laughed softly. "I am not," she said. "They are eager and fast learners, or at least Douglas mostly is when he is not pining away for women. He is so excited about this feast that he and Myles went into the village of Presteigne and purchased perfume to attract women. I think they smell like a rubbish fire, but they are convinced the scent will attract women."

Dustin rolled her eyes and turned back to her sewing kit. "God help us," she said. "I suppose I should see my sons and assess the damage of the rubbish fire perfume. I do not want them shaming the entire family."

"Nay, do not," Elle said, turning back for the mirror to check her careful hairstyle, which was simply a braid that had been intertwined with blue ribbon and pinned in a circle around the back of her head. "They will know I have told you, and I do not want them to think I am gossiping about them. If you must see to them, then do not tell them I mentioned it. I do not want to embarrass them."

Dustin looked at her. "You have a kind heart, lass," she said. "From what Chris told me, I had wondered. And worried. But I can see now that there's no hate in your heart for my lads."

Elle turned away from the mirror, looking at her. "There was, once," she said honestly. "I was taught to hate your sons and men like them. But a strange thing happened when I married Curt—I discovered a world where hate wasn't the usual thing. A world where there was laughter and affection. A world where I was not scrambling to find my next meal or wondering if I'd have enough wood for the fire. I am not saying that I no longer feel strongly for my people, because I do, but I understand that hate will only bring hate. It does not help the Welsh for me to hate the English or my husband. And I do not hate him at all. I couldn't if I tried."

Dustin smiled as she shut her sewing kit. "I am happy to

hear that," she said. "I know from experience how difficult it is to marry someone you do not know, someone you'd rather not marry, and suddenly, you find yourself in his world, for better or for worse."

"Curt told me about your introduction to Lord Hereford," Elle said. "I was told you fell out of a tree right in front of him."

Dustin chuckled. "I did," she said. "Right onto my back. I thought I was dying. Then I looked up to see the biggest man I'd ever seen standing over me. I think I tried to strike him or kick him. I do not exactly remember, but I do remember seeing his face for the first time. It was like looking at the face of God."

Elle lifted an eyebrow. "Did you hear how Curt and I first met?"

"You charged him from the top of the wall?"

Elle nodded, sighing with some embarrassment. "It was... memorable."

Dustin laughed, going to her and taking her hand. "And look at you now," she said. "The Countess of Leominster, the future Countess of Hereford and Worcester. What a grand position you have now, my lady. I think you are going to do great things for your new family as well as for your people."

Elle wasn't used to such female encouragement, especially that of kindness and positive thinking. Considering her grandmother had only spouted poison, this kind of reinforcement from Curtis' mother was something quite new.

But something she knew she could come to like.

"Like what?" she said. "Both Curt and Lord Hereford have said I can do more for my people in this position, but I do not know what. Or how."

Dustin patted her hand as she led her toward the door. "Do what all fine ladies do," she said. "Go to the local church and become a patron. The priests will tell you where you can help. Mayhap it is feeding the poor or providing clothing. Mayhap it is helping school the children of your lands, helping them learn to read and write. I know that is not usual for poor families, but if children learn a skill, they can grow up to use it. They can become better than their parents and live a better life."

Elle liked that idea a great deal. "I already give alms to the poor when I can," she said. "I have given money to the church, but I wanted to do more than that. Do you think that's what they meant about helping my people? By making sure they have a better life?"

Dustin opened the chamber door. "I am certain of it," she said. "Your position is only limited by your imagination, Elle. Think great thoughts and make a name for yourself. We will all be quite proud of you."

She was smiling as she said it, leading Elle onto the landing so they could take the stairs down to the keep entry. But Elle was still thinking on what Lady Hereford had said—*we will all be quite proud of you*. God's Bones, was that really true? Was there someone out there who would actually be proud of something she accomplished, even if it wasn't killing Englishmen or hating them to their very guts?

A novel concept, indeed.

And a good one.

CHAPTER SIXTEEN

"**D**OES SHE KNOW I have been invited?"

"She will when she sees you."

Gruffydd had been the one to ask the question of Curtis as they stood on the wall of Brython Castle, something he was quite familiar with. He'd arrived a short time earlier, having received the invitation to the feast as an ally of the House of de Lohr, only to discover his sister didn't know he had been on the guestlist.

That changed things a bit.

At least Gruffydd knew where he stood. He was to be a surprise. But he could see by the expression on Curtis' face that it might not be so bad.

Hopefully.

"Don't you think you should have told her?" Gruffydd said. "Given our history, it would have been the kind thing to do."

Curtis shook his head. He was already tipsy from the fine wine he'd been drinking throughout the afternoon, and now, as the guests arrived in earnest and great lords were being admitted into Brython while their escorts set up camp beyond the castle walls, the drink had gone to his head a little.

But the entire day had been filled with joy.

So much joy.

It all started when he'd told his father that Elle was expecting their first child and made him promise not to tell anyone until he and Elle could make the announcement together. He and his father had toasted the coming de Lohr heir, and even now, in the presence of Elle's brother, Curtis could hardly keep his mouth shut. Or his joy contained.

It was a struggle.

"She is a changed woman," he said. "Trust me, Gruffydd. I think you will find that much of her has changed."

Gruffydd wasn't convinced. "I've known her longer than you have," he said. "You will forgive me for doubting this great change."

Curtis looked at him. "You are a de Lohr ally," he said. "She is going to have to become accustomed to that. She hated you, in large part, because you sided with the English, but now she is married to an English knight and her child will be half English."

"True."

"And it was your grandmother who instilled that hatred in her."

"Also true."

Curtis shook his head. "Your sister has learned to see more of the world than what your grandmother narrowly allowed," he said. "I am not saying she will throw herself in your arms, but I do not think she'll be as bitter as she has been. With me, she has changed a good deal."

Gruffydd shrugged. He didn't know what to make of this situation—his sister or the great feast. But he'd come at the request of Curtis, to celebrate the great alliance with the son of Gwenwynwyn, but also to celebrate the alliance with English marcher lords who were allied with the House of de Lohr.

And there were many.

"I suppose we shall soon discover what she thinks of my presence here," he said after a moment. Then he pointed to the land beyond the moat of Brython where, two months ago, the de Lohr army had sent up their encampment. Now, it was an encampment for several great houses, all of them setting up their colorful tents with banners snapping in the sunset. "Tell me who has arrived. For a Welshman, it is a bit disconcerting to see all of the English camped out there."

Curtis grinned, looking over the field as the sun set in the west, bathing the sky in shades of lavender and pink. "Myles and Hugo have been settling them since they started arriving yesterday," he said, pointing. "The blue and red standard closest to us? You should recognize that one. Sean de Lara, Lord of the Trilaterals. That is Trelystan, Hyssington, and Caradoc Castles."

Gruffydd nodded in recognition. "De Lara," he muttered. "My father knew him."

"I'm sure he did."

"He was a great knight with King John, was he not?"

Curtis nodded. "He was one of William Marshal's greatest spies," he said. "The man is a legend, so treat him with all due respect. Frankly, I am surprised to see him because he is getting up there in age, like my father."

"I was told once that great knights never die."

"If that is true, then de Lara shall live forever," Curtis said. Then he pointed to the larger encampment behind de Lara. "See the green and black? That is the Earl of Wolverhampton, Robert de Wolfe. The House of de Wolfe and the House of de Lohr go back many years. Robert's father, Edward, was my father's best friend. In fact, Robert's full name is Robert Richard Christopher."

Gruffydd squinted to see the green and black standards. "I've never met de Wolfe," he said. "Warstone Castle, isn't it?"

"Aye."

"Who else is here?"

Curtis was looking over the recognizable standards. "I see my brother, Peter," he said. "Lord Pembridge of Ludlow Castle, he is. To his south is Sherry, Christin's husband."

"Who is Christin?"

"My sister," Curtis said. "Alexander de Sherrington is the most fearsome killer you've ever come across. On his way back from the crusade of Richard, he spent a few years in Rome at the Lateran Palace, committing dirty deeds for the pope."

Gruffydd looked at him in surprise. "Is that so?" he said. "Impressive. But I'll be sure to stay away from him."

Curtis snorted softly. "He has become a family man in his old age," he said. "As he tells it, all of that assassin madness is well in his past. He's the garrison commander of Wigmore Castle, one of my father's properties, and my father recently gifted him with the title of Lord Barringdon. It was a title that belonged to my mother's father, a courtesy title, so my father gave it to Sherry. Being married to Christin, he has earned it."

Curtis had a grin on his face with what could be construed as slander toward his eldest sister, and Gruffydd shot him a long look. "You have a troubled sister, too?"

Curtis shook his head. "She's no trouble, at least not these days," he said. "But confidentially, she was a spy, too, years ago."

"Is that so?"

"It is. She's as fearsome as her husband, I think."

Gruffydd shook his head, returning his attention to the land below. "You English are full of trouble," he said. "Who else has come?"

Curtis pointed. "The red and white standards are of Caius d'Avignon of Hawkstone Castle," he said. "Another former spy of William Marshal's. They used to call the man the Britannia Viper in the Levant. And the group to his right with the crimson standard is none other than the Earl of Wrexham, Tristan de Royans. Yet another agent of William Marshal, not to mention the bastard son of Henry the Second."

Gruffydd frowned. "Sounds like a powerful man."

"He is," Curtis said. Then he squinted off to the southwest. "See that standard of red and black and white? Out there?"

Gruffydd had to lift his head to see it. "Aye," he said. "I think so. Who is that?"

"That is the husband of Ajax de Velt's eldest daughter," Curtis replied. "De Velt has several border properties, castles he acquired through a good deal of blood and mayhem many years ago. Bretton de Llion married Jax's eldest daughter, and he commands the properties for Cole de Velt, who inherited his father's empire. I've not seen Bretton in many years, so I'm glad he has come. My father and Jax de Velt were close friends."

"De Velt," Gruffydd said with some distaste. "I remember the stories about him. My father used to speak of the terror that man brought with him wherever he went."

"Very true."

"And your father was his friend?"

"Indeed, he was."

"Are your friends all made up of spies and killers?"

Curtis laughed. "It would seem like that," he said. "But there are other warlords camped out there, lesser warlords, who don't have such terrifying reputations. I will introduce you to those men as they enter the hall, but for now, you know the major lords. These are men who have shaped the history of England, my father included. They are great men, all of them."

Gruffydd could hear the reverence in Curtis' tone. "And you grew up with them."

"I did," Curtis said. "I grew up surrounded by giants. I can only hope that some of that greatness has rubbed off on me."

Gruffydd turned away from the edge of the wall. "Your command of Brython will be exemplary," he said. "You will make a name for yourself, I am certain. But when do you intend to invite Welsh warlords to feast?"

They headed for the tower with stairs that led down to the bailey. "That is an excellent question," Curtis said. "The answer is soon. What I did not want is to invite many to this gathering with a host of English warlords. I think something like that, even in a social setting, would be a recipe for disaster. One spark and the entire thing would go up like kindling. I must ease the Welsh into the idea of an English knight being in charge of such a legendary castle. Already, I am certain they do not like that I have a castle that holds such significance for them."

Gruffydd took the stairs first. "You mean the portal to the Otherworld?"

"Exactly."

"Have you looked for it yet?"

"I have," Curtis said. "Ellie says it is under a pond down in the vault."

Gruffydd shook his head. "I do not think that is where it is."

"Why not?"

"Because that means the Otherworld would be flooded," he said. "No one can get to the entry if it is buried underwater."

"Then where do you think it is?"

They reached the bottom of the stairs, and Gruffydd looked at him, smiling. "Beneath the stable."

Curtis' eyebrows lifted. "What?" he said, incredulous. "Why do you say that?"

"Because there is an old door secured with a chain under one of the stalls," Gruffydd said. "The door is extremely old, with very old writing on it. So old that no one can make it out. And something is anchoring it shut. We have tried to pry it open, and it will not budge."

Curtis found that very interesting. He was about to reply when he caught sight of his father heading in his direction. He lifted up a hand, catching the man's attention.

"Papa," he called. "Where did you disappear to? I was looking for you earlier."

Christopher gestured over toward the keep. "I was speaking to your younger brothers," he said. "Douglas is very unhappy here, Curt."

Curtis shook his head at the ridiculousness of that statement. "Of course he is," he said. "And do you know why? Because of the lack of women and the fact that he has to share the attention of what women there are with Andrew, who is a kind and handsome lad. Papa, he's utterly ridiculous, puffed up like a peacock, thinking he is above everyone else. He harps on Westley constantly, and then I find myself breaking up fights."

Christopher cleared his throat unhappily. "I was afraid it was something like that," he said, noting Gruffydd standing next to Curtis. "But we shall speak of it at another time. Lord Gruffydd, it is agreeable to see you again."

Gruffydd dipped his head respectfully to Christopher. "Lord Hereford," he said. "It is an honor, *fy arglwydd.*"

He addressed him formally in Welsh, and Christopher acknowledged the respect with a dip of his head. "Is this your first visit to Brython since Curt married your sister?" he asked.

Gruffydd nodded. "It is, my lord," he said. "As you are aware, my sister and I do not get on well, but Lord Leominster is telling me that marriage has changed her. I suppose we shall see."

Christopher smiled faintly. "I suppose we shall," he said. "Meanwhile, has Curtis told you of everyone who has arrived so far? It is only English this time. We must discuss potential Welsh allies with you first before we invite anyone here to parlay."

"Agreed," Gruffydd said. "English alliance is a delicate subject here."

Christopher waggled his eyebrows in agreement. "Of that, I have no doubt," he said. Then he turned to his son. "Speaking of delicate subject, I saw that you invited Lord Munstone."

Curtis nodded. "He is small, but he's always been a good ally," he said. "Why?"

"Because I wonder if you know who he married."

"Who?"

"Larue la Dechy."

Curtis looked at him in surprise. "He did?" he said. "But he's old enough to be her grandfather!"

Gruffydd was looking between them. "Who is Larue la Dechy?" he asked.

As Curtis groaned and put a hand over his face, Christopher answered. "A young woman from a very wealthy family who used to be quite sweet on Curt," he said. "Her father tried very hard to buy his daughter a husband, but in the end, I simply didn't want her for him. Curtis was destined for great things, not the daughter of a merchant. Even if he did have more money than God."

"Is that so?" Gruffydd said with interest. "It seems she found a husband after all."

"One that is very old and quite rich himself," Curtis said. "Larue was pretty enough, but as petty as a child. She probably married Munstone because she's hoping he'll die soon so she can use his money to buy herself a harem of men. She tended to like a few suitors at one time."

Christopher chuckled, thinking on the young lady who wore the jewels of a queen and demanded the attention of many young men. "Be that as it may, I thought I should warn you that she married Munstone," he said. "Clearly, she knows this is your garrison, and she knows she is going to see you. I would be on my guard if I were you."

Curtis lost his humor. "I am hesitant to tell Elle," he said. "I do not want to upset her. She is already nervous enough about this feast."

Christopher's expression suggested that it was probably a good idea not to let Elle know that there was a woman in attendance who once fancied Curtis. There was no use in upsetting the woman. But the truth was that Christopher never told his son how much negotiating went on that he wasn't aware of, because Larue was used to getting what she wanted. Her father threw half his fortune at Christopher in exchange for a betrothal, but in the end, Christopher wouldn't do it. He wouldn't consign his son to a woman who, in his opinion, had been ill-mannered and shallow. He'd saddled him with a banshee who was a Welsh princess by blood, but that had been different—Elle was intelligent and a deep thinker. There had been something about her that he had liked. But with Larue…

There was nothing he had liked.

He found himself on his guard, as well.

"Papa! *Papa!*"

Jolted from his train of thought, Christopher turned to see Rebecca and Olivia Charlotte bolting in his direction. Olivia Charlotte eventually crashed into him, but Rebecca was more poised and in control. At twenty years of age, she was a graceful young lady, while Olivia Charlotte was still in the throes of awkward childhood.

"Greetings, my love," Christopher said, kissing Olivia Charlotte on the top of her blonde head. "Where is your mother?"

"She is coming," Rebecca said. "She sent us to tell you that she and Lady Leominster are coming down."

"Call her Elle," Curtis admonished her softly. "Lady Leominster is so formal. She is your sister."

"A sister whom they do not know well yet," Christopher reminded him. "When Elle gives them permission to address her informally, they will."

Curtis simply shrugged, but he held out his hand to Rebecca, who took it quickly. With that, he began to lead his family toward the great hall of Brython, which had recently seen repairs, much as the rest of the castle had. With Myles and Hugo at the gatehouse welcoming the guests and directing them toward the great hall, the rest of the de Lohr family, and Gruffydd, entered the hall with its roaring fire and carpet of fresh rushes upon the floor. Servants were already putting out pitchers of wine, and there was a sense of excitement in the air.

The festivities were about to begin.

CHAPTER SEVENTEEN

IT HAD BEEN so very easy to get in.

It had all started when Amaro neared Brython from the south, knowing there were farms along the road, and slipped into one of the farms and stole some clothing that had been out to dry after a washing. Nothing more than a used tunic and breeches, but he'd confiscated them along with a rough canvas cowl and hood that farmers sometimes used to protect their heads from sun or the elements. He traveled further down the road and was able to find more items to wear, an old oil cloak hanging on a barn door and a pair of muddied shoes that were a little too small. But he could accept that for a means to an end.

He headed to Brython looking like a servant.

Because he'd pushed himself and his horse swiftly from Lioncross, he reached Brython before the day was out. But he had a plan—because the village of Rhayader was closer to Brython than the English villages were, and because he wanted to move about undetected, he went into Wales and stabled his horse at a livery in Rhayader. He'd paid the man well to tend his horse and borrowed a smaller, less spectacular horse that the man had at the livery. He used that horse to travel to Brython, arriving just as several important warlords were setting up their encampments, including Christopher de Lohr.

After that, it was a simple thing to blend in.

Because of all of the visitors, the gatehouse of Brython was open. Security was more relaxed than it would normally be. Amaro entered the visitor encampment from the west side, secured his horse in the trees, and made his way into the camp of Bretton de Llion. The man flew a black and red standard, and the knights, squires, and even the servants were wearing those colors. Amaro managed to grab one of the servants by the neck, drag him into the trees beyond, and kill him for the tunic he wore. Leaving the body in the woods, he donned the colors and hastened back into the encampment, picked up a bucket that was on the ground by one of the tents, and continued on toward the castle.

There was nothing less suspicious than a servant with a bucket.

Not strangely, no one stopped him. He kept his head down, hidden by the cowl he'd taken from the farmer's laundry, so his hair and features were concealed. As he approached the gatehouse, he could see that Christopher had set up his camp right at the mouth of the gatehouse, which concerned him. Christopher had brought some of his senior knights with him, men who would recognize Amaro in a flash, so he kept his head lowered as he passed on the perimeter of the de Lohr encampment and made his way through the gatehouse.

As he'd hoped, no one was checking a man's identity and no one was paying any attention. Therefore, accessing Brython was fairly simple. Now, he had to conceal himself and wait for that perfect moment.

And the moment, for him, would come.

He'd make sure of it.

CHAPTER EIGHTEEN

THE FIRST FACE Elle saw upon entering the great hall of Brython was that of her brother. Gruffydd was near the dais, in conversation with Christopher, and, for a moment, she was surprised to see him.

Beyond that, she wasn't sure how she felt about it.

So many feelings were swirling within her chest as she watched her brother. He was the mild-mannered sort, so there was no animation as he spoke to Hereford. He was calm, as he always was. But it occurred to Elle that Curtis must have known that Gruffydd was coming, because he had clearly invited the man, yet never said a word about it.

She felt strangely betrayed by that.

"There you are," Curtis said, coming up behind her and taking her hand. Still holding her hand, he stood back to look at her. "God, you're beautiful. The dress is magnificent. Did my mother amend it?"

Elle nodded. "She was able to," she said. "I like your mother. She is very kind."

Curtis nodded, kissing her hand. "She is," he said. "She will be very helpful to you if you will allow, but you will have to ask her. She would never do anything you did not ask her to do."

"Like fix a dress."

"Exactly. She's not one to push herself onto others."

Elle smiled weakly. "I hope she and your father remain after the feasting is finished," she said. "I would like to spend more time with your mother and come to know her better."

Curtis smiled, kissing her hand again. "I am certain they can be persuaded," he said. "Were you able to speak with Rebecca and Livvy?"

"You mean that child with the long name, Olivia Charlotte?" Elle said, grinning when Curtis laughed softly. "Your mother told me that she and your father could not agree on names for her, so they call her by both."

Curtis nodded. "They are both stubborn people," he said. "I hope we will not have the same trouble with ours."

Elle shook her head. "We will not," she said. "I will make a bargain with you."

"What is that?"

"You will name the boys and I will name the girls."

His face lit up. "I love that suggestion," he said. "I accept."

"I thought you might."

"The truth is that I already have a name in mind if the child is a boy."

She cocked an eyebrow. "It is no wonder you agreed to my suggestion so easily," she said. "Well? What is it? We are not going to name him after a king, are we? Because I do not like the names John or Henry."

Curtis chuckled. "I would not name my son after those two," he said. "But if it is a lad... I would like to name him after my father."

They both turned to look at Christopher, in conversation

with Gruffydd, and Elle moved closer to Curtis, putting an arm around his waist. "I like that name," she whispered. "I cannot think of a more pleasing name."

His expression turned adoring. "Thank you," he murmured. "I mean that from the bottom of my heart. It means a great deal to me."

"I know," she said. "And I agree—if it is a lad, he should be named for a man you love very much."

"You're sweet," he said, kissing her on the forehead. "But if it is a lass, what will you name her?"

Elle cocked her head thoughtfully. "I do not know," she said. "If we are naming children after parents, I do not want to name her after mine. What was the name of your mother's mother?"

"Mary."

"Then we will name her Mary."

He grinned, giving her a quick squeeze, but as he did so, he noticed that guests were beginning to come in through the hall entry.

"Our guests are arriving, Lady Leominster," he said. "We should go to the door and greet them."

Elle could see them, too. "Of course," she said. "But before we go, I assume you deliberately did not tell me that Gruffydd was going to be here. Am I correct?"

Curtis didn't hesitate. "You are," he said, his features softening as he looked at her. "I know you have a long history with him, Ellie. I know it has been fraught with tension and unhappiness. But you are a great lady now, with great responsibility. You are a woman of substance. I am wondering if it is possible for you to peacefully coexist with your brother, who is a valuable ally. If you would at least be civil to him, for my sake,

I would be grateful."

She pursed her lips wryly. "When you put it that way, how can I refuse?"

He gave her his best smile, laughing softly when she rolled her eyes. "You cannot," he said, before kissing her swiftly and then pulling her toward the entry door. "You are the best of me, Ellie. Let us show everyone that, including your brother."

His words hit her. *You are the best of me.* Only a crazy man would say such a thing, but Curtis wasn't crazy. He was bright and brilliant and patient and loving, and she believed he was the greatest creature God had ever created. She never imagined she would think such a thing about any man, especially an Englishman, but she thought that about him.

And he clearly thought that about her.

You are the best of me.

He was the best of her, too.

With Curtis by her side, and eventually Christopher and Dustin, Elle met men with names like Bretton and Caius and Sean. Big, scarred, older knights who had seen much action in the course of their lives. Curtis would introduce her and then whisper in her ear about who the men were and what made them so special, summarizing their careers for her.

It was a parade of legends.

Spies and assassins and agents passed into the great hall, as well as the Earl of Wrexham and the Earl of Wolverhampton. Great, powerful lords who had shaped the history of England and even Wales and Scotland, and in the middle of it was Christopher, whom everyone revered greatly. Peter and Alexander and their wives had arrived, and Elle was introduced to Liora de Lohr and Christin de Sherrington. Beautiful, graceful women who were more than happy to hug her and tell her how happy they were to meet her.

Acceptance.

Kindness.

Elle was overwhelmed by all of it.

Myles had arranged for musicians to play for the evening, having lured them over from a tavern in a village south of Brython, so music filled the stale warmth of the hall as everyone mingled and drank. There was a party atmosphere. Elle had been commandeered by Christin and Dustin and Liora, who took her to the dais and sat at the end of the table, conversing over the noise of the men and music. Other wives were in attendance, like the Countess of Wolverhampton, Giselle, who had come with her husband. The two of them had Christopher cornered. Still other wives—de Lara, d'Avignon, and Wrexham—had been unable to come due to sick children or pregnancies.

Truthfully, Elle was glad. She was already overwhelmed with so many people and, in particular, so many women. Melusine, who had been mostly in the kitchens while Elle led a gay social whirl in the hall, finally joined the ladies and sat next to her cousin, holding her hand, and somewhat fearful of all of the Englishwomen around them.

But Elle wasn't afraid.

She'd never in her life known such kind and curious women.

They weren't her bitter grandmother. They weren't her mother who had run out after she'd been born, never to be heard from again. These were women who knew and loved one another, who shared similar experiences, and who spoke to Elle as if she was part of them. She'd never been part of anything in her life.

The overwhelming feeling began to turn into gratitude.

The tears began to come.

Before Elle realized it, they were streaming down her cheeks and she'd had to lower her head, discreetly trying to wipe them away, when she heard a soft voice in her right ear.

"Are you weary, sweetheart?" Dustin asked softly. "Would you like to lie down for a while? Everyone will still be here when you return."

Elle lifted her head, trying to smile. "Nay," she said. "I… I am not weary. It's just… It's just that…"

She couldn't finish. The other women were concerned that she was weeping, and she was trying to smile and assure them that nothing was terribly wrong. But she couldn't quite get the message across, and they were growing more concerned.

"It is nothing, truly," she finally said, wiping furiously at her eyes. "It's simply that… that other than Melusine, my cousin, I've never had any women to speak to. My mother left after I was born, and the only other woman I've spent time with was my grandmother, who was resentful and hateful. I have come to realize that. Now, I'm sitting with you lovely women, and to experience this… this kindness and camaraderie… It is simply overwhelming. I've never known anything like it."

They understood. Dustin put her arm around Elle's shoulders and gave her a gentle hug, knowing that the woman's upbringing and background was far rougher and more brutal than she let on.

"You are one of us now," Dustin said. "We will come to know you, and we will value you very much, I promise."

Elle laughed softly, a nervous sort of laugh, as she wiped away the last of her tears. "I am being silly," she said. "Forgive me."

Dustin kissed her cheek. "There is nothing to forgive, my love," she said. "But if you are feeling poorly, I will take you back to your chamber. You should lie down for a time and rest. This gathering will still be going on when you return, I promise."

Elle shook her head. "Not before we eat," she said, looking to Melusine. "Are we ready to bring the food out?"

Melusine nodded and stood up. "I will see to it," she said. "It will only be a moment."

The ladies watched her scurry off as Elle spoke softly. "I have given her the task of managing the kitchens," she said. "Everyone has tasks here at Brython, and the kitchens are hers, although I help her. She has been doing very well. She likes standing in those hot kitchens more than I do."

"You are fortunate to have the help," Christin said from across the table. "And she is content with her role?"

Elle nodded. "She is," she said. "Melusine has more experience in managing kitchens than I do, so it is something that comes easily for her. She, too, has come to see that living with the English is not such a bad thing. It helps that she is fond of one of the warriors."

The ladies grinned at each other, knowing how the distraction of a man could change a woman's life because they had all experienced the very same thing. "And you, my lady?" Liora asked, seated next to Christin. "What tasks do you have here?"

Elle smiled, perhaps in embarrassment. "Truthfully, I have never been good with things women are expected to tend to," she said. "I have no training, not the way all of you have. If Curtis has told you anything about me, then you know I was in command of Brython when Hereford and his army came."

Dustin nodded proudly. "She held Chris off for an entire

month," she said to the group. "She is to be commended."

The women giggled, knowing what a blow that must have been to Christopher and his pride. "Then you are helping Curt with his army?" Christin asked.

Elle shrugged. "A little," she said. "I know the warlords of these lands, so we discuss that a good deal. I give him my opinion on their strengths and loyalties. When I am not doing that, I tend to the keep and the kitchen stores. But Curt and his knights have been very generous in teaching me what they know about managing a house and hold, at least as much as they are able. I have been keeping the ledger of accounts for Curt, of what we spend and how much money we have. I make suggestions on income that do not include taxing his vassals."

"Oh?" Dustin said, interested. "What have you suggested?"

Elle was reluctant to answer, given that she was so new to the concept of finding income for a castle. She didn't want to sound foolish in front of these women who had been doing it all their lives, but she figured that saying something would be better than avoiding the question. She didn't want to appear rude when the truth was that she was simply uncertain.

"It is not really my idea," she said timidly. "But Curt told me that Lord Hereford has herds of cattle for income. I... Well, I have suggested that we buy some and have our own herd. You see, in the life I led before my marriage, I never had enough money to buy cattle or anything else, but now, we have the money to purchase what we need to make Brython thrive, and it seems logical that we must create income not dependent on taxation."

Dustin smiled broadly. "Well done, my lady," she said. "You are clearly brilliant. My son is very fortunate to have married such a bright mind."

Elle smiled modestly. "The past two months have been quite an education for me," she said. "I have had to learn quickly. I have had to change my way of thinking, with many things. And… and I think I like it."

As Dustin and Christin continued to congratulate her and discuss other ideas worthy of making money for a castle and its inhabitants, Elle caught sight of Gruffydd. He was standing by himself as Christopher and Curtis were off speaking with other lords and their wives.

I've had to change my way of thinking.

That meant with her brother. All Curtis had asked her was to be civil to him. Perhaps they would never been the best of friends, but he was her only living sibling. As she gazed at him, he could feel herself easing when it came to Gruffydd. Had he ever wronged her? She honestly couldn't think of a time he had. If she thought very hard, she remembered a time in her life, when she'd been very young, that he'd sung her a song or tried to help her catch a fish. Little things.

But things she remembered as being… pleasant.

But she'd grown older, and he went away. She went to live with her grandmother. And when she came back from her grandmother, Gruffydd was on a different path than she was. His was diplomacy; hers was fighting. The never agreed on anything, and her animosity toward him grew to the point where she'd given him a sleeping potion and thrown him in the vault.

And now, they were here. At a crossroads. Did she want to hate the man for the rest of her life because he chose to ally with the English and she didn't agree? Now, she found herself married to an Englishman. Her life was changing for the better.

Perhaps she needed to rethink her attitude toward

Gruffydd.

Perhaps it was time to put the hostilities aside.

"Will you excuse me a moment?" she said to Dustin and the others. "I see my brother. I should like to greet him now that Curt is not taking all of his attention."

The ladies waved her off as they continued their conversation about revenue and running a castle. Elle stood up from the table, making her way around it and toward the hearth, where Gruffydd was nursing a cup of wine. It was warmer over here because the hearth was blazing like mad, spitting sparks and smoke into the hall. Most people were congregating away from it, in the center of the room, and Elle came up behind Gruffydd as the man swallowed a big gulp of wine and then burped.

"Is the wine to your liking?" she asked.

Startled that she'd snuck up on him, Gruffydd turned to her quickly. "It is very good," he said, eyeing her warily. "Your husband told me that it was from Burgundy."

Elle nodded. "Aye," she said. "He had it brought from Lioncross. It seems that the family buys it by the shipload."

"The English do indeed like their fine wines," Gruffydd agreed, but he quickly moved to the meat of the situation between them. There was no use in avoiding it. "I know you were not told that I was invited, but I did not realize that until I arrived. Had I known, I might not have come. If my presence here is upsetting, know that I had nothing to do with it."

Elle could see that he was gearing up for what he thought was going to be a fight. "I know," she said evenly. "Be at ease, Gruffydd. I come in peace. I know this was my husband's doing."

That seemed to relieve him but also confuse him, as if he weren't certain how to act now. "Right," he said, a bit nervous.

"Then try not to be too hard on him. He wanted all of his allies here. If that displeases you, then I am sorry."

Elle could hear the same old Gruffydd in his tone, in his words. The man was a diplomat. He'd never been much of a fighter. That had fallen to her. She cocked her head as she gazed at him, perhaps through new eyes. Or perhaps she was *trying* to see him through new eyes. Marriage to Curtis was causing her to see many things differently.

Even Gruffydd.

"I never did understand you," she said. "It occurs to me that much of it stems from the fact that you were never a soldier, Gruffydd. Always the diplomat, the peacemaker. Our father taught you that, didn't he?"

Gruffydd wasn't sure he wanted to speak on this subject, the root of every wrong between them, but he answered. "Aye," he said. "Elle... I have said this before and I will say it again. I am sorry that our father did not treat you well. I am sorry he ignored you. Do you remember when you were very small and I would come to you and tell you stories? And sometimes I would even take you with me when I went to be with Papa?"

Elle nodded. "I remember," she said. Then she snorted ironically. "In fact, I was just thinking about that. I remember all of that, but one day, you simply stopped coming to me."

"Do you know why?"

"Nay."

Gruffydd grew serious. "Then mayhap it is time for you to know," he said. "It wasn't because I wanted to. It was because I needed to."

"*Needed* to? Explain."

He lowered his voice. "Because Papa had grown... senile," he said. "There was some kind of madness in his mind. He was already an old man when I was born, and even older when you were born. There is eleven years between our births, Elle. You were, and always will be, my baby sister. But I stopped coming to you because Papa developed this madness and a real hatred toward our mother. Even the mere mention of you would cause him to rage. I stopped coming because he needed to be managed. And I needed to keep that rage away from you."

Elle looked at him in shock. "But… no one ever said anything about madness," she said. "I never heard anything at all."

"I know," Gruffydd said, somewhat agitated. "There were only a few of us who knew, and we tried to keep it very quiet. There was no knowing what would happen if it got around that Gwenwynwyn ap Owain suffered from madness. It would have destroyed his rule, his control over his own vassals, and it would have given Llywelyn a great opportunity to seize Powys. But I never had a chance to tell you, for you were sent away to our grandmother, and when you returned, you reflected all of the bitterness and love for Llywelyn that she had. Certainly, I would not have told you then."

Elle was feeling a good deal of astonishment at the revelation. "Of course not," she said. "It would have gone straight to Llywelyn."

"Exactly," Gruffydd said. "After our father died, you were as angry as ever. I know you thought I was a traitor to our people for continuing Gwenwynwyn's legacy, and mayhap I am, but he felt that an alliance with the English was something that would survive Llywelyn. He knew the English would defeat him, at some point, and our father's hope was that we would be given his lands. It was all quite political, really. But you saw the opposite… You saw Llywelyn in command of our lands once I was ousted."

Elle could see the very clear picture that Gruffydd was painting. "I did," she said. "Up until I married Curt, that's exactly what I saw."

"Do you still see it?" Gruffydd asked. "God, Elle, if you still see that, does Leominster know? Because if you betray him, you will ruin it for all of us. You will not be giving Brython back to the Welsh, but you will be bringing all of England down on us. Powys will be ruined, and when Llywelyn is defeated, our people will be at the mercy of the English more than you can ever know."

She could see that he was verging on panic, and she hastened to reassure him. "That is no longer my opinion, Gruffydd," she said. "In fact, that was what I wanted to tell you. Growing up, all I knew was rejection and hardship. But since I married Curtis, I have discovered what it means to be valued and respected and loved. I have a husband who is madly in love with me, and I am madly in love with him. I would rather die than betray him, I swear it."

Now, it was Gruffydd's turn to be shocked. "Is this true?" he gasped. "You... you mean it?"

"Every word."

He blinked in response, his mouth hanging open. "But... how?" he finally asked. "Are you so easily swayed away from something you have believed your entire life?"

She smiled wryly. "What did I believe in?" she said. "I believed in Welsh rule for Welsh people. I believed in our way of life. But our way of life brought me starvation and cruelty and brutality. It brought me people who treated me poorly and ignored me. I believed in it because that was all I knew. But Curt has shown me a wonderful world of happiness and love and respect... I would much rather have that than what I had before, and if that means I have been swayed, then it is true—I have been. I've been swayed by love, Gruffydd. That is the greatest power of all."

Gruffydd could hardly believe what he was hearing, but in the same breath, he'd never been so happy or relieved. His warring sister, who would rather use a sword than her words, had been changed by marriage. By love.

It was truly astonishing.

"But what about our people?" he asked. "You still believe in our cause?"

She nodded. "I do," she said. "But as it was pointed out to me, I can do more good as a great lady than as a rebel. I have the money and the name to do great things, Gruffydd. I can feed the poor or educate children. I can make a difference in ways I could have never made it before. *That* is the cause I believe in—helping our people to thrive. Even if I am not changing a nation, I am doing what I can. I will make my mark. As for you... I misjudged you, Gruffydd, and I am sorry. I understand much more than I did before. I hope we can be at peace with one another in the future."

Gruffydd smiled in delight and a little surprise. "I would like that," he said. "In fact, I plan on marrying Hawise next month. I would like it if you and your husband could attend."

Elle returned his smile, perhaps the first genuine gesture of peace between them in an entire lifetime together. "I would be honored to come," she said. "I hope this is the beginning of something better between us, Gruffydd. I truly do."

Gruffydd extended his hand to her, and, after a moment's hesitation, Elle placed her hand in his. He gave it a squeeze.

"As do I," he said. Then he chuckled. "I suppose I was wrong."

"About what?"

"I once told Hereford that trying to make a good wife out of you was like trying to tame the wind," he said. "I told him it could not be done. But I was wrong."

Elle chuckled, somewhat embarrassed. "It was probably not the first time you were wrong," she said. "Truthfully, I would not have believed it, either, had someone told me two months ago that I would be my happiest with an English warlord at my side."

"But you are? Happy, I mean?"

Elle nodded sincerely. "Verily," she said. "More than I could have dreamed."

Gruffydd liked hearing that. In truth, the entire conversation with her had been a revelation to him, but a good one. And he'd never been happier to have been wrong.

Perhaps the English were wind tamers after all.

CHAPTER NINETEEN

"I UNDERSTAND THAT you already know my wife, Lord Leominster." Sir John Munstone indicated the slender, pretty woman next to him covered in jewels. "I hear that you are old friends."

Curtis found himself looking at Larue la Dechy, the woman who had long pined for him, but a woman he'd had absolutely no interest in. She hadn't aged well, unfortunately, and he could see that she'd painted her cheeks with rouge to an obnoxious degree. Everything about her screamed of excess.

He smiled politely.

"Aye, we are," he said, focused on Larue. "Congratulations on your marriage. Lord Munstone is a good friend of the House of de Lohr."

Larue was gazing at Curtis with the look of a hunter sighting prey. "I know," she said. "When we received your invitation for tonight's feast, I was most excited to see your mother and father again. Where are they, by the way?"

Curtis turned and pointed to the dais across the hall. "My mother is over there with my wife," he said. "You've not met Elle yet. I should like to introduce you."

Larue's pleasant expression faded. "I'm sure she is busy with your mother now," she said. "There will be time later. I would much rather speak to you and hear about your new command. Brython is quite a prize, Curt. Well done."

There was that hunter again. Larue had always been about prizes and money and prestige. It reminded him why he never liked her in the first place, and he realized he didn't much want to speak with her any more than he had to. At the risk of being rude, he fumbled for an excuse to cleave the conversation quickly.

"Thank you," he said. "It wasn't only me, but my father and brothers as well. We had a good deal of help. In fact, please excuse me. I see someone over there I must speak with. Please enjoy yourselves."

With that, he pushed his way through some of the gathered men and women, apparently on his way to speak with someone more important the either John or Larue. Munstone didn't seem to mind, but Larue was positively livid.

"How rude," she said. "The man never did have good manners. Living on the wilds of the marches has given him rough edges."

John never paid much attention to his wife, who liked to complain too much for his taste. "He is a busy man, my dear," he said. "Come—let us find a table and sit. I would like some wine."

He was already moving for a table, leaving her behind. Larue was still looking for Curtis, seeing his blond head on the other side of the hall. Frustrated, she considered following him and asking him what he intended to do to make up for his rude departure. It had been years since she last saw him, but those years hadn't removed her lust for Curtis de Lohr. They'd only dulled it a bit.

But it was back now.

There was no man more beautiful in all of England than Curtis de Lohr.

"Good eve, Larue." A woman with faded red hair and a bejeweled wimple sauntered up to her. "Back in Curtis de Lohr's realm, I see?"

Larue glanced at her friend, a woman she'd known many years who had been seeking a husband the same time as her. Not really a friend as much as she had been competition at one time. Lady Rosalie de Nage had grown up in the same town as Larue, in Brookthorpe, just south of Gloucester, and both of their fathers had thriving businesses. Both fathers had ambitions for their daughters, but it had been Larue's father who took the leap for the big fish of de Lohr. Rosalie's father had been a bit more pragmatic and found her a minor warlord in Bromyard, a town between Hereford and Worcester.

Minor as Lord de Nage was, he was still part of the marches alliance, which was how Rosalie also found herself at Brython Castle, and she knew the history between Larue and Curtis very well. She'd heard the rumors and gossip about it for the better part of a year.

But Larue had little patience for Rosalie's taunts.

"I'm surprised to see you here, Rosalie," she said. "Your husband is not nearly so important that he should have a de Lohr alliance, is he?"

Rosalie stiffened. "He's important enough to have received an invitation, just like your husband did."

Larue still had her focus on Curtis. "Charming," she said drolly. "How long must you stay?"

"Long enough to see Curtis ignore you."

Larue's gaze snapped to her, eyes narrowed. "Only momentarily, darling," she said. "I would stop gloating if I were you."

Rosalie laughed when she saw how angry Larue was. "Be at ease, my dearest," she said. "I come in peace, truly. In fact, I heard a little something about the new Lady Leominster that you might be interested in. If you'd like to make Curtis truly miserable for ignoring you, that is."

Larue could always count on some good gossip from Rosalie. That was probably the only connection they'd ever had. "Oh?" she said. "What is that?"

Rosalie stepped closer, looking around to make sure they were not overheard. "We arrived earlier today," she said, lowering her voice. "I sent my maid to the castle to find out what she could about Lady Leominster. No one knows anything about her, other than she's a Welsh princess, of course, but my maid discovered plenty."

Larue was all ears. "What did she discover?"

Rosalie leaned toward her. "She did not go to her marriage bed a virgin," she whispered. "Evidently, she had been living with a bunch of Welsh rebels, if you know what I mean, and Hereford plucked her out of obscurity and demanded she marry Curtis."

Larue's eyes widened. "A whore?" she gasped. "But why did he force Curtis to marry her?"

Rosalie snorted. "Look around you," she said. "This castle was hers. Now it belongs to him. Her father was the ruler of Powys, so I can only imagine the lands that belong to Curtis now. She had made him rich, so certainly, Hereford was willing to overlook her indiscretions."

Larue put her hand to her mouth in shock. "Are you certain of this?"

Rosalie nodded. "It is all the English servants can speak of," she muttered. "She's of royal blood, and that was all Hereford cared about, so poor Curtis has been forced to marry the leavings of Welsh rebels."

Larue shook her head in disbelief. "So Curtis has married a Welsh whore," she said. "What else have you heard?"

Rosalie shrugged. "Isn't that enough?" she said. "Now, if those rumors were to get around the feast this evening, it might shame Curtis sufficiently that he will be looking for comfort. Surely you could console him because he was forced to marry a Welsh strumpet. Certainly he would appreciate your... comfort."

Larue was seized with the very thought of it. She knew that spreading the rumor about Curtis' wife was a horribly nasty thing to do, but if it meant driving a distraught Curtis into her arms when his fellow warlords shamed him because of who he married, Larue was more than willing to be understanding enough. Besides... it would punish the man for not marrying her in the first place.

What a lovely, wicked thought.

"You have always been a true friend, Rosalie," she said with insincere sweetness. "Mayhap I could very well comfort Curtis when news of his wife gets around."

Rosalie nodded, moving her gaze out over the sea of mostly men and a few well-dressed women. "I will tell my husband," she said casually. "He likes a bit of gossip."

"Does he?"

"Enough that he will not keep it to himself."

"Even if it is about Curtis?"

Rosalie looked at her. "What man would not like to take a de Lohr down a peg or two?" she said. "To be truthful, I think some of these men are only allied with Hereford because they are afraid of him. A bit of gossip like this is sure to knock him down a peg or two."

Larue rather liked that idea, since it had been Hereford himself who rejected her father's offer of a betrothal between her and Curtis. Perhaps he did indeed need to be knocked down.

Perhaps the whole family did.

With a scheme in place, Larue and Rosalie parted ways.

The evening was about to get interesting.

CHAPTER TWENTY

DUSTIN HAD BEEN watching the dancing for the past two hours.

But something was amiss.

Perhaps it was simply her overactive imagination, but something didn't seem quite right. Curtis and Elle were dancing in front of the snapping hearth as the minstrels played, along with Myles, Douglas, Christin, Liora, Melusine, and Asa, but neither Myles nor Douglas could seem to find partners, which was why they'd ended up dancing with Christin and Liora. The single women, who had come with their fathers or brothers, didn't seem particularly interested, not even when handsome Andrew tried to persuade them. One young woman, from the House of de Lave, did dance for a little while, but after two dances with Andrew and Douglas, her father demanded she sit down with her mother.

It was quite strange.

And Dustin was watching all of it, trying to figure out what was going on. The music was good and the wine was flowing, but no one seemed to be having a good time. Christopher, who had been in Curtis' solar in the keep with Peter, Caius,

Alexander, Bretton, Robert, Tristan, and Sean, eventually came out and rejoined the people in the hall. Most of them headed for the dais, collecting cups and leftover food as they sat. Christopher, cup in hand, sat next to his wife and smiled at her before taking a hefty swallow of the wine.

"This is good," he said, smacking his lips. "After sending so much to Curt, I think our own stores are running low. I must send for more."

Dustin didn't respond to his comment as he drank more wine and muttered something to Alexander about taking a trip to Burgundy to find other, more delicious wine. She was fixed on the dancing.

"Chris," she finally muttered.

"Aye, love?"

She pointed to the group dancing. "Does something seem odd to you?"

Alexander and Peter, the closest, heard her. "What seems odd, Mama?" Peter said. "Other than Douglas being angry that he has to dance with a sister, nothing looks odd to me."

Even though Dustin wasn't his mother by birth, she had raised him, so Peter always addressed her as his mother. As he and Alexander snorted about Douglas pitching fits because Andrew drew in the unmarried women before he did, Dustin pointed to the dancing group again.

"Do you think it strange that the only people dancing are de Lohr family members?" she said. "Look—it is only those from our family. With music like this, there should be dozens of dancers out there."

Christopher simply shrugged. "Mayhap they do not feel like dancing tonight," he said. "It is no great mystery."

But Dustin wouldn't let go. "Look at them," she said, gesturing to the guests on the other side of the hall. "They are not even looking at the dancers. Everyone is crowded away from them. There is no cheering, no joy. No one is even here at the dais, speaking to us. We may as well be eating alone."

Now, Christopher was starting to see what she meant. "It does seem odd," he said. "Do we all smell horribly? Is a foul odor driving everyone away?"

Dustin was becoming increasingly annoyed with it. "Sean," she said, turning to the man across the table as he sat in conversation with Caius. "Will you and Cai see what you can find out? You do not bear the de Lohr last name, so if this is some kind of strange vendetta against us, maybe they will tell you. Find out why no one is dancing and no one is speaking to us, but be discreet."

Sean, perhaps one of the greatest spies England had ever seen, had heard most of the conversation. He looked to the dancers, musicians, and finally the hall full of people that seemed to be oddly removed from the party going on around them.

"What is wrong with them?" he said, frowning. "There should be twenty dancers out there, not eight. If my wife were here, she would dance until dawn."

"That is exactly what I said," Dustin said. "Will you see what you can discover?"

Sean stood up. "Come along, Cai," he said, nudging Caius. "Let's find out what is wrong with this crowd."

Caius stood up, following Sean as they left the dais and headed toward the throng of guests. As they moved with the stealth of panthers, blending in with the crowd, a young woman rose from her seat and headed for the dancers near the hearth. It took both Christopher and Dustin a moment to realize it was

Larue, and when they became aware that she was moving toward Curtis, they passed glances between them. Larue, in close proximity to Curtis, was never a good thing, especially with Curtis' rather volatile wife nearby. But they didn't comment on it. They didn't have to.

They knew what the stakes were.

What they didn't know was that, thanks to Larue, the evening was about to break loose.

ᔔ

IT HAD BEEN a lively tune, and Elle was very nearly worn out. She'd been dancing for a couple of hours and was very much enjoying herself, but she was winded. So winded. Curtis had spun her around too many times, and her tender tummy didn't appreciate it. As the music wound down, she came to a halt with her hand on her heaving chest.

"God's Bones," she said, breathing heavily. "Is this what happens at every great feast? People dance themselves into exhaustion?"

Curtis was sweating from exertion, but grinning. "Indeed," he said. "You wanted to dance, so here we are."

"I wanted to dance, not cavort in a frenzy and collapse in a heap."

Curtis laughed, and was going in to embrace her when Myles grasped her by the hand and pulled her away.

"It is my turn to be your partner," Myles said. "Let Curt dance with Christin. She is stepping on my feet too much."

Christin, nearly bent over in exhaustion from the lively dancing, suddenly straightened up, her eyes widening dramatically at the insult. "Consider yourself fortunate that I am your partner," she said imperiously. "I can just as easily force my husband to dance. He doesn't complain."

Myles shot her a long look. "He would rather die a thousand painful deaths than dance, and you know it," he said. "Dance with Curt for a while. I want to dance with Lady Leominster."

Even as Myles pulled her along, Elle was trying to beg off. "Please, I must rest," she said. "Let me sit for a few minutes and then I will dance with you, I promise."

"*What*?" Curtis gasped in mock outrage. "You are promising him a dance? Then it is over between us, Lady Leominster. I do not care if you are the most beautiful, brilliant, and witty woman in the world. I'm through with you, you ungrateful wench."

He was a little drunk and far too dramatic. Elle bit her lip to keep from laughing. "As you wish," she said. "I'm certain I can find others who would be interested, so I do not need you, either."

"How dare you!" Curtis declared. "Show me these men and I will slay them where they stand."

"Then it *is* true. She *can* find others."

Suddenly, there was a woman in their midst whom Elle didn't recognize. She wasn't unattractive, with jewels around her neck and on her ears, and her hair in a careful coif that was slightly disheveled. She interjected herself into the conversation, interrupting, and she was looking at Curtis with a decidedly inebriated expression. In fact, if Elle didn't know better, the expression seemed to border on seductive. But even if Elle didn't recognize her, Curtis did.

All of the humor left his face.

"Lady Munstone," he greeted her. "I apologize, I did not quite hear what you said."

The woman shook her head sadly. "Poor Curtis," she said. "I heard what happened. Everyone has heard. You have our sympathy."

Curtis had no idea what she was talking about, and neither did anyone else. Irritated that Larue had interrupted his conversation with his wife, Curtis gestured to Elle.

"I do not believe you have met Lady Leominster," he said. "This is my wife. Elle, this is Larue, Lady Munstone. Her husband is an ally."

Larue turned to look at Elle, weaving unsteadily as she did so. She was appearing more drunk by the moment. She looked Elle over, from head to toe, and returned her focus to Curtis.

"Dance with me," she said. "I have come all the way to Brython, and I want you to dance with me."

Curtis wasn't pleased that she had been rude to Elle. "Greet my wife, Lady Munstone," he said, his voice low. "It would be the polite thing to do."

Larue rubbed one eye, nearly throwing herself off balance as she did so, before looking to Elle. "*Lady* Leominster," she said in a catty display before returning her attention to Curtis. "We've all heard how this marriage came about, and you have our sympathy. Mayhap your wife should know that our loyalty is to you, Curt. What your father did to you was not fair."

"What are you talking about?" Myles said, frowning. "Sit back down, Lady Munstone. You're drunk."

Curtis held up a hand to silence his brother, but Larue lashed out at him. "Why couldn't it have been you?" she said, her voice lifting as she glared at Myles. "Why did it have to be Curtis? If your father was going to force one of you to marry a Welsh whore, why did it have to be Curtis?"

Liora and Elle gasped at the blatant insult as Christin, who had been listening to the entire exchanged, moved like lightning. Before Curtis could stop her, she was on Larue, her fingers biting into the woman's arm.

"Get out of here, you drunken fool," she said. "Get out of here before I cut your tongue out."

Larue gasped in pain as Christin squeezed, and Myles and Curtis were forced to separate them. Curtis had hold of Larue, turning her in the direction of her husband's table.

"Return to your husband, Larue," he growled. "For the insult you have dealt to my wife, tell him to go back to your encampment. He is not welcome at Brython, and nor are you. Get out."

But Larue wouldn't be pushed around. She slapped at Curtis' hands, stumbling away from him.

"Don't touch me!" she nearly screamed. "You… you stupid beast! I know all about your wife and how she was not a virgin when you married her! I know how she kept company with Welsh rebels, warming their bed! We all know that you were forced into this marriage because she is of Welsh royal blood, but royal blood of the Welsh is no better than the blood of dogs. You married a dog when you could have married me!"

The entire room had fallen into shocked silence as Larue shouted her venom. There wasn't one person in the hall who hadn't heard her. Through it all, Elle stood stock-still, unmoving and hardly breathing. She was so shocked that she couldn't do anything but stand there, cut to the bone by the woman's accusations, but Curtis wasn't silent in the least. It occurred to him that Larue was repeating what she had heard because someone on this night had been spreading rumors. He didn't know who, or why, but something had been going on.

Something nasty.

He, too, had wondered why no one else was dancing on this night when it should have been filled with merry revelers. Instead, the guests seemed to be keeping to themselves as the de Lohr family enjoyed the food and wine and music. When the dancing first started, he'd wondered why no one joined them, but because Elle had been having such a good time, he didn't think any more about it. He was focused on her, as he should be. But now…

Now, he could see that something was most definitely afoot. That was why no one was dancing or singing or celebrating. Like the small-minded bastards they were, someone had started a rumor about a Welshwoman and the others had listened. Elle was not one of them. She wasn't English, so the crowd was more than willing to believe any slander spoken against her. They were showing their true colors.

Now, he was about to show his.

"So this is what has happened," he said, looking at Larue with unmitigated disgust before looking to the group of guests. Enraged, he leapt onto the nearest table, scattering the empty cups as he shouted. "Is that what has happened? You have all heard some vicious gossip and, suddenly, you have decided to shun my wife? Is that why you're all crowded away from the dais?"

His voice was reverberating off the roof by the time he finished. He could see Robert de Wolfe and Tristan de Royans near the entry, but they weren't part of the group that was huddled together. When they heard him shouting, they came away from the entry and moved past the other guests, going to take a stand near Christopher and Curtis and the de Lohr family. Bretton de Llion had been with them, and he, too, moved over to the de Lohr side. Sean and Caius, who had blended into the group to discover why they'd been so standoff-ish, now had their answer. They, too, began to move away. All of them moved over to the de Lohr family, as something quite serious was evidently happening.

They would side with de Lohr to the death.

Even against petty rumors.

But Curtis was beyond livid. He was still drunk, which made his actions more dramatic, but he was a very big man with a very nasty temper when aroused, and the guests and allies he'd invited for a celebratory feast were going to find that out firsthand.

He spoke with great animation.

"Since some of you have chosen to listen to slanderous gossip about my wife, let me be plain," he said. "Elle was married before. She is a widow. That is why she was not a virgin coming into our marriage, if it's any of your damn business. As for warming the beds of Welsh rebels, nothing could be further from the truth. My wife is the daughter of Gwenwynwyn ap Owain, and she has spent her life fighting for the rights of her people. Rather than sit on her arse and dictate to others, like so many of you do, she chose to fight alongside them, and that is noble and admirable. And as for my being forced into this marriage, let me assure you that it was not the case. While the marriage was arranged, I love my wife and we are very happy. That is something most of you cannot claim, so if you must gossip about a woman you do not know simply because she is Welsh, then I believe I must rethink my alliance with the lot of you."

John Munstone, who hadn't paid much attention to his wife until she spouted off about the rumors regarding Lady Leominster, stepped forward. He had seen his wife earlier in the evening, whispering rumors to others, and with her most recent explosion, he realized that she was largely to blame for the situation.

John didn't want to lose the de Lohr alliance.

"Forgive me, my lord," he said, heading in Larue's direction even as he was begging pardon. "I... I do not believe my wife meant any harm. We were only concerned for you and your reputation."

Curtis scowled. "How dare you lie to my face," he said. "You were concerned for *your* reputation, not mine. You were concerned how you would be viewed if you associated with a man married to a woman with a sullied reputation, so your lies are unbecoming, Munstone. You are supposed to be a great warlord, but you clearly have the mind of a muddled fishwife. All of you do."

John cleared his throat nervously, glancing back to the group of shocked people. "You are correct," he finally said. "It is... regrettable."

Curtis wasn't in a forgiving mood. "Regrettable?" he said. "Is that all you have to say? I do not even care who started these rumors, but you listened to them and you believed them and you repeated them. Against a woman who has never done you any harm. Do you know why I arranged for this feast tonight? Because I wanted to introduce her to you. To everyone. I wanted to show her how noble and loyal our allies are. But you made me a liar. I told her you were good people, and you made a liar out of me."

John appeared truly remorseful. "Sometimes it is... difficult," he said, trying to make excuses. "Your wife is Welsh, after all. Most of us have lost friends and loved ones to the Welsh. It is harder to accept the Welsh sometimes."

"And easier to believe any slander about them."

"Unfortunately, it is."

That only fueled Curtis' fury, and he unleashed on that small, timid man. "If you'd like to spread rumors that are actually true, let us speak of *your* wife and how many beds she warmed before you married her," he said angrily. "I know that for a fact because she tried to worm her way into my bed on more than one occasion. I do not think there is an aroused manhood between Hereford and Brookthorpe that she hasn't put her mouth on, so before you go spreading foul rumors about others, you had better keep your own house in check, Munstone. If you are looking for whores, look no further than the one who bears your name."

It was a low and cutting blow, but he'd meant it that way. His fierce defense of Elle called for it. Larue burst into tears, rushing past her husband and running out of the hall. Curtis watched her go, utterly sickened and disgusted with her and the horrific situation she had started. He began to say something else, but someone climbed onto the table beside him, and he turned to see his father.

"No more, Curt," he said quietly. "You've said enough."

Curtis could see that the man was pale with distress. "You think so?" he said incredulously. "I think they deserve all that and more for what they've done. They haven't heard half of what I intend to say to them."

Christopher looked at him. "I know," he said quietly. "And I agree, they deserve it. But you must take Elle out of here. She is close to swooning."

That had Curtis moving off the table, rushing for Elle, who was standing where he had left her, shocked and trembling. She was positively ashen. He scooped her up into his arms, holding her tightly as she wrapped her arms around his neck and buried her face in his shoulder. Dustin and Christin moved up beside them quickly.

"Take her out through the servants' entrance," Dustin said quietly. "I will follow. Christin, go with them."

Christin did. In fact, Alexander joined her, and they shoved people out of the way as Curtis carried Elle out of the great hall and into the keep. Alexander lit a torch and illuminated their way up the narrow stairs, kicking open the master's chamber door while Christin rushed in and began lighting tapers. Between Christin and Alexander, they lit up the room and started a fire in the hearth as Curtis laid Elle down on the big bed that they shared.

Her eyes were closed, tears streaming onto her temples, as he put a big hand on her forehead, feeling as terrible as he possibly could. Christin came up beside him, bending over to kiss Elle on the head before she turned to her brother.

"Let me tend to Larue," she said. "Let me do this, Curt. *Please*."

Curtis knew what she meant. His sister had been a trained spy and assassin long ago, serving William Marshal in all manner of risky situations. Quite literally, she wanted to end Larue.

God, it was tempting.

"Although I love you for asking, not now," he said. "Papa would skin us both, so not now. But ask me again in a week. I may have a different answer for you."

Frustrated, but understanding his hesitation, Christin turned away, folding her arms angrily across her chest. Alexander eyed his rather unpredictable wife with some concern before going to Curtis.

"Do you need anything?" he asked softly. "What can we do for you?"

Curtis looked at him. "Burn down the great hall, mayhap?" he said with some irony. "Just make sure everyone we love is out of it and burn the bastard down."

Alexander knew he wasn't serious. Well, not *too* serious. But there was anguish in his expression. "If I thought you meant it, I would do it without hesitation," he said. Then he put his hand on Curtis' shoulder. "I'll leave you to tend your wife, and I must tend mine. I'm not entirely sure she is not going to go after Munstone's wife, regardless of what you say, so I will need to talk her out of it. And I will probably need to calm your father down."

Curtis nodded quickly. "Go," he said. "And Sherry… thank you."

Alexander gave him a brief smile before going to collect his wife, who was secretly planning how to end Lady Munstone's life and make it look like an accident. As Alexander put an arm around her and escorted her from the chamber, Curtis stood over Elle and watched her with great concern. His heart was breaking for her in so many ways. He only hoped he could repair the damage that had been done this night.

In truth, he wasn't entirely certain he could.

What a mess.

"May I have some water?"

Elle asked the question so pathetically that Curtis immediately went to the pitcher they had in the chamber, the one that had boiled water and fruit juice. Elle wasn't hugely fond of wine, and her pregnancy was making her gag with ale, so the watered fruit juice was the only thing she could really drink. He poured her a cup and quickly took it over to her just as she was sitting up. He helped her to drink it, all the while watching her anxiously.

"Can I get you anything else?" he asked. "Bread, mayhap?

She lay back down, closing her eyes. "Nay," she said softly. "I just want to sleep."

"Of course, my love," he said, pulling the coverlet over her and tucking it around her. Then he sat there and watched her, his heart absolutely breaking. "I'm so very sorry for this. If I had to guess, I would be willing to bet my life on the fact that Larue started those unsavory rumors. I'm so deeply sorry."

Elle didn't open her eyes as she rolled onto her side. "You know her."

"I do."

"She wanted to marry you."

He nodded regretfully. "She did," he said. "I should have told you."

"Did you know she was going to be here tonight?"

"Nay," he said. "I did not know she'd married Munstone until my father told me this evening."

"Yet you did not tell me," she said. "Just like you did not tell me about Gruffydd. What else have you not told me, Curtis?"

Suddenly, he could see trouble. There was a trust issue now, and the realization cut him to the bone. "Nothing, I swear it," he said. "I did not tell you about Gruffydd because I needed you to find some peace with him for the sake of our alliance and for no other reason. If you knew he was coming, I feared it would have clouded your entire evening, and I wanted you to look forward to it. As for Larue, it simply did not occur to me. Had she behaved herself, there would have been no issue, but given what I know about her, I should have anticipated trouble. That is my failing, and I apologize for it."

Elle didn't answer right away. He thought she had fallen asleep, and he'd stood up to bolt the door and prepare for bed when she spoke softly.

"Now, that entire group knows our most private secrets," she muttered. "They know *my* private secrets. They know I was not a virgin when you married me. They know I am a widow who fought alongside Welsh rebels. But they will never fully believe you when you told them I was not a whore. They will always think terribly of me."

He looked at her. "That's not true."

"It is."

"Then what do you want me to do?" he asked in a tone bordering on pleading. "Do you want me to go back to the hall and speak to each one of them? I will if you want me to."

Her eyes suddenly opened, and she sat up in bed. "And tell them more intimate details of me?" she said. "Of course not. The less they know about me, the better. Your family has been warm and wonderful, Curtis, but your allies are exactly as I imagined the English to be. Petty, nasty, and vile. Do not give them any more information on me. I do not care what they think. But you should have told me about Gruffydd, and you should have told me about Larue. It makes me wonder what else you've withheld from me in spite of your denials."

He went to stand in front of her. "I do not lie," he said, his voice low. "I will swear to you that there is nothing else I've not told you. If you do not believe that, then we do indeed have a problem."

She eyed him before lying back down and closing her eyes. "Please leave me alone," she said. "I want to sleep, and I want to do it alone. Go back to your family, Curtis. They've come a long way to see you, so you must not ruin their evening. But I will not go back into the hall as long as your allies are there."

"I do not blame you," he said. "But know this—I love you, Ellie. With all that I am, I love you. If I could have prevented what happened tonight, had I known it was coming, then I would have stopped it. I will defend you to the death. I hope you know that."

The tears began to trickle out of her eyes again. "I know you love me," she whispered. "I love you also. But love didn't stop the hurt and humiliation. It didn't stop you from withholding information from me. I had a right to know what I was facing tonight, and you took that away from me. You left me vulnerable and then tried to protect me after the fact. All I know is that I would have never done such a thing to you."

Curtis felt as if he'd been hit in the gut. He felt desperation as he'd never felt in his life. She was hurt and she was withdrawing, and the last thing he wanted was for her to return to the woman she was when he met her… guarded and suspicious. Had something been damaged tonight that could not be repaired?

It made him sick to think about it.

A soft knock at the door caught his attention, and he went to open it. He pulled back the panel to reveal Melusine, who was looking at him anxiously.

"I came to see if I could help," she said softly. "Is Ellie well?"

Curtis looked over to the bed where Elle was huddled up. "I do not know," he said honestly. "But I think she would rather not have me here right now, so do come in. At least someone will be with her if she needs something."

Puzzled, Melusine came in while Curtis went out. As he headed down the stairs, she closed the door and threw the bolt, moving toward the bed with hesitation. She peered at her cousin with great concern.

"Elle?" she said timidly. "What did he mean by that?"

Elle's response was to burst into gut-busting sobs.

CHAPTER TWENTY-ONE

F ROM WHAT HE'D heard, the feast had been interesting, to say the least.

The morning after what was supposed to be Curtis' triumph, all anyone could speak of was how he had berated one of his allies when the man's wife spread vicious gossip about Curtis' new Welsh wife. Something about her being a whore and having illegitimate children, or stealing an old man's wealth when he died. There seemed to be a few versions. The rumors were flying fast and furious, even though Curtis had set his friends and family straight the night before. He'd been in a rage for the rest of the night, becoming blindingly drunk and then trying to fist-fight men who attempted to calm him down. Rumor had it that he actually hit his brother, Myles, right in the face, and the man was sporting a lovely black eye this morning as a result. Whatever the truths were, it sounded like quite an eventful party.

And one that had not accomplished what Curtis had hoped.

Even now, as Amaro hung around the kitchens, carrying wood and pretending to repair broken kitchen implements, he could hear the servants whispering about the *terribilis vesper-*

um—the terrible evening. Most of the lesser warlords had already left by the time the sun rose, including the Munstone party. The rumor was that Lady Munstone was Curtis' former lover, and she was the one who had started the trouble. True or not, the party left very quickly as the sun appeared over the horizon, escorted out by several de Lohr soldiers.

Amaro had a grin on his face. He simply couldn't help it at the thought of Curtis' failure. He was becoming more and more entrenched in the kitchens and stables of Brython, mostly because they didn't seem too particular about their help, and also because he was in far less danger of being noticed because he'd stopped shaving and his beard was growing in, red and bushy. He'd smeared a layer of dirt on himself to further conceal his identity, so he wasn't particularly worried about being recognized any longer.

But he was still lying low, as much as he could.

Since his arrival yesterday, he'd seen Lady Leominster once as she came out of the keep with Dustin de Lohr at her side. She didn't look at all like the lady he remembered—the skinny, dirty woman who hissed like an angry cat. Two months of being married to Curtis had seen her cleaned up and fattened up and dressed in finery, so she really was quite beautiful when properly adorned and washed. But that was the only time Amaro had seen her, though he'd been told she tended to spend time in the kitchen and yard, helping her cousin. Amaro had seen Miasma, the only name he remembered her by, but he didn't care much about her.

He only cared about Lady Leominster.

That little bitch was his target.

After an evening like the one last night, he wasn't entirely sure he was going to see her at all today. Surely she would be off licking her wounds. Therefore, he simply went about the chores he'd been asked to do by a kitchen maid who had too much to handle herself. He'd tossed out the rubbish in the kitchen, throwing it to the pigs in their sheltered pen in the yard, and hauled water for the kitchen servants. He'd swept the entry and pieced together another broom that someone had broken, all the while wondering how long he could remain unnoticed by Miasma if she spent as much time in the kitchens as he'd seen last night. She was the one he'd seen the most of. At some point, she could very well notice him even through the hair and dirt. If that happened, she was a dead woman. He needed to keep his presence secret until he did what he'd come to do.

But he truly had no idea when that would be.

The morning began to head toward the nooning hour, and he had finished repairing two brooms. There was an area next to the well where women did laundry, and he'd hauled water up from the well to pour it into a small pool where they did their scrubbing. Ash was added to the water to give it some substance to clean away the stains. An older maid had come out to do some washing, leaving newly clean linens out to dry, but she was called into service by the cook, a woman Amaro recognized from Lioncross.

Yet another woman to hide his identity from.

Closer to the nooning meal, all of the focus seemed to be on the kitchens as they began to prepare for the evening meal, the largest meal of the day, which meant the kitchen yard was vacant for the most part—except for Amaro. He grabbed a shovel he had repaired earlier and sat on a stool, pretending to mend the shovel when he was really looking around for anyone he recognized. He could see the stable yard from where he was, and he could see the west side of the great hall.

At one point, he saw Myles and Hugo, which sent him into a panic because he was certain Hugo would recognize him, but he was too far away and Hugo was focused on Myles. When those two passed out of his range, he breathed a sigh of relief. He was coming to think that he needed to wander the bailey a bit to see if he could spy Curtis or his wife, or both, because he was too out of the way, hidden back in the kitchen yard, to see much at all. With the shovel still in hand, he stood up with the intention of walking out into the bailey and looking as if he was busy with a task. He hadn't taken two steps when, coming through the kitchen door, the very object of his search appeared.

Lady Leominster was directly in front of him.

And she was alone.

CHAPTER TWENTY-TWO

H E HADN'T COME back.

Elle had wept intermittently most of the night, finally falling into fitful sleep right before dawn, which only lasted an hour or two. She awoke to a bed devoid of her husband while Melusine snored over on the lounge. Knowing that Curtis had spent the night elsewhere left her feeling sick and alone. Perhaps he'd even spent the night with his old love Larue, though she quickly discounted that idea. It was a cruel one, coming from a confused and hurt woman. It wasn't fair to him. Unable to sleep any longer, Elle rose and prepared for the day.

She didn't know if any of the allies were still there. Not that it mattered. She didn't plan on dressing in lovely garments and parading around for them. Quite the opposite. She planned on going about her day as she usually did and ignoring the bastards who thought so poorly of her. She didn't plan on ignoring Curtis' parents, however, but perhaps they had left also. It wasn't as if there was any reason to stay now.

The feast had been a disaster.

As she moved about with her morning routine, Melusine awoke, yawning and scratching her head as she sat up on the lounge.

"What time is it?" she asked, yawning again.

Elle was over at the water basin. "Early," she said. "This sun is just rising."

Melusine's eyes were closed as she scratched her head with two hands now. "Did you sleep?" she asked.

"A little. Did you?"

"A lot."

That was the truth. Elle snorted. "You could sleep through the return of Christ and his angels," she said. "You have always been that way."

Melusine grinned, yawning yet again as she stood up and stretched. "I know," she said, but she stopped yawning long enough to look at the bed. "Did Curtis return?"

"Nay."

That seemed to wake Melusine up a little more when she realized how sad that must have made Elle. She went over to her as the woman washed her face.

"I would not worry," she said softly. "I am certain he went to be with his family. He has not seen them in a while. He will be back this morning, I'm sure of it."

Elle dried her face off. "As am I," she said with more confidence than she felt. "Everything will be just as it was."

Melusine thought her cousin sounded a little too cheery, but she didn't push. For once in her life, she didn't push. That young woman who often spoke before thinking was becoming more controlled these days. Being with Asa, and watching his temper, had helped her grow up a little.

She had some maturity these days.

"I'm sure it will," she said. "But... are you well after last night?"

Elle nodded. "I am over the situation," she said. "It happened, but it is finished. We move on."

Melusine could see that she was trying hard to be brave. "That is the best way to look at it," she said. "If my opinion matters for anything, I believe Curtis defended you admirably."

"Did he?" Elle said, looking at her. Then she thought about it. In fact, she'd had all night to think about it. "I suppose he did. He was certainly angry enough."

Melusine nodded. "He was," she said, putting a hand on Elle's shoulder. "I do not know why he left last night and did not come back, but he loves you, Elle. You could search your entire life and never find a man who would love you as much as he does. Whatever you are angry about—whatever chased him from this chamber—I would not be too harsh on him. Not only has he possibly driven away allies over what they've said about you, but now you've chased him away, too. It must be very hard on him."

It was shockingly apt advice coming from Melusine. She was absolutely right. Elle smiled her thanks for the woman's counsel, and Melusine smiled in return before heading for the door.

"If you no longer require me, I must return to my chamber to bathe and dress myself," she said. "I promised Asa that I would break my fast with him."

Elle waved her on. "Go," she said. "I have chores this morning. Come and find me in the kitchen yard when you are finished with Asa."

Melusine gave her a smile that suggested she might never be finished with Asa as she unbolted the door, passed through, and shut it behind her. That left Elle with a smile on her face, thinking of Melusine and the wild-tempered Asa. But it also made her think of Curtis.

She missed him dreadfully.

You could search your entire life and never find a man who would love you as much as he does.

Elle knew that to be true.

Dressed in a linen surcoat with a light shift underneath and a leather belt around her still-slender waist, she braided her hair and tied a kerchief around her head to keep her hair out of her face. Elle was a woman used to doing things for herself, and that included things that most noblewomen left to servants. Sweeping, scrubbing, and laundry were more than part of it. Today was laundry day because she had a few things she needed to wash, including two tunics that smelled horribly because her husband tended to wear clothing for days at a time, until she couldn't stand the smell any longer.

It made her smile to think of how quickly she had learned that aspect of him.

Curtis had lived a man's life before her, without any female influence other than his mother, so he wasn't hugely aware of things like smelling clean or brushing his hair or even farting at the table. She had been married to him for two days when the cook had made a stew of beans and pork, and the knights had eaten massive portions of it only to start letting loose with gas a couple of hours after the meal. As Elle and Melusine tried not to breathe through their noses, Curtis and his men farted up a storm to the point that the women had to flee the hall or suffocate. Curtis had no idea why they were running until he followed them outside, watched them head for the keep, and then returned to the hall only to walk into a wall of smell that nearly knocked him off his feet. Then he knew.

And he had apologized for it.

As Elle gathered the laundry into a bundle to tie off and carry down to the laundry, she giggled when she remembered the Notorious Night of Beans. They'd had beans since, but the knights were now polite enough to go outside if they needed to clear out their bowels, even if they were running outside every few minutes. It made for a better-smelling hall, at least.

But it *had* been rather funny.

With her laundry bundled up and ready to go, Elle went to the wardrobe in the chamber and pulled forth a sack of dried rosemary and lavender. The old cook had given her that helpful hint to make the laundry smell fresher, and she liked it very much. She especially liked it on her shifts. She would throw it into the laundry water and scrub the clothes with it, leaving the scent behind. Gathering the sack, she was bending down to pick up the laundry when the chamber door opened. She looked up from her laundry to see Curtis walking into the room.

The man looked like hell.

"May I come back, please?" he asked before she could say a word, tears glistening in his eyes. "Elle, I've spent almost eight hours away from you, and I cannot stay away any longer. If I must beg for your forgiveness for the rest of my life, I will, but please do not make me stay away any longer. I cannot bear it."

Instantly sympathetic and feeling horribly guilty, Elle rushed to him and threw her arms around his neck, kissing him deeply as he responded with passion she'd never before experienced from him. He held her so tightly that he was in danger of squeezing her to death. It was difficult to breathe, but she didn't pull away. He was so terribly distraught that she let him do what he needed to do. If that meant holding her in a viselike grip, then so be it.

"I am sorry if I was angry at you," she whispered between

heated kisses. "I should not have been so cruel to you. Please forgive me, my dearest."

He was responding to her kisses feverishly. "It was my fault, all of it," he said. "I should have told you about Gruffydd, and I should have told you about Larue. It was wrong of me not to. It was wrong of me to let her into the castle after I knew she had married Munstone. I should have turned her away, alliance be damned."

She ran her fingers through his blond hair. "You were trying to balance an alliance against a woman you hoped had forgotten you," she murmured. "I do not blame her that she has not. I cannot fault her for her good taste. But please do not withhold information like that from me again."

"I swear upon my life that I won't," he said. "This has been something of a learning situation for me, Ellie. I've never had to consider anyone else's feelings before, at least not like this. I thought I could control the situation, but I was wrong. Very wrong. It'll never happen again."

She believed him.

After that, they simply held one another. No lust, nothing sexual, but something that went beyond the physical. It was the melding of souls, the blending of minds, body against body as they drew strength from one another. Curtis had his face buried in the side of her neck, inhaling everything about her. He'd spent a horrible night of too much drink and too much emotion, so much so that he couldn't even sleep it off. He'd been awake all night with his father and brothers and brother-in-law, understanding what it meant to love a woman so much that he couldn't breathe or talk or think without her. His father and Peter and Alexander understood that, even if his younger brothers didn't. It was a night of reflection and regrets. As soon as the sun rose, he was on her doorstep whether or not she wanted him.

Thank God she wanted him.

"I do not say this often to you, my love, but you look terrible," Elle finally said, loosening her grip so she could look him in the face. "Truly, truly terrible, Curt. And I think you may still be drunk. I can smell it."

He started laughing, trying to turn away from her, but she wouldn't let him. She put her hands on his face and kept him from turning away. He let her go and tried to pull away, still laughing, but she hung on to him until he tripped and fell on the end of the bed. Then he threw his arms over his face so she couldn't look at him. All she could see were his mouth and jaw. Hands on her hips, she stood over him and shook her head.

"You *are* still drunk," she said, fighting off a grin. "Admit it."

He sighed heavily. "I am," he said. "I did not sleep last night. I stayed awake, drinking with my brothers and my father and even your brother. Gruffydd stayed with us. And I am not surprised that I look terrible, because I feel terrible. Guilt and remorse will destroy a man's soul when he's hurt the woman he loves."

She eased up on her harsh manner. "That is in the past now," she said, leaning over him as he took his arms away from his face. "Where is my brother?"

He looked at her with red-rimmed eyes. "The last I saw, he was heading home."

"This morning?"

"Aye."

"He was up all night, too?"

He nodded. "He told me that he was glad you spoke," he

said. "He also said to tell you that he will see you at his wedding next month."

Her lips twitched with a smile. "I will, indeed," she said. "So will you."

"Then I am to assume all is well between you two?"

She shrugged. "I think it is going to be," she said. "It will take time, but I feel confident that it is going to be. Where are your parents, by the way?"

"Neither one of them went to bed until it was nearly dawn."

"And the rest of your family?"

He reached up and pulled her down against him. "Myles and Douglas went to bed about the same time I came up to see you," he said. "Peter and Sherry, too. Liora and Christin went to bed last night, but I assume they will be up shortly. Christin... Sherry had to very nearly restrain her from harming Lady Munstone. My sister was determined to seek vengeance on your behalf. She probably still is. I do not think Lady Munstone is going to be safe for the rest of her life."

Elle smiled faintly. "I like your sister a great deal," she said. "I see a lot of myself in her, I think. She seems passionate for what she believes in."

He rolled his eyes. "You have no idea," he said. "She has seen, and done, quite a bit in her lifetime."

"And the sister that is closest to her?" Elle said. "Brielle? Is she the same way?"

"Worse," Curtis said. "Brielle is as tough as they come. She married a de Velt, you know. You met Bretton de Llion last night—he married Brielle's husband's sister. Very strong, very determined, very deadly people."

Elle began to toy with his blond hair. "I think the same could be said for the entire de Lohr clan," she said, growing serious. "I hope you are not disappointed that I did not stay and defend myself last night. Mayhap I should have, but I was so sickened by it... I could not speak."

He was shaking his head before she finished speaking. "You should not have had to defend yourself," he said. "Moreover, the vendetta was against me. You happened to be the tool that was used by a petty woman with a small mind. I found out that she and another woman, a friend of hers who was married to another allied warlord, spread the rumors. They were hoping to create a divide between us. My father took their husbands aside and essentially threatened them. If one does not wish to feel the wrath of the Earl of Hereford, then mayhap he should control the mouth of his ruthless and stupid wife."

Elle grew serious. "But there was a grain of truth to what they said," she said. "I did not go into our marriage a virgin, and I did live with rebels. They did not make up those details. Someone had to tell them."

"True," he said. "It was probably servants or soldiers. You know how they talk. But they heard those details and decided to spread the lies, which was a very bad decision on their part. But last night, my father and I spoke to all of the allied warlords and straightened out the situation. They have asked me to express their apologies to you, and they hope you will give them another opportunity to make it right. But that is your decision, love—I will not force you."

Elle was glad that the situation had worked itself out, but she wasn't sure about giving a former enemy the chance to hurt her again. "I will think on it," she said quietly. "But thank you for telling me."

He smiled and pulled her to his lips for a gentle kiss. "I have asked those close to our family to stay tonight so that we may have another feast without petty dramas," he said. "Wrexham and Wolverhampton and de Llion and the rest. They are good men, Ellie. I hope it was agreeable with you that I asked them to remain even after the others have gone home. It means a great deal to me that you know them and that they know you."

She shrugged. "If it means so much to you, I am not troubled if they remain," she said. "If you value them, then I am certain I will, too."

He smiled, kissing her again. "I hope so," he said. "But meanwhile… May I sleep this morning, my lady? And will you lie with me?"

She grinned slyly as she pushed herself off him. "If I lie with you, you most certainly will not sleep."

"Please?"

She shook her head. "It is not because I do not want to, but because you have been up all night and you need your rest," she said. "You need to sleep off the drink that is still in your veins."

"But where will you go if you are not here with me?"

She pointed to the bundle of laundry on the ground. "There are things to wash," she said. "I will do that while you sleep."

He crooked a finger at her, and she went to him, cautiously, but he suddenly reached out and grabbed her. Giggling, she resisted, but in the end it was just too much. He slid a hand in behind her neck, pulling her mouth to his, and his gentle kisses increased in force very quickly. His tongue invaded her mouth, licking her, tasting her, and Elle was quickly succumbing. He was trying to disrobe her, and she threw caution to the wind and helped him, pulling off the surcoat and the shift, leaving her in nothing but her slippers.

Those came off, too.

Pulling her onto the bed beside him, he stroked her face

tenderly, sucking on her jaw line. Elle was already hot for him, her body responding to his attention as it had done every day since their marriage. There was no longer any unfamiliarity or hesitation between them. If they wanted it, they took it or they asked for it. This time, she was going to ask for it. Taking his hand, she placed it on her wet heat, and he growled.

Curtis grew more demanding, and Elle came alive. The early pregnancy and usual nausea were forgotten as she responded to him without restraint. Curtis rolled onto his back, taking her with him, and her mouth left his before kissing his magnificent chest as his enormous hands wound themselves in her silken hair. He pulled the kerchief off and unwound the braid, letting that marvelous hair flow over him. She suckled at his nipples, slipping her hand between his legs to fondle his rock-hard manroot. The more she fondled, the more he groaned with pleasure.

Curtis could only take a few seconds of her touch before he was pulling her up by the hair, fusing his mouth to hers. They rolled sideways, kissing and fondling, until they nearly rolled off the bed. Curtis actually ended up on his knees, on the floor, but he had a plan in mind. Turning Elle onto her stomach, he pulled her up so that she was on her hands and knees on the mattress. Grasping her hips, Curtis drove into her from behind.

Elle groaned loudly as he filled her with his body, gripping the coverlet as Curtis thrust into her repeatedly. She was already begging for release, putting her hand between her legs to feel him as he made love to her. She touched him, and touched herself, feeling his power as he moved. His hands shifted from her hips to her breasts, and his face was against her back as he fondled her nipples from behind. Her breasts were full and luscious now, just like the rest of her, and all he could feel was unadulterated joy in this woman who had become his entire reason for living.

She was the very air he breathed.

His hands moved from her breasts to the junction between her legs. But the moment he touched her, she shuddered with a powerful climax and collapsed forward. Curtis continued to hold her up by the hips, thrusting into her until he achieved his own exquisite release. Together, they fell onto the mattress, riding the wave of ecstasy down to the ground, back to the world of reality.

It was heavenly.

Elle must have dozed off, because when next she realized, Curtis was snoring into the back of her head. Opening her eyes, she could see that it was brighter in the chamber now, a sure sign that the morning was in full bloom. She tried to move, but she realized that Curtis had her firmly pulled back against him, one big arm around her waist and the other one underneath her, his hand on her left breast.

Carefully, she began to disengage from him. She didn't want to wake him because he was clearly exhausted. She was able to worm her way onto her back, but he shifted in his sleep. His head ended up trapping her left arm, and his lips were on her breast. He must have sensed it somehow, because he started suckling her left nipple. As much as Elle loved it when he did that, she had things to do that morning, and he needed to sleep. If she let him suckle much longer, she would end up on her back with him between her legs again, so she gently pushed his mouth away from her breast and continued to slide out of his grasp. In order to get completely free, however, she had to slither to the floor before she could stand up.

Curtis just lay there, spread out all over the bed, and snored.

Grinning at her husband and his sleepy-time antics, she put her clothing back on, fixed her hair again, and found her slippers. Grabbing the bundle of laundry and the sack of lavender and rosemary, she silently slipped out of the chamber and shut the door, leaving Curtis to sleep as the world around him went on.

With a smile on her face and a spring in her step, Elle headed down the narrow spiral stairs. She was quiet, not wanting to wake anyone who had been up long into the turbulent night before. The entry level to the keep had servants bustling about because Christopher had used the solar the night before and they were cleaning it out, but she moved past them and out into the bailey.

The servants were all from England, from Lioncross and other de Lohr properties, and at first they'd whispered with disdain about the Welsh wife of Curtis de Lohr who liked to sweep floors and wash their clothing. It had been a breach of protocol for them. But these days, they'd grown used to her heading into the kitchen yard to do her husband's laundry. Some even thought it was a gesture of love and submission to the de Lohr heir, and that had drawn approval from even the stuffiest traditional servants.

Therefore, no one gave her a second look as she lugged the laundry bundle around.

They respected her for it.

The kitchens were smelling strongly of baking bread this morning as Elle entered the kitchen yard. The laundry area was ahead, near the yard wall and near the well, and she headed for it. What she didn't know was that Melusine had seen her crossing the bailey through her chamber window and was hastening to join her down in the laundry area. If Elle was going to work, then surely everything was well again. Things could get back to normal and petty rumors could be forgotten.

The world moved on.

As Melusine was on her way, Elle set her bundle of laundry on the table that was near the well. She opened up the bundle and took out the garments inside, putting them into the ashy water. There didn't seem to be enough water for her taste, so she asked a nearby servant to draw water from the well and add it to the basin. As the man with a shovel in his hand went to draw water, Elle went to the kitchen door and asked the cook for a couple of buckets of hot water, which were brought out by servants and dumped into the basin.

The servants retreated and the yard emptied as Elle focused on her laundry. Taking the rosemary and lavender from her sack, she tossed a few handfuls into the laundry and began to rub one of Curtis' tunics with a clean rock soaked in the ashy water. She scrubbed it and soaked it a few times, lifting it up to smell it and realizing that it still smelled like her husband's smelly, unwashed body. Wrinkling her nose, she scrubbed it harder, wondering if she should use the same soap she used for her body on the clothing. If it was good enough for skin, then certainly it should be good enough for clothing. Surely, it would work.

But that was her last calm thought before someone grabbed her by the back of her head and slammed her face down into the water, submerging it.

After that, the fight was on.

CHAPTER TWENTY-THREE

M ELUSINE WASN'T IN a big hurry.

She came scurrying out of the keep, following Elle's trail to the kitchen yard, but the entire time, she was keeping an eye out for Asa. That enthusiastic, sometimes irreverent Englishman whose entire family was Jewish. Asa was something of an anomaly, determined to fight like a warrior because that was what he'd wanted to be his entire life, yet he had the delicate skills of a jeweler that his father had taught him.

Bold yet gentle at the same time.

The man had made his own sword with the help of a smithy, and it was the most exquisite sword anyone had ever seen. Christopher had tried to buy it from him several times. Curtis had also tried to buy it, as had Myles, and Douglas actually stole it from him once. When Asa caught him, Christopher gave him permission to punish Douglas, and he had—by throwing eggs at him for a solid hour. Douglas was covered in eggshells and splattered egg, forbidden to wash it off for a day and a night.

To date, he had never stolen again.

Melusine was very fond of Asa. As she had told Elle, she

knew the man wanted to marry her, but she had neglected to tell Elle that he hadn't exactly asked. His affections were clear, but he'd never actually said the words. Still, Melusine knew what was in his heart. She knew that he very much wanted to marry her, and she wanted to marry him. She wasn't afraid to convert to his religion, either, though he hadn't asked her to. But she was confident that he would.

Someday.

But Asa didn't seem to be in any hurry.

As Melusine passed through the bailey, she heard someone calling to her. Turning toward the sound of her name, she could see Christin coming up behind her.

"Good morn, my lady," Christin greeted her pleasantly. "I wanted to tell you how much we enjoyed your food last night."

Melusine liked Lady de Sherrington, at least what she knew of her. She'd had a chance to speak with the woman at the feast last night before the chaos erupted, and she found Lady de Sherrington to be kind and curious.

A nice lady... for an English lass.

"I am glad to know that," Melusine said. "The cook and kitchen servants worked hard on the meal, so I will tell them that you appreciated it."

Christin nodded. "Please do," she said. Then she glanced around the bailey. "I was looking for Lady Leominster. Have you seen her?"

Melusine nodded. "I was just going to her," she said, pointing in the direction of the kitchen yard. "She is off to wash clothing."

Christin's brow furrowed. "Washing?" she repeated. "Does she not have a maid for that?"

Melusine shook her head. "She prefers to do it herself," she said. "She considers it a wifely duty."

Christin grinned. "Ah," she said. "Then I shall go with you. My brother is a very lucky man to have married such an industrious woman. Has she always been like that?"

They began walking toward the kitchen yard as Melusine nodded her head. "Always," she said. "Ever since she was a child, she has been very busy. She is not afraid to sweep a floor or pick up a sword in equal measure. She is brave and determined."

Christin laughed softly. "I think I have seen a bit of that," she said. "My father told me how my brother and his wife met. Did she really throw him off the wall in battle?"

Melusine grinned in spite of herself. "That is what I have heard, too," she said. "As Elle tells the story, she saw a very big knight come to the top of the ladder as he prepared to mount the wall. She was so angry that she charged him, and they both fell off the wall together."

Christin had to cover her mouth to keep from laughing out loud. "God's Bones," she muttered. "And I thought I was bold."

"Are you?" Melusine said, having no real idea of Christin's background. "Your mother seems to be a direct sort of woman, too."

Christin half nodded, half shrugged. "My parents met in much the same way that Curtis and his wife met," she said. "I think it is in the blood with de Lohr women to be rude to the man you are going to marry when you first meet him."

"Were you rude to your husband?"

Christin did laugh out loud then. "The great Alexander de Sherrington?" she said, feigning shock. "Surely not. I was so in awe of him I could hardly speak."

They were walking past the western side of the great hall at that point, with the kitchen yard directly ahead. There was a wall around the yard, covered with vines, and a gate in the middle of it. Melusine led Christin toward the gate.

"Then if you could hardly speak to him, how did you convince him to marry you?" Melusine asked with genuine curiosity. "Did your father speak to him?"

Christin shook her head, frowning. "My father did not want us to marry," she said as they reached the gate. "He thought Sherry to be too old for me."

"Was he?"

Christin reached out and opened the gate before stepping through with Melusine. "Of course not," she said, her attention moving to the kitchen yard and the search for Lady Leominster. "He was just the right age. In fact, he…"

Her sentence ended unnaturally fast as she spied something over near the laundry. A servant was holding someone down into the laundry basin. Someone in a linen dress who was struggling fiercely. Melusine's gaze fell on the same scene, and she immediately screamed, which spurred Christin into action.

She took off at a dead run.

Christin had been trained for survival and protection. She wasn't a wilting flower or a weak woman. She was a de Lohr, and they were the best of the best, the toughest women in England. A servant was clearly trying to drown a woman, and her instincts took over. As she ran for the laundry basin, she grabbed the first weapon she came across, which was a heavy piece of wood for the fire beneath the great cauldron in the kitchen yard. It was a rough piece of wood, with small branches sticking out of it like spikes, and she ran at the servant, who had yet to see her.

She used that to her advantage.

Flying up on the servant's blind side, she swung the wood with all her might, right at his head. She ended up catching him in the neck, causing him to stagger away from the struggling body he'd been on top of. As the person came up for air with a great, ragged gasp and Christin saw that it was Lady Leominster, she charged the servant again and hit him twice more in the face and chest with the wood. It was enough to send him backward and rip the cowl from his head. As he fell to his knees, Christin got a look at his face.

Bewilderment filled her.

"Amaro!" she gasped. "It's *you!*"

Amaro knew he was in a bad way, now recognized by Hereford's eldest daughter, who had been a trained assassin long ago. This was no feeble woman who had attacked him.

He had to fight back.

The shovel he'd been carrying before he attacked Lady Leominster was a few feet away. When Christin swung the wood at him again, he batted it away and lunged for the shovel. Meanwhile, Melusine was pulling a dazed and nearly drowned Elle away from the laundry basin as Christin did battle against a significantly larger opponent. When Christin saw that Amaro was going for the shovel, she threw the wood at him as hard as she could, clipping him in the face. Unfortunately, it didn't stop him, as he managed to grab the shovel.

Christin darted away.

"Run," she commanded Elle and Melusine. "*Run!* Find help!"

Elle wasn't able to move very fast. She still had water in her nose and lungs, so every breath was a struggle. Melusine was trying to pull her along, but Amaro was moving to cut off their exit. As Christin picked up an iron poker used to tend the cauldron fire, Amaro pulled out a dagger from somewhere around his waist. All good knights carried an assortment of daggers, and even though Amaro was posing as a servant, he was not unarmed.

Unfortunately for them.

The fight had just become more dangerous.

The dagger in Amaro's hand went flying at Melusine, catching her in the center of her chest before she could get out of the way. As she toppled over, he produced another dagger and hurled it at Elle. She was too weak and dazed to dodge it, and it slammed into her upper chest, near her neck.

She went down as well.

Horrified, Christin waited for a third dagger to come flying at her. She began screaming, trying to attract attention, and much to her surprise, Asa suddenly appeared in the yard entry. The truth was that her screams hadn't attracted him. He'd seen Melusine and Christin go into the yard, and, wanting very much to see Melusine, he had followed.

But what he stumbled upon was a horrific scene.

"Asa!" Christin screamed. "Help us! He is trying to kill us!"

Asa went into battle mode. He didn't have to see more than he'd already seen or hear more than he'd already heard. His broadsword, that magnificent piece, was pulled from its sheath, and he charged across the yard, heading for Amaro, as more men began to run toward the yard. Christin's screams had brought them from all over the bailey.

Asa raced at Amaro, who had another dagger in his hand. Prevented from throwing it at Christin, who rushed to Elle and threw herself on top of the woman to prevent Amaro from injuring her further with another flying blade, he turned the dagger on Asa and threw it. Because Asa was a moving target, it caught him in the thigh, but it didn't slow the man down. He came down on top of Amaro with that beautiful sword and nearly cut the man's left arm off.

Suddenly, the yard was filling with men, including Hugo, who had command of the gatehouse because the other knights all seemed to be sleeping. In fact, he'd had command of Brython since last night, since the beginning of that eventful feast. As he came into the yard and saw the carnage, he saw Asa standing over Amaro, who was trying desperately to escape the man. As Hugo watched, Asa brought the sword down and planted it squarely in Amaro's chest. The man collapsed, never to move again.

Having no idea what was happening, Hugo caught sight of Christin as she pushed herself off a wet and bloodied Lady Leominster. A few feet away lay Melusine, flat on her back, and as Asa ran to Melusine, Hugo ran to Christin.

"My God," he said, absolutely horrified at what he was seeing. "Lady de Sherrington, what happened?"

Christin was close to panicking. "We came into the yard and Amaro was trying to drown Elle," she said, her voice lifting in terror. "Hurry! Rouse Curtis! Rouse my father! We must get the ladies into the keep!"

Hugo turned to the soldiers who had crowded in behind him and gave them the commands to rouse the knights. As the soldiers fled and the alarm was raised all over the castle, Hugo dropped to his knees beside Elle, who was only semiconscious. A quick assessment of the dagger had him shaking his head at Christin.

"We need to get her into bed, where this can be removed," he said. "If we remove it now, we risk having her bleed to death in front of us. I will take her!"

He scooped Elle into his arms with Christin's help, and as he turned for the keep with an escort of frantic soldiers, Christin went to Asa as he held Melusine in his arms. The man was sobbing, rocking Melusine's limp form back and forth.

"Asa, put her down," Christin said urgently. "Let me see her. Asa, *put her down!*"

But Asa wouldn't do it. He continued to hold her, tears and mucus running down his face. "He killed her," he wept. "He *killed* her!"

Appalled, Christin had to forcibly pry Melusine away from him. She had a dagger sticking out of the center of her chest, right between her breasts. There was an enormous red bloom that radiated out from the dagger's entry point, and Christin put her fingers to Melusine's neck to feel for a pulse.

There was none.

Christin opened an eyelid to see that Melusine's eyes were fixed. There was no movement. She felt for another pulse at her wrist and put her hand on the woman's chest for any hint of breathing, but there was nothing.

Everything was still.

The realization that Melusine was dead swept Christin, and tears of shock came. She slapped a hand over her mouth, looking at Asa as the man wept with grief. Bold, brilliant, aggressive Asa, whom she'd known since he had been a boy, was suffering through something unspeakable. She put her hand on the man's head to comfort him, weeping with him, as Alexander burst though the yard gate. Half dressed, as he'd just been yanked from his bed by anxious soldiers, he began bellowing for his wife.

"Christin!" he shouted. "*Christin!*"

"I am here," Christin said, standing up so that he could see her. "Here, Sherry. I am here."

Catching sight of her, Alexander rushed in her direction, throwing his arms around her when they finally came together. For a brief moment, Christin gave in to his strength and warmth, because his arrival signified that she was safe. After the terror of the past few minutes, she was finally, and truly, safe. Alexander was here and nothing could hurt her, not ever.

"What in the hell happened?" Alexander said, finally releasing her long enough to clutch her head between his two big hands and look her in the eye. "What is going on?"

Now that the fight for her life was over, Christin was trying desperately not to weep. "It was Amaro," she said. "When Melusine and I came into the yard, he was trying to drown Elle in the laundry basin. I stopped him from killing her, but he began producing daggers and throwing them. He struck Melusine and Elle, but Asa came before he could throw one at me. Asa killed him."

Alexander still wasn't over his terror. His heart was beating so fast he thought it might beat right out of his chest. "Amaro?" he said incredulously. "De Laraga?"

"Aye."

"But he was at Lioncross," Alexander said, baffled. "At least, he was supposed to be."

Christin shook her head. "He was here," she said, gesturing to Amaro's body several feet away. "I do not know how he got here, but he was here and he was trying to kill Elle. Sherry, he killed Melusine. She's dead."

As she said that, Asa suddenly stood up. He was gasping like a madman, weeping and hysterical, and he staggered over to Amaro, pulled his sword out of the man's chest, and began stabbing him again and again. As those in the kitchen yard watched, Asa cut Amaro's body to pieces in his grief.

It was a heartbreaking sight.

"God," Alexander muttered, watching a man's agony play out. "My God, the poor man."

Christin was watching as well, softly weeping. "What do we do?"

Alexander shook his head and turned away. "Leave him," he said. "If there is any justice in this world, he is dispensing it. Let him do what he needs to do."

Christin simply nodded, wiping at her eyes as she turned to look at Melusine. Other than the massive red stain on her chest and the dagger sticking out, she looked as if she were sleeping. It was tragic in so many ways. Silently, Christin knelt down beside the woman, gazing at her still face for a moment before smoothing back her hair and kissing her on the forehead.

"I am sorry, my love," she whispered. "So very sorry. But you needn't worry—we will take good care of Asa for you. And Elle. You may rest well, darling, I promise."

With that, she took hold of the dagger and yanked it free of Melusine's chest, handing it to Alexander when he knelt down beside her.

"She seemed like a sweet lass," Christin whispered tightly. "I did not know her well, but I know that she spent the last few moments of her life trying to help someone who was in danger. That is a brave ending, Sherry. It is a warrior's ending."

Alexander nodded sadly. "It is, my love," he agreed softly. "Very brave, indeed."

"Make sure Asa knows that. I am not sure I can tell him."

"I will."

Christin's gaze lingered sadly on Melusine for a moment longer before she turned away. "I must go to Elle now," she said bravely, trying desperately to focus on the living and not the dead. "Curtis may need my help. Will you stay with Melusine and see she is taken care of? She must be well tended, Sherry. Please see to that. Be gentle with her."

He nodded, kissing her temple and helping her to stand. As Christin headed from the kitchen yard, Alexander sent men to collect something soft to wrap Melusine in as Asa continued to carve up Amaro. If anyone understood that kind of raw and horrible grief, it was Alexander. He'd seen much of it in his lifetime. But when Asa had exhausted himself and Amaro was in several different pieces, he returned to Melusine, took her in his arms, and stayed there for the rest of the day.

For moral support, and to show respect to a woman who had died trying to save Lady Leominster, so did Alexander.

CHAPTER TWENTY-FOUR

"**W**HAT IN THE bloody hell happened?" Curtis exploded. Having just been awoken from a deep sleep by pounding on his door, he'd slipped on his breeches from the night before and yanked the door open, only to find Hugo carrying a bloodied Elle in his arms. Suddenly, it was as if the entire world was bursting into his chamber as Hugo, followed by Dustin and Christopher and Peter, rushed to the bed and laid Elle upon it.

After that, it was chaos.

"Is she breathing?" Dustin demanded, sitting on the bed beside her while Christopher took up position on the other side. "Can you tell?"

Christopher was leaning over Elle, carefully inspecting the dagger that was jammed into her shoulder right at her neck. "She's breathing," he said. "Her heartbeat is weak and fast. She's in shock. Why is she all wet?"

"Because he tried to drown her!" Hugo said, distraught. "It was Amaro! He was here!"

Curtis, who was barely holding on as it was, looked at Hugo in horror. "*Amaro?*" he nearly shouted. "He did this?"

Hugo nodded, looking to his liege with the greatest of re-morse. "He did," he said. "My lord, I feel as if this is my fault. I should have told you… I should have told you what he was capable of!"

Curtis' mouth was hanging open in shock, in terror. "Tell me *what*?"

Hugo was in great distress. "The things he said," he mut-tered. "He would make threats toward the lady, toward her cousin. He said you were not allowed to punish him for anything he did, but when he went to Lioncross, I thought he would forget. I thought the threat was over. But he came back!"

Curtis couldn't decide what to do at that moment—go on the rampage, snap Hugo's neck, or push his parents out of the way to get to Elle. Perhaps he would do all three, but his brain was broken in the sense that he couldn't make a choice. He just stood there and quivered. He ended up emitting something of a roar of pain before turning for the door.

"Where is he?" he boomed. "Where is Amaro? I will kill him!"

Peter and Myles were in the chamber, too, grabbing Curtis before he could get away. But it was like trying to stop a raging bull. He'd already slugged Myles the night before in a drunken rage, and here he was again, fighting with his brother, whom he loved dearly. He elbowed Peter in the belly when the man grabbed him from behind and threw him into a bear hug to stop his forward momentum. As this was going on, Caius and Sean came into the chamber because they'd heard the alarms, only to see a full-blown fight going on between Curtis and his brothers while Curtis' wife lay on the bed between Dustin and Christopher, a dagger sticking out of her chest. When Christo-pher saw Caius and Shawn, he threw a finger toward Curtis.

"Help them," he bellowed. "Cai, help them calm Curt. Sean, I need you!"

Caius and Sean split up, Caius going to the tussling de Lohr brothers and Sean going straight to the bed. As Caius entered the struggle, Sean leaned over Christopher's shoulder, getting a good look at Lady Leominster.

She was a bloody, wet mess.

"What happened, Chris?" Sean asked quietly, urgently.

Christopher sighed sharply. "Amaro de Laraga has tried to kill my son's wife," he growled. "Curtis is trying to escape this chamber to find the man and kill him, but I need him here. I need him calm for his wife's sake, not running around like a madman."

"Where is de Laraga?" Sean said ominously. "I will take care of him."

Christopher shook his head. "I do not know," he said. "But find out where he is. Find out what happened and where this happened. I want to know how this came about. And when you locate de Laraga... make it hurt, Sean. Cause him pain."

It was a command to the man once known as the Lord of the Shadows. He brought pain with him wherever he went, and no one escaped his wrath. Nodding grimly, Sean headed out of the chamber on a mission. As he cleared the room, Christopher looked to Hugo, who was standing a few feet behind him, looking as if he was ready to collapse. But Christopher would have none of the man's guilt or grief. It wasn't his right.

"De Bernay," he snapped. "Look at me and listen."

Hugo's gaze immediately shifted from Curtis and the men trying to calm him to Christopher. "My lord?" he said, his voice quivering.

"Find a physic," he said. "We will do what we can, but she

needs a physic."

"We do not have one, my lord," Hugo said.

"Then go to the nearest town and find one," Christopher nearly shouted. "I do not care where you go, but find one. Send men out to comb the area for one. You will also have the servants send up hot water and clean, boiled rags. The same ones they use for the wounded soldiers. Lastly, send Wrexham to me, now. I am in need of de Royans. *Hurry!*"

He shouted the last word, and Hugo fled. Meanwhile, Elle was starting to come around, and Dustin had to practically lie on the woman to keep her still.

"Easy, lass, easy," Dustin said soothingly. "Be at ease. We will take good care of you."

Coming out of a dark and unpleasant fog, Elle had no idea what was going on. She was staring up at the ceiling, hearing Dustin's voice, before finally turning her head slightly and catching sight of the woman's strained face.

"My... my lady?" she said hoarsely, puzzled. "What is it? What has happened?"

Dustin forced a smile. "Be still, love," she said softly. "There has been a little trouble, but we will take very good care of you."

Elle still had no idea what she was talking about until she began to remember being in the water. Someone was holding her down in the water. She tried to fight back but couldn't seem to gain any headway. She remembered panicking, and then someone pulling her out of the water. After that... Was she running? She thought Melusine had been there. But the feelings of panic returned, and she tried to sit up.

"The water," she babbled, somewhat incoherently. "There was water. Where's the water?"

Both Dustin and Christopher attempted to push her back

down again, but the moment she jostled the knife in her shoulder, she cried out and fell back to the bed. In fact, that cry stopped Curtis in his tracks as he was fighting three men to get out of the chamber and find Amaro. That feeble cry had him pushing them aside so he could get to his wife.

His focus shifted.

"Ellie?" he said, his voice cracking. "Ellie, I'm here, my love. I'm here. Everything will be well, I promise. I'm here."

Dustin had to move aside, because he was going to his wife's bedside whether or not his mother was in the way. As Dustin moved away, helped by Myles, Curtis collapsed beside the bed, his big arm across Elle's chest to keep her from moving.

"I was in the water," Elle said, clutching at him with the only arm that was pain-free to move. "Someone pushed me into the water. They tried to drown me!"

Curtis laid his head on her shoulder, that horrible knife in his line of sight. "I know, my sweetest love," he said softly. "But you are safe now."

Elle wasn't convinced. She was also still dazed. As she started to weep purely out of fright, Curtis looked at his father in agony.

"We must remove the dagger," he hissed. "Help me, Papa."

Christopher put his hand on his son's blond head. "We need something to stop the blood before we can," he said. "Dustin, you must get your sewing kit. We must get this out."

Dustin was already on the move, sending Myles running for her kit. There was wine in the chamber, something to use for cleansing the wound, so she went around collecting what they needed in order to remove the dagger and plug the hole. As she looked for something to use as a rag, because she wasn't sure they could wait much longer, Caius came up beside her.

"You cannot be sure that dagger did not puncture a lung," he whispered. "If it has and you remove it, the lady will not be able to breathe."

Dustin nodded. "I know," she murmured. "We must be able to make a hole in her chest to make breathing easier, which will not be a simple or a painless thing."

Caius lifted a dark eyebrow. "There is also something else to consider," he said. "There is very little blood coming from the wound. Either it missed everything vital, which would be the best of all things, or it is holding back the flow."

Dustin knew the implications. If they were unable to stem the tide, Elle could bleed to death in minutes. But they both knew that they simply couldn't leave the dagger there. One way or the other, it had to come out.

Dustin sighed heavily.

"God help us," she muttered. "We need a physic!"

There was desperation in her tone, and Caius patted her on the shoulder. "I will see to the rags," he told her. "Go and keep Curt calm. He needs you."

Dustin nodded, squeezing his arm gratefully before returning to the bedside. As Caius headed out to see what was keeping Hugo and the things Christopher had demanded, Curtis remained with his wife, his head on her shoulder, his enormous arm across her chest to hold her still.

He'd never felt so helpless in his life.

"Everything will be well, I promise," he said softly, trying to distract her because he could hear people scrambling behind him, preparing to remove the dagger. "When you are feeling better, and before our son is born, mayhap we can journey to some place lovely and warm. I've heard that there are beaches of white sand to the south, though I've never been. I think my father has. I hear they are very nice. Would you like to go to a warm beach of white sand?"

Elle was still weeping softly, but her eyes opened as he spoke. "A beach?" she said. "What beach?"

"To the south," Curtis said, lifting his head to look at her. "I have always wanted to go. My father says they are beautiful. Aren't they, Papa?"

Christopher, sitting on Elle's other side, had been listening to the conversation. When Curtis looked at him, he smiled weakly. "They are, indeed," he said, watching Elle focus on him. "When I was young, I went with Richard to the Levant. I spent years there, fighting on sand the color of clouds. And you've never seen water as blue as the water there. It was so clear that you could see all the way to the bottom of the sea."

Elle sniffled. "It… it must have been beautiful."

"Verily," Christopher said, noticing that Caius had returned with not only de Royans on his heel, but also with Christin in tow. Servants were filing in after them, bearing the things he had asked for, but his focus remained on Elle in an effort to keep her calm. "It can be very hot there, so unless you are prepared to melt, you may want to think about staying in England, where the weather is much more agreeable. There are some lovely beaches to the south, at Brighton for one. Or mayhap Curt will take you to our townhome in London and you can lounge on the banks of the Thames."

"I did not know you had a home in London."

Curtis nodded. "Lonsdale," he said, seeing that Myles had also returned with Dustin's sewing kit. The time had come to remove the blade. "My lady, we must remove the dagger in your chest. There will be some pain, but I promise we will remove it as quickly as we can. You must be brave just a little while longer."

Elle seemed to be calmer than she had been when she first awoke. "I can see something sticking out of me," she said. "I have been afraid to look."

"It is a dagger," Christopher said.

"That is what is causing me such pain?"

"Aye."

She smiled, without humor. "In all the years I have taken up arms, I have never been wounded," she said. "This is a first."

Christopher smiled ironically. "Then you have joined the ranks of Curtis and myself, and even Lady Hereford," he said. "We have all been wounded in some way, at some time."

Elle's smile faded. "You told me of your wound at Tickhill."

Christopher's smile brightened, though it was forced. "I survived," he said. "And so will you. You will survive and thrive, and my grandson will be born fat and happy. Everything will be as it should."

Elle believed him. This man, who had once been her greatest enemy, was now someone she trusted. She knew he would never harm her or be dishonest. Much like his son did, Christopher had her respect.

She was in good hands.

"Then do what needs to be done," she said, turning her head to look at Curtis. He was gazing at her with such distress that she forced a smile, just for him. "Your father says everything will be well. I believe him."

Curtis nodded, too choked up to respond. As Christopher stood up and went to de Royans to ask the man to take command of the castle while everyone was wrapped up with this tragedy, Christin, who had been standing out of the way, slipped into the space her father had occupied.

"You will be feeling better very soon," she said, smiling at Elle. "Is there anything you want? Anything I can get for you?"

Elle felt some comfort with Christin there. She had come to like the woman a great deal. "Mayhap you can help me change into dry clothing when this is over," she said. "I seem to be wet."

Christin's smile faded, no matter how hard she tried to remain positive. "I will seek out fresh clothing for you right now," she said. "When your wound is bandaged, I shall be ready to help."

She tried to move away quickly, but Elle stopped her. "Where is Melusine?" she asked. "She can help you. But you must be gentle when you tell her what happened. She will be quite upset."

Something in Christin's eyes flickered when she realized that Elle must not have remembered what had happened in the kitchen yard. She glanced at Curtis, who seemed to be waiting for an answer too. *He doesn't know*, she thought. Therefore, she proceeded carefully.

"I will be gentle," she said after a moment. "Now, you must lie still and quiet. I will take care of everything."

As Christin darted away, Elle's gaze moved back to Curtis, who smiled bravely and kissed her hand repeatedly. Comforted, but quite weary, Elle closed her eyes to rest as Dustin and Christopher brought everything they would need over to the bed. Dustin gently shooed Curtis out of the chair she wanted to take, next to Elle, and as Curtis stood up, he could see Christin motioning frantically to him. Leaving his parents with Elle, he went over to her.

"What?" he asked curiously. "What is it?"

Christin was clearly upset. "Her cousin was killed in the attack," she whispered. "I could not tell her, Curt. It would only upset her more. Let Mama and Papa do what needs to be done, and then you will tell her, please?"

Curtis closed his eyes tightly for a moment, greatly distressed at the news of Melusine's death. "You know she is dead for certain?" he said. "Did you see her?"

Christin was fighting back tears. "Aye."

Curtis was expecting more of an answer. "Well?" he demanded, trying to keep his voice down. "What happened?"

Christin sighed heavily before answering. "Curt, I am the one who stopped Amaro from killing your wife," she hissed. "I was just coming into the kitchen yard with Melusine as Amaro was trying to drown Elle in the laundry basin. That's why she is all wet. I attacked Amaro and drove him away, but as Melusine was pulling your wife out of the water and trying to flee with her, Amaro produced daggers from somewhere on his body and began throwing them. That is why Elle has a dirk sticking out of her chest. Amaro threw one at Melusine, also, but it hit her right between her breasts. She was probably dead before she hit the ground."

Curtis was listening in horror, his hand over his mouth. "My God," he gasped. "Is… is *that* what happened?"

Christin nodded. "With God as my witness, it is," she said. "I am so sorry, Curt. I wish the outcome had been different."

He shook his head, his hand coming away from his mouth. "This is not your fault," he assured her. "None of it is. But what about Amaro?"

Christin could see that he was getting worked up again, and she grasped him by the shoulders. "Asa came to our rescue," she said. "He killed Amaro, and when he realized Melusine was dead, he hacked the man's body to pieces. I do not know what has happened after that, but Sherry is with him. He is making sure that both Melusine and Asa are taken care of."

Curtis digested what had happened. It was the first time he'd heard the entire story. When he realized what his sister had told him, and how close Elle had come to death, the situation overwhelmed him. Closing his eyes tightly, he felt tears stream down his face as Christin tried to comfort him.

"Don't weep," she said softly. "Elle will survive. Mama and Papa will take great care of her."

He shook his head, his hand coming away from his mouth as he suddenly threw his sister into a tight hug. "You saved her," he murmured. "You saved her and risked your life to do so. How can I ever thank you enough for that, Cissy? You saved my life, too."

Christin hugged her emotional brother before finally forcing him to release her. "Everything will be well and good again," she assured him, wiping the tears from his face. "It was not my intention to tell you everything right now, but I had to because your wife has asked for her cousin. Melusine died bravely, Curt. She died trying to take your wife to safety, so she must be well remembered for that."

Curtis nodded, taking a deep breath and trying to steady himself. He heard his mother calling for him, and he turned to see her waving him over.

"They are going to begin," he muttered. "I must help them hold her still. But Cissy… truly, you have my deepest gratitude. I love you for it."

She smiled, encouraging him to go to his wife's bedside, where their parents were beginning the process of removing the dagger in Elle's chest. As she watched, Curtis knelt down next to his wife's head, holding her left arm still while Myles got in behind their father and held her right arm. The entire de Lohr family was pulling together to save the young woman who had become Curtis' all for living. Perhaps they didn't know her very well, but that didn't matter. She was precious to Curtis, and that made her precious to the rest of them. Like a pride of lions, the House of de Lohr banded together. When one was hurt, they were all hurt.

This was their way of preventing any more hurt to one of their own.

Elle was going to live.

The de Lohr family would make sure of it.

CHAPTER TWENTY-FIVE

H E'D BEEN TOO late to warn them.

Jeffrey had arrived about a day after Amaro's chaos. He quickly discovered that Amaro had moved through Brython like a tempest, injuring Lady Leominster and killing her cousin. But he hadn't made it out alive, thanks to Asa and Sean de Lara, who had disposed of the pieces of Amaro's body in a manner they wouldn't disclose. Hugo, who had known of Amaro's vendetta, had been so distressed about the situation that Christopher sent him back to Lioncross. The man had been a wreck. But no one felt guiltier about the situation than Jeffrey. He felt as if he'd failed the entire family by letting Amaro slip away from under his watchful eye, even when Christopher had assured him that it wasn't his fault.

But Jeffrey didn't see it that way.

The day after he'd arrived, word was that Lady Leominster was doing well. She was eating and arguing with her husband about getting out of bed, which was a good sign. Everyone seemed to breathe a sigh of relief. She'd been told about Melusine and, quite naturally, she was grieving it deeply. Her desire to get out of bed was because Curtis had sent word to the priests at St. Nicholas because they needed to bury Melusine, and Elle was adamant that she attend the burial. Unfortunately, Curtis would not let her go, and that only compounded her grief. She was angry and upset, and he'd spent two days trying to comfort her.

Meanwhile, the guests who had come for Curtis' celebratory feast had all departed for home. This included Caius, Sean, Wolverhampton, Wrexham, and even Peter and Alexander. Although Christin in particular was loath to leave, the truth was that she had young children who needed her, as did Liora. Dustin had Christin take her son as well as her younger sisters with her, removing Andrew and Rebecca and Olivia Charlotte from the madness, while Dustin and Christopher remained behind. It was with great sadness that Curtis bade everyone farewell, promising to see them at a more favorable time.

Jeffery had watched the departures from the wall, unable to shake the feeling of doom that had settled on him. His guilt was endless. But his arrival was fortuitous, because the de Lohrs seemed to be consumed with Elle and the situation at hand, so Jeffery took command of the castle when Tristan de Royans headed home. Perhaps he didn't feel so much like a failure when he could do something useful. But as he, and everyone else, prayed for Lady Leominster's recovery, dark forces were seemingly at work. Two days after surviving the attack on her life, Elle began showing signs of a fever.

By nightfall, she was on fire.

The hope that had so recently been present as Elle's healing began was dashed when a poison took hold. Hugo's men, the ones sent to find a physic, had gone into England looking for such a man, and every qualified individual they found refused to go that far into Wales. Realizing the difficulty of convincing an English physic to enter Wales, the men shifted tactics and headed to Rhayader, the closest village, and were referred to Pliny, who knew Elle and agreed to come. But what he saw upon his arrival did not please him.

He was in for a fight.

Elle slept fitfully most of the time as the first day of fever stretched into the second and the third. She was worried for her baby, not for her own life, as Pliny forced a willow bark potion down her lips every few hours whilst working to create something he called rotten tea, an ancient recipe for healing those with poison in their bodies. Unfortunately, it took time to produce what he needed, so all he could do in the meanwhile was give Elle what he had and hope that was enough.

But fevers were unpredictable things.

The fever would ease, only to come back more strongly than before. On the sixth day, Curtis could barely rouse Elle, who slept heavily and sweated profusely. Her wound was festering, and although Dustin had washed the wound out as best she could with wine before stitching it, Pliny was convinced that some bit of fabric or another foreign body was causing the poison to rage.

That meant opening the stitches and cleaning out the wound again.

It was with a heavy heart that Curtis, Christopher, and Dustin held Elle down as Pliny removed the stitches and began to probe a wound that didn't seem to want to heal. Elle's lungs hadn't been compromised by the puncture, which was good news, but she screamed in pain as Pliny probed the wound, cleaning out clots and pus until he finally came to a small bit of linen from Elle's shift that had been shoved deep into the wound when the blade made contact. Elle had finally passed out from the pain, and Pliny quickly removed the fabric, cleaning the wound once more and stitching it up. Bandaging it tightly, he told a very pale-faced Curtis that all they could do at that point was wait.

Wait to live.

Or wait to die.

Only time would tell.

So, they waited.

On the seventh day, Christopher was in the bailey with his sons, getting some much-needed fresh air. Elle had slipped into unconsciousness at that point, and had been for over a day, so the mood was solemn. No one wanted to voice what they were thinking, which was the fact that Elle was going to die. The fever was going to kill her. Myles had even sent word to Gruffydd the day before to let the man know what had happened. But no one would speak the words aloud, even if that was the general consensus.

Christopher had to seriously wonder what her death was going to do to Curtis.

"Papa!" Douglas shouted, sitting atop a very big horse with shaggy hair. "What do you think of him?"

Distracted from his morose thoughts, Christopher caught sight of his son as he emerged from the stable yard. "Think of what?" he said. "It looks like you are riding a haystack with legs."

Douglas frowned. "This is a very fine animal," he told his father as he drew close. "The man I bought him from says that he has seen many a battle. He is big and tough. See?"

Christopher could only see a very beaten-down nag of a horse. Westley came up behind Douglas, stick in hand, and began to poke at the horse, hoping to annoy it enough so it would dump his brother. As Christopher stood there, a dubious expression on his face, Myles walked up beside him.

"Ah," he said. "I see that Douglas is showing you that horrible creature he bought."

Christopher was trying not to scowl. "When did he buy that thing?"

Myles snorted. "A few weeks ago," he said. "He had saved enough money and was determined to buy his own horse."

"And he bought *that*?"

Myles nodded. "We tried to stop him," he said. "Curt did, I did, but he would not listen. The man at the livery in Presteigne saw a fool in my younger brother and convinced him that the horse is a relative of Pegasus. The truth is that the old horse has one foot in the stew pot."

Douglas was clearly thrilled with his purchase. He reined the horse in circles as Westley held on to the horse's tail and tried to smack it with his stick. Douglas saw what his youngest brother was doing and tried to kick at him to get him to stop.

Christopher just shook his head at the antics.

"Would it be best for me to take Douglas back with me to Lioncross?" he said, scratching his head irritably. "I fear those two have been creating havoc for Curt, and he does not need that right now."

Myles' smile faded. "I think you should take them both back," he said. "Curtis does not need to worry about them. As much as I love to watch my younger brothers beat on each other, the truth is that they are young. They are annoying. If you do not take them back with you, you may find them tied up and dumped on your doorstep someday. Ellie was the only one with any patience for them, and now…"

He trailed off abruptly as they ended up on the subject of

Elle. Christopher instinctively turned his attention in the direction of the keep, his eyes finding the windows that were part of Curtis and Elle's bower.

"Your mother thought she might have been better this morning," he said. "The apothecary managed to brew that foul-smelling potion, and he started pouring it down her throat yesterday. He thinks it will help a great deal."

Myles was looking to the keep also. "Is she awake yet?"

"Not the last time I saw her."

Myles let out a heavy sigh and looked away. "What is going to happen if she dies, Papa?" he finally asked. "Curt will go out of his mind. You must stay until we know which way Ellie will go, because I surely cannot handle him by myself. This entire place is in chaos because of Amaro. Asa is useless because of Melly's death, Hugo is nearly as useless because he feels responsible, and that leaves me to manage everything. I cannot do it all."

Now, he was voicing what they had not yet been able to voice. He was speaking of death and consequences. It was like opening the door for the devil to step in and take her. Christopher put his hand on Myles' shoulder.

"I know," he said, trying to be of some comfort. "But you are Curt's rock right now. He needs you, so do not collapse under the strain."

"I will not," Myles said. "But what about Roi? Can you not send him here?"

Christopher shook his head. "Roi is in London," he said. "Henry is having problems with Richard Marshal, and Roi has gone to give counsel. You know that Henry relies on him."

Myles looked at him. "I would say the possible death of Curt's wife is more important than Henry's issues with Richard

Marshal," he said. "You must send word to Roi and have him come. He is needed here more. Or at least send Sherry back. You cannot leave me alone with this."

Christopher knew that. But he also knew that Peter and Alexander were important garrison commanders, and to pull them away from their own commands was beneath them.

"They have their own mighty commands," he said. "I cannot do that. What about leaving Jeffrey here?"

Myles shook his head. "You know I love Jeffrey, but he is far too old," he said. "He would be fine commanding, but he wouldn't be much in a fight. I need men with strong swords."

Christopher's gaze moved to the wall where Jeffrey was. He could see him near the gatehouse. "This situation has him broken," he said. "He feels responsible that he let Amaro slip away from Lioncross."

"It is not his fault," Myles said. "He should not take any blame."

Christopher sighed heavily. "I know," he said. "I told him so. What if I send Staff to you? I will if you think he would be of help."

Myles knew Stafford de Poyer, a keen and intelligent knight who had served his father for a couple of years. Stafford's father, Keller, had been a knight sworn to William Marshal, so Myles had known the family for several years. Stafford had only recently come to Lioncross, beefing up the border castle's stable of capable knights.

"If you will do that, I will be grateful," he said. "I would feel much better with Staff here. He can help me manage this beast of a castle, but I would like another knight if you can spare him."

"Who?"

"Rhys d'Mearc."

Christopher grunted unhappily. "I hate to part with him."

"I know, but he is needed much more here than at Lion-cross."

"Why would you say that?"

Myles frowned. "Because you have a dozen junior knights at home," he said. "Plus, you have Jeffrey and Staff's brother, Cal. Those two could take on an entire army by themselves and win."

Christopher smiled, looking up to the wall where he could see Jeffrey, who was now completely gray, with a big white beard. "Jeffrey would scare them into submission, to be sure," he said. "And Cal is hideously frightening when he wants to be. Who do you think keeps our junior ranks in line?"

It was Myles's turn to grin. "He takes after his father," he said. "Keller may be incredibly old, but he is still vital. Like you."

Christopher's eyebrows rose. "Are you saying I am incredibly old?"

Myles started to laugh. "Never," he said. "You're ageless, Papa. You'll outlive us all."

Christopher's smile faded. "I hope not," he said. "I do not want to outlive my children. But I would say, on the whole, that—"

He was cut off when the sentries lifted a cry, announcing an incoming visitor. Christopher and Myles headed for the gatehouse, strong and long since repaired, to see what the fuss was about. The gatehouse of Brython faced east, toward England, but the road leading to the entry curved around from the south. As they peered through the portcullis, they could see a group of people coming up the road, heading for the gatehouse.

Curiously, Christopher and Myles watched them come closer. It wasn't a military group, but rather a collection of peasants. No one seemed to be armed. There were a few on horseback, but most were walking. Some were carrying things. Christopher ordered the portcullis lifted, and when it was high enough, he and Myles went out to greet the throng.

The sight of two armed knights coming out of the castle slowed down the procession. There was a man in the front with a walking staff, and he held up a hand for the group to come to a halt. When Christopher and Myles came to a stop several feet away, the man with the staff took a few steps in their direction.

"*Cyfarchion, fy arglwydd,*" he said. *Greetings, my lord.* "*Rydym wedi clywed am helynt y ferch.*"

They were speaking Welsh. *We have heard of the daughter's trouble.* Myles looked at his father in confusion, but Christopher suspected whom they were speaking of. He answered in fluent Welsh.

"Do you speak of Lady Leominster?" he asked.

The man nodded. "Aye," he said. "I am Cadell. My wife and I are bakers. Sometimes, the lady comes to our shop and buys our bread. We have heard of her troubles and have come to pay our respects."

Christopher nodded. "It is kind of you to come," he said. "All I can tell you at the moment is that the lady is very ill. She is not receiving visitors."

Cadell's fair face tightened with sorrow. "That is terrible news, indeed," he said. "We were told that she was in a bad way."

"Who told you?"

"Pliny," Cadell said. "The apothecary. Before he left the

village with the men who had summoned him, he told others that the lady was ill."

Christopher's gaze moved over the group behind him. "She is," he said. "But I will tell her husband that you have come to give your best wishes for her recovery. That will mean a great deal to him."

Cadell gestured to the group behind him. "When someone is ill in our village, it is a tradition that we bring them gifts to help them recover," he said. "The lady is part of our heritage, my lord. Her father was a great ruler, but she has not known a great life. We all know that. Pliny told us that marriage to the Saesneg has made her very happy. We've come to show our gratitude for the happiness he has given her."

Christopher was rather touched by that. "It is very kind of you to do that," he said. "I have been told that Brython is a special place to the Welsh, and to have an English commander is probably not what you would like. But know that the lady and her husband are ensuring that this place of legend is protected."

Cadell gestured to the castle. "Brython is thriving," he said with a smile. "We can see that for ourselves. When the lady comes to town, she buys food from all the bakers. She spends money at the apothecary and the merchant. She has prospered, and she comes to town to ensure that we prosper, too. It was never like that before the English came. *She* was never like that before the English came."

Christopher smiled faintly, looking to Myles. "Cadell, this is my son, Myles," he said. "He is the brother of Lady Leominster's husband."

Cadell dipped his head to Myles, but his attention returned to Christopher. "And you, my lord?" he said. "Who are you?"

"Christopher de Lohr."

That brought a buzz of excitement from the group. Even Cadell seemed surprised by the answer.

"Hereford," he said in realization. "You are Hereford."

Christopher nodded. "I am."

"You were the one who took Brython from Gruffydd."

Christopher didn't want to get into the fact that he'd conquered a Welsh castle in the presence of Welshmen. "Gruffydd is an ally," he said. "Since the lady has been ill, we have sent him word. He knows."

"Who knows?"

The voice came from the gatehouse, and they all turned with surprise to see Curtis coming through. He was unshaven, unwashed, and looking like a wild man with a growth of beard on his face. But he was coming toward his father and brother, his gaze fixed on Cadell.

His eyes flickered in recognition.

"I know you," he said. "You are the baker."

Cadell nodded. "I am," he said, replying in the language Curtis had spoken. "I was telling your great father that we have come to see how the lady is faring. We heard she was ill."

Curtis had spent too many sleepless nights to adequately keep his composure at the sight of so many people coming to see how Elle was doing. Any conversation about her had him verging on tears these days, which wasn't usual for a man who was normally in control of himself. But he nodded shortly to Cadell's statement.

"She is," he said. "She is very ill. I am moved that you would take the time to come all the way to Brython to see to her health."

Cadell quickly turned around, motioning frantically to someone, and the crowd parted to reveal a couple of men pulling a handcart. As the men came forward, Cadell turned to Curtis.

"You and the lady have been good to our village," he said. "Because Brython prospers, you have helped us to prosper, too. As I told your great father, the lady spends money in the village with as many merchants as she can. She spends it until she has no more. She leaves money at the church so they can give alms to the poor. I do not know if you have realized that. Her prosperity has been our prosperity, and her happiness is reflected in her actions. It is because of you, my lord. Marrying her has changed our lives, too."

By the time he was finished, Curtis was choked with emotion. He could only nod his head, blinking back tears, as the men with the handcart came to a halt and Cadell reached into the cart to display the contents.

"I have brought the lady many loaves of honey bread," he said, holding up a loaf. "We have brought her baked eggs and currant buns and pies with honey and apples. We have brought baskets of food for her."

Curtis was stunned. He went over to the handcart to look at all of the treats, and a woman approached him with folded blue material in her hands.

"For your wife, my lord," she said, extending it to Curtis. "It will keep her warm."

Curtis took it from her because he didn't know what else to do. She was kindly offering it to Elle, so he took it. Before he could thank her, other people came forward, handing him things, mostly articles of clothing or blankets, telling him that they were meant for Elle and wishing her a swift recovery. A man, evidently a blacksmith, handed him a metal bracelet that he had made. It was simple and strong. Curtis took all of these things, completely in awe that so many people thought so well of his wife.

And it touched him more deeply than he could express.

"I will make sure she knows who brought these things to her," he said sincerely. "Please tell me your names. I will not forget them. But she will want to know who to thank."

"Gratitude is not necessary," Cadell said. "These are small things, just small things, to tell her that we will pray for her recovery. We want her to know that we are grateful to her. God rewards those who are generous and kind, and we know that God will heal her. Elle ferch Gwenwynwyn is a true Welsh-woman with a true heart. Mayhap she does not know the good that she does, but we do. You will tell her, won't you?"

Curtis was starting to get choked up again. "Aye," he said hoarsely. "May I borrow your handcart to take these things to her? I will return it, I promise."

Cadell nodded, motioning the villagers away from it, as Curtis put the items in his arms next to the baskets of food. The villagers, having delivered what they had intended, turned for the road.

"If the lady needs more honey bread, do not hesitate to send word," Cadell said. "We will send it along."

Curtis smiled weakly. "I am certain she will want to come and get it herself as soon as she can," he said. "She rather likes her jaunts into the village."

Cadell grinned. "Then I will make sure I have something special for her the next time she comes," he said. "Good day to you, my lord."

Curtis held up a hand in parting. "And to you, Cadell," he said. "And thank you. This means… It means a great deal."

Cadell simply waved a hand, herding the villagers back the

way they had come. They had delivered what they intended to, and now their business was concluded. Curtis, Christopher, and Myles watched them depart, heading down the road until they faded from view. At that point, Curtis turned to the handcart full of gifts.

"Rhayader is not a wealthy village," he said. "Those people can ill afford to give things away like this. They should not have done it."

Christopher came to him, resting a hand on his shoulder. "It does not matter that they cannot afford to do this," he said. "Do you not understand, Curt? Your lady has been kind to them, and they are showing kindness in return. This is the only way they could do it. Gifts like this are worth more than gold, lad."

Curtis did understand that, but he still felt bad that the villagers were giving over things of value. He wasn't sure how Elle would feel about it, knowing that they could ill afford it. But as a show of gratitude, his father was right—it was worth more than gold. Perhaps, in a small way, it was acceptance to him, too, as the Lord of Brython.

If the Welsh were accepting him, then extended peace was assured.

And that was why he'd married Elle... for peace.

It had come.

"Help me get this back, Myles," he said to his brother, who came to assist him with the handcart. "Since my wife is not eating these days, I suppose we could give it to the men before it spoils."

They turned the handcart for the gatehouse, with Curtis and Myles pushing it between them. Christopher followed alongside, peering at all of the food in the cart.

"Elle must be fond of the honey bread," he said. "There is a good deal of it."

"She is fond of everything the baker made," Curtis said. "If she knew it was here, she would rise up out of her bed and rush to eat it."

"Then take it to her and let her smell it," Christopher said, half joking. "If she smells it, it might rouse her."

Curtis smiled weakly. "Pliny says she is sleeping heavily now," he said. "The fever has gone down. He hopes it will soon break."

As they reached the gatehouse, pushing the cart through, Christopher put his hand on Curtis' shoulder. "That is good news," he said. "Is your mother with her?"

"Aye," Curtis said. "I've been sitting in the same chair since last night. Mama told me to get out and get some air. But I am going to take some of the honey bread and go back. Mayhap you are right—if I wave it under her nose and she smells it, it will rouse her. At this point, I am willing to try anything."

He sounded hopeless. Christopher felt bad for the man, with every day being a day of grief and sorrow. Well did he know what it felt like to worry over a wife that was loved more than life itself. As Myles shouted to Douglas and Westley to help with the handcart and take it to the kitchen, Christopher picked up a loaf of the honey bread and handed it to Curtis.

"Do not lose faith," he said quietly. "Women are remarkable creatures. They are far stronger than you think they are. I know this because your mother almost died giving birth to you. I endured days of horror as she struggled, and in the end, I had a horrible choice to make—your life or hers. That was what the physic presented to me. But before I had to make that choice, by a miracle, you were born. I will never forget that moment, Curt,

not as long as I live. I, too, had lost all hope. But your mother...
She dug deep down, tapping into that strength that all women
have, and willed you to be born. She wasn't going down without
a fight. And neither is Elle."

Curtis took the bread, hearing his father's words that
brought tears to his eyes. "I want so badly to believe that," he
whispered tightly. "I do. But every day that passes, she grows
weaker. Every day that passes is a day my hope lessens, just a
little. She cannot keep going on like this."

Christopher smiled sympathetically. "She will not," he said.
"This will be over, soon, one way or the other. All I am saying is
that you must have faith in Elle's strength. The woman threw
you over a wall in battle. She can fight off a fever."

In spite of his tears, Curtis started to laugh. Christopher
patted him on the cheek and pointed to the keep, a silent
command to return to his wife. Taking the bread with him,
Curtis obeyed.

The keep was warmly lit when he entered, with a fire in the
hearth near the door and torches lit to illuminate the stairwell.
He took the stairs two at a time, increasingly smelling the bread
in his hand, to the point of taking a bite, as he came to the level
where the chamber that he shared with Elle was. He realized
how hungry he was and took another bite as he headed toward
the chamber door, chewing with a very full mouth. Opening the
door, he swallowed part of the bite just as his gaze fell on the
bed.

It was empty.

Momentarily stumped, he nearly choked on the rest of the
bread in his mouth, spewing it out all over the floor as he
envisioned an empty bed.

Empty!

"Jesus," he gasped, panic filling his veins. "Oh, God. *Mother!*"

He bellowed at the top of his lungs, only to hear his mother answer him almost immediately.

"Curtis, hush," she said. "Why are you shouting?"

She was sitting at the window seat off to his left, the one that was set in a small alcove that contained chairs and a chest. Most of the windows in the chamber were lancet, but there was one big window sunk into the thickness of the wall, with two seats facing one another in front of it. It was Elle's favorite place to sit, and as Curtis' frantic gaze found his mother, with Pliny standing beside her, it took him a moment to realize there was someone sitting opposite her.

Elle turned to look at him.

"I'm here," she said softly. "Do not fret."

Curtis looked at her as if he were seeing a ghost. She was wrapped up in a robe, leaning weakly against the wall behind her, but she was alive. And she was speaking to him. For a moment, he couldn't answer. He pointed to the bed with the bread he was holding.

"You... But you were sleeping," he said, clearly unable to process what he was seeing. "I left, and you were sleeping."

"She was," Pliny said. "Her fever is completely gone, my lord. She awoke shortly after you left, and we told her you had gone outside. She wanted to see for herself."

Curtis stood there with his mouth open. Then he burst into quiet tears, covering his face with one hand to hide the emotions that were coming out all over the place. He took a few staggering steps in Elle's direction as Dustin jumped up and rushed to him, helping him over to his wife, who weakly put her arms up to guide him down next to her. As Dustin and Pliny wandered away to give the couple some privacy, Curtis put his arms around Elle and sobbed.

"I thought you were dead," he wept into the side of her head. "You were so ill, and I thought you were... *gone*."

Truthfully, Elle felt as if she *was* quite nearly gone. She was horribly weak, but even so, she had demanded to sit by the window. Dustin had told her that she forced Curtis out into the fresh air, so she knew the man would return shortly. Elle was counting on it. What she hadn't counted on was his falling to pieces in front of her. He'd been so terribly frightened that his fear brought tears of her own. She hugged him as much as she could, trying to reassure him.

"I am quite alive," she said, pulling back to look at him. "See? Look at me. I am not dead, I swear it."

Curtis grasped her face, gazing into those miraculous blue eyes. "God, I hope I am not dreaming."

"You are not."

"You're real?"

Elle smiled weakly. "I am real."

He fought to regain his composure now that his shock was wearing off. "But why are you here?" he said. "You should be in bed."

She leaned against the wall again, her hands on his face. "My entire body aches from having been lying in bed for so long," she said. "The moment I awoke, it was screaming to get out. I am sorry that I could not wait for you to help me."

He shook his head, kissing her twice, tremulously. "That does not matter," he said. "But... Oh, God, I keep saying this, but I cannot believe it. You're alive."

Her smile grew. "I am," she said. "Did you really think I was going to leave you, Curt?"

He lifted his big shoulders. "Sometimes we have no control over things," he said. "My father told me to have faith. He said that women are stronger than we know."

"Your father is very wise," Elle said, watching him lift her hand to kiss it reverently. "How could I leave you? We have a son coming in a few months. We have a life to live. I could not let you live it without me."

He put his hand against her belly, on the heavy robe in between. "And he is well?" he said. "He has not suffered?"

Elle put her hand over his. "Pliny says that if he has survived my troubles, then there is every chance that he has not suffered," she said. "I suppose we will find out."

Curtis simply couldn't speak anymore. He was overwhelmed. He pulled Elle into his embrace, finally picking her up and carrying her back to bed, because he wasn't comfortable with her sitting in the breeze of an open window. Elle didn't put up a fight, letting him do what he wanted to do. She simply went along with it. But when he set her down on the bed, she finally noticed what he'd been holding in his hand the entire time.

She pointed.

"Is that honey bread?" she asked.

He shook his head, putting it behind him. "It is nothing."

"Show me."

"You must conserve your strength."

Elle was lying back on the pillows, looking up at him. "Curtis?"

"Aye, my love?"

"Show me what is in your hand."

With great reluctance, and fighting off a grin, he produced the honey bread with two big bites taken out of it. Dustin, who was back at Elle's bedside now, put her hand over her mouth to keep from laughing as Elle sighed faintly.

"You promised not to lie to me again," she said softly.

He closed his eyes for a brief moment, knowing he was caught. "I did not lie to you," he said. "I simply said that it was nothing at all."

Elle shook her head at her guilty husband. "I am too weak to punish you, but know that when I am feeling better, my punishment shall be swift," she said. "Do you have anything to say in your defense?"

He smiled and sat down on the bed next to her. "There is more of it in the kitchens that is untouched and waiting for you," he said, reaching out to take her hand. "The villagers brought it as a show of gratitude. They wanted you to know that they were praying for your swift recovery."

After hearing that, of course she could not become angry. In fact, she was quite touched. "Will you bring me some of it?" she said. "I think I could eat something."

That was a good sign, but Pliny put up a hand. "Broth for you, my lady," he said. "You have not eaten in days. We must introduce food slowly so that your belly will become used to it again."

Elle was disappointed, but she understood. "Very well," she said. "May I have some broth, then?"

Pliny nodded, looking to Dustin, who grinned as she leaned over to kiss Elle on the forehead. "Of course, my love," she said, stroking Elle's blonde head. "I will fetch it for you. Welcome back. We have missed you."

As she headed off to retrieve the broth, Curtis held Elle's hand, smiling at her, still incredulous that he wasn't dreaming this whole event. Elle smiled in return, caressing the big hand that held hers. He was holding her like he was never going to let go.

Ever.

Nor was she.

"You will have to tell me everything that happened since I've been… asleep," she said softly. "How is Asa?"

Curtis squeezed her hand gently. "Much as you think he would be," he said. "He is mourning Melly deeply. We all are."

That brought tears to Elle's eyes. "When I am feeling better, will you take me to her crypt?"

He leaned down and kissed her hand. "Of course, love," he said. "As soon as you wish."

Elle wiped at her eyes. "It will seem strange without her," she said. "But she was happy when she went, Curt. That is very important to me. Melly spent so much of her life unhappy, but I know that here, with us, she was very happy."

Curtis didn't want her becoming emotional over Melusine and exhausting herself over something that she could not change. "Brython has been a happy place for me, too," he said. "It brought me to you, and for that, it will always have my deepest fondness."

"Even after Amaro's rampage?"

"Even after."

She watched his face, seeing that he was sincere. "That is something we must strive to forget," she said. "I do not want it clouding what Brython has become to us. It was a terrible event, of course, but we have many happy things awaiting us here. A home and children. They will be born here, children of two worlds. Your father said that to me once."

Curtis kissed her hand again. "He was right, in every way," he said. "I remember when he told me that I was to marry you, and I very nearly refused. He said something to me that seems more important now than it was then. He said that he had made his mark on the marches, and with my marriage to you, it was time for me to make my own mark. I knew what he meant, or at least I thought I did, but now I think I have it figured out."

"What do you mean?"

He smiled at her, putting her palm against his unshaven cheek. "I mean you," he said softly. "It wasn't that I was to make my mark on the marches. It was that you were to make your mark on me. You *are* the mark, Ellie. You are *my* mark. And you have given me a life I could have never imagined."

It was a sweet thing to say. "Nor I," she murmured. "Do you remember when we first met and I told you of the Otherworld? How the Welsh are waiting for our greatest prince to rise and free us from English tyranny?"

He grinned. "I do," he said. "How Brython protects the gate to the Otherworld."

She grinned because he was. "Prophecies are meant to give hope," she said. "They are meant to give the downtrodden a reason to live, a reason to fight. I am not saying that it is a foolish legend, but I think that you have changed that prophecy."

"How?"

"Because you have brought hope with you," she said, her eyes glimmering with warmth. "You have given me a gift greater than any prophecy, greater than any army. You have given me yourself, Curtis de Lohr, and that is all I will ever need."

Curtis leaned over her, touching his forehead to hers in a moment of complete and utter adoration. The love he felt for her, and she for him, had propelled them beyond prophecies and armies. It had moved them beyond English and Welsh. Now, they were on a plane that few people achieved in their lifetimes. Only the fortunate few would know what they knew. That the phoenix of hope could rise from the ashes of hate, and that love was the only thing that mattered in the end.

For Curtis and Elle, it was their calling.

And yet another legend of a great and timeless love was born.

EPILOGUE

1240 A.D.

THERE WAS A war going on in the keep of Brython.

If Christopher, Arthur, and William de Lohr had any-thing to say about it, they were going to capture their cousins James, Vaughn, and Westley. Sons of Rebecca, their father's sister, it was three determined boys against three determined boys.

The battle was on.

Eleven-year-old Christopher Titus de Lohr was at the head of it. The name Christopher after his grandfather, the name Titus because his mother had liked it. He went by the name Chris sometimes, the General other times. Whatever he was called, he was all de Lohr. As his father said, he was born a man.

And he was ready for his cousins.

He could hear them coming. They were on the floor below, listening to someone tell them to stay out of the way. It was moving day at Brython Castle, and Chris' parents, Curtis and Elle, were moving their possessions out of the keep and into great wagons in the bailey. The king had decided that Brython should be given back over to the Welsh as part of a peace treaty with Powys, and, oddly, Gwynedd, and that meant the Earl of Hereford had to surrender the garrison to their Uncle Gruffydd. It wasn't a hugely difficult transfer from what they'd heard from their parents, because Uncle Gruffydd was a good man, but it was more the fact that they had to move at all.

Brython had been their beloved home.

Chris and his brothers, Arthur and William, weren't helping with the move at this time. They had been earlier, with smaller things, until the heavier items were moved and their mother had told them to go entertain themselves. So they were. They were going to entertain themselves by ambushing their cousins, who were coming up the stairs. They could hear Westley, named for their Uncle Westley and mostly called Mouse because he had brown eyes and brown hair and a little nose and moved rapidly, just like a mouse. James and Vaughn, the twins, were bigger and meaner than Mouse was. They were coming up the stairs with sticks they'd found somewhere. Once they hit the top of the stairs, the fight began in earnest.

Chris was the first one out of his hiding place, a toy sword in hand as he charged Vaughn and sent the boy to his knees. Arthur was next, a very big lad with red hair and a temper, who rushed out and kicked James in the shins. As James went down, Mouse saw William coming at him and screamed, rushing back down the steps and falling over the last few stairs so that he ended up at the bottom with scraped hands and a big bump on his chin. William was right behind him with a rope he'd stolen from the kitchen yard, and as Mouse sat at the bottom of the stairs and wailed, William tied his cousin's hands together and started dragging him back up the stairs.

That was until Elle came up on the scene.

"William!" she gasped. "What on earth are you doing?"

William dropped the rope as his mother rushed over to untie Mouse's hands. "Playing," he said as innocently as a seven-year-old could. "We are all playing."

Elle could hear the grunting and scuffling on the floor above. She looked at her son as if the lad was a hardened criminal, with horror, before shouting up the stairwell.

"Chris!" she said. "Arthur! Are Vaughn and James with you?"

The scuffling stopped immediately, and there was a long pause before Chris answered.

"Aye, Mama."

Infuriated, Elle scowled. "All of you," she shouted. "Come down at once!"

There was some hissing and shoving. She could hear that, too. Someone either tripped or fell. Then there was the marching of little feet, of boys coming down the stairs like prisoners coming down to face their execution. As Elle waited for the gang to arrive, Curtis appeared from the floor below.

He, too, had heard the wailing.

He pointed at Mouse.

"What happened to him?" he wanted to know. When he noticed William standing there, he suspected he knew the answer to his own question. "Ah… What have you been doing, William?"

William smiled at his father. "Playing, Papa."

"Playing?"

"Aye, Papa. *Playing.*"

Curtis happened to look at his wife, who was just pulling Vaughn off the stairs, but he saw what she was holding. "Why does your mother have a rope?" he asked.

William simply grinned and shrugged, entirely innocent of

any wrongdoing, but Curtis knew that wasn't the case. As he stood there and wondered how he was going to plead the case of William to his mother, Elle lined up Chris, Arthur, Vaughn, and James. Chris had a scrape on his face, Arthur had a bloodied nose, Vaughn had the beginnings of a black eye, and James was bloodied around the mouth. Curtis tried desperately not to laugh at the bruisers before him as Elle stood in front of the boys, her expression stern.

"Today is an important day at Brython," she said. "And what do I find? Six boys trying to kill one another. What have we told you about that? Chris? What do you have to say for yourself?"

As the oldest, Chris knew he'd take the brunt of his mother's rage. His father was standing a few feet away, but he knew the man was utterly powerless against his mother. It had happened too many times before. Therefore, he knew how to handle his mother.

With logic.

"We were practicing, Mama," he said.

She frowned. "Practicing what? Death and mayhem?"

He shook his blond head. "We are traveling to Monmouth Castle," he said. "It is a long journey. We were practicing in case we are attacked along the way. We must be prepared to fight off the outlaws who will attack us."

Elle's eyebrows flew up at her son's original excuse. "Is that so?"

Chris nodded seriously. "Aye," he said, daring to look at his father. "Papa said we must be ready to fight."

Elle turned to Curtis, who now found himself the object of her disapproval. He scowled at his son. "Many thanks, lad," he muttered wryly. "Now she will take a stick to *me*."

Elle wouldn't let him get away so easily. "Did you really tell them that?"

Curtis sighed. He decided to confess everything and hope for the best. "I did," he said. "It is a long journey to Monmouth Castle, and I did tell them that we should be prepared, but I did not give them permission to beat each other bloody."

Elle shook her head reproachfully at her husband before turning to the boys. "Mouse, stand up," she told her nephew. "All of you will go to the kitchen yard and wash off your faces and hands. Clean yourselves up. Then you will go to the great hall, sit down, and stay there. Do not move until I come to you. And keep your hands off one another. Am I clear?"

The boys nodded solemnly. Elle pointed to the stairwell, a silent gesture to get on with it, and the six of them slipped away, hissing and whispering angrily as they headed down the stairwell. That left Elle and Curtis standing alone. Once the boys were out of earshot, Curtis broke down in giggles.

"God's Bones," he muttered. "They remind me so much of my brothers and me that it is frightening sometimes."

Elle was fighting off a grin. "They are just like the lot of you," she said, trying to sound disgusted. "But mark my words—one of these days, someone is going to be seriously injured. They play far too roughly with each other."

Still chuckling, Curtis went to her and wrapped her up in his arms. "You must let them be true to themselves," he said, kissing her cheek when she tried to turn away. "I know you do not like to hear that, but it is true. They must learn and they must grow, but they can only learn by doing."

Elle was trying to avoid his seeking lips but she wasn't trying very hard. "I do not think ambushing each other is learning," she said. "That is Asa's fault. He has encouraged them to do that."

Curtis finally managed to kiss her on the mouth. "That is because he only has two daughters," he said. "The man lives for a good fight, so he finds it in our boys."

Elle couldn't keep the smile off her face after that. "*Uncle Asa*," she said, shaking her head. "Who knew they'd have a Jewish uncle?"

"One who likes the thrill of battle, no less."

She chuckled. "But he has made an excellent addition to our house, hasn't he?" she said. "Who knew he would find another Welsh lass to marry in the end?"

Curtis nodded. "It is a good thing he did, for I do not know what I would do without him and his sword," he said. Then his hand found her gently rounded belly. "Speaking of sword, mayhap this one will be another girl. Then we'll have three of each, and we'll only have to worry about the boys because the girls will be perfect."

She thought on her blonde, curly-haired daughters. "Mary and Valeria are angels," she agreed. "Although Valeria is more like the boys. She certainly has your grandmother's spirit, from what your father says."

Curtis couldn't disagree. Their daughters were five years and four years old, respectively, and absolutely the apples of his eye. "She will ride into battle with me someday, just like her great-grandmother," he said. "Where are the girls, anyway?"

"Where do you think?" Elle said wryly. "They are with your father, attached to him by invisible cords. When he is around, I hardly see them."

Curtis grinned. "He adores them, and the feeling is mutual," he said, but his smile soon faded. "But I will be honest when I say that I wish he had not come."

Elle knew what he meant. Christopher hadn't been well as of late—not terribly so, but enough to worry his sons, who fretted like women sometimes when it came to their beloved papa. Putting her hands on his face, she kissed him before letting him go.

"Your mother says he would not stay away," she said, taking him by the hand and leading him toward the stairwell. "She says he has been feeling well enough, and this is a big move for us, so he wanted to be part of it. He's well enough if he's simply sitting down and not trying to exert himself."

Curtis was still greatly saddened. "He's very old," he said. "The physic says his heart—"

"His heart is fine," Elle said, not wanting Curtis to drift into the melancholy that so often consumed him when speaking of his father's deteriorating health. "He is here and he is well enough. Be grateful for that and spend as much time with him as you can, Curt. In fact, find the boys and take them to your father. He will want to hear what they've been doing."

Curtis sighed heavily and nodded. "He will," he said. "Those six make him laugh."

"They make me crazy."

Curtis smiled weakly at her. "Admit it," he said. "You love every minute of it when you're not swatting behinds."

She tried not to smile but wasn't doing a very good job of it. "I must have been mad when I agreed to let Rebecca's sons foster here," she said. "How is it we have raised such wild animals?"

He shrugged. "I cannot speak for Rebecca, but in our case, look at their parents," he said. "Our boys were bound to be battle-born, my love. There was no way around it."

That was true. Elle paused before taking the stairs, looking around the floor, at the landing and the doors. Behind those doors were chambers where memories had been made for the past twelve years.

It had been a wonderful place to bring up a family.

"We *have* had good times here, haven't we?" she said.

He paused, too, looking at the doors, the walls, the windows around them. "Aye," he said, putting his arm around her shoulders. "Violent children notwithstanding, it has been a place of dreams. I am going to miss it."

There was more of an impact for Elle. She moved away from the stairs, walking to the area where the boys had been lined up. She reached out to touch one of the stone walls, remembering all of the things that had happened at Brython since she had been part of the place.

"I go back a very long time here," she finally said. "The first time I saw it, I remember thinking how intimidating it was. But also how proud I was that it belonged to the Welsh, even if it wasn't Welsh-built."

"It was Norman-built with Welsh stone," Curtis said. "Those mystical blue stones that the Welsh seem to revere so much."

She nodded, leaning against the wall and looking at him. "Blue stones to protect the gate to the Otherworld," she said. "There's so much about this castle that is legendary and mystical, but so much about it that is simply normal in an everyday sense. The sounds of our children, for example. Our five bright, beautiful children who carry the blood of Welsh royalty and English nobility. They *are* the new world. I never forgot what your father said to me those years ago about that, but I also didn't truly believe him until Chris was born. Then I saw it."

"What did you see?"

She smiled. "Something you said to me once," she said. "*Open your eyes to the world around you, and I promise you will not regret it.* Do you remember that?"

He smiled in return. "Of course," he said. "And did you open your eyes?"

She nodded. "I did," she said. "And you were right. I did not regret it."

Curtis chuckled softly, going to her and putting his arms around her. It was true that they were leaving Brython for a new de Lohr post, the great and mighty Monmouth Castle, as part of the de Lohr expansion along the marches, but they were leaving behind a place that was precious to them both.

Years ago, Curtis had come to Brython with the intention of conquest. What he'd found was so much more than he bargained for. He had conquered a castle, but what he received in return changed his life forever. A firebrand of a woman who refused to surrender, who had fought him every step of the way, and who had finally become his all for living. To him, that was the legacy of Brython.

Open your eyes to the world around you, and I promise you will not regret it.

He had opened his eyes, too. Elle had done that for him.

Much like her, he didn't regret it, either.

☙ THE END ❧

Children of Curtis and Elle
Christopher "Chris"
Arthur
William
Mary (After Dustin's mother)
Valeria (After Christopher's mother)
Nicholas
Adam
Jasper
Callum
Powell

KATHRYN LE VEQUE NOVELS

Medieval Romance:

De Wolfe Pack Series:
Warwolfe
The Wolfe
Nighthawk
ShadowWolfe
DarkWolfe
A Joyous de Wolfe Christmas
BlackWolfe
Serpent
A Wolfe Among Dragons
Scorpion
StormWolfe
Dark Destroyer
The Lion of the North
Walls of Babylon
The Best Is Yet To Be
BattleWolfe
Castle of Bones

De Wolfe Pack Generations:
WolfeHeart
WolfeStrike
WolfeSword
WolfeBlade
WolfeLord
WolfeShield
Nevermore
WolfeAx
WolfeBorn

The Executioner Knights:

By the Unholy Hand
The Mountain Dark
Starless
A Time of End
Winter of Solace
Lord of the Sky
The Splendid Hour
The Whispering Night
Netherworld
Lord of the Shadows
Of Mortal Fury
'Twas the Executioner Knight
Before Christmas
Crimson Shield

The de Russe Legacy:
The Falls of Erith
Lord of War: Black Angel
The Iron Knight
Beast
The Dark One: Dark Knight
The White Lord of Wellesbourne
Dark Moon
Dark Steel
A de Russe Christmas Miracle
Dark Warrior

The de Lohr Dynasty:
While Angels Slept
Rise of the Defender
Steelheart
Shadowmoor
Silversword
Spectre of the Sword

Unending Love
Archangel
A Blessed de Lohr Christmas
Lion of Twilight
Lion of War
Lion of Hearts

The Brothers de Lohr:
The Earl in Winter

Lords of East Anglia:
While Angels Slept
Godspeed
Age of Gods and Mortals

Great Lords of le Bec:
Great Protector

House of de Royans:
Lord of Winter
To the Lady Born
The Centurion

Lords of Eire:
Echoes of Ancient Dreams
Lord of Black Castle
The Darkland

Ancient Kings of Anglecynn:
The Whispering Night
Netherworld

Battle Lords of de Velt:
The Dark Lord
Devil's Dominion
Bay of Fear
The Dark Lord's First Christmas
The Dark Spawn
The Dark Conqueror
The Dark Angel

Reign of the House of de Winter:
Lespada
Swords and Shields

De Reyne Domination:
Guardian of Darkness
The Black Storm
A Cold Wynter's Knight
With Dreams
Master of the Dawn

House of d'Vant:
Tender is the Knight (House of d'Vant)
The Red Fury (House of d'Vant)

The Dragonblade Series:
Fragments of Grace
Dragonblade
Island of Glass
The Savage Curtain
The Fallen One
The Phantom Bride

Great Marcher Lords of de Lara
Dragonblade

House of St. Hever
Fragments of Grace
Island of Glass
Queen of Lost Stars

Lords of Pembury:
The Savage Curtain

Lords of Thunder: The de Shera Brotherhood Trilogy
The Thunder Lord
The Thunder Warrior
The Thunder Knight

The Great Knights of de Moray:
Shield of Kronos
The Gorgon

The House of De Nerra:
The Promise
The Falls of Erith
Vestiges of Valor
Realm of Angels

Highland Warriors of Munro:
The Red Lion
Deep Into Darkness

The House of de Garr:
Lord of Light
Realm of Angels

Saxon Lords of Hage:
The Crusader
Kingdom Come

High Warriors of Rohan:
High Warrior
High King

The House of Ashbourne:
Upon a Midnight Dream

The House of D'Aurilliac:
Valiant Chaos

The House of De Dere:
Of Love and Legend

St. John and de Gare Clans:
The Warrior Poet

The House of de Bretagne:
The Questing

The House of Summerlin:

The Legend

The Kingdom of Hendocia:
Kingdom by the Sea

The BlackChurch Guild: Shadow Knights:
The Leviathan
The Protector

Regency Historical Romance:
Sin Like Flynn: A Regency
Historical Romance Duet
The Sin Commandments
Georgina and the Red Charger

Gothic Regency Romance:
Emma

Contemporary Romance:

Kathlyn Trent/Marcus Burton Series:
Valley of the Shadow
The Eden Factor
Canyon of the Sphinx

The American Heroes Anthology Series:
The Lucius Robe
Fires of Autumn
Evenshade
Sea of Dreams
Purgatory

Other non-connected Contemporary Romance:
Lady of Heaven
Darkling, I Listen
In the Dreaming Hour
River's End

The Fountain

Sons of Poseidon:
The Immortal Sea

Pirates of Britannia Series (with Eliza Knight):

Savage of the Sea by Eliza Knight
Leader of Titans by Kathryn Le Veque
The Sea Devil by Eliza Knight
Sea Wolfe by Kathryn Le Veque

<u>Note:</u> All Kathryn's novels are designed to be read as stand-alones, although many have cross-over characters or cross-over family groups. Novels that are grouped together have related characters or family groups. You will notice that some series have the same books; that is because they are cross-overs. A hero in one book may be the secondary character in another.

There is NO reading order except by chronology, but even in that case, you can still read the books as stand-alones. No novel is connected to another by a cliff hanger, and every book has an HEA.

Series are clearly marked. All series contain the same characters or family groups except the American Heroes Series, which is an anthology with unrelated characters.

For more information, find it in **A Reader's Guide to the Medieval World of Le Veque**.

ABOUT KATHRYN LE VEQUE

Bringing the Medieval to Romance

KATHRYN LE VEQUE is a critically acclaimed, multiple USA TODAY Bestselling author, an Indie Reader bestseller, a charter Amazon All-Star author, and a #1 bestselling, award-winning, multi-published author in Medieval Historical Romance with over 100 published novels.

Kathryn is a multiple award nominee and winner, including the winner of Uncaged Book Reviews Magazine 2017 and 2018 "Raven Award" for Favorite Medieval Romance. Kathryn is also a multiple RONE nominee (InD'Tale Magazine), holding a record for the number of nominations. In 2018, her novel WARWOLFE was the winner in the Romance category of the Book Excellence Award and in 2019, her novel A WOLFE AMONG DRAGONS won the prestigious RONE award for best pre-16th century romance.

Kathryn is considered one of the top Indie authors in the world with over 2M copies in circulation, and her novels have been translated into several languages. Kathryn recently signed with Sourcebooks Casablanca for a Medieval Fight Club series, first published in 2020.

In addition to her own published works, Kathryn is also the President/CEO of Dragonblade Publishing, a boutique publishing house specializing in Historical Romance. Dragonblade's success has seen it rise in the ranks to become Amazon's #1 e-book publisher of Historical Romance (K-Lytics report July 2020).

Kathryn loves to hear from her readers. Please find Kathryn on Facebook at Kathryn Le Veque, Author, or join her on Twitter @kathrynleveque. Sign up for Kathryn's blog at www.kathrynleveque.com for the latest news and sales.